THE TIDE OF NEW BEGINNINGS

THE TIDE OF NEW BEGINNINGS

RONALD SAVAGE JR.

Ronald Savage Jr.

Acknowledgements

Thank you to God who helped me see this book to completion.
Thank you to my family and friends for your support.
Thank you to the readers who continue to trust me to tell them a good story.

Genealogy

This is the genealogy of the Brown family of Creeke.
Hiram Jones married Molly Jones. And he begat two sons, Garland Jones and Rosario Jones. Garland never married.

Rosario married a woman named Lilly Harvey. He begat twelve daughters -Susan Jones, Loretta Jones, April Jones, Josephine Jones, Ophelia Jones, May Jones, Charlotte Jones, Cara Jones, June Jones, Agnes Jones, Louise Jones, Leanne Jones - and one son, Gabriel Ray Jones.

Gabriel married Mavis Clara Ellis. And Gabriel begat one son, Abel Joel Jones, and two daughters, Abigail Elizabeth Jones and Marianne Solomon Jones. Abel and Abigail died at birth.

Marianne married Damian Lee Parker for four years. Damian begat one son, Terrence Lee Parker, and one daughter, Ruth-Anne Grace Parker. And Damian had one brother, Arthur Lee. And Arthur married Tasha and begat one daughter, Danielle.

Terrence married Sarah Eileen Martin who had no prior familial roots in Creeke; and he begat two sons, Terrence Lee Parker Jr., and Michael Damian Parker, and a daughter, Angela Ray Parker.

Ruth-Anne married Arnold Green and begat one daughter, Naomi Green. Thus, the Parker line became the Green line through Ruth-Anne.

Marianne married Leonard Calvin Brown, whose parents were Calvin and Denise Brown. And Leonard begat two sons, Jeremy-Micah Kyle Brown and Torrance Dean Brown, and one daughter, Marie Denise Brown. Thus, the Jones line became the Parker line and the Brown line through Marianne.

Jeremy-Micah married Francine who had no prior familial roots in Creeke, and begat one son, Alexander Tanner Brown.

Marie married Alejandro Garza, who had no prior familial roots in Creeke. Alejandro begat Mariana Isabela Garza and Mariella Adelaida Garza. Thus, the Brown line became the Garza line through Marie.

Torrance married Leilana Ernestine Allen, whose parents were Jared Allen and Ernestine Brooks. And Torrance begat six children with Leilana – Drake Jared Brown, Karla Elizabeth Brown, Mary Ann Brown, Andre Joel Brown, Adrianna Ernestine Brown, and Antoine Marvin Brown. Torrance and Leilana divorced after eleven years of marriage. And Leilana married Forrest Hall, and begat one daughter, Layla Esther Hall.

This is the genealogy of the Brown family of Creeke.

-

How Did We Get Here: A Prelude

Torrance Brown is the name,
And this is my game,
To tell you about my life,
Leading up to my new wife,
That I'll marry soon,
Cuz she's my boon,
But let me take you back,
 To where it all began.

Born the youngest of five,
Arrival ruined lives.
Oldest two were from my mama's first,
While the other two were from my mama's worst.
And I guess I came from her worst too,
But I don't claim him like he didn't do,
For me.
I was only raised by my granddaddy,
Gabriel Jones, the realest man I know,
Even though he could sometimes be ice cold,
But that's okay cuz he was my old man.
And he's the one made me a music fan.
And not a day passes me by,
When I don't think how much I miss that guy.
He's the one I'll always call my dad,
Cuz he's the only dad I ever had.

Since we're talking about fathers,
I got sons and daughters.
There's Drake, Karla, Mary, Andre,
Adrianna, Antoine, they make my day.
They are the kids of my first wife,
She left me after a time of strife.

She said she left cuz I was always angry.
Maybe I was, but I said maybe.
If she'd been through what I'd been through,
She'd probably be very angry too.
I try to do my best for my kids,
But it gets hard when you're over six,
With strong personalities,
That are all needing me.
I've got to be my best,
Till there's nothing left.

I consider myself to be a great dad,
There's just no way I could've done as bad,
As my supposed father.
I don't know why he bothered,
To have me since he was garbage.
He's the type you leave in a ditch.
He talked about some he didn't know,
But all the evidence was right there though.
I have the misfortune of having his face.
Why on earth is this my stupid fate?
Why must I be cursed to look like that man,
Of who I'm clearly not a fan?
Got a right fist with his name on it,
And a left one if he want to get slick.
As long as he stay from around me,
We won't have no issues you see.

Like I was saying I'm a great dad,
My kids have no reason to be mad.
They get what they need and get what they want,
And on top of all that they get my love.
My oldest son Drake is out on his own,
And sometimes doesn't know how to use a phone.

Karla of course lives with her mommy,
And it ain't really a bother to me.
My baby Mary got my music skills,
I hope she blows up so she can help with these bills.
Andre, Andre, as smart as his father,
His only problem is he needs to try harder.
Adrianna is daddy's dancing pearl,
I think I should say I'm proud of my girl.
And Antoine that's my techno boy.
All of my kids bring me so much joy.

And now I'm getting ready to marry again,
To my one and only love Gretchen.
I don't know what she sees in me,
But somehow I bring her a lot of glee.
Hope this second time goes better than the first,
Cuz I guarantee there won't be a third.
I'm looking ahead to my future,
When it'll just be me and her,
And all my kids will be out my place,
And I'll finally get to have my space.
But I've still got some work to do,
To raise my kids to not be fools.
We're nearing the end of my tale,
Of my life story that I tell.
There's other stories to be told,
And I want to see how it unfolds.

A-Side

Drake Brown

To Drake Jared Brown

Your mama named you Drake,
And it rhymes with snake.
I don't like it cuz you should bear my name.
Since I am the dad from which you came,
I think that you should be called T.J.
But your mama went and ruined my day,
And gave you the name of a comic book guy.
And I really just don't understand why,
Cuz I was standing here on the sideline.
If she needed a name, she should've used mine.
And your middle name came from her daddy,
Cuz I ain't got one as you can clearly see.
All I got is the last name Brown for you,
So I guess that makes me oh and two.
Your name was a battle that I lost,
But my love for you was worth the cost.

-

Friday

Drake Brown was in an expensive predicament. He had borrowed five thousand dollars from Matthias Harrison the previous September, and the deadline to repay it was almost upon him. But Drake did not have the money. In fact, he did not have even half of it. Bills and adult responsibilities had severely limited his saving efforts, his two jobs did not pay highly, and his music career was still in its unpaid infancy. Nothing less than a miracle could save him.

Drake knew his parents could help, but he was reluctant to ask them, especially his father Mr. Torrance Brown. During their last heated argument before Drake had moved out, Mr. Brown had told him: *'Don't come crying to me when you need help, since you're so tired of dealing with me!'*. Those words had driven Drake and his hot-tempered father apart in more ways than one. And he did not want to place a financial burden on his mother and stepfather either. He had agreed to repay Matthias by the time of his father's wedding. With Mr. Brown getting married the following weekend to his fiancée, Gretchen Nelson, Drake had to man up and face the music.

"Jesus, how I love you, you're everything that I need," sang Drake. His workday at the local gospel radio station was concluding. Although he preferred his job as a soundboard operator to his second job as a waiter, it was still a job, and he was ready to enjoy his weekend.

"Drake, this is the third worship song you've played in a row," chided his boss, Mr. Delroy King, from his office. "The next one better have some praise in it."

"Yes sir," said Drake. Drake liked and respected Mr. King, but sometimes the man could be nerve-wracking. He was a fifty-year-old dark-brown music head set in his ways like Drake's forty-one-year-old father.

Drake had not seen his father since Christmas. They both had December birthdays, with Drake having been born a week after his father's twentieth. As the oldest of his siblings, Drake had learned early that he could either have a birthday or Christmas, but not both. But that past Christmas, his father had surprised him.

"I want to give you something," said Mr. Brown that day. He had handed a rectangular gift to Drake and said, "It's something special to me and I want you to have it."

"I didn't get you anything," said Drake.

"I don't need anything. Open it."

Drake had unwrapped the gift and his eyes had bulged when he saw what it was. The gold lettering on the brown leather cover had caught his eye immediately. He had flipped through the marked-up pages until there was nothing left to do but gaze at his father's smiling face.

"Great-Grandpa's hymnal?"

"I want you to have it," repeated Mr. Brown. He had rubbed the back of his neck and glanced away, saying, "He always said music brought people together and..."

Mr. Brown had trailed off his sentence, but Drake had gotten the message. His father wanted to bond over their love of music like Drake had wanted to during the fall. They had begun to during that time before the revelation of Mr. Brown's biological father had sidetracked everything and caused the big argument that led to Drake moving out.

"Thanks," said Drake. "I'll take good care of it."

The worship song entered the final chorus, and the next one had to be upbeat. There was a song called 'Rejoice' by his brother Andre's favorite Christian rock band, 'THE CA113D', that Drake liked, but he had already played it with his other go-to upbeat songs. And the current gospel music trend was long, slow worship songs that continuously repeated the same lyrics.

Despite this challenge, there was one genre Drake knew always provided upbeat songs: the rap genre. He also knew Mr. King heavily despised the genre, but he hoped Mr. King would make an exception.

Drake placed his sister Mary's favorite gospel rap song into the rotation and hoped for the best.

I love God, and he loves me,
He gave His son to set me free.

"What in the–?!" cried Mr. King. He rushed into the room and hollered, "What are you doing?!"

"Sir?" responded Drake, anticipating a lecture.

"You know we only play rap during the rap hour on Fridays! I run a gospel station, not a rap station!"

"These are gospel artists."

"That's what they claim," sneered Mr. King. "But they be out there living any old type of way and then try to cover it in Jesus and act like it's alright. The listeners of this station don't want to hear that crap when they're driving home from a long day at work. They want to hear something positive and uplifting. You keep that crap off the air, you hear?"

"Yes sir," said Drake, trying to hide his exasperation.

Drake found Mr. King's dislike of rap fascinating. Mr. King used to be King Roy of Mr. Brown's favorite old-school rap group, The Boombox Boyz. His son, KV, and his niece, DJ Mousie, were also rappers who credited Mr. King as their mentor. Drake did not understand how Mr. King could have such heavy ties to the genre and despise it so much.

After finishing his workday, the only thing Drake wanted to do was go home and kick his feet up. But before he did that, there was a special someone he wanted to see. His girlfriend, Tamela Kane, would be finishing her college classes around the same time Drake got off. He figured he could catch her before she went home and called her to see if it was possible.

"Hello?" said Tamela.

"Hey Tam," said Drake. "Have you left campus yet?"

"I'm about to. Why?"

"I'm swinging by," said Drake, pumping his fist triumphantly. "I want to see you."

"I don't know...," said Tamela. "I need to get home."

"It'll be quick."

"How far are you?"

"Leaving the station."

"I don't think I can wait that long."

"I really want to see you."

"And I really need to get home."

Drake pursed his lips and silently exhaled through his nose. He did not know when seeing his girlfriend had become such a rare occurrence. When she had told him she was switching to the university in the city, Drake had figured it was because she wanted to be closer to home and him. And in a way, he had been right. Tamela *had* wanted to be closer to home. But it was because her mother's cancer had returned, and Tamela needed to be home to help take care of her.

"Tam, is everything alright?" asked Drake worriedly. "Did something happen to your mom?"

"Everything's fine," sighed Tamela. "I just need to get home."

"Okay. Hug Mrs. Reesy for me and tell her I'll stop by to visit this weekend."

Tamela did not answer.

"Tam?"

"I don't think that's a good idea."

"It isn't?"

"She doesn't want any visitors right now."

"Oh."

"I'll tell her you said hi though."

"Okay. I'll let you go. Love you."

Tamela paused before saying, "I love you too."

"I'm home," called Drake, entering the apartment he shared with his best friend, Andrew Stone.

"Hey," said Quentin while keeping his eyes trained on the video game before him. Quentin Lloyd lived in the apartment across from Drake's, but he spent more time in Drake's apartment than he did his own. He was Andrew's friend, but over time Drake had also developed a level of friendship with Quentin.

"Hey Que," replied Drake. "Where's Titan?"

"Taking his post-gym shower," answered Quentin. He had shaved off his blonde mohawk and returned to his natural black hair color. Quentin paused the game and looked at Drake. "You got a minute?"

"What's up?"

"I've got a music opportunity for you. A friend of mine is looking for background singers for his next project and it's paid too. I brought your name up as a potential singer for him."

"Who is it?"

"I can't say yet. But if you're interested, I'm meeting up with him tonight."

"I don't know. I'd prefer to know who it is we're meeting."

"Come on Drake. You know I wouldn't put you in a situation. Andrew would kill me if I did."

"What would I kill you over?" asked Andrew, entering the room and heading straight for the kitchen.

"Que said he has an opportunity for me to sing background for someone but won't tell me who," said Drake.

"Oh yeah?" said Andrew. "Why not?"

"The information isn't public yet," said Quentin. He grinned and added, "Besides, you both wouldn't believe me if I said who it was anyways. Plus, I'm protecting his identity for his sake."

"He got enemies or something?" asked Andrew, filling a cup with water.

"Yeah, but nothing to worry about."

"Is he a bad man?" asked Drake.

"Nah," said Quentin. "It's a guy I grew up with and went to high school went."

"A Pirate, huh?" teased Andrew, referring to the mascot of Creeke High School's biggest rival, Preston High School. "Is he a drug dealer?"

"Why would I bring you to a drug dealer?" snapped Quentin.

"Well, what am I supposed to think? You're being all mysterious about who he is, and you said he got enemies. And he's a Pirate. That's three strikes."

"Will you just trust me?"

"I don't like this," said Andrew, sitting between Quentin and Drake.

"Me neither," agreed Drake. "The last thing I need today is more things to worry about."

"Is that why you've got that look on your face?" asked Andrew.

"What look?"

"That Mr. Brown look that he gets when something's wrong."

"I uh..."

"You can talk to me if you want."

"I just had a long day at work."

"Alright," said Andrew, picking up Quentin's game controller. "That means it's game time."

"Hey!" whined Quentin. "I was playing that!"

"You can play later," said Andrew, saving the game for Quentin before closing it. "Right now, Drake needs to talk about something."

"Nothing's wrong," said Drake.

"Do you want to fight, race, or play basketball?" asked Andrew.

"Does it matter? Either way, you're going to win. And I keep telling you nothing's wrong."

"Let's fight today," said Andrew.

"Alright," sighed Drake.

"Should I go?" asked Quentin.

"You can stay because there's *nothing wrong*," said Drake.

"You say that now," snorted Andrew. "I'm sure you'll be ranting in no time."

Andrew chose a boxer, while Drake chose whoever wore his favorite color purple. Unlike his brother Antoine, Drake was terrible at video games, especially the fighting ones Andrew was fond of. He repeatedly jabbed at Andrew, hoping at least one would hit him. While he seemed to do better than usual, Andrew would block most of the hits and occasionally use a powerful move against him that would flatten Drake on his back.

"I wanted to see Tam today and she didn't have time," said Drake, continuing to jab at Andrew. Occasionally, one would make it through Andrew's defense and hit him in the face. "She never has time."

"You do know her mom is sick, right?" said Andrew, launching Drake across the arena with a left hook and a right uppercut to the chin.

"Of course I do!" cried Drake, lying on the ground. He wondered if Andrew would attack if he remained there. His body stood up on its own and resumed jabbing. "And that's another thing! Every time I ask about her mom, she gets all evasive."

"Maybe she's not comfortable talking about it," said Andrew, executing another move that left Drake on the ground again after various blows to the gut. He jokingly added, "Especially to an unapproachable ball of stress. She's got a lot to handle already between school and her mom. She doesn't need you stressing the both of you out even more than she probably already is."

"But she won't let me be there for her either. It's like I've been shut out."

"Yeah, I could see how that would be frustrating."

"What do you think I should do?"

"Be her boyfriend," advised Andrew. "Be there for her in ways that don't stress her out."

"But how?"

"That's for you to figure out," said Andrew. "Finish me off."

"How do I do that?" asked Drake. He had somehow managed to wear down Andrew's health while most of his still remained.

Andrew did the finisher for him, and Drake watched as he executed a special kicking move he did not know he could do.

"Was that the best you could do?" said Drake, espousing his victory line with a smug grin.

"I don't believe it!" cried Quentin. "You let him win!"

"Did you really?" asked Drake, looking at Andrew.

"What is this, a courtroom?" said Andrew defensively. "Is it so hard to believe Drake could beat me fairly?"

"Yes!" said Quentin. "Drake sucks at this game! He didn't even know how to finish you off! There's no way he'd win by just mashing the jab button!"

"It's not impossible," stated Andrew.

"You let him win!"

"Titan, be honest," said Drake. "Did you let me win?"

"I didn't 'let you win'," said Andrew. "I just prioritized our talk over the game."

"I knew it!" cried Quentin.

"So what?" argued Andrew. "It's not that big a deal."

"You never let me win! I want revenge!"

"Revenge...?" muttered Andrew, his face clouding over. "Are you challenging me?"

"Careful Que," advised Drake. "Andrew is the best player in the house."

"He may be good but he's not invincible," said Quentin. "I can take him!"

"Are you challenging me?" re-asked Andrew.

"Yes, I am!"

Andrew left the room.

"He's pulling out his headband," chuckled Drake.

"What headband?"

"Back during freshman year of high school, a senior challenged him to a fighting game when he was wearing this red headband. They both had won a round and during the last round, the senior had taken Andrew down all the way to near defeat while he still had half his health. Somehow, Andrew managed to come back and beat the senior with a speck of health left. So now, anytime he pulls out that headband, it means he's not going to let himself lose."

"Oh really?" said Quentin, rolling up his sleeves. "We'll see about that."

"I hope your role-playing skills are good."

"Role-playing skills?"

"Yeah."

"I didn't think he was one of those live-action role-playing guys."

"It was something he did with Simon."

"Oh."

"You know in two weeks it will be four years since Simon's death."

"Really?" gasped Quentin. "Man, now I feel bad for getting on his head."

"Who dares challenge Andrew The Titan?" bellowed Andrew, emerging from his room with a red headband tied around his forehead.

"I do?" said Quentin confusedly.

"And thou art?"

"Quentin...?"

"Quentin who?"

"Your friend?"

"Titan has no friend named Quentin," said Andrew, narrowing his eyes at Quentin.

Quentin looked at Drake confusedly.

"Play along," whispered Drake.

"I...," said Quentin. He glanced at Drake, then took a fighting stance and stated, "I am Quentin the Destroyer. I've come to destroy you, Titan!"

"It is you who shall be destroyed!" taunted The Titan. "And I only need one round to do it!"

"We shall see about that!" declared The Destroyer.

Drake watched as the two men duked it out. Sometimes it seemed like The Titan would win, and other times The Destroyer. They fought long and hard, each claiming a victory for themselves. But in the end, it was The Titan who was the winner, finishing The Destroyer off with his ultimate special move.

"Consider yourself destroyed," said Andrew.

"Darn it!" yelled Quentin.

"Next time you speak of revenge," said Andrew. "Watch your mouth, my boy."

"Yeah, whatever," grumbled Quentin. "Are we meeting with my music opportunity or am I going solo?"

"Was that a music pun?" laughed Drake.

"It wasn't meant to be."

"Oh."

"We'll go with you because I've got to see this mystery man," said Andrew, removing his headband. "What time you trying to go?"

"I'm supposed to meet him in an hour."

"Alright, but don't have us out all night," said Andrew in a paternal-like tone. "Especially if things get out of hand."

"Worried you'll have to put those boxing lessons to use and fight for real?" joked Quentin.

"It's not me I'm worried about," said Andrew, glancing at Drake.

"I had one fight when I was fifteen," griped Drake.

"And it was pretty bad," said Andrew. "And you did all that at eight-thirty in the morning. Anyone who gets riled up that early is dangerous."

"I'm not dangerous," said Drake. "I am a grown God-fearing man who is more than capable of avoiding fights."

"Good," said Andrew. "Let's keep it that way."

Downtown was packed. Everyone was out celebrating the beginning of spring break. Drake, Andrew, and Quentin walked up the street, admiring all the nice cars driving by.

"Look at that one!" exclaimed Quentin.

"That's nice," said Andrew. "What do you think Drake?"

"It's cool," said Drake.

He hoped whoever they were meeting was legitimate. The last thing Drake wanted to do was waste time on someone else's music when he could put that same energy into his own.

Drake dreamed of becoming a successful recording artist. He had a notebook full of songs he had written, he played various instruments, he had an amazing singing voice, and even though he was not as gifted a dancer as his sister Adrianna, he could still do a little two-step.

He also suspected his great-grandfather had had the same dream. In the back of his hymnal, Great-Grandpa Gabriel Jones had scribbled some of his own compositions. Drake suspected those were not the only songs his great-grandfather had penned, and he just never had the opportunity to showcase them. And his father also had had minor success as a recording artist. But his career had been cut short at the local level, and whatever music he had written, he kept hidden away in the jungle he called a room. If he could, Drake wanted to honor them both by bringing their songs to the world.

Everything Drake needed to succeed was there. All he needed was an opportunity to propel him. And this could be that opportunity.

"How long will ye simple ones love simplicity?!" cried a dark-brown woman with a white headwrap. Her white t-shirt had the named 'WISDOM' drawn on it in black permanent marker, but Drake knew her as twenty-three-year-old Camille Abernathy from church.

"Hey Wisdom," said Drake.

"Huh?" said Camille, turning to face him. Upon recognizing him, she smiled and said, "Oh hey! What are you doing here?"

"Just walking," replied Drake. "You?"

"Preaching and handing out flyers for the church. You're going to be at prayer tomorrow, right?"

"Of course," said Drake. "When have I ever missed prayer?"

"You know how young folks are when it comes to the things of The Lord."

"Are you not also a young folk, ma'am?"

"I am," said Camille. "But I'm also serious about my Jesus."

"So am I."

"As you should be," said Camille. "Hey Brother Andrew. Brother Quentin."

"Hey," answered Andrew and Quentin.

"I'll see you both at church on Sunday, right?"

"I can't wait for the day you upgrade to Church Mother Camille," joked Andrew. "You've already got the role down pact."

"Uhn uhn, that's reserved for seasoned saints," laughed Camille. "I'm not quite there yet. But I won't keep you guys from your plans. Just remember, that whatever you're about to do..."

"We know," said Quentin. "Use wisdom and discernment."

"That's right," said Camille. "Many lives have been saved because they yielded to The Holy Ghost. I'll see you guys later."

"Bye Wisdom," said Drake.

"That Camille is something else," laughed Andrew as they walked on. "Alright Que, where's this mystery man at?"

"He's around here somewhere," said Quentin. "Search for a green sports car. That's his car."

The men looked around for a few minutes. When they did not spot the car, Quentin called.

"Say man, where you at?" said Quentin. "You see us? I don't see you. Blink your lights. Oh, there you are. Alright. See you soon."

"Well?" said Andrew.

"He's across the street in that parking lot," said Quentin. "He drove his cousin's car."

Quentin led them to a tan car parked in a gas station parking lot. When they approached the car, the tinted window rolled down, and Drake's breath hitched in his throat. Sitting inside the car was the rapper Knokout. Drake looked at Andrew to confirm what he was seeing and found Andrew was doing the same.

"If it ain't Que," laughed Knokout. "What's good, man?"

"Shoot, I could ask you the same thing," said Quentin. "You and Rak been out here going at it."

"Man, that's him," said Knokout. "He's claiming I stole some stuff from him, but everything he got I got. I think it was someone on his security team but you know how he is."

"Yeah, I know," said Quentin. "But did you have to hit him upside the head with that bottle?"

"He ran up on me and I defended myself," said Knokout. "I'm just mad Zion got mixed up in it when it had nothing to do with him.

Thankfully, they cleared him of involvement and he wasn't fired from his job, but I haven't been so blessed."

"That's what happens when you fight in public," said Quentin.

"Again, he ran up on me," repeated Knokout. "I was just sitting there chilling and minding my business. I didn't even really want to be there in the first place but my manager had already booked it and I didn't want to back out."

"You don't have to explain nothing to me," said Quentin, holding his hands up. "What you and Rak got going on is between you two."

"Anyways," said Knokout. He motioned to Andrew and Drake. "Introduce me to your friends."

"Muscleman is Andrew," said Quentin. "The other one is the one I was telling you about."

"The singer?"

"Yeah, that's him. Drake Brown. He's got a great voice and I think he'll be perfect for your next project."

"Nice to meet you," said Knokout, offering his medium-brown hand to Drake.

Drake accepted the handshake but was too stunned to speak back.

"So, you sing?" asked Knokout.

Drake nodded. Knokout had a friendly smile that emphasized his brown eyes. It also helped Drake feel more comfortable around him.

"Did you know you were meeting with me today?" joked Knokout.

Drake shook his head.

"You could've at least told him who he was meeting with, Que," laughed Knokout.

"He wouldn't have believed me," said Quentin.

"Let's start over," said Knokout. "I'm Vincent, but you can call me Vince."

"Okay...," said Drake, recovering from his shock. "I'm Drake."

"Hi Drake," said Vincent, disarming Drake with his smile again. "I'm glad you can talk. Hopefully you can sing too. How about we go for a drive?"

"Okay."

"You guys can come too."

"See Andrew?" said Quentin, shoving a still-stunned Andrew into the car. "I told you he wasn't a drug dealer."

"A drug dealer?" snorted Vincent. "The only thing I'm dealing is good music. And that's what I want to talk to you about, Drake. I'm working on my first album under my new label, and I need session singers to do background. Does that sound like something you'd like to do?"

"Sure," answered Drake. "What genre of music is it?"

"It's... I don't really know yet," admitted Vincent with a laugh. "I want it to be uplifting and addressing real life issues and I want it to have a choral type of sound for it. That's what the background singers are for."

"Hmm."

"I'll be holding auditions about two weeks from now," said Vincent. He handed Drake a business card and said, "Just contact me before then if you're interested and I'll send you the info."

"Okay," said Drake.

"So, about this new label," said Quentin, leaning over Vincent's seat.

"Sit back nosy," snorted Vincent. "It's called Baby Bag Productions."

"How many people are on the label?"

"Just me so far."

"Plan on signing anyone else?"

"Maybe one day when I can afford it," said Vincent. "I was thinking we hit the pool hall tonight. You down?"

"Sure. I don't think Andrew and Drake would like to go there though."

"I'll drop them off wherever they want to go."

"You can drop them off at my car," said Quentin. He handed his keys to Andrew and said, "Andrew, I'm trusting you with my baby. Do not wreck it."

Andrew nodded.

"Where's your car?" asked Vincent.

"By Seaweed's," said Quentin. "You might get stuck in the traffic though."

"And?"

Vincent turned the radio up. The next song to play was KV's new song 'Rite of Passage', which sampled The Boombox Boyz's 'Rite of Passage'.

Hey Rak, what in your opinion makes a man?
Why are you asking me that?
Well, King Roy said–!
I know what my Pops said. But I'm King Rak. And I say a man needs paper, respect, and love.
So, you're saying your Pops was wrong?
Nah. I'm just saying a man only lives once. And why shouldn't he get to enjoy life while he has it? Why can't a rite of passage be fun? You know what, give me a beat.
Duh-dun dun dun dun dun, duh-dun dun dun dun, duh-dun dun dun dun dun, duh-dun dun dun dun...
Yeah, now speed it up.

Trying to find my babe out here
And trying to get paid
I'm enjoying my manhood
Through my rite of passage

This ain't your daddy's rite of passage
Because we're living in a new age
Ain't nobody trying to hear all that sadness
We out here trying to get into some madness
Trying to get myself to a bag
But it won't be a baby's that I snag
And speaking of snagging babies
I got me a whole gang of ladies
And I'm trying to see what they're about

Drake expected Vincent to cut the song off after the first verse. But he did not. They listened to the whole thing.

"Hmm," said Vincent. "Not his best."

He changed the radio to the old-school soul station and dropped Andrew and Drake off. The car ride back to the apartment was silent, with both men still processing what had happened.

"So, what do you think?" asked Drake when they got home.

"I can't believe we just met Knokout," said Andrew. "I didn't even know Que knew him! You think he knows KV too?"

"From their conversation, it sounds like he does."

"This is crazy!"

"What do you think of his offer?"

"You should take it," said Andrew. "This could be your big break. A lot of famous singers started out as background singers."

"Yeah," said Drake.

He hoped Andrew was right. Even though the opportunity would not pay out until after his deadline with Matthias, he was still hopeful it would lead to something.

It had been an eventful day for Drake, and he was ready to call it a night. But before he did, there was still one person he needed to talk to: his dad. He typically called his mother in the mornings and his father in the evenings. And while he had consistently called his mother daily, his impending deadline with Matthias had caused him to call his father less frequently. All his father wanted to talk about lately was the wedding, but the wedding was the last thing Drake wanted to think about.

"Hello?" said Drake.

"Hello," said Mr. Brown.

"Hi Dad."

"Hi. When do you plan on coming down here?"

"Uh... probably Friday," said Drake.

"Friday?" repeated Mr. Brown. "That's the day before the wedding."

It was an opportune moment for Drake to explain his financial troubles and why he wanted to stay away from Creeke as long as possible. But his father's infamous words rang in his ears and stopped him.

"I still have to work next week," said Drake.

"You're just down the road," said Mr. Brown.

"I don't want to drive back and forth every day."

"You got to work both jobs?"

"Yes sir."

"I don't miss those days."

Before his father was a teacher and his mother a housewife, Mr. Brown had worked as a janitor. His grandfather had been a janitor and had gotten Mr. Brown hired at his old job after graduating high school. Drake remembered those days when his mother worked as a secretary and he barely saw his father because he worked day and night shifts at two different janitor jobs. Once he had added college classes on top of them, Mr. Brown had seemed like an angry zombie to Drake. He did not miss those days either.

"I'll be down there Friday," said Drake.

"Okay," said Mr. Brown.

There was not much else to say. Drake's thoughts were consumed with his finances, and since those were off-limits with his father, there was nothing else to talk about. They ended the conversation, and Drake prepared for bed. Before he fell asleep, he got on his knees and prayed.

He prayed about everything else before finally touching on the topic that tortured him most.

"Lord, I really need your help," prayed Drake. "I need to pay Matthias this money back, but I don't think I'll have it for him in time. Can you make a way for me... or at least keep Matthias from breaking my face?"

Closing his prayer, Drake climbed into bed, hoping The Lord would see fit to answer him.

My Daddy Was My Hero

Daddy was my boyhood hero,
He could never do wrong.
But when I was a boy of ten,
My hero said so long.

His wife had left him behind with
Six kids to raise alone.
And then I became the hero,
For my hero had gone.

Monday

Monday was a bright, sunny day. But like any bright, sunny day, it could always suddenly turn dark and stormy. Drake hoped it would remain a good day because he did not need anything else in his life going wrong. He chatted with his mother, First Lady Leilana Hall, on his way to work his morning shift as a waiter.

"Hey Mom," said Drake.

"Hey," said First Lady Hall.

"How'd yesterday go? Karla said you preached the sermon."

"Child, I tried."

"Uh oh. Sounds like it didn't go so well."

"All I'll say is next time your stepfather goes out of town, I'm going with him."

"Oh dear," said Drake. "Well, just know you're not alone. Yesterday, our Bishop's son Hosea preached his first sermon too."

"A mess," sighed First Lady Hall. "I can't wait till your stepfather gets home."

"I know," said Drake. "I'm almost to work. I'll call you later, okay?"

"Okay. Have a good day son."

"I will. Love you."

"Love you too."

The conversation ended, and Drake turned up his radio. He liked listening to other stations in the area because it helped him develop ideas on what did and did not work on air.

"You're listening to the Royal Court, your number one morning show for all things hip hop and R&B."

"So Empress, you went and saw that new Drake Malone this weekend?"

"Yeah Emperor, I went and saw that new Drake Malone."

"How was it?"

"It was so good. They need to get some awards for this movie. I'm talking Best Actor for Baby Luke, Best Actress for Irina Frazier, Best Director and Screenplay for Morgan Abernathy, and Best Soundtrack. The whole movie was phenomenal."

"I want to talk about this surprise track we got from the movie."

"Right? For those of you who don't know all four of our hometown heroes The Boombox Boyz reunited on the Drake Malone movie soundtrack."

"What?!" gasped Drake.

"And Tony-P and NikNak appeared in the movie too!"

"They did?"

"Yeah. I won't say too much but it was definitely good to see them in there. But yeah, like I said all four Boombox Boyz reunited on the soundtrack. Now Baby Luke told us they would be recording a new song for the soundtrack, but we all assumed it would be the trio like it's been for years. Then when the track listing dropped and King Roy was listed on the track, you know we all got excited but some people said they probably used his voice from a previous track or in a sample and had to credit him. BUT! I'm here to tell you firsthand, that it's a new track and King Roy is really on there for real. And they're not rapping either but they're singing! Baby, if they wanted to cross over into R&B, they'd be just as successful there too."

"Oh wow. We've got to celebrate this. Coming at you is a certified classic. It's The Boombox Boyz with Rite of Passage!"

Boyz, I got a question for y'all.
What's up Roy?
What, in y'all's opinion, makes a man?
Here you go getting all deep again.
Nah nah I'm just asking, Tony. What makes a man? Nik?
A man ain't a man if he ain't got no paper.
So it's money that makes a man? Is that what you think Baby?
I think money's important, but a man also needs that respect.
Now we on to something? How does he get that Baby?
By proving he's not the one to mess with, that's how.

How does he prove it?

By any means necessary.

Hmm... Tony what you think?

I think any man worth his salt needs him a little sweet thing on his arm.

Aaaah! Right on!

So... money, respect, and women? That's what makes a man?

Roy why you asking us this?

I don't know. I just feel like as Black men, we don't have no real rite of passage.

No what?

A rite of passage. Think about it. How did we know when we became men? What were we taught that manhood was? Money, respect through violence, and women? That's all we are? That's all we value?

"Well dang. Now I feel bad about my answer.

Don't feel bad Nik. You should be glad that your eyes have been opened because now you can change things.

How?

By using what God gave us. Nik, gimme a beat.

Duh-dun dun dun dun dun, duh-dun dun dun dun, duh-dun dun dun dun dun, duh-dun dun dun dun...

Good good. Now Tony, gimme a hook man.

Trying to find my way out here
Trying to be the change
I'm coming into my manhood
Through my rite of passage

King Roy here to rock the mic
And take you on a trip back in time
When we were warriors and we were kings
And we were creating most everything
See our history didn't start on boats
That's just the water they're shoving down our throats

We can do more than just survive
If we apply ourselves than we can thrive
They thought we were expendable
But they didn't know we're unkillable
Destroy the body if you want
But the spirit will live on and haunt
The spirit of freedom knows no rest
For it won't stop till it has the best
And if to get it I've got to die
Then I'll die with a warrior's heart inside

Trying to find my way out here
Trying to be the change
I'm coming into my manhood
Through my rite of passage

Nik nak patty wack give a dog a bone
It's NikNak here to take you down a road
To a time when the brothers put up a fight
Against the injustice in their sight
They took to the streets and stomped it out
And risked getting put six feet in the ground
All so I could have the right to be
And to be myself and completely free
In a country that shows me no love
And looking for a reason to spill my blood
They try to tell me being Black is a curse
But I can think of several things that's much worse
Like being hateful and being deceitful
And just straight up being evil
Black men know hardship from a young age
Is that supposed to be my rite of passage

Trying to find my way out here

Trying to be the change
I'm coming into my manhood
Through my rite of passage

Baby Luke here coming off the milk
To give you a taste of something real
This country was built on our backs
And yet we still cannot relax
My brothers don't you see that you're in chains
And your freedom is going up in flames
They got us out here warring on each other
When we should be warring on the lover
Of evil who loves himself some division
And factors it into all his decisions
We got to do so much better than this
And I don't want you thinking this is a diss
Because it's not it's a wake up call
To put the guns down and stand up tall
And to remember just who you are
A warrior, a king, a man, a star

Trying to find my way out here
Trying to be the change
I'm coming into my manhood
Through my rite of passage

Trying to find my way out here
Trying to be the change
I'm coming into my manhood
Through my rite of passage

Trying to find my way out here
Trying to be the change
I'm coming into my manhood

The song ended as Drake arrived at work. He loved the message of it, and he loved how the beat was made using only drums and handclaps. It made Mr. King's stance on rap even more baffling, but also justified when compared to KV's Rite of Passage.

Drake stared at his job and released a quiet sigh before exiting the car.

"Lord, please let it be a good day today," muttered Drake as he walked in.

To his surprise, the morning shift had been fine. Usually, he had at least one difficult customer per shift, but all his customers that morning had been pleasant and good tippers. He even genuinely smiled instead of plastering on the fake customer service smile that kept his boss off his back. When Drake's shift ended at noon, he felt so good about the day that he was sure his radio station afternoon shift would be just as positive.

"Afternoon Drake," said the host for the midday show.

"Afternoon," answered Drake.

"You look happy today."

"It's a good day," said Drake. "Is Mr. King in?"

"Not yet. He's been busy all morning with interviews."

"Interviews?"

"All the local news outlets wanted an exclusive with him about The Boombox Boyz reunion. He's going to be my guest on the show today too."

"Okay."

The station phone rang, and Drake answered it.

"How can I help you?" said Drake.

"Hi. This is Ralph Brewer from The Creeke Courier. I'm calling to request an interview with Mr. Delroy King on his return to The Boombox Boyz. Just a few questions that'll take no more than three minutes. Is he available?"

"Ralphie?"

"Yeah. Who is this?"

"It's Drake."

"Drake!" exclaimed Ralph. "I didn't know you worked there! This is perfect! Do you think you could help a brother out?"

"Mr. King isn't available at the moment."

"Aw, come on Drake," begged Ralph. "You know I'm the real deal. And you'd be doing a great service for your uncle's newspaper."

"He's literally not available," repeated Drake. "I'll take a message."

"Alright," said Ralph disappointedly. "Tell him to call Ralph Brewer at The Creeke Courier at his earliest convenience."

Ralph left a callback number and hung up. Mr. King walked into the station that day, and his attitude was dark.

"Good afternoon, Mr. King," said Drake. "You got a call from a reporter wanting to interview you on your return The Boombox Boyz."

"Alright," grumbled Mr. King. "Who was it?"

"Ralph Brewer from The Creeke Courier."

"How convenient," said Mr. King, side-eyeing Drake.

"I didn't tell him to call here."

"Sure, I believe you. He a good reporter?"

"Yes."

"Is it a good paper?"

"Yeah. My uncle runs it."

"So, a reporter from your uncle's newspaper in your hometown happens to call the radio station that you work at..."

"They are part of the local news so it's not unlikely."

"Mhmm," uttered Mr. King, giving Drake another side glance before sitting at the table. "Alright."

Mr. King always came down hard on Drake, even when it was not his fault. But Drake understood it was only because he cared. His father was the same way, and from the stories Mr. Brown had told, Drake's great-grandfather had also been the same way too. He was grateful to be working for Mr. King because even though he had a rough exterior, his heart was generous and compassionate. It was that generous, compassionate heart that had given him the job.

When he first moved to the city, Drake started attending Andrew's church and quickly joined the choir. One Sunday, it was announced that Mr. Delroy King was still accepting interns at his gospel radio station. Although the opportunity had interested Drake, he was not going to apply at first because he had felt unqualified and was still new in town. But he felt led to give it a shot, so he did. A week after applying, Mr. King granted him an interview.

"Drake Brown?" said Mr. King.

"Yes."

"How old are you?"

"I'll be twenty-one in December."

"You in school?"

"No sir."

"You working?" asked Mr. King, raising his eyebrows.

"Yes sir."

"Alright then," said Mr. King, slightly nodding. "I can't stand no able-bodied person that's lazy. Especially able-bodied young men."

The two had discussed where he worked and why he had been interested in interning at the radio station. It had been a good conversation, and Drake had hoped he had made a good impression.

"You know, typically this type of role requires you to be in school," said Mr. King.

"I see," said Drake disappointedly. He started preparing to leave. "Thank you for your time."

"Hold on, I ain't done yet. I said 'typically'. But since I make the rules here, I'm going to give you a chance without that requirement."

"Really? Thank you!"

"You'll do a three-month internship. After those three months, if I decide that you're a good fit, then I'll hire you as a staff member."

The two people who had been chosen for internships were himself and Camille. And while Camille had completed her internship and returned to school, Drake had completed his and been hired as a soundboard operator. Getting the job at the radio station had been a great blessing for him, especially since his rent had doubled only a month after moving in with Andrew.

Having his rent increased on him had strained Drake financially and emotionally. He had been so broke in November and December that he could barely afford his basic needs let alone put aside money to pay back Matthias. But January had brought a new spark of hope with him starting his second job.

Had he had more time, Drake could easily pay Matthias back in a few months. But he did not have more time.

"We've got our station owner Mr. Delroy King in the building," said the host, snapping Drake out of his thoughts. "How you doing, Mr. King?"

"I'm blessed and highly favored," answered Mr. King. "How about you?"

"I'm good sir, I'm good," said the host. "Now, Mr. King, I know this isn't necessarily gospel, but there's no way I couldn't get you on the air for this when you're my boss. You reunited with The Boombox Boyz and didn't tell nobody nothing."

"Yeah, well Luke called me and told me the group was doing a new song for the movie and they wanted to know if I'd be interested in doing it with them."

"That's incredible," said the host. "Honestly, we all thought you left the group because it got a little too real between you guys."

"Nah, the Boyz are my brothers," said Mr. King. "I wanted to go into making gospel music and they understood. They supported me, promoted my music, even came to some of my performances. We never fell out."

"That's good to hear. Have you seen the movie?"

"Of course I did. I liked it."

"Why didn't you cameo with Tony-P and NikNak?"

"Scheduling conflicts."

"Ah. Now everybody's talking about how there was no rapping on this new track. Those of us who came up listening to The Boombox

Boyz always remembered it being Tony-P as the singer and everybody else was rapping."

"Yeah, I told them I didn't want to do any rapping. And they respected that, and Tony decided we'd do an R&B track instead and arranged it to suit all our voices. We all collaborated on the lyrics, and I made sure there wasn't no craziness added in there."

"Why didn't you want to rap if you don't mind?"

"Hip hop has changed so much since I first started in the game and my opinion on it has changed. And it wouldn't be right for me to get on a track and rap knowing full well what my opinion of the genre is."

"Wait, what's your opinion?"

"I'm about to ruffle some feathers, but I just feel like the state of music today is sad," said Mr. King bluntly. "Especially gospel music. There's too much of the world in today's gospel music, and not enough of The Word. Today's gospel artists are too busy trying to conform to the ways of the world and be seen instead of focusing on what is truly important which is glorifying God. Especially all these so-called hip hop gospel artists."

"Well, Mr. King, wouldn't you say that it's possible for The Lord to reach people through any genre of music?"

"He can, and I know some will disagree with what I'm saying," said Mr. King, shooting Drake a sideways glance. "But I also believe that we as believers in Jesus Christ have a personal responsibility not to misrepresent who God is. Hip hop is too worldly. When you hear rap do you think of God or do you think of partying and riotous living? And I'm not saying that the artists who make those songs aren't living for Jesus. But what I am saying is their sound is too worldly. And some of them are even remixing secular songs into gospel songs! If that's not backwards I don't know what is! It's already bad enough hearing these secular remixes like that awful 'Rite of Passage' remix I heard earlier today blasting out of some young man's car. Seriously, he had the volume up so loud it was vibrating his car and mine!"

Drake gulped. The thought of a car's volume vibrating the surrounding cars made him think of Matthias and the speaker in his car trunk. And that made him think of the money he owed Matthias.

"That original song had an intention to inspire and discuss real-life issues, even if it is worldly," continued Mr. King, causing the host to smile at Drake in a way that made Drake feel like he had missed something important. "All that remix does is promote riotous living. And then that's another issue. Artists like KV are putting on a show, portraying people they're not, and then you find out they came from two-parent, God-fearing families who did NOT raise him to act like that! Why would you as a gospel artist want to emulate that? Why would you want to associate yourself in a genre with people who act like that? As a believer, you are to be set apart!"

"Whew!" said the host. "Mr. Delroy King, everybody. We're going to take ourselves a quick music break and be back shortly."

Drake closed all the microphones and started the music. The radio host excused himself to go to the bathroom, and Mr. King eyed Drake knowingly.

"I know you got something to say," said Mr. King.

"I don't agree with what you said just now," said Drake.

"Figured you wouldn't. My ideas are probably a little too old-school for you."

"It's not that. I listened to your Rite of Passage today. What you said on there was powerful and real."

"I didn't think someone your age would know anything about that part of my life."

"You're one of my dad's favorite rappers. I grew up on your music."

"Really?"

"Yes really," said Drake. "I think you're wrong."

"You want to know what I think?"

"That I should shut up and do my job?"

"Uh... no," said Mr. King. "That would be rude."

"Oh," Drake said with an embarrassed frown. He realized there were some differences between his father and Mr. King after all.

"Let me tell you what I know," said Mr. King. "What I know is that I was raised by two God-fearing parents, but I wanted to be a prodigal son and explore life for myself. So, I did. I started rapping for profit with The Boombox Boyz. When I rededicated my life to Jesus, I left the group and started rapping for Jesus. But the people of God didn't want to hear it. It was devil music to them. But I wanted to prove them wrong, so I kept rapping. And I met a wife who supported me and had a son."

"KV."

"Ra'Kaveon," corrected Mr. King.

"Ra'Kaveon."

"I raised him, and I raised him right. He and his friends took a liking to rap and like an idiot I let them and even taught them. And now look where they're at. Lost to the world. My own son taken by the very thing I tried to use to prove everyone wrong. Devil music. That's what it is."

"Maybe he'll end up being a prodigal son like you were."

"He loves that lifestyle too much. All I can do is pray that one day The Lord will open his eyes and show him that lifestyle is not worth living."

"I still think you're wrong," said Drake. "Your music had a huge impact on my dad's life."

"But your dad is a listener. He's never had the responsibility that comes with making music for others."

"He's the choir teacher at our high school. And he made a gospel album once."

"What's his name?"

"Torrance Brown."

"What?!" gasped Mr. King. "The little boy with the eyepatch from The Brown Family Band?! That's your father?!"

"Yeah?" said Drake surprisedly. "What do you know about The Brown Family Band?"

"What do I know?! Boy, what do you know?! Do you know how popular your father was with the saints back in the day around here?!"

"Not really. He never talks about it. In fact, I just found out about it last year."

"What?! Aw man, his song was the best song on the album! I still remember when they performed at the church all those years ago and his shoe came flying off his foot while he was up there singing and dancing."

"Yeah, that's my dad," laughed Drake. "Can't keep his shoes on to save his life."

"What happened to them?" asked Mr. King. "I remember they dropped that one album and then just kind of disappeared."

"Personal matters," answered Drake. "My dad actually prefers rapping to singing now. He says you were one of his inspirations."

"You see?" said Mr. King. "Your dad's wasting that beautiful voice because of rap. Devil music."

"I don't think he is, just like I don't agree with your opinion of rap."

"Just like a young person. They never listen to the advice of their elders until after they bump their heads."

Drake had seen some elders bump their heads pretty hard too. Especially his father. But he did not say so. Instead, he finished his workday and went home. On the way home, the radio station played KV's Rite of Passage, so Drake decided to listen to it in more closely.

Drake had to agree with the general opinion that the song paled compared to the original. He thought the beat was nice though. But the lyrics were not that great or memorable.

When he got home, he found his friend, Dorothea Burton, sitting on his couch, playing Andrew's gaming system.

"No Phil?" said Drake, referring to their other friend, Philomena James.

"Phil went home for spring break, so I'm out here by myself with nothing to do," said Dorothea.

"Why didn't you go home?"

"Didn't feel like it," said Dorothea. "It's not as special when home is just down the road."

"Is Andrew here?"

"Yeah. We're getting ready to head to the park. Want to come?"

"What's at the park?"

"A basketball court. I've got to whoop Andrew in a game of twenty-one real quick."

"As if," snorted Andrew, entering the room. "You couldn't whip me even if I gave you a twenty-point lead."

"We'll see when we hit the court."

"Yeah, we'll see."

"Ready to go now?"

"Yeah, come on."

Drake followed Dorothea and Andrew to the park down the street from their apartment complex. It was almost like old times. Almost. All they were missing was Tamela.

Drake missed Tamela. The way things were with them at the moment reminded him of how things had been before they became friends. Tamela had not liked Drake at first because she thought he was annoying. She had started thawing out towards him in eighth grade, and they were dating by sophomore year of high school. But Drake felt like he was being iced out of her life again and he did not understand why.

"Hey Mr. Brown," teased Dorothea, waving her hand in front of Drake's face. "Do you know where your son went? I can't find him under all that frowning."

"You guys finished already?"

"Yeah," said Dorothea. "He got me with a three. He was nice enough not to dunk on me though."

Andrew victoriously sauntered up to them.

"You didn't let her win?" asked Drake.

"I never let Do win," said Andrew. "She only got as close as she did because I got distracted by your sulking face."

"Oh yeah, blame it all on Drake," mocked Dorothea.

"What had you over here looking all sad?" asked Andrew, ignoring Dorothea.

"I was thinking about how this was just like old times," said Drake. "All we're missing is Tam."

"Yeah," sighed Dorothea. "I don't know how that girl is still standing. I'd have lost my mind by now if I was in her shoes."

"What do you mean?"

"Huh?"

"Do you know something I don't?"

"Like what?"

"Like what's going on with her."

"Only what she's told me," said Dorothea. "I'm sure it's the same stuff she told you."

"She hasn't told me anything. She just says everything's fine."

"Oh," said Dorothea quickly. "Yeah she's told me that too. You guys hungry?"

"Starving," said Andrew.

"Why don't I make us something?" offered Dorothea.

"Sure," said Andrew. "I'll help."

"Absolutely not," said Dorothea. "I'm not letting you anywhere near my food just so you can slip something spicy in it while I'm not looking."

"Come on, Do," whined Andrew. "When's the last time I pulled a prank on you?"

"I know you," said Dorothea, eyeing Andrew suspiciously. "I get too comfortable around you and next thing I know poor Drake will be breathing fire."

"Now why am I in it?" muttered Drake.

"I would never mess up the food that I'm also going to eat," said Andrew. "Nor would I pull a prank on you that affected innocent bystanders."

"Oh, I know," said Dorothea. "You'll probably set some to the side for yourself and Drake and *then* tamper with it."

"Come on Do," said Andrew. "Have a little faith."

"In you?" snorted Dorothea. "Never."

Dorothea ended up cooking hot dogs for them, which she figured was something Andrew could not possibly mess up. Throughout dinner, Drake noticed how Andrew and Dorothea would throw playful jabs at each other. They talked about things he had limited knowledge of like sports, video games, and fitness. But what Drake noticed most was how Andrew kept Dorothea laughing up until she left.

"Do you like Do?" asked Drake after Dorothea was gone.

"Yeah," answered Andrew, cleaning up the kitchen.

"Romantically?"

"Er... no," laughed Andrew. "Not like that."

"You two seem to have great chemistry."

"It's called friendship."

"Do you think you'll ever find someone?"

"I better," laughed Andrew. "How else am I going to have twelve kids?"

"Twelve?!" exclaimed Drake. "Why so many?"

"I want my own little basketball team."

"So, why not just coach little league or something?"

"I could do that," said Andrew, scratching his chin. "But I still do want a big family."

"You don't think twelve is a bit much though?"

"Sir, you are the oldest of seven and possibly counting."

"Exactly," said Drake. "Who do you think is going to be raising that basketball team of yours?"

"Me and my wife."

"That's what you think," snorted Drake. "And you're going to be a doctor too? You're practically never going to be home, and it'll all be left to those poor older kids of yours."

"You didn't have to crap all over my dreams like that," muttered Andrew.

"I'm just giving you the perspective your older kids will have."

"I'm an older sibling."

"There's a difference between being the oldest of two and the oldest of seven and possibly counting."

"Alright, Mr. Brown Jr.," said Andrew. "I just wanted a big family, that's all."

"Yeah, but if you have one you need to be able to manage it."

"How many kids are you and Tamela going to have?"

"We've got to get married first."

"At the rate you're going, that'll be sooner than you think."

"There's no way I could support a marriage right now," said Drake. "I'm broke and I can't even get Tam to tell me what's going on with her. She obviously tells Do more than she tells me."

"Do is her best friend."

"Yeah, but I'm her *man*. She should be able to open up to me as much as she does Do if not more than her."

"Have you told her what's going on with you?"

"What?"

"You keep complaining that she won't tell you her problems, but are you doing the same with her?"

"I uh...," muttered Drake.

"You've got to practice what you preach, man," chided Andrew. "And you still haven't answered my question."

"What was it?"

"Kids. How many you want?"

"I'll just leave it up to her. She's the one having them."

"And you are a contributor," joked Andrew. "How many contributions do you want to make?"

"Not as many as my dad that's for sure," said Drake. "And definitely not as many as you plan to make."

"Well, I'm not making any contributions to anyone until I'm a doctor," declared Andrew.

"That could take a long time."

"Becoming a doctor is the most important thing to me right now. I can't let myself get distracted because the road's only going to get tougher."

"Mhmm."

"What about you?"

"What about me?"

"You going to take Knokout up on his offer?"

"I don't know," said Drake. "I want to but how trustworthy is he really? I mean he is facing accusations of stealing right now and then he's facing charges for that whole brawl in that nightclub a few months ago. What if that whole chill, nice guy thing is just an act?"

"What would he gain from that?" asked Andrew.

"Free labor, for one," said Drake. "I'll have messed around and got paid in 'exposure' if I'm not careful."

"Yeah, but Que vouched for him," reasoned Andrew. "And Que wouldn't put you in a tough spot like that."

"Not willingly maybe," said Drake. "But he could also be getting lied to."

"Well, let's say Knokout does end up being a snake," said Andrew. "You could still take the opportunity and flip it to make more opportunities. You could network with the others involved in the project and maybe they'll consider you for future projects. You could start doing tutorials on background singing. You could sing on the street for tips. *You could finally release the music I hear you working on every night.*"

"It's not ready yet," whined Drake.

"If you keep being a perfectionist, it'll never be ready."

"You sure do know a lot about business to be a broke college student."

"You don't become a sponsored gamer sitting around doing nothing."

"I'm still in awe that you get paid to play video games."

"Because I put myself out there," said Andrew. "And I'm taking full advantage of it while I still have the time. Take that first step of faith and God will take care of the rest."

"You're right," said Drake.

"I know I am," said Andrew. "Now if you'll excuse me, I've got some new DLC to stream."

"Make that money," said Drake. He only knew what DLC was because of his brother Antoine, who sometimes gamed with Andrew.

Drake knew Andrew was right. He would not get anywhere unless he took the first step. But he just wanted to be sure the first step did not send him hurdling down a cliff.

The Father's Rite of Passage

Torrance Dean here to share a rhyme,
About a very special time,
When I had my own rite of passage,
When I was twenty years of age.
To me fatherhood was something new,
Because I had so much to do.
It wasn't all about me anymore,
I had someone I was responsible for.
I know I'm far from the perfect dad,
But I don't think I've done that bad.
I had it tough when I was coming up,
But I wanted his way up to be full of love.
So, I cleaned up behind other's mess,
To make sure he had the very best.
That's all I want for all my kids,
To have better than what I did.

Tuesday

Drake was once again on his way to work his morning shift. Everything was the same as the day before, with the exception that the hosts of The Royal Court were interviewing DJ Mousie. Although Drake had never met her personally, Quentin had told him she was sweet and down to earth. And he could hear that it was true while listening to her radio interview.

"Welcome back to The Royal Court," said Empress. "We're sitting here with DJ Mousie who dropped by to promote her new project, 'Alice'. So, Mousie, how did 'Alice' come about?"

"It was just time," said DJ Mousie. "I've been DJing for KV and just got my degree, so I figured it was time to do something for myself."

"Congratulations on graduating by the way," said Emperor.

"Thank you!" laughed DJ Mousie. "It wasn't easy, but I did it."

"You sure did," said Empress. "So, you mentioned you had been DJing for KV, but word on the street is you guys split."

"Professionally, we did part ways," said DJ Mousie. "I was ready to take my career in a new direction."

"There's no bad blood?" asked Emperor.

"Of course not," said DJ Mousie. "That's my family. We're always going to be good."

"I want to talk about 'Love Me Back' which is the lead single on 'Alice'," said Empress. "That has been my song since it dropped."

"I was very passionate about writing 'Love Me Back'," said DJ Mousie. "I've had people tell me I've only gotten this far because of my looks or who I'm related to. People also claim I don't write my own stuff and I just wanted to put it all out there and get paid off it at the same time."

"Do you think some of the backlash has to do with you being KV's cousin?"

"Some of it, yeah," said DJ Mousie. "I got a lot of backlash early in my career because people claimed I used him to jumpstart my own career and that he was the one writing my stuff. In reality, I was doing music before him, and I've been DJing since high school. And our styles are similar because we were both mentored by his dad. Then there's the people who claim I've gotten as far as I have because of my looks and I'm just like 'I can't help it that I'm pretty'. And that's why I love this 'Alice' project. It shows me as I am and all my talent not just as an artist but also as a producer. I'm still DJ Mousie, but I'm Alice King first and I want the listeners to get to know Alice King."

"I know that's right," said Empress. "We're going to take a break and listen to 'Love Me Back'."

DJ Mousie, make 'em scream yo!

Drake listened to the song and found it to be good. He arrived at the radio station thirty minutes before his shift started. There was enough time to get lunch, but he was unsure what he wanted. As he waited for the cars to pass so he could turn into the parking lot, he noticed Camille standing on the street corner and called her.

"Hello?" said Camille.

"I see you, Wisdom," joked Drake.

"Where are you?" asked Camille, looking around.

"I'm in the radio station parking lot," said Drake as he parked his car.

Camille turned around and spotted his car. She waved and hugged him when she reached him.

"Out here witnessing again?" asked Drake.

"Not right now," answered Camille. "I was actually on my way to catch the bus to the library."

"I could drive you."

"That's alright. I don't want you to be late for work."

"You hungry?"

"Am I hungry?"

"I've got some time to get lunch before my shift starts. If you want, you can join me."

"I am a little famished...," said Camille. She exclaimed, "I know this great place where we can go! Come on!"

Camille grabbed Drake's hand and started leading him up the street.

"I can drive us there."

"It's not that far," said Camille. "Plus, we can exercise our temples and not get stuck in lunch hour traffic."

"I think you're the only person I know who refers to our bodies as temples," chuckled Drake.

"The Bible says–!"

"I know what it says. I've just never heard anyone actually reference it that way."

"Well, I'm not everybody. I'm a daughter of The King and He said my body is a temple of The Holy Ghost."

"Are you always this chaotic?"

"I rebuke that. Chaotic is not a Christian trait."

"You know what I mean."

"I do," giggled Camille. "I'm just myself. Nothing more, nothing less."

"So... the answer is yes."

"Have you always been this snarky?"

"I'm myself. Nothing more, nothing less."

"Well, I'm glad we know ourselves."

"What's at the library?"

"I'm working on a project for my film study class."

"You're interested in film?"

"Well, my major is journalism, but I took this class as an elective," explained Camille. "My professor wants us to do a presentation on lesser known people in the industry and their lives. I'm doing mine over Cindy Frazier."

"Who's that?"

"She was an actress in the seventies," said Camille. "She was in a lot of blaxploitation films, and her father was an actor too. She's also Irina Frazier's mother."

"Oh," said Drake. "I didn't know her mother was an actress too."

"A lot of people don't."

"Is she still alive?"

"No, she died," said Camille sadly. "Once the blaxploitation era ended, she retired from acting because the roles dried up."

"That's sad."

"Yeah."

"What are you doing after the library?"

"I'll probably nap and then do some witnessing."

"You witness every day?"

"Of course. A servant of God never rests!"

"Yes we do. The Lord literally tells us to rest in the Bible."

"You knew what I meant."

"I did. Do you like witnessing?"

"It's not about what I like. It's about what needs to be done."

"My stepfather says God doesn't need anything."

"He doesn't. But He still wants us to preach the gospel."

"And you enjoy the way you do it?"

"Yep."

"Don't you ever get scared though? Being out there on the street by yourself and approaching random people?"

"If God is for me who can be against me? I trust God to protect me while I'm out there witnessing. And the people I talk to are people who take interest in what I'm saying. Some of them can be jerks but some of them are also people who want to hear about God. Talking and sharing God with those people makes dealing with the jerks worth it. And if God decides to let someone kill me while I'm witnessing then at least I'll be in Heaven."

"Don't say that," chastised Drake. "Power of life and death is in the tongue."

"You're right," agreed Camille. "That's definitely not how I would like to die."

"You're as bad as my stepfather," said Drake. "He'll get carried away preaching and say stuff he doesn't actually want to happen to him."

"What does your stepfather do?"

"He's an accountant and a pastor. He's the head pastor of our church in my hometown."

"So you're a preacher's kid?"

"Well now I am. But I didn't grow up as one."

"How's that work?"

"My mom married my stepdad when I was twelve, but I lived with my dad."

"Really? I thought kids usually went with the mother."

"He was in a better financial position than my mother was."

They passed by the movie theater and Drake noticed Camille frown. She had glanced at the poster for the new Drake Malone movie, 'Drake Malone: Back In Action'. Drake glanced at the poster, wondering what she had seen wrong with it. Standing in the forefront was the titular Drake Malone, played by Baby Luke under his real name, Lukas Mc-Kinney. Forty-eight-year-old Baby Luke was the youngest member of The Boombox Boyz, and Drake Malone had been his first lead acting role. Behind him was his partner, Karla Klein, played by Irina Frazier. At forty-eight, Irina Frazier was still one of the hottest Black actresses in more ways than one. Drake, like his fictional namesake, was mesmerized by her beautiful medium-brown face.

"Do you plan on seeing the new Drake Malone movie?" asked Drake.

"I don't know yet," said Camille. "There's just so much craziness in the movies these days."

"I still can't believe we're getting a sequel twenty years after the first movie. And I can't believe Baby Luke and Irina Frazier came back."

"Why wouldn't they? The first one made them movie stars."

"Well, you know how some people are about doing sequels."

"Yeah."

"I just hope it's as good as the first one."

"Well, her husband is the one making it again and I doubt he'd write, direct, and produce a terrible movie for his wife to star in."

"How ironic that we're talking about Morgan Abernathy and that's your last name too."

"Mhmm," said Camille quickly. "I'm sure this new movie will be great. I'm sure the acting will be great too. Especially hers. My favorite role of hers is when she played A'shyra in this indie movie called... well A'shyra."

"I don't think I've seen that one."

"It's one of her earlier roles before she did the first Drake Malone movie. It was also the first time she worked with Abernathy."

"Oh," said Drake. "I'm definitely excited to see her in this new Drake Malone though."

"You and every other man in existence," said Camille with a smirk while tilting her head toward him.

"Hey!" whined Drake. "For all we know you could be going to see the movie for Baby Luke."

If I'm going to see the movie, it's because I want to see the movie," said Camille. She quietly added, "No matter how fine Baby Luke is."

"Well, I for one am glad you find him attractive," said Drake. "Because it would be terrible to be named after a character that was ugly."

"What?" snorted Camille. "There's no way you're named after him."

"I'm serious," said Drake. "My mom named me after Drake Malone, and my sister after Karla Klein."

"I don't believe you."

"I'll prove it," said Drake.

Drake called Karla.

"Hello?" said Karla.

"Sister, I have you on speakerphone," said Drake. "What's your name?"

"What?"

"What's your name?"

"Karla?"

"And who are you named after?"

"Why are you asking me this? You know full well Mom named me after that Karla Klein character just like she named you after Drake Malone."

"My friend didn't believe we were named after them."

"I wouldn't either," said Karla. "Let me tell you about what your sister did today."

"Oh Lord," said Drake, taking Karla off speaker. "What'd she do?"

"What didn't she do?!" ranted Karla. "This don't make no sense! I have to take her over to Tavia's because she don't know how to act! Sitting up throwing tantrums!"

"I was not!" cried Layla.

"Yes you were! Now sit back and be quiet!"

"You sound like her mama," chuckled Drake.

"At this point I am her mama!"

"No you're not!" said Layla.

"Girl, if you don't sit your narrow behind down in that backseat!" warned Karla. "I don't understand why this little girl don't know how to act today! Why am I the one always having to take care of somebody's kids?!"

"Because you like kids."

"That don't mean I always want to watch them! I swear, your parents always give me their kids to watch!"

"I know," said Drake. "I was there watching them too. You've got to remember that Layla is six."

"So?"

"Do you remember what you were like when you were six?"

"Not like her!"

"You were worse."

"You know what, bye! Sitting up playing on my phone!"

"Don't get mad because it's true."

"Byyyyyyyye-uh!" said Karla.

"Byyyyyyyyyyyyyyye-uh!" said Drake.

"You and your sister are funny," laughed Camille.

"Do you have siblings?"

"I have a sister and two brothers. I'm the oldest."

"Me too. I have two brothers and four sisters."

"And one of them is six?" blurted Camille. Realizing what she said, she blushed and added, "I... I wasn't listening, I just... overheard."

"That's alright. My youngest sister is six."

"How old are you?"

"Twenty-one."

"That's crazy. You're twenty-one and your youngest sister is six. My youngest brother is sixteen. And my other brother is the same age as you."

"So, you're twenty-three, your brother is twenty-one, and your other brother is sixteen. That just leaves your sister."

"She's seventeen."

"Ah. Yeah, me and most of my siblings are stairstep children. I'm twenty-one, Karla's twenty, my second sister Mary is nineteen, my younger brother Andre is turning eighteen on Thursday, my third sister Adrianna turns sixteen next month, my youngest brother Antoine will be fifteen in May, and then my youngest sister Layla will be seven in June."

"Your parents didn't have to be fruitful and multiply that quickly. And why that big gap between the brother and the youngest one?"

"She's the stepdad's."

"Oh."

"My dad's getting married Saturday and I think he plans on adding more children to his tribe."

"Oh Lord," said Camille. "Yeah, my parents are definitely not having any more kids."

"Sometimes I think my parents had so many kids because there isn't much else to do in my hometown."

"Where are you from?"

"Creeke."

"Where's that?"

"You don't know where Creeke is?"

"Should I?"

"It's just down the road."

"Oh."

"I take it you're not from this area."

"What makes you say that?"

"You didn't know where Creeke was."

"Am I supposed to?"

"No, I guess not. So, what brought you out here?"

"My dad's from here."

"You live here with your family then?"

"No, they live elsewhere. I'm out here by myself."

"By yourself?"

"By myself. My dad moved everyone closer to him so I'm here all alone. Just me and God."

"No boyfriend either?"

"You're a nice guy Drake but–!"

"I have a girlfriend already."

"Oh?" said Camille, raising her eyebrows. "Does she go to the church?"

"Not up here. She's in Creeke."

"So, it's a long-distance relationship."

"I wouldn't call it long distance."

"You live in different cities. It's long distance."

Camille's spot was a food truck run by a woman named Ms. TiTi in a food truck park. Taped to the side of the truck was a flyer for a singing contest happening that Thursday. Drake took note of it.

"Camille!" squealed Ms. TiTi.

"Hey Ms. TiTi," said Camille. "Can you get me my usual please?"

"Sure thing," said Ms. TiTi. She looked at Drake and said, "And for you honey?"

"Uh...," said Drake, looking at the menu. "I'll have what Camille is having."

"I'll have that right out for you guys," said Ms. TiTi.

"How's business been?" asked Camille.

"Business is better than ever," said Ms. TiTi. "I thought I would take a huge hit to my sales when Sepia got shut down, but it turns out this new location is way more profitable and way safer!"

"God is good," said Camille.

"All the time," said Ms. TiTi.

Camille's usual turned out to be a catfish plate with collard greens, and macaroni and cheese. The pair started back toward the radio station.

"Do you like working at the radio station?" asked Camille.

"Yeah," said Drake.

"Do you plan on being there a long time?"

"It's a start. But what I'd really like to be is a singer."

"You're already a singer. You sing in the church choir."

"A professional singer."

"Well, you're certainly under the right man who could teach you some things. I personally wish he'd make some more music himself."

"You listen to rap?"

"Christian rap, yeah."

"That's interesting."

"Why?"

"I didn't think you'd like the genre."

"I'm not an old maid, Drake," laughed Camille. "Did you think I was one of those beatless worship people?"

"Beatless worship?" chuckled Drake.

"You know," said Camille. "One of those people who claim every instrument is demonic even though God is the one who created instruments and there are several instances of instruments being used during praise breaks in the Bible."

"That's... an interesting perspective."

"Well, you better get used to perspectives like that if you want to be a professional artist."

"It almost sounds like something Mr. King might say," said Drake. "Sometimes I wonder if Mr. King would really help me if I asked him to."

"Can't say I blame him," said Camille. "That industry will have you doing some strange stuff to stay relevant if you're not careful."

"You talk as if you've been there," observed Drake.

"I...," said Camille. "I just want you to be mindful, that's all. I know you'll succeed. But when you do, be careful. You could completely lose yourself and not realize it until it's already happened."

The pair arrived back at the intersection where they met.

"Well, this is where I leave you," said Camille. "The bus should be arriving soon. Thanks for lunch."

"You're welcome."

Camille began walking but stopped and turned to Drake.

"You're a really nice guy, Drake," said Camille. "I'm glad we're friends."

And then she was off. The way she tilted her head when she said it was uncanny to Drake. He had seen it somewhere before, but he could not place where.

Compared to the previous day, his radio station shift was uneventful. After work, Drake was determined to speak to Tamela. Sometimes she answered his calls, and sometimes she did not. It took everything in him not to rush down to Creeke and see her in person. She needed space, and he respected that, but it did not make him worry any less.

"Hello?" said Tamela, answering his call.

"Hey," said Drake. "Can you talk?"

"For a little bit," yawned Tamela. "I'm about to go to bed."

"Okay," said Drake. "I just wanted to check on you."

"I'm doing okay."

"How's school?"

"School's fine. I might be able to graduate early in December."

"That's good. I'm proud of you."

"Thanks. It definitely hasn't been easy."

"I know it hasn't. But you know I'm here for you if you need me."

"I know."

"How's your mom?"

"She's good."

"How's her treatments going? Does it seem like she's getting better?"

Tamela did not answer right away. When she did, she sounded as if she were holding back tears.

"Drake, I'm really tired and I have to get up early tomorrow. Do you mind if I call it a night?"

"Sure. Get some rest."

"Thank you. Goodnight."

"Goodnight. I love you."

"I love you too."

Drake knew something was wrong. Tamela had not answered his questions. He wanted to be by her side and hold her and comfort her. But he could not do so if she did not want him to, and it hurt. It hurt terribly.

The Oldest Son's Rite of Passage

Trying to find my way out here,
Trying to be the change.
I'm coming into my manhood,
Through my rite of passage.

The most intriguing job I have,
Is the oldest brother.
Even if they won't to admit it,
I'm like second father.

Trying to find my way out here,
Trying to be the change.
I'm coming into my manhood,
Through my rite of passage.

I can't count the number of times,
"You're not the boss of me!"
Has escaped from my siblings' mouths.
I've never tried to be.

Trying to find my way out here,
Trying to be the change.
I'm coming into my manhood,
Through my rite of passage.

I didn't ask to have this role,
Sometimes it's such a pest.
But if it were left up to me,
I'd still be the oldest.

Trying to find my way out here,
Trying to be the change.

I'm coming into my manhood,
Through my rite of passage.

Wednesday

By Wednesday, Drake was ready for the week to be over so he could enjoy his weekend. Then he remembered his father's wedding was that weekend, which made him remember the money he owed Matthias. Drake was in the middle of his radio station shift, mulling over his three options to handle the situation.

The first was to miraculously scrounge up five thousand dollars in two days. But it had taken him almost six months just to save what little he had, so the first option was unlikely. His second was to beg Matthias for more time, and the outcome of that depended entirely on Matthias. Drake feared that Matthias would possibly be just as ruthless in taking his five thousand dollars back as he was generous when he had loaned it out.

Drake's final option was to ask his father for help. It was the safest, surefire, and most reasonable option, but Drake was uncomfortable taking it. Every time he worked up the nerve to ask, he heard his father saying those words and decided against it. He had done alright for himself so far and made it through the terrible fall without having to ask his father for help. Therefore, he figured he could make it through his present crisis too.

Drake exhaled frustratedly and looked at the clock. There were three hours left in his shift. The four o'clock show would not start for another hour, and Drake had already programmed all the music to play for the three o'clock hour. He had nothing to do and no one to talk to. Calling or texting Tamela was out of the question because she was in class, but Drake doubted she would respond even if she were not. She was hiding something from him, but the last thing he wanted to do was make things harder on her by badgering her for the truth. It seemed like every aspect of Drake's life was a mess, and he had no way of fixing it.

As Drake was lost in thought, he heard someone enter the station. He looked up, and his eyes almost bulged out his head. Standing in the station was Ra'Kaveon King. Drake should not have been surprised to see him since he was Mr. King's son, but the reality was that Ra'Kaveon had never visited the station since Drake had been there.

"Hey," said Ra'Kaveon. "Is Mr. King here?"

"No... not yet," said Drake, finding his voice. "He should be here in a bit though."

"Alright, I'll wait," said Ra'Kaveon. He sat in one of the radio guest chairs and propped his feet on the table. "I ain't never seen you around here before. You new?"

"Yes."

"What's your name?"

"Drake."

"Got a last name, Drake?"

"Brown."

"Drake Brown. What do you do here?"

"I run the soundboard."

"A sound guy," said Ra'Kaveon, nodding his head approvingly. "Cool. I'm sure you already know who I am, but you can call me Rak."

"Okay."

There was a moment's silence until Ra'Kaveon spoke again.

"You like working for my Pops?"

"Yeah."

"Cool. You from around here?"

"I'm from Creeke."

"Oh," sneered Ra'Kaveon. "You're one of those Cowboys from down the road."

"Yeah, I went to Creeke High," said Drake, feeling the need to defend his alma mater.

"What made you want to work here?"

"I needed a job."

Another silent moment.

"Were you here when my Pops was ranting about me over the air?"

"Yeah."

"What'd you think of that?"

"It's not my business."

"You mind the business that pays you, huh?" laughed Ra'Kaveon. His smile slowly faded, and it seemed like he wanted to say more. But he just frowned and stared off into space.

Mr. King entered, and his eyes went straight to his son.

"Ra'Kaveon Armand King, take your darn feet off my darn table!" hollered Mr. King.

"Pops!" snapped Ra'Kaveon, standing up to meet his father. "Why'd you dog me out like that over the radio?"

"I told the truth about what I thought!"

"You could've told it to me first! Why I got to hear about it over the radio?!"

"Don't raise your voice at me, boy! You got yourself looking stupid trying to portray someone you're not! Running up in that nightclub and starting a brawl?! Letting your cousin walk around with a gun on him?!"

"How was I supposed to know D'Marko had a gun on him? I'm not his pops!"

"You're his older cousin! You're supposed to look out for him! Now he's in jail behind some mess that you started!"

"Look, I told Vince it was on sight when I caught him."

"That's not how your mother and I raised you and you know it!"

"I'll handle my business how I see fit. And the next time you got something to say, be a man and tell me to my face!"

"Don't talk to me that way! It's already bad enough that you're out here making devil music!"

"How come my music is devil music, but you have nothing to say about Alice's music?"

"Because you're the one acting a fool!" ranted Mr. King. "Take this so-called Rite of Passage remix for example! I mean listen to some of these lyrics!"

Drake could not believe his ears. He had never imagined Mr. King saying some of the phrases he read off.

"Wow Pops, I've never known you to talk like that," said Ra'Kaveon with a smirk.

"Boy…!" growled Mr. King. "And the music video is even worse! Men throwing up gang signs, women running around half-naked women and gyrating and degrading themselves!"

"I didn't tell any of those people to do that."

"You're in the video cheesing, throwing money, grabbing all over them, and even holding up scorecards based on how much they gyrate!"

"It's not my fault the only dance moves they know how to do is shake their butts, just like it's not my fault those guys stood behind me throwing up signs. We told them to dance and that's what they chose to do."

"Ra'Kaveon, you are an independent artist just like I am an independent artist. Everything from the song to the video goes through you for final approval, so don't try and bullcrap me. I don't like nothing you're doing! You reach and influence a lot of people through your music. What type of impact do you want to make on them?"

"I'm just trying to give them something that's fun and makes them feel good!"

"There are lots of things that make you feel good and lead you straight to Hell. Is that what you want? To lead people to Hell?"

"I didn't come here for this. I just dropped by to tell you that if you've got something to say about me, you can say it to my face. You don't have to put me on blast over the air."

"It's my station and I'll do as I see fit."

"Alright Pops," said Ra'Kaveon, nodding and pursing his lips. "Alright."

"Yeah, alright," said Mr. King. "Now if you don't mind, I've got work to do."

Ra'Kaveon stormed out of the station.

"Young folks these days!" ranted Mr. King as he went into his office. "Ain't got none of the sense The Good Lord gave them!"

Drake kept his head low and focused on his job. He already had enough going on, and the last thing he needed was to be dragged into someone else's problems. The workday could not end fast enough for him, but when it did, he rushed home to finally have a moment to think for himself. But as usual, Quentin was sitting on his couch playing Andrew's video game.

"Hey," said Drake.

"Hey," answered Quentin. "You going to church tonight?"

"We'll see," said Drake. "I met Rak today."

"You did?"

"He came to the station and argued with Mr. King."

"Sounds about right. You decided on what to do with Vince yet?"

"Still thinking on it."

"Don't think too long," said Quentin. "My name is on the line here."

"Okay," said Drake. "Do you think he stole from Rak?"

"Why are you asking me?" answered Quentin. "I wasn't there."

"Because if he'll do his best friend dirty, then he'll do me dirty, and I don't have time for that."

"I see your point," said Quentin. "Honestly, I've never known Vince to be a thief. He's always been real laidback and only focused on his music. From what they both told me, they were filming the video for a song they were preparing to release, but Rak couldn't find the chains he was going to wear in the video. They found them mixed in with Vince's stuff, and Vince claimed he didn't take any of it. They both just assumed their stuff somehow got mixed together and let it go. Then a week later, some money and the chains came up missing from Rak's place. And Rak thinks Vince did it because he had recently been over there the day they went missing, and he'd already been caught with the chains once before. Vince keeps saying he didn't do it, but Rak is the type of guy where once he settles on something in his mind, it's hard to change it."

"Just like his dad," sighed Drake.

"Yep," agreed Quentin. "Just like his dad."

Drake ended up attending church that night. Hosea was once again preaching the service. While Drake listened to the message, he caught himself playing with the cross necklace he always wore. It was a gift his father had given him and his siblings, and it made Drake realize he had not spoken to his father in a few days. After service ended, he called his father on the way home.

"Hello?" said Mr. Brown.

"Hi," said Drake. "Are you at church?"

"Church ended a while ago," chuckled Mr. Brown. "What's going on?"

"I uh... was just calling to say hi."

"Oh."

"I'll be down there Friday evening."

"You already told me that."

"Oh yeah."

There was a silent pause. It was another opportunity to ask his father for help, but he could not do it.

"So... we just going to sit in silence?" asked Mr. Brown.

"No, I...," said Drake. "Just making sure you knew when I'd be down."

"Okay..."

"I'll see you Friday then."

"See you Friday."

Drake hung up. He realized he could not ask his father for help. Therefore, he had to go with his next best option: begging Matthias for mercy and more time.

I Miss You

You know you barely call.
When you do talk is small.
Don't talk like we used to.
What's going on with you?
What is life like now,
That you aren't in my house?
Are you doing okay?
Did you have a good day?
Do you need anything?
Can I help with something?
Why won't you talk to me?
What could the problem be?
Why'd I let you go when,
I know I wasn't ready yet?
I don't know what to do.
Don't you know I miss you?

-

Thursday

It was Andre's birthday.

Drake's younger brother had turned eighteen. Instead of calling his mother first, Drake called Andre.

"Hello?" answered Andre sleepily.

"Happy birthday," said Drake.

"Thanks," said Andre.

"How's it feel to finally be a man?"

"Okay, I guess."

"Got anything planned for today?"

"Not really."

"Okay. I'll let you get back to sleep."

"Bye," Andre yawned, hanging up the phone.

Drake hoped Thursday would be one of those days that flew by. He was trying something new that night and participating in the singing contest he had learned about earlier that week. It was at a lounge, and the winner received one thousand dollars as a prize. If Drake won, it would place him a lot closer to paying Matthias off.

"What's got you all excited today?" asked Mr. King.

"I have something planned for after work," answered Drake.

"Oh? Hopefully nothing that'll get you in trouble."

"It won't," said Drake. He thought about what Camille had advised him to do and decided to test the waters. "Mr. King?"

"Yeah?" answered Mr. King.

"Do you think a music career is worth it?"

"It depends on what you're trying to do."

"Singing...?"

"Singing huh?" repeated Mr. King, scratching his chin. "It's a lot of people out there trying to break into that one."

"You don't think it's worth it?"

"I wouldn't say that," said Mr. King. "I'd say it'd be a good idea to have other ventures alongside the singing."

"I see."

"But I'd also say that you should take the risk," added Mr. King. "You never know where The Lord will lead you with it."

"Let's say I did take a risk like that," said Drake. "Would you help me?"

Mr. King did not answer right away. Drake could see he was seriously considering his answer.

"It depends on what you'd want my help with," said Mr. King after careful deliberation.

"What could you offer?"

"Old man advice and singing lessons."

"How much would it cost?"

"The advice would be free. Singing lessons would be fifty an hour."

"Okay."

"Okay."

Mr. King returned to his office. Drake knew that Mr. King had a lot of great advice to offer, having been a professional music artist since the late eighties. And while he knew he was a great singer, Drake also knew he could always benefit from working to improve. The offer was a good one, and Drake was inclined to seriously consider it.

By the time the contest rolled around, Drake was jittery with excitement. Andrew was not home when he left, so he went by himself. But he soon learned it would not stay like that for long. When he arrived at the lounge, he spotted his eighteen-year-old cousin, Mariana Garza, sitting near the stage.

"What are you doing here?" asked Drake approaching her.

"What are *you* doing here?" responded Mariana. She glared at him with the blue eyes she had inherited from her father.

"I'm entering the singing contest," said Drake. "And I'm grown."

"I'm grown too."

"Barely. And you still haven't said why you're here."

"I'm... entering the singing contest too," said Mariana, blushing.

"Oh?" said Drake. "Let's sing together then. We can win and split the prize money."

"Absolutely not," said Mariana. "I'm going to sing by myself and win by myself."

"Alright. But I'm not holding back. I plan on winning too."

"And? I'm just as good a singer as you are. Probably better because I can sing in more than one language."

"Well, I have the better range so what's your point?"

Before she could respond, Mariana was interrupted by another arrival at their table.

"Are you nervous?" asked an older woman to Mariana. She was tannish brown with black curly hair.

"A little," answered Mariana.

"Oh my gosh, you have to try these!" said another girl, sitting at the table with a tray of nachos. Drake had never seen the girl or the woman before. But the girl sounded familiar to him. She was light-brown with straightened brown hair and multiple ear piercings and bore some resemblance to the older woman. The girl looked at Drake and asked, "Who's this?"

"My cousin Drake," said Mariana. "This is my friend Jada and her mamá Mrs. Serafina."

"Mhmm," said Jada. "I see the resemblance."

The name Jada sounded familiar. Drake felt like one of his siblings had mentioned her at some point, but he could not remember who. But who Jada was or why Mariana was there no longer mattered. It was time for the contest to begin, and Drake had gone into game mode.

Drake shined in front of a crowd, and he knew it. He had done choir and theatre in high school and had always been one of the go-to's for leading roles. Some people claimed nepotism because his father was the choir teacher, and the theatre teacher, Mr. Troy Lewis, was his stepfather's brother-in-law. But regardless of the connections, Drake had the talent to back it up, and he knew it.

The last time he had had to compete against someone musically was sophomore year of high school when he had auditioned against Jonathan Haynes for a role in a school play. That play had resulted in his first and only fight because of Jonathan's jealousy. Drake allowed himself to drift into the memory as he waited for his turn.

It was for a role Mr. Lewis had played as a senior at Creeke High School. Everyone thought Jonathan would get the role because he was a senior and had already played lead roles in previous productions. And he was one of Mr. Lewis's favorite students. But the lead role had singing parts, and Drake was a better singer than Jonathan. Since he was a sophomore, he was also eligible to audition for the lead role. So, he did.

Everyone was shocked that a sophomore would go against a senior for the final production of the year. They all figured Drake should have let Jonathan have it and waited until his time came. But Mr. Lewis allowed Drake to audition, and in the end, Drake got the lead role over Jonathan. Instead of being a good sport, Jonathan had chosen to spread rumors about Drake and make fun of his singing voice. But what had upset Drake most was Jonathan saying that Mr. Brown had cheated and gotten the role for Drake.

Drake had not cared if Jonathan trash-talked him, but trash-talking his father was another story. When he had gotten to school that morning, he had met up with Andrew and then seen Jonathan. He did not remember anything after punching Jonathan in the face. According to Andrew, Drake had punched Jonathan a few more times before Jonathan had started wrestling with him. By that point, Andrew had recovered from his shock and helped separate them. Then, Drake had started yelling and threw his shoes at Jonathan before being escorted to the principal's office. It was in that office, sitting beneath the glare of his angry father's eye, with a torn shirt and missing shoes, that Drake had regained his composure.

"You see this belt around my waist?" Mr. Brown had asked. He had leaned against the principal's desk with his arms folded across his chest. Drake had glanced at the aforementioned leather belt and nodded. "You

got one chance to convince me why I shouldn't take it off right now and wear you out in front of this whole school."

"Because I did away with corporal punishment at this school," Principal Arthur Lee had said, trying to de-escalate the situation.

"You want to be next?" threatened Mr. Brown.

"No," squeaked Principal Lee.

"Then sit there and shut up," commanded Mr. Brown. He had turned back to Drake and asked, "Why were you fighting?"

"Because Jonny was talking smack."

"About what?"

Drake had not answered, hoping it would somehow make his father less angry. It had not.

"You better answer me, little boy," growled Mr. Brown.

"About you," answered Drake.

"And what? You're my defender now?"

"I'm not going to let him talk smack about my father!"

"I don't care what some stupid kid says about me! You going to fight every person that says something bad about me?!"

There had not been much to say after that. Drake had been sent home from school and his mother had to pick him up.

"So... a fight, huh?" First Lady Hall had said.

"Yeah," Drake had said with a sigh.

"You know better than that."

"I'm not just going to let someone just disrespect my father."

"Yeah, but now you're suspended for three days, and both your father and mother are mad at you. Was it worth it?"

"Yes."

"Alright," First Lady Hall had warned. "We'll see in a few days if it was worth it."

His mother had been right. In the end, both Drake and Jonathan were dropped from the play and the role was tweaked to suit Mr. Lewis's daughter, Brianne.

"You were right," Drake had said to his mother when he found out he had lost the role.

"What about?" First Lady Hall had asked.

"The fight wasn't worth it. I lost the lead role in the play."

"And there's the big, hard lesson. Always think and consider everything you have to lose before you act. And if you decide that losing everything you've got is worth it, don't call me to bail you out because I will leave you in jail for being stupid."

"Thanks Mom," Drake had grumbled out.

"I'm serious! I'm over here being the level-headed parent to balance out your father's anger but really I want to smack you upside the head. Because if you think I'm going to have my children out here acting straight-up fools, you've got another thing coming. It's already bad enough you all be flinging shoes and screaming..."

His mother had ranted for a while, and his father even longer. And they both used him as an example to his siblings on what would not be tolerated. But despite it all, Drake had learned his lesson. And he knew that it would serve him well for years to come.

Drake was the fifth and last person to compete in the singing contest. Mariana sang a Spanish song that wowed the audience, while Drake had relied on an R&B classic that got everybody in the groove. He knew they were truly the best, but it was popularity with the audience and not talent that would win the contest. Still, Drake had fun even if he did not win.

"Contestant Number Four!" said DJ Yip-Yap, waving his hand above Mariana's head. She got a lot of cheers.

"Contestant Number Five!" said DJ Yip-Yap, waving his hand over Drake's head. It seemed like the whole room exploded in applause for him. "I think we have a winner."

The one-thousand-dollar cash prize was his. He was one step closer to paying Matthias back, and he was elated.

"You did good," said Drake to Mariana.

"If I did so good then why didn't I win?" griped Mariana.

"You're not always going to win," said Drake. "What's important is that you did your best and had fun."

"Says the winner," scoffed Mariana.

"Oh my gosh you did amazing!" said Jada, latching on to Mariana. "I told you you'd do great!"

"I guess," said Mariana.

"And you did amazing too Drake!"

"You both did a really good job," said Mrs. Serafina. "We should be getting home girls. It was nice meeting you Drake."

"Yeah, nice meeting you!" echoed Jada.

"Nice meeting you too," said Drake as he watched them leave.

Drake felt good about himself. He had won the singing contest and felt he stood a good chance of becoming Vincent's background singer if he chose to audition.

When he arrived home, he found Andrew sitting in the dark, watching television.

"Hey," said Drake. "You alright?"

"I'm good," said Andrew. "I had a great workout today."

"How do you find time to do it all?" said Drake.

"It's all about being organized," said Andrew. He laughed, adding, "Besides, I can't afford to slack off. My future wife could be one of my patients and I want to make sure I look my absolute best."

"Well, in a year you'll be graduated and off to the next step toward becoming the world's greatest doctor. So, it's only a matter of time until you find Mrs. Stone."

"Yeah," said Andrew.

"What kind of doctor do you plan on being?"

"I'm not sure yet."

Andrew was Drake's best friend and was the nicest, most laid-back guy Drake knew. But Drake was also well acquainted with Andrew's dark side. It's why Drake could tell Andrew was putting on a happy front for him. In a week, it would be the anniversary of his brother's death, and he knew Andrew still hurt from it, especially during March.

"Do you want to fight, race, or play basketball?" asked Drake, handing a controller to Andrew.

"Let's race," said Andrew.

The racing game did not go as terribly as Drake thought it would. He even beat Andrew once.

"Oho!" cheered Andrew. "You're getting good at this game!"

"Oh please," said Drake. "You probably let me win again."

"Nah, not this time. This time you actually did win."

After the race, Andrew sat his controller down and leaned back on the couch.

"That was fun," said Andrew with a smile.

"Are you ready to talk?" asked Drake.

Andrew's smile faded, and a sigh escaped his lips.

"I miss Simon," admitted Andrew. "I was thinking about him today."

"I know," said Drake.

"And you know what the worst part is?" said Andrew with a cynical chuckle. "He didn't have to die."

Drake nodded. He knew Simon had died from sickness resulting from a misdiagnosis, but Andrew had never told him fully what had happened.

"We waited in that waiting room for hours and they told us he just had a cold," said Andrew. "They didn't even bother running any tests. Just looked at him and said it was a cold. It wasn't a cold. It was pneumonia. We knew it wasn't just a cold, but they wouldn't believe us. They wouldn't listen to us. And by the time they did it was too late. I was there when he took his last breath. I saw him leave with my own eyes."

Andrew brought his knees to his chest and hid his face in them to muffle the sobs that escaped his lips.

"He should still be here," uttered Andrew. "I want to kill that doctor for letting my brother die. I wish I could knock that smug look off his face that he had that day. When I was hitting the bag today, I imagined I was punching him in his face. And no matter how much I punched it wasn't enough. It didn't stop the pain. It won't bring Simon back. I hate that man. I know it's wrong but I do. I hate him and anyone who thinks like him."

Andrew wiped his face and turned his reddened eyes on Drake.

"I'm going to be a better doctor than he was. I won't let what happened to Simon happen to someone else."

"I know you won't," said Drake. "And you know I'm here for you."

"I know," said Andrew. "You're a good friend Drake. A real good friend."

-

Does Daddy Respect Me?

I've been his sidekick since age ten.
Does Daddy respect me?
When he could not, I raised his kids.
Does Daddy respect me?

I still love him despite his flaws.
Does Daddy respect me?
I hope he loves me flaws and all.
Does Daddy respect me?

I've felt the heat from his fire.
Does Daddy respect me?
I took the brunt of his ire.
Does Daddy respect me?

I still love him despite his flaws.
Does Daddy respect me?
I hope he loves me flaws and all.
Does Daddy respect me?

I called out his flaws to his face.
Does Daddy respect me?
And manned up into my own space.
Does Daddy respect me?

I still love him despite his flaws.
Does Daddy respect me?
I hope he loves me flaws and all.
Does Daddy respect me?

Now there is trouble in my way.
Does Daddy respect me?

And I hope it's not here to stay.
Does Daddy respect me?

I still love him despite his flaws.
Does Daddy respect me?
I hope he loves me flaws and all.
Does Daddy respect me?

I wish I could tell my daddy.
Does Daddy respect me?
That this money is stressing me.
Does Daddy respect me?

I still love him despite his flaws.
Does Daddy respect me?
I hope he loves me flaws and all.
Does Daddy respect me?

I do not know what I will do
Does Daddy respect me?
But I'm praying God will come through.
Does Daddy respect me?

I still love him despite his flaws.
Does Daddy respect me?
I hope he loves me flaws and all.
Does Daddy respect me?

I have grown into my own man.
Does Daddy respect me?
But there's soreness with my old man.
Does Daddy respect me?

I still love him despite his flaws.

Does Daddy respect me?
I hope he loves me flaws and all.
Does Daddy respect me?

Friday

The dreaded moment had arrived. Friday afternoon, Drake arrived in Creeke and drove straight to Pastor Derrick Harrison's house to see Matthias. He had no doubt some saw him driving through the town. Pastor Derrick and his wife, Mrs. Kiana, lived on two acres of land on the outskirts of Creeke. It was within walking distance of the creek, but sometimes Drake wondered if it was really a creek because it was deep enough to swim in.

As he drove up the dirt path, he wondered what he would say to Matthias. He considered turning around and maybe avoiding Matthias altogether. But he quickly abandoned that idea because Matthias knew Drake would be at the wedding the next day and would find him there if necessary. Drake knew he had to rip the bandage off and get it over with. So, he knocked on the front door and waited to seal his fate.

It was Mr. Marlin Harrison who answered the door. Drake had not seen Mr. Harrison since he and Mr. Brown had fought at Creeke High. Mr. Harrison's house had been damaged by a fire in the winter, so he and his family were staying with his father until it was repaired. He stared blankly at Drake, waiting for Drake to state his business.

"Uh… is Matthias here?" asked Drake.

"Yeah," said Mr. Harrison.

"Can you ask him to come here please?"

Mr. Harrison disappeared, and seconds later, Matthias came out onto the porch.

"I don't have your money," said Drake before Matthias could say anything.

"Hi, hello, how you doing?" griped Matthias. "We don't do that no more?"

"I wanted to get to the point."

"Well, you really need to stop doing that."

"Matt, what is he talking about?" questioned Alexander Brown, stepping outside.

Drake realized he had messed up. He had not realized his cousin Alexander was visiting. In hindsight, he should have because he had parked beside Alexander's truck. But he had been so wrapped up in his thoughts he had not paid attention to his surroundings and had created an uncomfortable situation.

"Nothing," answered Matthias.

"Doesn't sound like nothing," said Alexander.

"It's none of your business."

"Matthias."

"Alexander."

"What money is Drake talking about?"

"It's none of your business."

Alexander began circling the pair, almost like a shark circling its prey.

"Matt, you know you're my boy," said Alexander.

"Yeah."

"And you know that I've always got your back."

"Yeah."

"But Drake is my family," said Alexander, stopping beside Drake. He put his hand on Drake's right shoulder and said, "You know my family comes first, just like I know your family comes first."

"Yeah."

"So, what is he talking about?"

"None of your business."

"You're really trying to bring the old Alex out today, aren't you?"

"Bring him out," said Matthias. "That dude was fun."

"So, you're really not going to tell me?"

"What have I told you about questioning a man on his money?"

Alexander released a frustrated sigh and spun Drake around to face him. Drake wished he were anywhere but under the heat of that gaze.

"Well?" demanded Alexander.

Drake glanced between Alexander and Matthias. One looked ready to kill him if he did not tell, while the other looked ready to do the same if he did.

"Don't worry about him," said Alexander. "Tell me what's going on."

While Drake loved and respected his older cousin and did not want to lie to him, he did not want to burden Alexander with his problems either. The situation was one that Drake wanted to handle alone, and that's what he intended to do.

"There's nothing to tell," said Drake.

"Then why are you here?"

"To talk to Matthias."

"About what? You never talk to Matthias."

"You don't know what I do."

"I know you said you don't have his money. What money are you talking about?"

"I have nothing to say."

"You know I won't let him do anything to you. So, if he's holding something over you–!"

"He's not."

"Then what's going on?"

"I have nothing to say."

Alexander gritted his lips and glared at Drake. He shot one final look at Matthias, then stormed off and drove away.

"He's mad at us," said Drake.

"He'll get over it," said Matthias. "How much you got?"

"I can give you what I do have."

"Let me have it."

"I'm sorry I don't have all of it," said Drake, handing Matthias the money he had saved.

"Okay."

"What are you going to do to me?"

"Nothing."

"Seriously?" gasped Drake. He had been fully prepared to face Matthias's wrath.

"I'm trying to live right," said Matthias. "Plus, Alex will get mad if I even breathe on you wrong."

"So I've been worried for nothing?"

"I still want the rest of my money if that's what you mean."

"And I'll get it to you as soon as I can," said Drake. "I promise."

"If you were anyone else, I wouldn't trust you to do it," said Matthias. "But I know you're good for it. Don't let me be wrong."

"I won't," said Drake.

He left before Matthias could change his mind. It felt like the weight on Drake's shoulders had lightened. The money he needed to pay back was still a priority, but it felt more possible than it had before he had talked to Matthias. Drake had two more stops to make before he went home.

His first stop was to visit his mother and Forrest. When he arrived, he found Layla napping on the couch and his mother nowhere in sight. Drake did not want to wake her, so he slipped past her into Forrest's office.

"Well, look who it is," said Forrest with a big grin.

"Shh!" shushed Drake. "Layla's sleeping."

"Ain't He good?" whispered Forrest. "That girl is just a nonstop ball of energy. That's probably why your mother snuck off with Karla to go get her hair done."

"Ah," said Drake. "Karla called me earlier this week ranting about Layla."

"Yeah, she's a handful," said Forrest. "I can't hardly imagine what she'll be like when she hits her teenage years."

"The Lord only knows."

"He sure does. So, how long are you in town for?"

"Just the weekend. I'm going back Sunday."

"Okay. You enjoying living on your own?"

"It's an interesting experience. Very expensive one too."

"Sure is. And with how expensive everything is nowadays I'd advise you to save every penny you can."

"Yes sir."

"Daddy!" called Layla.

"And she's up," sighed Forrest. "I'm in my office!"

Layla entered the office, and her dark-brown face lit up when she saw Drake.

"DRAKE!" hollered Layla, running to hug him. "Daddy! Daddy! Drake's here!"

"I see him big girl," said Forrest, smiling. "What did you want to tell me?"

"Mommy's home."

"She is? Well, where is she?"

"Forrest, are you in here?" asked First Lady Hall, entering the office. She saw Drake and smiled, asking, "When did you get here?"

"Just now," answered Drake.

"That's good," said First Lady Hall. "Have you been to see your father yet?"

"Not yet."

"Oh boy. I'll warn you now. It's a den of chaos over there."

"How come?"

"You know how your father is and you know how your brothers and sisters are."

"Maybe I should just stay over here..."

"Boy, don't be ridiculous," chided First Lady Hall. "Go on and go see your father. He should be home by now."

"Okay," said Drake. "I'll stop by again before I leave."

"I hope so," said First Lady Hall, walking him to the door. "It seems like my kids only remember they have a mother when something goes wrong."

"I love you too Mom."

"I know. I love you too."

Before going to his father's, Drake stopped to visit Derek Harrison. Derek had been Drake's friend since high school, and he was dating Adrianna. He had last seen Derek at the Creeke Church revival, but since then, Derek had had some troubles of his own, and Drake wanted to check on him. When he entered Derek's room, he found him lying in bed with his cast-covered leg propped up.

"Hey," muttered Derek.

"Sir, where are your clothes?" asked Drake.

"You and your sister say the same thing," grumbled Derek.

"You don't wear clothes when she visits?" questioned Drake.

"She just kind of drops by unannounced," answered Derek. "Last time, she went through my whole wardrobe and made fun of my clothes."

"Well, you do have... interesting tastes."

"It's not my fault I can pull anything off."

"I didn't say you couldn't," said Drake. "How you been?"

"Fine."

"How's things with you and Dria?"

"She's pissed at me."

"Why?"

"Ask her."

"I'm asking you."

Derek glared at Drake. Drake glared back.

"I did something wrong," admitted Derek.

"To her?"

"No. But she's pissed about what I did."

"What'd you do?"

"I can't tell you."

"Why not?"

"Because you'll be pissed at me too."

"Why would I be pissed at you?"

"Because you would."

"Hey," said Drake. "You know you can talk to me if something's wrong, right?"

"I'm fine."

"Well, when you're not fine, you know how to reach me," said Drake. "How's your leg?"

"Still broken," muttered Derek. He had been the victim of a hit-and-run during the winter. "It won't be fully healed until after graduation."

"That sucks."

"I won't get to dance at prom, I won't get to walk across the stage at graduation, and I'll spend most of the summer in rehab," complained Derek. "This is so annoying and unfair."

"Yeah," agreed Drake. "But at least you still have your leg."

"I guess..."

"You going to the wedding tomorrow?"

"Yeah."

"That's good. I should get going but I'll be here till Sunday if you need to talk."

"Alright."

Drake felt bad for Derek. But he also wondered what Derek had meant when he said he had done something that would upset Drake. As Drake arrived at his father's house, he figured he could get an explanation out of his sister.

Mr. Brown sat in the kitchen, shining his shoes. Shoes in the hands of his father always made Drake nervous. Although Mr. Brown had promised to no longer throw them, there were no guarantees of that promise's fulfillment when his temper was lost.

"Hi Dad," said Drake.

"Hi," said Mr. Brown, keeping his attention on his shoes.

Drake sat across from his father. The last time they spoke while his father shined his shoes was when Drake learned why his father had stopped singing. It had seemed like ages ago.

"You eaten yet?" asked Mr. Brown.

"No," answered Drake.

"Good. I'm having a family dinner tonight."

"A family dinner?"

"Me, you, your brothers, and your sisters. Including Karla. But not Layla."

"Why'd you have to specify?"

"Because Layla is not my child, but she is your sister," said Mr. Brown. "This dinner is for my specific children."

"I figured that's what you meant."

"I just wanted to be clear."

"You ready for tomorrow?"

"I'm getting there."

"You're getting there?"

"It just feels like there's so much to do before tomorrow," said Mr. Brown. "And it doesn't help that your brothers and sisters all decided to lose their collective minds this week either."

"What'd they do?"

"I'm not in the mood to discuss it."

That's where Drake let the conversation end. He went in search of Adrianna, who was in her room lying on a bed he did not remember her having the last time he was there. Her hair was wrapped up in a scarf, preserving the style she had just gotten done for the wedding.

"Is that my bed?" asked Drake.

"It's my bed now," said Adrianna.

"How you just going to take my bed?"

"It's not like you live here anymore to use it."

"You know what, where's Mary?" asked Drake.

"I don't know," answered Adrianna. "She's been out all day."

Drake was surprised. Out of all his siblings, Mary was the homebody and when she did go out, it was never for extended periods. As he looked closer at Adrianna, he noticed another surprise that he was not used to seeing.

"What's that all over your eyes and lips?"

"Makeup?"

"Since when do you wear makeup?"

"Since Mom said I could."

"I'm sure Dad wasn't too excited about that."

"Dad, like you, needs to stay out of women's business," said Adrianna. "Now, what did you come in here for?"

"To say hi," said Drake. "I went to see Derek today."

"Don't even mention him to me," scoffed Adrianna. "I'm so mad at that boy right now."

"What'd he do?"

"Act a fool in front of his little friends."

"That bad, huh?"

"I just can't with him right now."

Adrianna obviously did not want to discuss what Derek did. Drake accepted he might never know what happened and went to his old room that he had shared with his brothers. His bed had been traded with the bunk bed that used to be Adrianna and Mary's. Antoine had moved from the top bunk of the bed he had shared with Andre to the bottom bunk of the other bed. That meant Drake would have to sleep above one of them.

"Where's Antoine?" asked Drake, choosing to sleep above Antoine, who had the cleaner side of the room. Andre, like their father, was not the tidiest person by any means.

"Probably somewhere making money," answered Andre.

"He trying to get a new game or something?"

"He owes Dad two-hundred bucks."

"Why does he owe Dad two-hundred bucks?"

"He accidentally took too much money off Dad's card."

"Why'd he have Dad's card?"

"Dad gave it to him."

"Dad gets a new wife and starts acting brand new," joked Drake.

"You can say that again," muttered Andre.

"Do you know what happened between Dria and Derek?"

"Did she tell you?"

"No," said Drake. "And when I went to see him, he wouldn't tell me either."

"Oh."

"Do you know what happened?"

"I was there. But if they didn't tell you what happened, I don't think I should either."

"Look, I get that Derek is our friend, but Dria is our sister. If he's done something to her–!"

"He didn't do anything to her," said Andre. "And he's your friend, not mine."

"What?"

"I don't want to talk about this anymore."

"You can't just say something like that and then drop the subject. What do you mean he's not your friend?"

"He's not."

"Did he do something to you?"

Andre looked away.

"He did, didn't he?" said Drake. "That's why he said I'd be pissed if he told me. What'd he do?"

"This is for me to handle," said Andre.

"What are you handling?" demanded Drake. "Is he bullying you or something?"

"No, we just...," said Andre. "Look just let me handle it, okay?"

"Handle what?"

"Oh my gosh!" snapped Andre. "If I said I'm fine, I'm fine! Now leave me alone!"

The outburst shocked Drake. In fact, the state of the whole family shocked Drake. Everyone was acting out of character. His mother had been right: his father's house had turned into a den of chaos, and he was bringing a new wife into it in less than twenty-four hours. Drake went to sit on the porch to clear his head.

"Well, look who decided to finally show their face in town again," said Karla.

"You could always come visit me," said Drake. "I'm just down the road."

"I was just out there yesterday," answered Karla.

"Why didn't you say something?"

"I was with Mimi and Angie."

"And nobody told me nothing!"

"Boy, we went shopping and had lunch. Besides you were at work."

"So? You could've still something."

"What are you doing out here on the porch?"

"Everyone in there has an attitude."

"What else is new?"

"Poor Gretchen is moving in tomorrow and this is what she has to look forward to."

"She chose it just like she chose him."

"I'm sure she didn't expect it to be like this though."

"She'll learn soon enough. I tried to warn her, but we'll see if she listened. Besides it's not our problem because we don't live here anymore."

Drake sighed. At least Karla acted like herself. But Drake wondered if it was because of what she had said. Neither she nor he lived with their father anymore. And yet, within mere minutes of returning, he had fallen back into his old role of being an additional parent to the household.

It amazed Drake how easily he had fallen back in line. How easy it had been to take up his old seat at his father's dinner table; on his father's right, between Mary and Karla and across from Antoine like when they were children. What amazed him most was how normal it felt to sit at that table and avoid his father's eyes. Everyone looked un-happy sitting at that dinner table. And all Drake could do was wonder what he had missed that made everyone so tense.

Karla Brown

To Karla Elizabeth Brown

Sweet precious daughter of mine,
Your mother named you after Karla Klein.
You are my second child,
And I think it's a bit wild,
That I had a daughter and son,
By the age of twenty-one.
I've never been one to drink,
But the day you came I couldn't think.
And besides I was grown too,
And nobody couldn't tell me what to do.
Or at least that's what I thought.
Grandpa caught me and we fought.
He said he didn't raise me that way,
It was only one drink to calm me that day.
And I'll never do it again,
Because I want me, Grandpa, and Karla to be friends.

Friday

Karla had always been the furthest from her father. Furthest in looks, furthest in opinion, and furthest in relationship. He had caused that distance between them by driving her away with his misdirected anger, just as he had driven her mother away. With his upcoming wedding, Karla wondered if a second marriage would help her father change his ways. She also wondered if he planned to bring more children into his dysfunction.

"Jesus, how I love You, you're everything that I need," sang Karla, listening to the radio station Drake worked at as she braided Layla's hair.

"To You I give my praises, my life is incomplete without thee," sang Layla, completing the rest of the chorus.

"Mmhmm," said Karla, chuckling at her six-year-old sister's knowledge of the lyrics. "Mommy is definitely still wearing that one out in the car."

"Are you done yet?" asked Layla, squirming impatiently.

"Almost."

"When will you be done?"

"When I'm done."

"When is that?"

"When I'm done, Layla."

"When?"

"Little girl," griped Karla. She paused to calm herself, then exhaled out, "Sit still, okay? I'm almost done."

"Okay..."

Karla shook her head, then chuckled as she remembered when she had been in Layla's position. When her father had first tried doing her hair following his divorce, he had been so rough that Karla had snatched the brush from his hand. He yelled at her for it and had continued yelling at her for things over the years until Karla had had enough. On her eighteenth birthday, she had packed all her stuff and wordlessly walked past her father out the front door. And he had not tried to stop her.

"Alright," said Karla, snapping the final barrette into place. "You're done."

"Finally!" cheered Layla, running to the bathroom mirror to admire herself.

Karla began putting away her supplies when the smell of cocoa butter wafted up her nose, informing her that her stepfather, Pastor Forrest Hall, was near.

"Hey," said Forrest.

"Hello sir," said Karla, acknowledging her stepfather.

"I'm leaving out soon, so I came to say goodbye to my girls."

"Layla ran off to the bathroom. She'll be back soon."

"I said my *girls*," said Forrest. "That includes you too, Karla. Like I've said before…"

"I know, I know," sighed Karla. "You have four daughters, not one."

"That's right," said Forrest. "Four daughters and three sons. You, your brothers, and your sisters are just as much my children as Layla is."

"I know."

"I know you know," said Forrest. "You've been living here for two years now, I'm sure you know by now that I always mean what I say."

"Just like my–!"

"Daddy!" cried Layla, running to her father.

"There's my big girl!" cheered Forrest, scooping Layla up in his arms.

Just like her father. That's what Karla was about to say. Her daddy was long gone. At fifty-two, Forrest was calm, cheerful, and encouraging, unlike Karla's moody and overly critical forty-one-year-old father.

Karla did not hate her father by any means. Despite their issues, she loved him dearly. She just figured the best way to love him and maintain her peace of mind was to do so from afar. And though Forrest was not biologically her father, she appreciated that he was willing to also be a type of father to her.

"Layla Esther," instructed Forrest, lifting Layla to eye level. "You be a good girl for Mommy and Karla, you hear?"

"Yes sir," said Layla.

"That's my big girl," said Forrest, kissing Layla on the forehead.

"When will you be back?" asked Karla. Forrest was preaching at another church that Sunday. First Lady Hall would preach Creeke Church's main service at his request, and she was not excited about it.

"Monday at the latest," said Forrest. "Take care of your mother for me, okay?"

"I've been taking care of her all my life," joked Karla.

"Well, hopefully you can take a rest after I get back," said Forrest, hugging her.

Karla blushed at the affectionate act. Forrest had always let her set the pace of their relationship. As she stood on the porch with her mother and sister, watching him drive away, she remembered how wary she had been of him at first. And it had all been because of her father.

Mr. Brown had made Forrest out to be a terrible man who had seduced his wife away from him. But after becoming an adult herself, Karla realized her father had just been bitter. Forrest had become youth pastor when Karla's parents were seniors in high school, and while Mr. Brown had grown close with Forrest during that time, her mother had barely known him because she and her family had barely attended church.

Her mother had become romantically involved with Forrest a year after the divorce. They had both been set up on blind dates at the same restaurant but had ended up eating together after they were stood up. Things had taken off from there and as quickly as her mother had fallen in love with Forrest had been how quickly her father had started hating him.

Karla remembered her father always believing that he could win her mother back. He had treated Forrest horribly, but Forrest had always been forgiving despite the mistreatment. Once Forrest had married his new First Lady Hall, Mr. Brown stopped hoping she would come back to him and accepted defeat. Over time, he had moved on from First

Lady Hall and they all had since gotten to a place where they could be friendly. First Lady Hall even asked Mr. Brown to watch Layla once when she had no other option, claiming that since she trusted him to care for her first six kids, it would not make sense to distrust him with her seventh. But Karla could never forget how he had been during that time because he had taken out all his frustrations on her.

"You ready for your father's wedding next weekend?" asked First Lady Hall later that night when they were alone.

"I don't know," answered Karla.

"Well, I am," said First Lady Hall. "I'm glad he's finally accepted our divorce and moved on. Hopefully he'll be a lot happier with Gretchen."

"She seems to make him happy."

"All the kids like her too," added First Lady Hall. "I just hope she's prepared to handle that house full of strong personalities."

"I hope so too," agreed Karla. "So, what are you preaching about Sunday?"

"Lord, don't remind me," sighed First Lady Hall. "I tried to get Mr. Derrick to do the main service but he refused. I wish we could just skip this Sunday and wait for Forrest to come back."

"Skip church?" gawked Karla. "Are you sure you're my mother?"

"Haha, very funny," said First Lady Hall. "But you're right, we can't skip church. We've got to go through this."

"That's right," agreed Karla.

"And you remember how Mrs. Stone stopped me to talk last Sunday?"

"Yeah."

"Guess who we were talking about?"

"Andrew?"

"Mhmm. She wanted to let me know he was doing well in school and very much single."

"What's that got to do with you?"

"Well, she figured that maybe we could try getting our very much single children together."

"Which single child did she mean?" asked Karla, arching her eyebrows.

"Well, you don't see me having this conversation with Mary, do you?"

"Me date Andrew?!" choked Karla. "No! That's Drake's best friend! That would be so awkward!"

"I agree," said First Lady Hall. "But *is* there a special young man in your life?"

"Jesus."

"Now Karla," snorted First Lady Hall.

"If I had a man you'd already know."

"I was just checking."

"I'm not interested in anyone right now," said Karla. "I just turned twenty. I want to live a little first."

"That's funny," chuckled First Lady Hall. "I was already married to your father and with a child by the time I was your age."

"How? I feel like my life has barely started."

"Your father and I were young, and we both thought we were so in love."

"Do you regret marrying him?"

"No," said First Lady Hall. "Your father wasn't a bad guy by any means. I loved him but he had... has issues to work through and he has to want to work through them. I thought if I loved him enough and stuck by him through his anger it would be enough to help him move past it, but it wasn't. All it did was tire me out until I couldn't handle it anymore."

Karla nodded with understanding.

"When you finally do start dating, don't do what I did with your father," advised First Lady Hall. "Don't go into it believing you can fix him because you can't. Only God can do that."

"Yes ma'am."

Karla appreciated her mother's advice but did not see herself using it anytime soon. She planned to finish college and live her life before she got married. Any man that could take her off track from that had to be extraordinary. And by Karla's standard, there was not a single man in Creeke extraordinary enough to do so.

My Daddy Was The Problem

Mommy, Mommy, I really want to know,
And please tell me the truth and not a lie.
Why is it that you had to up and go?
And why is it that you left me behind?

Is there something that I did that was wrong?
Something wrong you couldn't forgive me for?
Why is it you couldn't take me along?
Why did you leave me staring out the door?

I look back now and know it wasn't me,
Because I'm not the one who made you sad.
Whatever broke between you and Daddy,
Changed him and hurt you leaving you down bad.

I don't know what you told the rest of them,
But I know my daddy was the problem.

Monday

Sunday service had been a disaster. A good chunk of the regular congregation had not shown up, and those who did had suffered through First Lady Hall's sermon. That Monday afternoon, First Lady Hall sat at her parent's kitchen table, filling them in on all the gory details of how terribly the service had gone.

"It wasn't that bad, Lana," encouraged Gran Ernestine Allen. "Honestly, it wasn't."

"Ernie don't lie," said Grandpap Jared Allen. "That girl looked like she was dying up there."

"Jared!" gasped Gran Ernestine. "Don't say that about your daughter!"

"Lana's been my daughter for a long time. She knows how I talk."

"Lord, have mercy."

Karla could not help but agree with her grandfather on both statements. He was sixty-eight, and Karla had always known him to be slick at the mouth. Gran Ernestine was sixty-four and was just as witty as Grandpap Jared, but she at least had sense enough to leave some thoughts in her brain.

"Daddy's right," sighed First Lady Hall. "I shouldn't have been up there. And I know most of the people didn't show up because they don't like me as First Lady."

"That ain't got nothing to do with you, Buttercup," said Grandpap Jared. "You got up there and did what you were asked to do and that's all anyone can ask of you."

"That's right," agreed Gran Ernestine. "If they didn't want to come hear the message and missed out on their blessing, then that's on them."

"I just wish Forrest were here," said First Lady Hall glumly.

The sounds of children laughing and playing drifted into the house. Layla was outside running around with the neighboring children, enjoying her spring break away from school.

"Well, at least someone's happy today," said Gran Ernestine.

"And she'll sleep good tonight too," added Grandpap Jared.

"You would think so," said First Lady Hall. "But it's like that girl never runs out of energy."

"Just like Andre," said Grandpap Jared. "That boy couldn't quietly sit still if his life depended on it."

"Just like a certain someone else I know," said Gran Ernestine.

"What you trying to say?"

"That you can't sit still and be quiet to save your life either. He probably gets it from you."

"Mom, I'm going to go visit Aunt Ruthie while we're over here," whispered Karla.

"Alright," said First Lady Hall. "Just have one of them drop you off at home when you're done."

Karla walked the few streets to her Aunt Ruth-Anne's house. Aunt Ruth-Anne had the most immaculate house in the whole town. Her yard was always well-maintained, and the one-story white brick house she lived in with her husband, Uncle Arnold Green, always looked like they had just moved into it. It was a stark contrast to Mr. Brown's house, which, while not a total mess, was nowhere near as clean as Aunt Ruth-Anne's.

When Karla arrived, she found her cousins Angela Parker and Naomi Green on the porch, rocking away in rocking chairs. Angela had recently turned twenty-six in January, and Naomi would soon be twenty-six in April. Both Angela and Naomi were light-brown like Karla was. And while Naomi looked like an even mix between her parents, Angela had inherited almost everything from her father, Uncle Terrence Parker, and almost nothing from her mother, Aunt Sarah Parker.

"Hey!" greeted Karla.

"Hey Kay!" said Angela, getting up to hug her. "What you doing on this side of town?"

"Visiting my grandparents."

"Well, the sun has certainly been good to you," laughed Naomi.

"That's how you know it's springtime," said Angela. "When Kay starts going from looking like her mom to looking like Uncle T."

"Right," agreed Naomi. "By the time summertime hits, she'll look like the rest of her brothers and sisters."

"Well, we have Layla to thank for that," said Karla. "That girl stays wanting to play outside and I'm always the one outside with her."

"Well, that is your child," laughed Angela.

"She's my sister," said Karla.

"Child, that girl spends most of her time with you. Layla is your daughter at this point. Your mother just had her for you."

"Whatever," laughed Karla.

Karla's skin had always been her defining feature in her family. She heavily resembled her mother, and it was most noticeable in fall and winter. But the arrival of spring and summer meant that her time as her mother's child was ending, and her time as her father's child was beginning.

Karla's skin raised many questions about her paternity because it did not match her father's more caramel-brown skin. It was the same ignorant thinking that had caused her father to grow up questioning his paternity after his father denied him. Her father never denied her though, and a summer spent in the sun when she was four stopped all the rumors by revealing her father's contributions.

"What are you two up to?" asked Karla.

"Nothing," answered Angela. "Just being stressed out by nursing school, that's all."

"I don't know why I did this to myself," whined Naomi.

"You and me both," added Angela. "If I'd known nursing school would be this stressful, I would've chosen something easier like what Kay's doing."

"My major isn't easy," griped Karla.

"I said easier."

"It's not easier."

"Your daddies are showing," joked Naomi, causing Karla and Angela to laugh.

"They sure do go at it all the time," said Angela.

"Two peas in a pod," said Karla. "Always upset about something."

"Always stressed about something," said Angela.

"Always yelling about something," said Naomi.

"But that's still my daddy and I love him," said Angela. "I wouldn't trade him for anyone else."

Karla did not respond. Her daddy had left the same day her mother had. The man who had cherished Karla and loved her mother beyond "being in a good place" was gone. Sometimes, Karla would catch glimpses of him with Gretchen, but they were only shadows of who had once been there. She loved her father, but not the same way she had loved her daddy, and she missed him.

"There goes Beverly," said Angela, waving at the car that drove past.

"Who's car is she driving?" questioned Karla.

"Probably her boyfriend's," answered Angela. "You know she's dating Marcellus Campbell now."

"No way!" gasped Karla. "I never would've pictured those two together."

"You know who else I never pictured being together?" added Naomi. "Dani and her new boyfriend."

"Who's she dating?" asked Karla.

"Derik Harrison!" exclaimed Naomi and Angela together.

"Which one?" asked Karla, her stomach knotting up.

"The youngest one that works for Daddy's newspaper," said Naomi.

"Okay," sighed Karla, relaxing with relief. "You guys have to specify! You guys know Dria's dating the other one. I thought he was out here cheating on her!"

"Girl, we're sorry," said Angela. "But yeah, him and Dani are dating now."

"I never would've seen that coming," said Karla.

"It's a lot of things around here I would've never seen coming," said Angela. "Like Junior deciding to become a cop for example."

"He probably just wanted to help Uncle Noah out," said Naomi. "You know Mr. Bud quitting on him put him in a tough spot. He can't police the town with only two men."

"Why can't he?" said Angela. "He's done it before."

"At least Junior's doing something with himself and not sitting around being useless," said Naomi. "You should be proud of him."

"I am proud of him," remarked Angela. "But sometimes Junior can be pretty irresponsible."

"If by 'irresponsible' you mean 'runs his mouth a lot' then yeah, I agree," said Naomi.

"That's exactly what I mean," said Angela. "He talks more than he listens, and he and Daddy already get into it enough as it is because he's overly goofy and Daddy's overly serious and strict. Just imagine them trying to police the town together like that."

"Well, if this doesn't work out, he can always be a delivery driver in the city like Mike," said Naomi.

"And that's the other thing!" said Angela. "Mike talking about he's thinking of becoming a truck driver!"

"What's wrong with that?."

"He's not even twenty yet!"

"He will be in August."

"We'll hardly get to see him!"

"He can't stay around here forever."

"But... but..."

"Give it a rest Angie. Mike's got to become a man at some point. He can't be your baby brother forever."

"Easy for you to say. You're an only child."

"And? I'm right and you know it."

Angela sighed and sat back in her seat. Karla understood what Angela meant regarding her brother Michael. She had experienced the same thing with Drake. They had always been an inseparable team, and their siblings had even jokingly referred to them as Mini-Mom and Mini-Dad. Whenever Karla needed someone to talk to, Drake was always the third person she went to after God and her mother. But after he moved away, Karla found that Drake had had less time for her. It was a change that Karla herself was still adjusting to, and she knew the faster Angela accepted it, the easier it would be for her to adjust to it too.

Aunt Ruth-Anne pulled into the driveway and came onto the porch with a cheerful, but tired smile. Karla could tell by how she walked that Aunt Ruth-Anne had had another long day at her nursing job.

"What you three doing sitting out here like a gang of old ladies?" laughed Aunt Ruth-Anne as she came up on the porch.

"Just talking and catching up," said Naomi. "Kay finally got some time away from her daughter."

"Daughter? I don't remember getting another niece."

"Layla," clarified Angela.

"Oh Lord," snorted Aunt Ruth-Anne "Don't pay them no mind Kay. Everybody used to do the same thing with me and your father. They always claimed he was my son because I was always the one having to watch him."

"How come he's so disorganized then if he was always with you?" joked Angela.

"Child, you tell me!" cackled Aunt Ruth-Anne. "Always making a mess wherever he goes."

It was a joke, but every joke held a hint of truth. Mr. Brown did make a mess wherever he went, and Karla knew it. His relationship with Karla was a mess, and it was his fault.

"Here Mommy, sit down," said Naomi, starting to rise.

"Girl, I'm alright," said Aunt Ruth-Anne. "I'm about to go in the house and put my feet up."

"As you should," agreed Angela.

"I saw your father on the way home," said Aunt Ruth-Anne to Angela.

"Did you honk to wake him up?" asked Angela.

"Didn't have to this time. He was wide awake, and all worked up."

"What happened?"

"Your Uncle Torrance has decided not to have a best man."

"Well, what's Daddy so upset for?" said Angela. "It's not like he would've been picked anyways."

"That's why he's upset," explained Aunt Ruth-Anne. "Your uncle claims he didn't want to choose between his brothers and Terrence thinks he only did that to spare his feelings."

"Child...," said Angela. "A mess."

After a few more stories and laughs, Angela took Karla home.

"You missed your brother," said First Lady Hall when Karla entered the house.

"Who?" asked Karla.

"Andre."

"What'd he want?"

"You know how it goes," chuckled First Lady Hall. "Something happens over there and suddenly everyone remembers they have a mom."

"What happened?"

"Nothing. He just wanted to talk."

Karla helped her mother tidy up the house for Forrest's imminent return. He returned around nine that evening. First Lady Hall allowed Layla to stay up long enough to see him.

"I'm home!" announced Forrest.

"Daddy's home!" hollered Layla, running to greet him.

"Hey big girl!" said Forrest, scooping Layla up. "What you still doing up?"

"We were waiting for you," said Layla.

"You were waiting for me?" repeated Forrest. "Were you a good girl for Mommy and Karla while I was gone?"

"Yes!"

"That's my big girl," said Forrest. "Now it's time for bed."

"Can you carry me?" asked Layla.

"Carry you?"

"Please?"

"Okay."

"Yay!"

"Say goodnight to Mommy and Karla."

"Goodnight Mommy! Goodnight Karla!"

"Goodnight," said First Lady Hall. "Come give Mommy a kiss."

"Okay!" said Layla. She kissed her mother and Karla goodnight, then allowed Forrest to carry her to bed.

"That girl is a mess," chuckled First Lady Hall.

"Mhmm," agreed Karla.

Forrest returned minutes later and walked over to his wife.

"Well," said Forrest with a smile. "If it isn't Sister Leilana."

"Hello Pastor Hall," said First Lady Hall, returning his smile.

"Just Forrest tonight," answered Forrest. "What's a good-looking sister like you doing here all by herself?"

"I'm supposed to be meeting someone here tonight," said First Lady Hall.

"That's funny," said Forrest. "I'm supposed to be meeting someone here too. I'm hoping that she'll be my First Lady."

"Well, I'm hoping the man I meet will be my second chance at love."

"Would you mind if I waited a bit with you?"

"Go ahead."

Forrest sat down. He made a big show of yawning and placed his arm behind First Lady Hall.

"Why Pastor," said First Lady Hall. "Are you trying to make a move on me?"

"I'm just stretching my arms," said Forrest. "If I wanted to make a move on you, I'd do this."

Forrest kissed First Lady Hall on the cheek.

"Your First Lady would be mighty surprised to catch you acting like this."

"Well it's a good thing that you're my First Lady."

"It is."

"How'd service go yesterday?" asked Forrest.

"Terrible," whined First Lady Hall. She wrapped her arm around her husband's rotund stomach and buried her head in his chest. "I never want to do it again. I'm so glad you're back."

"Aw, did you miss me?"

"Yes."

"Well, I missed you too," said Forrest, planting a kiss on his wife's forehead. He wrapped his arms around her and pulled her closer.

Karla left the couple to enjoy each other's company alone. She was glad her mother had found happiness in her second chance at love.

Problem Child

How do you know when you have a problem child?
Is it when they are no longer mild?
Is it when they always make you upset?
And on your last nerves they always get?
Is it when they don't get along?
And are always the off notes in your life song?
When does a kid become a problem?
Is it when it becomes you versus them?
When you're no longer the hero?
And have become a zero?
When they kick you while you're down?
And do things that get you tightly wound?
Is it when the good times are no more?
And the sour times are the norm?
What turns a sweet child sour?
What on earth has that power?

Tuesday

Karla's Tuesday started as usual, with her waking up at nine in the morning. Her mother had gone out to run some errands and Forrest was working in his office, which left Karla to watch Layla. Layla had seemed a bit cranky all morning, but she had still behaved herself, so Karla thought nothing of it. Things took a turn when naptime came along.

"I'm not sleepy," said Layla. "I want to color."

"You can color after your nap," said Karla.

"I want to color now."

"No. It's naptime."

"I don't want to take a nap!" screamed Layla, stamping her foot. "I want to color!"

"It's. Naptime," repeated Karla more forcefully.

"I want to color!"

"Little girl...," growled Karla.

"I want to color!"

"Layla, be quiet! Your dad is trying to work!"

"I WANT TO COLOR!"

"Girl!" snapped Karla, snatching Layla by the arm. "You stop all that screaming and crying before I give you something to cry about!"

"Daddy!" wailed Layla, running out of the room after wrenching herself free from Karla's grasp.

Karla shook her head and exhaled. She always did her best to avoid yelling at Layla because she herself did not like being yelled at. But sometimes Layla tried her patience, and before realizing it, Karla would lose her temper. Her temper was something she wanted to get under control because she did not want to be like her father, walking around with unresolved anger issues and taking them out on everyone else.

"Karla!" called Forrest. Karla sighed and prepared to be scolded. When she reached Forrest's office, he smiled and said, "Can you take Layla to Auntie Tavia's, please? I really need to get this work done."

"Okay," said Karla.

Karla strapped the rebellious Layla in and drove off to Tavia's house. Tavia Hall was Forrest's younger sister, and she was the band director at Creeke High School. She had recently reconciled with her estranged husband, Troy, and had moved back in with him, much to Forrest's delight. Forrest loved Troy and had hoped for the longest time that his sister worked things out between them so their brotherhood would not be destroyed.

"What is wrong with you?" asked Karla as she glared at Layla through the rearview mirror.

"I'm having a bad day," said Layla with a pout.

"What do you know about having a bad day?"

"I know that I don't feel happy!"

"Probably because you were up late last night and didn't get a good night's sleep!"

Drake called her before Layla could respond. She told him about Layla, and he annoyed her even more but also set her straight and encouraged her. He always told her what she needed to hear, and that was why she loved him. Karla and Layla arrived at Tavia's, who sat outside waiting for them. Forrest had no doubt called her to inform her of their imminent arrival.

"Hey!" said Tavia. "What's going on?"

"Your niece has been getting beside herself today," said Karla.

"I have not!" argued Layla.

"Layla," said Tavia, eyeing her niece sternly. "Have you been misbehaving?"

"No," said Layla. "Karla's been being a meanie!"

"Oh? What did she do?"

"She wouldn't give me my crayons!"

"Why not?"

"Because she's mean!"

"Girl!" snapped Karla. "That is not why, and you know it. You know full well I said you could color after naptime was over!"

"I'm not sleepy!"

"Alright you two, no arguing," said Tavia. "Here's what we're going to do. Layla is going to spend the day over here so Daddy can get his work done, okay?"

"Okay."

"Karla, you can stay if you want or you can go back home," said Tavia. "We got it from here."

"I'll stay for a bit," answered Karla.

"Fine with me," said Tavia. "Let's go inside."

Inside the house, Karla found Tavia and Troy's daughter, Brianne Lewis, lying on the couch with her eyes closed.

"Girl, you are not sleep," said Tavia.

"Shh," shushed Brianne. She opened one eye and whispered, "Dad doesn't know that. He just laid this blanket on me."

"Where is he?"

"In the family room."

"Come on Layla, let's go say hi to Uncle Troy."

"Okay!"

"Hey," said Brianne when she and Karla were alone. She sat up and asked, "You having a rough day too?"

"Rough is an understatement," muttered Karla.

"Tell me about it," sighed Brianne. "Girl, my dad has been asking me to run lines with him all day for this indie film he and Ms. Donna plan to shoot in the summer."

"Aren't you a theatre major?"

"Yes, but I am on *break*! I had to resort to pretending to nap on the couch!"

"Bri!" called Mr. Lewis. "I know you aren't sleep!"

"Darn it," groaned Brianne. "Sir?"

"Layla said she wants to play tea party with you! And bring my blanket back with you!"

"You know what that's better than running lines," said Brianne triumphantly. "Coming!"

Brianne left to go tend to Layla as Tavia entered the living room.

"I'm going over to Gretchen's to help with wedding prep," said Tavia. "Want to come?"

"What about Layla?" asked Karla.

"We can leave her with Troy and Bri," said Tavia. "They're good with little kids."

Karla was glad to have something to do besides looking after her sister for once. She loved her sister and did not mind helping her mother out, but Karla had her own life that she wanted to live too. Her mother understood that and tried not to rely heavily on Karla to parent Layla, but it had been one of the points of contention with her father while living with him.

Mr. Brown had often fallen back on Drake and Karla to help him maintain his household. Because they were the oldest, it was made their responsibility to look after their younger siblings. Especially Karla. Following the divorce, Karla had essentially become the new mother of the house. She had cooked, cleaned, looked after the others, and put up with all of Mr. Brown's rantings and ravings. And despite having to shoulder such a heavy burden, Karla had still been expected to stay in a child's place, and it had irked her.

It was why she left. But it was also why she hoped Gretchen would succeed as his wife. Gretchen would not be in Karla's position. She would be Mr. Brown's equal and would have a say in what went on in the home. In fact, she had already started having her say, and Karla loved it.

When they arrived at Gretchen's house, Gretchen had gone out with one of her bridesmaids, Ms. Shirley Lowe, to run some errands. Left behind were Gretchen's twin sister, Greta, and two of her other bridesmaids, Ms. Shirley's twin sister, Ms. Shirleen Lowe, and Ms. Jessica Rodriguez.

"Hey, hey," said Tavia. "How's everything going in here?"

"Child, I cannot wait for this to be done," said Greta, rubbing her temples. "Hey Karla."

"Hey," said Karla.

"Don't tell me she's gone bridezilla on us," said Tavia.

"Not her," sighed Greta. "I just got off the phone with my mother. She and my dad wanted to fly in from Havensberg today, but Gretchen booked their tickets for Thursday."

"It must've been an accident."

"It was not. They are not happy. She wanted to be here the whole week to help Gretchen prepare."

"What's wrong with that?"

"Let's just say Mr. and Mrs. Nelson tend to get overly excited about their daughters and what they have going on," said Ms. Jessica. She looked at Ms. Shirleen and giggled, "Remember the talent show?"

"I remember a certain someone went rogue and made us her backups mid-performance," teased Ms. Shirleen.

"Okay, I was sixteen!" griped Greta. "It's not my fault I had star power."

"Mhmm," said Ms. Shirleen. "Star power with a pink frilly dress and casket-ready make up thanks to your mom."

"It took forever to get that stuff off my face, and I broke out from it!" added Ms. Jessica. "Your parents set us up for failure!"

"And the whole time they both were just cheesing and smiling through the whole thing like it was their pride and joy to have us up there like that."

"It was," grumbled Greta. She held up a bouquet of black roses and said, "I think she might fall out when she sees these decorations though. It's going to look more like a funeral than a wedding."

"Well, we can't help that Gretchen's favorite color is black," said Ms. Jessica.

"Is the dress black?" asked Ms. Shirleen.

"Thankfully not," said Greta. "How's the hotel?"

"Great," said Ms. Shirleen. "We hired a new general manager so Shirley doesn't work herself to death."

"Doesn't stop her from trying though," added Ms. Jessica. "And Brad's gone too."

"Oh?" said Greta.

"He became too difficult to work with, so he quit," complained Ms. Jessica. "Our new bartender is a much better fit."

"I guarantee you he was bitter because you wouldn't take him back," said Ms. Shirleen.

"I think he's planning to open his own bar and Heather's one of his investors. I also think he's got a new girlfriend. Some girl that looked kind of like you kept visiting him a lot before he left."

"Good for him," said Greta. "I'm glad he's moved on. But he's still the biggest bullet I've ever dodged in my life."

Karla did not know all the particulars about the discussion because it all pertained to the Nelson twins' hometown, Havensberg. But she did know that Brad was Greta's ex-fiancé who left her at the altar over a decade ago and that Heather was someone neither of the Nelson twins had gotten along with in high school. Both had caused some drama between Mr. Brown, Gretchen, and Greta when they had visited Havensberg the previous summer, but Karla did not know exactly what had happened.

"Speaking of moving on," said Ms. Shirleen. "I heard you've got a special someone."

"Oh, they don't know about Bud?" asked Tavia.

"Tavia!" cried Greta.

"I want the whole story on how you met this man," said Ms. Shirleen.

"And I want to know when we'll get to meet him," added Ms. Jessica.

"You'll meet him at the wedding," said Greta. "Speaking of the wedding, Jessica be ready for Alejandro."

"Who's that?" asked Ms. Jessica.

"That's one of Torrance's brothers-in-law," explained Greta. "He's Afro-Latino and anytime he sees another Latino person he automatically assumes they speak Spanish."

"Oh," said Ms. Jessica. "He's going to be very disappointed then."

"Mhmm," said Greta. "The same thing happened with Zack's wife Serafina. That poor lady doesn't speak a lick of Spanish and he was so disappointed."

"I appreciate this heads-up but we're not going to ignore the subject," said Ms. Jessica. "We're supposed to be talking about how you met your new boyfriend."

"We met through his sister," said Greta, blushing. "You know, Jana?"

"Uh-huh," said Ms. Shirleen.

"She'd invited Gretch and I over to her place for a game night, and he was there. I hate to say it but when we first met, I thought he was a little uh... not smart. But he's not dumb! Sometimes things just go over his head."

"Oh, you're definitely in love with him," said Ms. Shirleen. "And I want to know how we got to that part."

"Well... uh...," stammered Greta, blushing harder. "Like I said, we met at a game night. And then in Havensburg, Jana started pitching him to me. And at first, I was like 'Ew no!'. But then I continued getting to know him. And Jana kept pitching him. And before I knew it, I started liking him. And then he invited me to the winter ball... and..."

"And...?" said Ms. Jessica and Ms. Shirleen.

"And...," repeated Greta, growing redder and sliding down in her chair. "And... at the ball he told me he liked me."

"Really?!" gasped Ms. Shirleen.

"Yeah," said Greta. "But I didn't believe him! I thought he was just drunk and saying stuff he didn't mean!"

"Was he?" asked Ms. Jessica.

"No," said Greta. "He confessed his feelings and before I knew it, we'd kissed."

"*Kissed?!*" squealed Ms. Jessica and Ms. Shirleen.

"Yes, we kissed."

"Now I need to know everything!" said Ms. Jessica. "You said his name was Bud, Tavia? That's really his name? It's not short for anything?"

"Some people jokingly call him Budrow but no," said Greta. "His name is literally just Bud."

"What does he do for a living?" asked Ms. Shirleen.

"He's starting a catering business... and wants to name it Daffodil's."

"Aw, after your favorite flower?" gushed Ms. Jessica. "He definitely loves you."

"I told him to call it Flowerbud's instead. I don't want him naming something so important in my honor."

"Why not?"

"Well... because what if we don't work out?"

"Lord, here she go," said Ms. Shirleen.

"What?" said Greta.

"You're doing that sabotaging mess again. Just like back home when we would try to set you up on dates after you and Brad broke up, you'd always find something wrong with the guys."

"And then swore off romance altogether," added Ms. Jessica.

"I don't sabotage myself!" argued Greta. "I'm just not wasting my time on guys who aren't worth it."

"Yeah, well this guy doesn't sound like a waste of time to me," said Ms. Shirleen. "You better hang on to him."

The doorbell rang. It was Ms. Jana Vaughn, arriving to help with wedding prep too.

"Hey!" greeted Ms. Jana. "I know you won't mind but I brought Bud with me. He wanted you to try something he made."

"Looks like we won't have to wait till the wedding after all," chuckled Ms. Jessica.

"I can't wait to meet this Mr. Right," said Ms. Shirleen, causing Greta to blush.

"What's going on?" whispered Ms. Jana to Tavia.

"You just brought your brother into the lion's den, that's what," snickered Tavia.

"I've got pound cake!" announced Mr. Bud as he walked through the door. He carried the cake into the kitchen and returned with a slice for Greta. "Here, try this! It's my mother's recipe and it's my first time making it. Tell me what you think. And if you like it, I might sell it."

"Okay," said Greta. She tried the cake and said, "Oh. This is good!"

"Yes!" cheered Mr. Bud. He began dancing, singing, "I did it! I did it! I'm the man! I'm the man!"

"Uh Bud," said Ms. Jana awkwardly.

"What?"

"I think you should greet the bridal party..."

"Hey," said Ms. Jessica and Ms. Shirleen.

Mr. Bud's bronze-colored face turned as red as the hair on his head.

"Ha...ha...hi...," stammered Mr. Bud. He glanced at Greta and asked, "How long have they been there?"

"The whole time," said Greta with a pursed smile.

"Okay...," said Mr. Bud with a wince. "Uh... I'm Bud. Bud Vaughn. I uh... nice to meet you."

"Hi Bud," said Ms. Jessica.

"So, Bud," said Ms. Shirleen. "What are your intentions with my best friend?"

"My intentions?" repeated Mr. Bud. He looked at Greta and said, "Uh..."

"Wait, let's not be too hasty," said Ms. Jessica. "How old are you?"

"Forty?"

"And when will you be starting this catering business?"

"As soon as possible?"

"Okay, I've heard enough," said Ms. Jessica to Ms. Shirleen. She looked at Bud and asked, "What are your intentions with our best friend?"

"Will you two cut it out?" griped Greta. "I'm sorry Bud, don't mind them. I liked the cake."

"Thanks," said Mr. Bud. "I should get going."

"What's the rush?" said Ms. Shirleen. "You just got here."

"I don't want to interrupt what you were doing," said Mr. Bud. blushing harder.

"You're not interrupting," said Ms. Jessica. "In fact, you showed up right on time."

"Again, don't mind them," said Greta. "Go ahead and go, I'll drop Jana off when we're done."

"Okay," said Mr. Bud. "I love you."

"I love you too," said Greta, blushing harder than she was before.

"Ooooh!" teased Ms. Shirleen and Ms. Jessica after Mr. Bud left.

"Shut up!" snapped Greta. "Both of you just shut it up!"

"Girl, he is so *cute!*" said Ms. Shirleen. "Let me know when the wedding is so I can book my flight now!"

"We just started dating," said Greta. "Don't get too ahead of yourselves."

"I agree with Shirleen," said Ms. Jessica. "I think he might be the one for real."

"Again, don't get too ahead of yourselves."

Even though Karla could see Greta was trying to be practical, Karla was inclined to agree with the others. Greta and Ms. Bud seemed like a perfect match for each other. And Karla was sure it was only a matter of time before they would make their way to the altar.

"I saw Soriah on the news today speaking at the Willard anniversary celebration," said Tavia when Ms. Jana sat down to help with decorations. "I didn't know that school had been open for one-hundred twenty-five years."

"Yeah, my mom was out there too because she's head of DEI for them," said Ms. Jana. "She tried to get me to go but I told her no. You know Soriah is the first black student to graduate from there, right?"

"No way!" cried Tavia. "Didn't she graduate in the nineties?!"

"Mhmm," said Ms. Jana. "Her picture is on the achievement wall and everything."

"What's the achievement wall?" asked Ms. Shirleen. "And what's Willard?"

"Willard is a private school," explained Ms. Jana. The achievement walls are walls in both schools' main hallways showing off students who have gone on to do great things."

"And what great thing has Soriah done?" chuckled Tavia.

"Be the first Black student to graduate," said Ms. Jana. "They put my picture up there too last year."

"What'd you do?" chuckled Greta.

"Be the first biracial to graduate," laughed Ms. Jana.

"You're kidding," said Tavia.

"I'm so serious," said Ms. Jana. "It was me, Soriah, and Soleya on the girl's side, and that was it. There's even been discussions recently to reclassify Bud from being the first Black graduate to the first biracial graduate for the boy's school and give the distinction to the second guy who isn't mixed.

"Okay, I'm still confused," said Ms. Jessica. "Can someone catch me up?"

"Willard is a private school for girls in the city," explained Greta. "It's split into The Janice Willard Academy for Girls, and The Roderick Willard Academy for Boys. They do all the grade levels, so you can literally be there from kindergarten up till you graduate high school."

"Like me and Bud were," added Ms. Jana. "The school's goal is to produce 'upstanding' men and women of society."

"In other words, the boys are prepared to be go-getters while the girls are prepared to be married to the go-getters," said Greta. "You know Soleya, the owner of Miss Leya's who is doing our hair for the wedding?"

"Yeah," answered Ms. Jessica.

"Her and her older sister went there but Soleya didn't graduate," continued Greta. "Her sister Soriah is who were talking about."

"Why didn't Soleya graduate?" asked Ms. Shirleen.

"She had her parents take her out of the school," said Ms. Jana. "She didn't like it there. I didn't either but I had no choice."

"I'm still stuck at Soriah and Bud being the first Black students and they both graduated in the nineties," said Tavia.

"Soriah wasn't the first Black girl student," corrected Ms. Jana. "She was the first one to graduate. Willard doesn't like to acknowledge the actual first Black girl who was Myrna Watson. She attended for half of her freshman year in the early seventies."

"Why don't they want to acknowledge her?" asked Greta.

"Because there was a big controversy after her parents pulled her out of the school," explained Ms. Jana. "She won class treasurer and then got attacked very badly by some of the students from both schools on her way home over it and Willard just swept the whole thing under the rug. They like to pretend she doesn't exist and prop Soriah up instead but us Black students that went there know about her because we always used to get warned by other Black people not to run for any of the student council positions."

"That's terrible," said Tavia. "I hope Myrna is doing alright."

"How many Black girls have gone there since?" asked Greta.

"Two, I think?" said Ms. Jana. "The boys have done a bit better with diversifying but it's just such an expensive school."

"A mess," said Tavia.

"Yeah," said Ms. Jana.

Karla was glad she did not have to deal with those issues when she was in school. Mostly everyone in Creeke was Black. But while she loved her community, Karla wondered how long she would truly stay there. At some point, she would have to venture beyond the town's limits and explore the world for herself. And when that time came, she hoped she would be ready for it.

Karla returned home that evening. She and her mother folded clothes while watching the latest episode of 'Legacies of Hip Hop', a reality show that her father called 'the place where music careers go to die'.

The show was in its seventh season, and amongst the various cast members was NikNak of The Boombox Boyz. He had been on the show since the first season, and his latest storyline focused on him opening his second Nik's Barbecue location in his hometown. Karla watched, however, as the grand opening was ruined by two of the other cast members arguing.

"So, what's up?" said one girl. "You said I ain't got no talent and that you could take my man if you wanted?"

"I did," answered the other girl.

"Why you ain't say it to my face scary?!" said the first girl, pointing her finger in the other girl's face.

"First of all, get your finger out my face."

"Get my finger out your face! You're scary and all you do is talk about people behind their backs! And that's why I know you won't do nothing!"

"Ain't nobody scary!"

"So, what's up?!"

The girls threw drinks at each other and were separated by security.

"No, we're supposed to be resolving this," said a third girl who had set up the interaction. "What are you doing?"

"Come here!" hollered the first girl, trying to get around security. "Come here!"

"Girl bye!" shouted the second girl. "You doing all that because security's here!"

NikNak watched with disdain alongside his wife, Chanda Hart.

"This night was supposed to be a celebration of my husband's success," said Chanda. "And these little girls can't even put their stuff aside and not act like hoodrats for one night! I'm so embarrassed for Nik because I know how hard he worked for this just for it to be ruined by these immature girls."

"I don't know why they're still on this show," said First Lady Hall. "He doesn't need it and it's done nothing for his career. And I'm pretty sure her toys are doing very well!"

"Maybe he needed a check," said Karla.

"If he needs a check that badly all he has to do is get in the studio and make a hit."

"They be in the studio every season."

"And yet, we haven't heard not one song from any of them. Like I said, this show isn't doing anything for them."

Karla agreed with her mother. NikNak was a hip-hop legend and the show had not progressed his music career. However, Karla heard great things about his restaurant. And his wife Chanda had formed her own toy company with her most successful product being her Chanda dolls. The Brown sisters had each had a Chanda doll growing up, and it was the first time Karla remembered seeing a doll that looked like her and her sisters.

Karla's Chanda doll was in Layla's room with Layla's Chanda doll. Troy had brought Layla home, who was coloring in her room. Karla was still heavily annoyed with her and was even more annoyed that Layla had basically gotten away with it and faced no punishment.

"Your daughter tried my patience today," complained Karla.

"Forrest told me," said First Lady Hall. "I probably shouldn't have let her stay up last night to wait for him."

"Was I like that too?" asked Karla, remembering what Drake had said about her being the same way at Layla's age.

"Um...?" said First Lady Hall, putting a finger to her chin. "You were just as headstrong and cute as she is."

"So... yes."

"Yeah. You were like Layla."

"Great."

"It doesn't have to be a bad thing," said First Lady Hall. "Layla is a good girl, just like you were. It was just a bad day."

"Kids don't have bad days," said Karla, echoing Mr. Brown's words.

"Don't bring your father's parenting style over here," said First Lady Hall. "If I say my baby had a bad day, then she had a bad day."

"How come I didn't get to have a bad day then?"

"Because your father wouldn't let you have one."

"You just going to act like you weren't the other parent?" said Karla, crossing her arms.

"Don't do that," said First Lady Hall.

"It's not fair that she gets to have bad days when I didn't get to."

"Well, Karla it may not be fair but it's what it is. I was still a new mother and learning with you. I'm still learning with her but now I have a better understanding of what does and does not work. And you also have to take into account that your father and Forrest are two different types of dads. Forrest isn't as strict as your father is."

"And I'm just supposed to accept that?"

"Not necessarily. But I do hope you understand that both your father and I did our best in raising you. And we may not have gotten everything right, but everything we did was always with your best interest in mind. And there may be some things that I do differently with Layla that I didn't do with you. She may get to do things you didn't get to do as a kid. But that's because I know better now and that's just what it is."

First Lady Hall bid Karla goodnight after the episode ended and retired to her room. That night, Karla lay in bed, replaying the conversation. She heard her bedroom door open and felt eyes upon her.

"Karla?" said Layla. Layla was the last person Karla wanted to see, so she ignored her. When Karla didn't answer, Layla called her again. "Karla."

Karla sighed heavily and opened her eyes. Layla stood at her bedside, looking at her with apologetic eyes.

"What, girl?" griped Karla.

"Are you mad at me?"

Karla wanted to say yes. She wanted to say she was mad that Layla had been a brat all day and had not been punished like she would have been.

"No," sighed Karla.

"Can I sleep in here with you tonight?"

"Why can't you sleep in your own bed?"

"Because I want to sleep in here with you."

"Lord have mercy," said Karla. She lifted her covers and said, "Come on."

Layla climbed into Karla's bed and snuggled close to her. As Karla lay there watching her baby sister fall asleep, she felt her heart soften toward her. It was hard to accept but her mother was right. She could not expect her mother to use the same parenting tactics with Layla when they had not even worked with her.

Problem Child?

What's it mean to be a problem child?
And who determines just what it looks like?
I've always thought those children were wild,
But I've been called one since I was a tyke.

What about me is such a big problem?
The fact that I speak my mind when I want?
Or that I value myself as a gem?
Why is it me this label chose to haunt?

Is it because I'm not a mindless drone
And choose to think with my very own brain?
Or is it that I've made it be known
That I am not one you can just contain?

Who was it that dared label me as so?
Me, myself, and I would just love to know.

Wednesday

Karla woke up on Wednesday with Layla's foot in her back. But her anger towards Layla was gone. She was determined to make the new day a good one, to make up for how terrible the previous one had been.

She decided to take Layla to the park, which sat across the street from the church. Karla had played at that park when she was a kid, as had her mother and father, and her mother's father, and her father's mother. The park held fond memories for Karla of a time when she was innocent and blind to the truths of life.

"Can I go play?" asked Layla.

"Yes," answered Karla. "But stay where I can see you."

"Okay!" yelled Layla, dashing to the playground.

Karla took a seat on a nearby bench. That same park also held painful memories for Karla. Whenever she wanted to be alone or got into it with her father, she would go to the park. Her mother used to do the same thing. Any time she argued with Mr. Brown, First Lady Hall would take Karla and her siblings to the park the next day.

Karla had never really thought about what her mother had experienced during those times. She would be playing, glance over at her mother, and see her staring off into space.

"Karla!" called Layla. "Look what I can do!"

Karla watched as Layla did a cartwheel, and then applauded her.

"Good job!" cheered Karla, causing Layla to giggle and run off.

It was ironic. Karla used to do those same things at Layla's age. She would see her mother zoning out and do something to get her attention and make her smile. But now, she was in her mother's position.

When they returned from the park Karla took a good look at her mother. A real good look. And for the first time, Karla saw her mother not as a mother, but as a woman. She saw a woman who had probably once had dreams, a woman who had once had her heart broken, and a woman who still pressed on despite it all.

"Why are you looking at me like that?" asked First Lady Hall with a smile.

"I was just thinking about when you used to take us to the park," answered Karla.

"Oh," replied First Lady Hall. Her smile became less pronounced.

"I think I sort of understand now why you used to take us when you did."

"And why is that?"

"You needed time to think."

"I did."

"Whenever me and Dad got into it, I would go sit in the park to think too."

"What'd you think about?"

"How I couldn't wait to move out of his house and be rid of him forever."

"Can't say I blame you," chuckled First Lady Hall. "Your grandmother used to do the same thing when I was a kid. Whenever times got hard for her, she'd take me to the park."

"Were things bad between her and Grandpap?"

"It wasn't your grandfather driving her to sit in the park," said First Lady Hall. "It was that awful Lady Sophia. I just know she considered quitting a few times while sitting there."

"And you'd be running around without a care in the world while she just sat there and thought," said Karla.

"Looks like we started a family tradition."

"It's kind of sad though, don't you think?"

"Maybe," said First Lady Hall. "It depends on how you look at it."

"Do you ever wonder what would've happened if you had stayed with Dad?" asked Karla.

"One of your parents would be dead and the other in jail for murder," answered First Lady Hall. "And it could've gone either way for who would be who."

"What was the final straw?"

"This lady at my old job had gotten flowers from her husband," said First Lady Hall. "And I was jealous because I couldn't remember the last time your father had gotten me flowers. And then I couldn't remember the last time we had done anything romantic together. Or even just been friends. I realized we were only still together because we had kids together. So, I come home, and of course your father's prepared this nice dinner and sent you all away. But I just couldn't do it anymore. I couldn't stay with him knowing I'd fallen out of love and pretend like everything was okay."

First Lady Hall shook her head and sighed. Karla had always understood why her mother had left, although it had hurt her deeply. But she placed the blame for the divorce on her father. He had caused it by being impossible to get along with. She was sure that if she were ever in a similar position to her mother, she would make the same decision as her mother.

"That's enough reminiscing for today," said First Lady Hall. She stood up and said, "Time to get ready for church."

Wednesday night service never lasted long because Forrest was an 'in-and-out' preacher. He taught what was necessary and avoided unnecessary theatrics. Some townsfolk felt he was not as strong a preacher as the Harrison men had been, but it was clear he had improved ever since Pastor Derrick returned to being the youth pastor.

The youth pastor was not the only new change at Creeke Church. Mr. Brown had taken over playing the piano for her Uncle Terrence during worship. Karla never understood why Uncle Terrence had been chosen out of all his siblings to be the music minister. He was the least musically inclined and the weakest singer. She thought if anybody should have been the music minister, it should have been her father.

Music was intrinsic to Mr. Brown's identity. It came naturally to him, and everything he did in life somehow connected back to music. Karla had not fully inherited her father's love of music, which was another thing in her life that made her the most distant from him. She was not a jack of all trades like Drake, or a composer like Mary. Her body did not attune to rhythms as naturally as Adrianna's did. Andre could play the guitar, bass, and drums, and Antoine liked experimenting with music mixing and beat-making. But Karla's interest in music only went as far as occasionally singing soprano in the church choir.

After the service, Karla talked with Mary. Mary had always been regarded by her siblings as Mr. Brown's favorite child, and Karla could see why. She had the most in common with their father, and he also tended to be a lot more easygoing with her. It was so unlike Karla's experience where everything seemed to be a battle with Mr. Brown, that she marveled at the fact that her siblings ever also considered her one of their father's favorites.

"Winter is definitely over," said Mary. "You're starting to look like me."

"It's all Layla's fault," said Karla. "Sometimes I just don't know what to do with that girl."

"I've got a children's book for her," said Mary. "That should keep her occupied for a while."

"Maybe five minutes before she runs off to do something else," snorted Karla.

"You know Dad plans on having another child, right?"

"I was hoping he wouldn't."

"I heard him and Gretchen talking about it. She wants a little girl."

"So, what you're telling me is, we might have another sister young enough to be our daughter?"

"Mhmm. She might even end up being around the same age as some of our own children."

"Do you even want children, Mary?"

"If it happens, it happens. What about you?"

"I honestly don't know," said Karla. "The last thing I'm thinking about right now is starting a family."

"Same. I wish I could say the same for Dria though. It seems like all she cares about is dance and Derek. She's probably already got the whole wedding planned and everything."

"The girl is fifteen. What do you expect?"

"We weren't thinking about boys when we were fifteen."

"You don't know what I was thinking about."

"Were you thinking about boys, Karla?"

"No."

"Exactly."

"How's your family research going?" asked Karla, changing the subject.

"It's going great," said Mary with a smirk that let Karla know she would allow the subject change that time. "I've already started getting the picture of why you're so light."

"Oh Lord," chuckled Karla. "Why am I so light, Mary?"

"So, there was some racial mixing on Dad's side," explained Mary. "I discovered that Great-Grandpa Gabriel was one-eighth White."

"Only one-eighth?" said Karla. "Some of his sisters looked even lighter than I do. Some of them could've even passed if they wanted to."

"His grandmother was half-White. Her father was a White slave owner and uh..."

"Just stop right there," said Karla, holding up her hand. "I can fill in the rest."

"But yeah. It's possible there was even more race mixing on Mom's side."

"As far as I'm concerned, I'm Black and my parents and grandparents are too."

"Speaking of grandparents...," uttered Mary. "I've got to tell you something."

"What?"

"It's a secret."

"Okay."

"And you can't tell anyone. But especially not Dad."

"If it's such a big secret, why are you telling me?"

"Because you're the only one I can trust it with. The only other person who knows is Grandma."

"Okay...," said Karla. "What is it?"

"I've been talking to Leonard Brown."

"What?!" gasped Karla. "Why?!"

"I'm just getting to know him!"

"You know full well you shouldn't be doing that."

"I'm nineteen years old," declared Mary. "I can do what I want."

"You know Dad won't like that."

"That's why you're not going to tell him."

"That man abused our father and wouldn't even acknowledge him as his son. Why would you even want to associate with him?"

"He's the only one who knows about the Brown's family history, and I need to know all I can."

"Is that really worth risking Dad finding out and getting super upset about it?"

"Yes," said Mary with determination in her eyes. "Yes, it is."

"Okay...," said Karla. "I hope you know what you're doing."

"I do."

Although Mary sounded sure of herself, Karla was not convinced. She could not believe her sister would do something so reckless. Not even Karla would think to betray Mr. Brown's trust in such a huge way, nor would she want to. Karla may have had her issues with her father, but there were certain things even she would not do to avoid hurting him. And establishing a connection with his abusive biological father was high on that list.

Problem Child Remix

How do you know you have a problem child?
How do you know you're not the one that's wild?
People used to say I was the problem kid,
But I didn't see what they all did.
So what if I had a few fights?
And walked around for years with half my sight?
But none of that means,
Something was wrong with me.
If I was a child with a problem,
Then as a man I'll wear it like an emblem.
Because the only problems that I had,
Were all the people who treated me bad.
So, if you got something to say,
Then bring your issue my way.
But don't get mad with the way I solve it,
Cuz you knew I was a problem and that's what you get.

-

Thursday

It was Andre's birthday. And Layla made sure Karla knew it as she ran through the house screaming Karla's name.

"Karla!" yelled Layla. "Karla! Karla! Karla!"

"Stop," said Karla when Layla finally reached her. "What?"

"Today's Andre's birthday!"

"I know."

"Is he going to have a party?"

"No."

"Why not?"

"He didn't want one."

"Did you get him a present?"

"No."

"Why not?"

"I just didn't."

"Won't that make him sad?"

"No."

"Why not?"

"Here, let's call him and he can tell you why."

Karla dialed Andre's number and waited for him to answer.

"Yellow?" said Andre.

"I have a certain someone here who wants to speak to you," said Karla.

"Who?"

"HAPPY BIRTHDAY ANDRE!" cheered Layla.

"Thank you, baby girl," chuckled Andre.

"Karla didn't get you a present," tattled Layla.

"That's okay," said Andre.

"Are you sad?" asked Layla.

"Why would I be sad?"

"Because Karla didn't get you a present."

"No, I'm not sad."

"Don't you want anything?"

"Girl, give me my phone," said Karla, snatching the cellphone from Layla's hand. "Go play."

"BYE ANDRE!" shouted Layla, running out of the room.

"That's definitely your sister," said Karla. "Loud and curious just like you."

"That's your sister too," laughed Andre. "She's got all your attitude."

"Rude," said Karla, causing them both to laugh harder. "What are you doing today?"

"I don't know yet," said Andre. "What are you doing?"

"Watching Layla as usual," sighed Karla. "Forrest has to work, and Mom has something going on at the church."

"Oh."

"Well, I won't hold you too long," said Karla. "I just called to wish you a happy birthday."

"Thanks," said Andre.

"Have a good day okay?"

"I will. Bye."

"Bye."

Karla hung up the phone and prepared to spend another long day watching Layla. She was unsure of what the two of them would do that Thursday. They had done every imaginable activity Karla could think of that week, and three days remained before they both returned to school. As Karla pondered on what to do, her phone began ringing.

"Hello?" said Karla.

"Hey," said Naomi. "Me and Angie are going to the mall. Want to come?"

"I'm watching Layla today."

"Okay," said Naomi. "If you somehow can manage to get away though, we're leaving in fifteen minutes so let us know by then."

"Okay."

Karla knew the selfless thing to do was to watch Layla. But she could not remember the last time she had had a real moment to do something for herself. Even when she was not watching Layla, she was helping someone else with something. And it was supposed to be her spring break too. So, even though Karla knew the selfless thing to do was watch Layla, her feet selfishly walked to Forrest's office.

"Sir?" said Karla, knocking on the door to Forrest's office.

"Hey!" said Forrest, smiling when he saw her. "What's up?"

"Uh...," began Karla. She could see he was hard at work and felt bad for wanting to ask if he could work and watch Layla. "Never mind."

"Is everything alright?" asked Forrest. "Did something happen with Layla?"

"No, she's fine," said Karla. "Angie and Mimi wanted me to go out with them today, but Mom's not back yet. And I know you have to work so–!"

"Go."

"Huh?"

"Go," repeated Forrest. "Go have fun with your cousins."

"You sure?" asked Karla. "I don't mind staying to watch Layla."

"I can watch her," said Forrest. "Go have fun."

Karla knew she should not have been, but she was shocked. Had the same thing happened with her father, the outcome would have been vastly different. The shock wore off once she was seated in the back of Angela's car. And then the guilt set in. She worried that Forrest might not be able to complete his work because she had chosen to be selfish.

"We just have to make a quick stop at Grampa's, and we'll be on our way," said Angela.

When they arrived at Mr. Damian Parker's house, he sat on the front porch eating peanuts with his brother, Mr. Lee. Mr. Damian was the ex-husband of Karla's paternal grandmother, Marianne Brown. He was generally a nice man, but the relationship between him and Grandma Marianne was still very sore. Despite his feelings toward her grand-mother though, Mr. Damian had a soft spot for Karla's father because

Mr. Leonard Brown had mistreated him along with Mr. Damian's children.

"Hi Grampa!" called Naomi as the three women walked up to the porch.

"My babies!" cheered Mr. Damian. He gave each of the girls a hug and asked, "What brings you over here?"

"Mommy made an extra lasagna for you and Mrs. Thelma last night and wanted me to drop it off," said Naomi.

"I told that girl I was still perfectly capable of cooking for us," said Mr. Damian. "I slip in the bathtub one time and the girl thinks I can't do anything now."

"I mean we can take it back," said Angela.

"No, we'll take it," said Mr. Damian. "I just wish Gracie would stop being such a worrywart."

"She's your daughter," said Mr. Lee. "She's going to be a worrywart over you whether you like it or not."

"Mimi, you can take the lasagna in the kitchen," sighed Mr. Damian. "Angie, stay here. I want to talk to you for a minute."

"And what about Karla?" joked Angela.

"Karla's a guest," said Mr. Damian with a smile. "She can go wherever she wants."

"I'll go with Mimi," said Karla.

Karla followed Naomi into the house. Mrs. Thelma was talking with Danielle while Mrs. Tasha Lee sat off to the side, on her phone.

"Hi Mrs. Thelma," said Naomi. "We brought you a lasagna."

"Oh!" exclaimed Mrs. Thelma. "Isn't that nice? Tell your mother I said thank you."

"I will," said Naomi. "So, what's been going on?"

"Nothing much," said Mrs. Thelma. "Me and Dani were just catching up."

"Mhmm," said Naomi. "I heard you got yourself a boyfriend."

"Yeah," said Danielle.

"How'd that happen?"

"It just did," said Danielle with a shrug.

Mrs. Tasha rolled her eyes and walked outside.

"What's wrong with her?" asked Naomi.

"Nothing," said Mrs. Thelma. "I hear cheer tryouts are coming up soon. You going to try out Dani?"

"Not if that lady is still going to be the coach," said Danielle.

Karla shook her head. Gretchen was the "lady" that Danielle was referring to. At the previous year's tryouts, Danielle had failed to pass the interview stage and claimed Gretchen had purposely added them to get her off the team. It had caused a falling out between Danielle and her friends who stayed on the team, and Danielle had given her father the cold shoulder when he had refused to override the decision.

"It's going to be your senior year," said Mrs. Thelma. "I think you should give it one more try."

"I don't see the point," said Danielle. "That lady doesn't like me, and I don't like her. She'll find any reason to keep me off the team."

The conversation drifted into everyone talking about what was happening in their lives until the three women were on their way again.

"What'd Grampa want to talk about?" asked Naomi.

"Daddy's fiftieth," said Angela. "He wants to do something special for it. What happened in the house?"

"What do you mean?" asked Naomi.

"I'm outside talking to Grampa, and Aunt Tasha comes out with an attitude asking Uncle Arty when they're going to leave."

"Nothing happened," said Naomi. "We literally said hi, asked Dani about her new boyfriend, and Aunt Tasha rolled her eyes and walked out."

"That lady," grumbled Angela. "She don't like Derik or something?"

"I don't know what's wrong with her," griped Naomi. "She's always got an attitude."

"Sometimes I wonder what Uncle Arty saw in her."

"I think he was just ready to get married and she was around."

"What makes you say that?"

"Think about it," advised Naomi. "He was in his thirties and still single while everyone else was married with kids. He didn't want to grow old alone, and Aunt Tasha was around."

"Girl, you should've been a psychology major with the way you be overanalyzing everybody," joked Angela.

"I just pay attention to stuff," said Naomi. "Uncle Arty is the perfect husband for her. He lets her do whatever she wants, pays for everything, and never gives her any pushback. He's low maintenance because he don't want to be alone and she knows that and so does Dani. Why do you think they were so pissed off when he put his foot down about the cheerleading thing? They're not used to him doing that."

"I want better for my uncle," said Angela. "I can understand not wanting to grow old and alone though. I can't even remember the last time I had a date."

"Me either," agreed Naomi.

"Well, if you two are looking for somebody in your field I have a great candidate," snickered Karla.

"Who?" said Angela and Naomi.

"Andrew."

"Stone?!" cackled Angela. "Girl, I thought you meant a real man. Andrew's a baby."

"He's a year older than me!" cried Karla.

"You're a baby too," countered Angela.

"Well, Mrs. Stone is looking for someone to be with her baby," said Karla. "I just thought I'd let you guys know."

"And I'm sure she'll find a great fit for him," said Naomi. "But it's not us."

"There's just really not a lot of options in Creeke," said Angela.

"There really isn't," said Naomi.

The trio had a great time at the mall and ate lunch in the food court. Karla was glad she had taken the time to go out. But in the back of her mind, she still felt a nagging guilt for dumping her responsibility on Forrest. He had been so gracious to her by allowing her to live in his home, and she had repaid him by forcing him to multitask when he should not have had to.

"Karla," whispered Naomi.

"What?" said Karla.

"Try not to be to obvious, but the guy at the table next to us keeps looking at you."

Although Naomi had cautioned her not to be too obvious, Karla looked straight at the man. Medium-brown, faded haircut, nicely dressed in a work uniform. He smiled at her, and she politely smiled back before turning back to her cousins.

"Well?" said Angela.

"Well what?" said Karla.

"He's cute and he's obviously interested in you," said Naomi.

"Well, I'm obviously interested in my plate," said Karla.

"The same plate you haven't touched for the past five minutes?" said Angela.

"Look, if he's interested then he needs to make the first move," said Karla.

"That can be arranged," said Naomi. "Come on Angie."

"Where are you two going?" asked Karla.

"We'll be back," said Naomi. "You just stay there."

Karla watched as her cousins left her alone at the table. She stared at the table before sneaking another glance at the stranger. He was looking at her again, causing her to blush and look away.

"Hi," said the stranger.

"Hi," said Karla.

"I uh... I noticed you here with your friends."

"Yeah."

"I didn't mean to stare or anything," said the stranger. "I just thought you looked nice."

"Thank you," said Karla. The stranger seemed kind of awkward but Karla found it kind of cute in a way. "You look nice too."

"Thanks," said the stranger. "I'm Hosea. Hosea Washington."

"Nice to meet you. I'm Karla Brown."

"Karla Brown," said Hosea, like he was savoring the name in his mouth. "Do you come here often?"

"To the mall?" snorted Karla.

"You're right, that is a silly question," laughed Hosea.

Karla laughed too. Before she knew it, they were having a full-blown conversation. Hosea was twenty-four and was a preacher's kid. He was beginning his own journey into pastoring but worked in one of the mall's stores for his day job. She was enjoying the conversation so much that she actually felt sad when his lunch break ended. The pair exchanged phone numbers and social medias, and then he was gone.

"How'd it go?" asked Naomi when she and Angela returned.

"He seems like a nice guy," said Karla. "Where'd you two go?"

"Shoe shopping," said Angela, pointing to the shoe store across from the food court.

"I can't believe you two," snorted Karla.

Karla returned that afternoon to find Forrest and her mother sitting on the porch. Layla was drawing flowers on the driveway with chalk.

"Forrest told me you went out today," said First Lady Hall as Karla ascended the porch. "Did you have fun?"

"Yeah, for the most part," said Karla. "Were you able to get your work done sir?"

"Yeah," answered Forrest. "I hope you weren't worrying about that while you were out."

"I just didn't want to leave you in a tough position," said Karla.

"Karla," said First Lady Hall. "I know everyone jokes that Layla is your daughter, but she's not actually your daughter. She's my and Forrest's daughter. She's our responsibility, not yours."

"I don't mind helping."

"We know you don't," said First Lady Hall. "But we want you to enjoy your life. Don't think you have to give up things for Layla or for anyone else for that matter. Okay?"

"Okay."

Karla went inside, thinking about what her mother had said and realizing she was right. She had grown so used to putting everyone else first that when she finally got an opportunity to do so for herself, she felt bad about it.

Her phone rang. Mr. Brown was calling her. He seldom called Karla.

"Hello?" said Karla.

"What are you doing tomorrow?" said Mr. Brown without saying hello back.

"Why?"

"I'm having a family dinner tomorrow with all my children," said Mr. Brown. "I want you to be there."

"Well, I would hope so considering I'm one of your children."

"Are you going to be there or not?"

"We'll see," answered Karla.

That was the end of the conversation. Karla considered not going. But she knew her father would not have asked her if he had not wanted her there. So, despite not wanting to, she decided she would go.

Does Daddy No Longer Exist?

Sometimes I see the smile on your face,
And I remember from a time ago,
Those moments I spent in your warm embrace,
Wishing the moment would always stay so.

More often now I feel your tongue's harsh lash,
Along with the glare you hold in your eyes.
I fear your heart has been burnt into ash,
And replaced with the coldest block of ice.

You, who dare to call yourself my father,
What have you done with that loving kind man,
Who treated me as his precious daughter,
As only a good loving kind man can?

Is this now truly who my father is?
Does Daddy truly no longer exist?

Friday

Karla was not looking forward to going to her father's house that evening. It seemed like every time she saw him, something went wrong. But she had no plausible reason to avoid the dinner, so she mentally prepared herself to once again sit at her father's table. That morning, she and her sisters went with their mother to get their hair done for the wedding. Since the style Adrianna wanted would take the longest, Karla drove her car so she and Mary could leave when they were finished.

Hair was the one choice Karla had been allowed to make for herself while living with her father. After his disastrous attempt at doing her hair, he had decided their mother would handle the girls' hair. First Lady Hall had allowed the girls to experiment with different hairstyles, which meant that Karla and her sisters, and not their father, decided how they wanted their hair. And over time, each girl found her preferred style. Mary liked her hair in its natural state as an afro and would leave it as such for the wedding. Adrianna liked to try different styles out and was having a weave installed for the occasion. Karla fell between her sisters, preferring her natural hair for everyday life, but straightening it for special occasions such as the wedding.

"Welcome to Miss Leya's Beauty and Barbershop, where you'll leave feeling just as good as you'll look," said eighteen-year-old Allison Harrison. "Who's going first?"

"Me," said Mary.

The wait for Karla's appointment was not long. After Mary finished getting her hair trimmed, she sat near the window while Karla took her spot in Nisha's chair. She could hear the men in the barber's side of the shop hollering and laughing through the wall.

"I'm thinking of hiring another girl for the salon," said Mrs. Harrison as she worked on First Lady Hall's hair. "It just being me and Nisha is not cutting it anymore."

"I remember when it used to be just you," said First Lady Hall. "Shoot, you better teach Allison to do some hair like you did Deidrick."

"I already did," said Mrs. Harrison. "But she wants to go into engineering."

"Ha!" laughed First Lady Hall. "That's what Andre wants to do too!"

"How ironic."

"You know what this means right?"

"What?"

"We're one step closer to getting them together."

"I don't see that happening anytime soon."

"It doesn't have to happen this minute. Just as long as it happens."

"And if it doesn't?"

"Then we'll just have to encourage them."

"You sound like my mother," snorted Mrs. Harrison.

"Oh Lord, let me stop," chuckled First Lady Hall. "Lord knows I don't want to have nothing in common with that lady."

"Lana."

"What? You know I don't like your mother. She did my mother dirty. All those years working for her and putting up with her snobbery just to be replaced with somebody younger with *no* warning."

"Okay, let's talk about something else," said Mrs. Harrison.

"Fine. How's your son?"

"Which one?"

"The youngest one."

"He's doing better," sighed Mrs. Harrison. "That whole kidnapping situation has turned the whole family upside-down. I took him to see a psychiatrist and they diagnosed him with anxiety."

"Anxiety?"

"Yeah. Mr. Harrison has been a great help with him because you know he has PTSD from his time in the war. But sometimes I'll find the boy asleep in my bed because he's too scared to sleep in his room."

"I'll bet Marlin doesn't like that."

"Marlin's the one who puts him there."

"He does?"

"Yeah. Apparently, he keeps tripping over him in the middle of the night when he gets up to use the restroom."

"Poor baby. But I guess it's a good thing Mr. Muscles does have a heart after all. How have things been between you two?"

"He loves me, but he's scared to say it," whispered Mrs. Harrison.

"Scared?"

"He thinks I'll think less of him."

"Now that's just silly."

"I know. But at the very least he for sure loves me. I can see it in his eyes."

"That's good," said First Lady Hall. "Listen, do you think seeing a psychiatrist helped your son?"

"For the most part. Why?"

First Lady Hall pulled out her phone and typed something. She showed it to Mrs. Harrison, whose eyes grew big with surprise.

"Seriously?" gasped Mrs. Harrison.

"I've suspected it for years," said First Lady Hall. "And with him going off on his own soon, I want to be sure that he'll be able to take care of himself. But up to this point I haven't been able to do anything about it because Torrance won't give me his approval, and we both have to agree on it first."

Karla became intrigued with the conversation between her mother and Mrs. Harrison. It was clear they were talking about Andre because her mother only needed Mr. Brown's approval for something that concerned their children. And Andre was the only one getting ready to 'go off on his own soon' after graduating high school. The talk of psychiatrists getting involved led Karla to conclude that her mother might have suspected that Andre was mentally ill and had been for years.

She did not know how to handle this conclusion. On the one hand, she did not want to believe anything was wrong with her brother. But on the other hand, many things about him would suddenly make sense.

Like why he always seemed easily distracted, all over the place, and always waited until the last minute to do things.

Nisha finished Karla's hair, and Karla and Mary drove home in an awkward silence.

"You ready for this dinner tonight?" asked Karla, breaking the silence.

"I guess," answered Mary.

"What do you think he's making?"

"I don't know."

Karla dropped the conversation after that. It was clear Mary did not want to talk. Something had happened between Wednesday and Friday, and it had put Mary in a horrible mood. After dropping Mary off, Karla went home to prepare for the dinner.

She did not know what, or rather, who to expect. Karla wondered which version of her father she would get that evening. It could be what little remained of her daddy in him, or it could be her father she barely got along with. Time ticked by until the fateful hour came, and Karla could no longer put off going to the house.

It saddened her that visiting her father seemed like such an ordeal. But every time she visited reminded her how hard living with him had been. She thought about how she had to grow up fast to help care for her siblings, and how her father yelled at her and criticized her for every little thing. Visiting her father should have felt like coming home. Instead, it felt like returning to a prison that she could not wait to leave.

When she arrived, the first person she saw was Drake, and it made her feel a lot easier. With Drake at her side, she knew she would at least have one ally if things went bad. He warned her that everyone in the house seemed to be in a bad mood, and after gathering her wits, Karla entered the house.

The first person she encountered inside was Andre.

"Hi," said Andre, hugging Karla.

"Hi," said Karla. She held onto Andre, a sadness overcoming her.

"You must really miss me or something," laughed Andre. "You've never hugged me this long before."

"Oh, shut up," griped Karla, trading her sadness for annoyance. But then she felt relieved. Andre was still her Andre. Her little brother that worked her every nerve.

After allaying that concern, Karla looked around and realized Drake had been right. Everyone seemed to be in a negative mood. And emerging from the kitchen clutching a pair of shoes was the one person Karla was nervous to see.

"Hey," said Mr. Brown.

"Hi," answered Karla.

"Glad you could make it."

That was all Mr. Brown said before he disappeared into his room. It had not been enough to gauge his mood or who she was getting. Karla realized she would have to wait and see how everything played out before she would know exactly who she had just spoken to. It would be a long night.

Mary Brown

To Mary Ann Brown

Here we go with baby number three.
We've decided to name this one Mary.
Even though she's named after my mother dear,
Naming her so was not my idea.
Since you're Mary Ann will you be mine?
Since my Marianne is with a man so unkind.
I wonder why it is that she's with him.
Does she like being on his life's rhythm?
Mary Ann I promise you that,
I will be the very best dad.
I won't ever deny you my love,
For you are a gift sent from above.
And all I ask from you in return,
Is that you allow me your love to earn.
I won't fail you this I promise,
And I seal it on your forehead with a kiss.

Friday

Mary had rarely gone against her father's wishes. Out of all her siblings, she had always been his most obedient child. But Mary was not a child anymore, and her curiosity had gotten the better of her.

She had committed the most grievous sin against her father: she had sought out a relationship with Mr. Leonard Brown. The accounts of his past evils, especially against her father, were known to her as they were to the rest of her family. And yet, their first fateful encounter the previous summer at Creeke Church had awakened something in her. A new craving to know who he was and everything about him.

She was like Eve in the Garden of Eden, drawn to the forbidden fruit of the Tree of Knowledge. But Mr. Leonard was both the fruit and The Serpent. And as Eve had hidden the nakedness of her sin from her Heavenly Father, so had Mary hidden the secret of Mr. Leonard away from her father.

The second time Mary talked to Mr. Leonard was in December. She had started a new job at the town's public library, and he had been looking for a book. Her back had been turned when he approached the desk.

"I'm looking for a book," said Mr. Leonard.

"What's the title?" asked Mary, turning around.

They had stared at each other.

"What's the title of your book?" asked Mary.

"Mary, right?" said Mr. Leonard after telling her the title of the book he had been looking for.

Mary had nodded.

"Since when do you work here?"

"Your book is in the nonfiction section."

"You're not going to answer my question?"

A smile had involuntarily spread across Mary's face. That had been enough to encourage him to talk to her some more. Before she knew it, Mr. Leonard frequented the library to talk to her. Then, those library trips turned into her visiting him at his house. She had tried to time her trips when Grandma Marianne was not home, but one day, she had gotten careless and been discovered. Mary had sworn her grandmother to secrecy and had freely visited Mr. Leonard since.

Mary visited Mr. Leonard again the week before her father's wedding. She was off on Fridays and Saturdays, and with her father at work and her younger siblings at school, she could go about her day in peace. When she arrived, she discovered Mr. Leonard was out. But Grandma Marianne was in.

"Hey Grandma," said Mary.

"Hey sweetie!" said Grandma Marianne. "I've got something here for you."

"What?"

"I've got a letter from my cousin Lora Mae's daughter, Lucy Ann, and a letter from my cousin Cleo," explained Grandma Marianne. She waved the letters around excitedly before handing them to Mary. "I wrote them and asked them to share everything they could about the Jones family history because I don't know that much."

"Thanks Grandma," said Mary.

Mary's quest to uncover her family's history had started as a desire to know more about Mr. Leonard. But he was reluctant to share in the same way Mr. Brown was regarding his own childhood. So, Mary had taken it upon herself to learn what she could apart from them. Grandma Marianne had been excited to see what Mary would discover and had spread the news of her exploits amongst the family. That caused everyone to request she explore their family lines as well, and Mary herself was curious about what she would learn. She sat at the kitchen table and opened the first letter from Cousin Lucy Ann.

Dear Cousin Marianne,

It's been a minute since we heard from you. I hope things are good down there in that town of yours, because we're doing just fine up here where I'm at. Mama's doing fine. She's not remembering much these days, but hearing your name brought a smile to her face.

As for what you wanted for your granddaughter, I've got the story right here and some pictures to go along with it. Aunt Ophi actually kept pretty good records of the family history, so everything I've got here came from her and Granny, as well as what Mama told me before her mind started to go.

According to Aunt Ophi, she traced our family line back as far as the Jones farm. Her grandmother, Molly, was a slave on that farm, and the master was her father. After emancipation, she married Hiram Jones, who had also been a slave on the farm, which is why they had the same last name. They stayed on that land as sharecroppers and had Uncle Garland and Great-Grandpa Rosario.

You already know Uncle Gabe went down there to where you live with his Uncle Garland. According to Aunt Ophi, the reason why was something to do with Aunt Lou's fiancé. Neither Aunt Ophi nor Granny would go into detail about it, but it was definitely something bad enough to make Aunt Lou hate Uncle Gabe for the rest of her short life and force the family to move from their hometown for good. Uncle Gabe went with Uncle Garland, while all the girls came here with their parents.

The pictures included are of the parents and the sisters. Hopefully, this will be helpful to your granddaughter. If she needs more, just let me know because there's plenty here.

Your cousin,

Lucy Ann

Mary looked over the photos Cousin Lucy Ann had sent. One depicted Cousin Lucy Ann with her mother, Lora Mae, and grandmother, Leanne. Aunt Leanne Clayton had been the last of her and her siblings, having died a year after her brother. Another photo showed all the siblings and their parents together when Great-Grandpa Gabriel was a little boy and had their names written underneath to identify them. All of them were varying shades of light-brown, with some of the sisters – Louise, Cara, Charlotte, May, and Ophelia – looking like they could be White women.

"Grandma, have you seen these before?" asked Mary, showing the photos to her grandmother.

"Let me see," said Grandma Marianne. A smile broke out on her face as she said, "No, I haven't."

Grandma Marianne looked through the photos, making comments such as, 'Look at mean old Aunt Susan!', and 'Aw Aunt Ophi was so pretty! It's a shame no one ever married her!'. She described how good of a cook Aunt Agnes was and how she never let anyone else be in the kitchen with her. How Aunt Charlotte was a smart schoolteacher and the only one to go to college. Then there was how funny Aunt June was, how kind Aunt April was, how everyone called Aunt Loretta "Floretta" because she liked gardening, how Aunt Josephine got on everyone's nerves with all her complaining, and how Aunt Leanne always smelled and dressed good. But through all the anecdotes Grandma Marianne shared, Mary noticed she never said anything about Aunt Louise.

"What about Aunt Louise?" asked Mary. "Do you have any stories about her?"

"Aunt Louise died before I was born," said Grandma Marianne glumly. "And all I know about her was that she hated my daddy."

"Oh," said Mary.

"I'll be back."

"Where are you going?"

"The bathroom. We can look at some more of the pictures when I get back."

While Grandma Marianne was gone, Mary read the second letter from Mr. Cleophus Taylor III.

Dear Cousin Marianne,

How are you? We've got to get together sometime. I've got everything you requested for your granddaughter.

Mary was shocked beyond words. The last thing she had expected to learn was that her great-grandfather had killed someone.

"Was there any good info in those letters?" asked Grandma Marianne, returning.

"Oh, uh...," answered Mary quickly. "Just explaining the family tree. Farthest they can go back is a farm run by someone named Jones."

"Really?" said Grandma Marianne. "Let me see."

Mary panicked. She did not want to give Grandma Marianne the letters exposing the truth about her father. But if she did not, her grandmother would grow suspicious, and Mary would have to explain anyway.

"Marianne!" called an old, rough-sounding voice.

"Oh Lord," sighed Grandma Marianne. "I'm in the kitchen!"

Mary silently praised The Lord for the timely interruption. The sound of a wooden cane crossed the living room into the kitchen. Mr. Leonard smiled and looked at Mary.

"Hey Mary. Didn't know you were here today."

"I was picking up some letters about the family history from Grandma," answered Mary. "You promised to tell me your family history, remember?"

"Not today."

"Okay," said Mary. "I'm going home Grandma."

"Why you want to run off as soon as I get here?" demanded Mr. Leonard.

"If you're not telling me anything, I don't see a reason to stay," said Mary.

"Well, go on then," huffed Mr. Leonard. "Get."

And that's what Mary did. She left knowing she would be back soon enough to try and coax Mr. Leonard into telling her of his family. It had been an ongoing struggle between the two, but Mary could feel that he was getting closer to sharing it all with her, and she just had to keep at it until he did. Especially because his family history was her family history too.

Mary returned home to find the kitchen had become a war zone. There were pots and pans scattered across the counters and broken pasta noodles on the floor. In the midst of it all stood her father at the stove, cooking what smelled like ground beef. He was pushing his falsetto to the limit, hitting notes that Mary did not think any man could hit, let alone her father, who had not sung consistently since he was fourteen. But even though Mary could tell that he had not properly warmed up his voice, he still sounded okay to her.

"I'm home," said Mary.

"*Hello*," sang her father. He chuckled and asked, "Where were you?"

"At Grandma's."

"Mrs. Ernestine's?"

"Grandma Marianne's."

"What?" said Mr. Brown, almost dropping his spoon on the floor. He scrunched his face and asked, "Wh... what were you doing over there?"

"Visiting."

"Visiting?" repeated Mr. Brown. "Your grandmother comes over every weekend."

"Well, I wanted to go to her house today."

"But why? You couldn't wait for her to come here?"

"You don't want me to visit her?"

"No... well... not *no* but...," stammered Mr. Brown. "I'd just prefer that you wait for her to visit here."

"So... are you saying I'm not allowed to go over there?"

"No, I...," began Mr. Brown. He thought about his response and sighed. "Just let me know when you go over there, okay?"

"Yes sir."

Mr. Brown did not sing anymore after that, and it saddened Mary. Her father had been having a good day, and she had come along and ruined it. Just the thought of her possibly being around Mr. Leonard had disturbed her father, and Mary did not want to imagine what the truth would do to him.

There was also what she had learned about her great-grandfather. He had been like a father to her father, with Mr. Brown even going so far as to claim him as such over Mr. Leonard. Learning that his grandfather had been a killer could have a great negative effect on Mr. Brown. So, Mary decided to keep both men a secret to preserve her father's happiness. And all she could do was hope that her father never found out what she was harboring from him because he would never forgive her if he did.

My Daddy Was Real

My daddy was like me.
And it was plain to see,
That he had my taste,
Like copy and paste.
To me he made sense,
Had the others in suspense.
But I knew him from the start.
He was like a work of art,
That had come alive.
And from him I derived,
Which made me an art piece too.
I was stuck to him like glue,
Cuz between me and him,
We were like synonyms.
And it was such a big deal,
Because my daddy was real.

Monday

Mary had spent all weekend trying to learn more about the Jones family. After two days of researching, she had not learned anything new. Coming home from work that Monday, Mary wanted nothing more but to clear her mind and take a break from researching. And so, she did by playing the family piano that Mr. Brown had inherited after Great-Grandpa Gabriel's death.

Music and reading books had always been Mary's second love after God. She could play multiple instruments, but her preferred instrument was the piano. And though Drake would never admit it, they both knew she was better at it than he was. But her brother made up for it by being better than her at everything else. He was technically the better singer, the slightly better lyricist, he danced better than her although neither of them could compete with Adrianna's ability, and he was overall the better performer. Mary, however, did not mind because she did not care to exhibit like Drake did. Her dream was to compose.

Mary had wanted to attend a prestigious music school after graduating high school. She had envisioned herself on the campus, had prepared herself for the admissions and audition process, and had discussed the cost of attending with her parents. But when the time to apply came, she felt unready. So, she took a year off and decided to apply the following year. And before she knew it, the following year had arrived.

She had already sent her application and transcript off to the school. All that remained was to complete her upcoming audition and interview in April. If she did well, she would be accepted to the school and on the road to pursuing her dreams and starting life on her own.

While she played the piano, Mr. Lee came by to visit. Although Mr. Lee and Mr. Brown were not related biologically or adoptively, they still treated each other like family. Mr. Lee was one of Mr. Brown's closest friends and vice versa. When he came to visit, he and Mr. Brown sat on the couch, talking about the quest he had begun the previous summer to find his biological family.

"So, how'd that thing with your birth family go?" asked Mr. Brown. "You said you found them, but you haven't said anything since."

"Man, do I got a story for you," said Mr. Lee. "I've got to tell it from the beginning."

"Okay."

"This whole time I'm thinking I'm a Black man dumped on somebody's doorstep as a baby in the freezing cold in the seventies, right?"

"Right."

"So, I take one of those blood tests that tells you what all you're mixed with. And while I waited on those results, I started looking for everyone with the last name Lee in the surrounding area. Of course, I was more inclined to research Black people with the last name, but I didn't want to rule out other possibilities."

"Makes sense."

"Torrance, I got those results. Now I'm thinking it's going to be like 'you're mostly Black, but there's some other stuff in here too but you're mostly Black' right?"

"Yeah?"

"Come to find out I'm Black and Asian."

"That explains a lot," said Mr. Brown. "Especially the eyes and the hair."

"You sound like Dani."

"Well, it's true."

"There were some other percentages in there too, but it was fairly clear that one parent was Black, and one was Asian. So, with this new discovery I was able to narrow down my search quite a bit. But then came the hard part. I had to start contacting people. There was a lot of frustration during that part because I had a bunch of dead ends with people who were hopeful, and I had some people flat out tell me they weren't interested in helping me. I was near the end of my rope, so I gave up."

"Then how–!"

"I'm getting there. About a week later, I received a phone call from this man named Harold Chang. He told me that he was doing family research and wanted to meet with me. I figured I had nothing left to lose, so I agreed. We met for lunch in the city, and when I saw him, I almost started crying because I could see the resemblance. We talked and got to know each other, and he decided we would do a DNA test. I was a little scared because I wanted my search to be over, but at the same time, if we were related, it would bring up a lot of new questions for me."

"Been there, done that," mumbled Mr. Brown.

"So, weeks went by as we waited for the results," said Mr. Lee. "I got to know Harold and his older sister Maureen. They're both younger than me, both very outgoing, and I could tell they really liked me a lot. But they never told me why they were so eager for us to do this DNA test. And then the results came earlier this month. And we learned that I was in fact their older brother."

"And you met the rest of the family this past weekend, right?" asked Mr. Brown.

"Yeah...," said Mr. Lee. "Some of the family accepted me, some didn't. That hurt a little, but I got over it. And I met my mother too. Her name's Marah. Marah Chang, but when she had me it was Marah Lee."

"How'd that go?"

"We talked. She was in her freshman year of college when she had me. My father died in the war. Her parents didn't like him, and they weren't very fond of me either, so she left home. She tried to care for me and ended up very poor. After two years, she took me to get a checkup at the clinic where my mom... er, Mrs. Parker, worked. She said my mom was very caring toward me and she decided she would give me to her because she wasn't able to care for me anymore. She followed my mom home and left me on her porch with a note explaining who I was. Harold found out about me because he saw me on the news during that time when Derik was kidnapped and noticed how much we looked alike. Marah was glad that I'd been so well taken care of and hoped we could get to know each other more."

"And what did Tasha and Dani think of all this?"

"Tasha hasn't really said much, but Dani doesn't like Marah for some reason."

"That girl," grumbled Mr. Brown. "Does she ever act right?"

"Dani is Dani," said Mr. Lee. "You know she's dating the younger Derik now."

"I heard," said Mr. Brown. "It's an interesting couple."

"If she's happy, then I'm happy," said Mr. Lee. "And Derik's a good boy. Very respectful."

"For the most part."

"Okay, he had one moment where he got disrespectful with you, but you have to admit that you started it."

"I don't have to admit anything," said Mr. Brown. "And I think you spoil that girl way too much."

"Look, I know she gets an attitude sometimes but she's not a bad girl," said Mr. Lee.

"Arty," said Mr. Brown. "How long are you going to lie to yourself about your daughter? She fell out with all her best friends in less than a year, gave you the silent treatment because you wouldn't break the rules for her to get back on the cheer squad, made fun of two adopted kids knowing you yourself are adopted, and now she doesn't like your biological family. What more proof do you need that your daughter is not a nice person?"

"Do you say all this stuff to your sister about her daughters?" said Mr. Lee. "Because last time I checked they were in my office too."

"Yes!" exclaimed Mr. Lee. "I tell both of you the same thing and you both make the same excuses. 'That's just how they are, they're not that bad, they're only teenagers.'. Do you see my children acting a fool? No! Because my children act like they have sense because they know I don't play."

"Because they're scared of you," mumbled Mr. Lee quietly.

"No, they're not," retorted Mr. Brown. "Mary, are you scared of me?"

"No sir," said Mary. She was not, and she was sure her brothers and sisters were not either, but she understood what Mr. Lee meant. Although she did not fear her father, she also knew he was not one of her little friends either.

"See?" said Mr. Brown.

"Well, I'm not you," said Mr. Lee. "I know Dani isn't perfect, and I talked to her about what she said to Latasia and Sami and how that hurt my feelings, and she said she wouldn't say it again. But I don't want her to feel like I'm controlling her life, and I also don't want her feeling like I'm not invested in it either. I used to worry that my parents would give me away like Mrs. Marah did when they decided they didn't want me anymore, and I don't want her feeling like that. I want Dani to know I'm here through it all. Good, bad ugly, pretty."

"I still think you spoil her too much," said Mr. Brown. "And you need to keep an eye on that Derik. He may be a good boy but he's still a boy."

"I could say the exact same thing to you."

"I don't have to worry about my Derek because I don't let him in the house."

"Don't you think that's a little overboard?"

"Nope. Ever since he and Dria started dating people have been speculating that he'll end up a teen father like his dad. I'm not letting that happen and especially not with my daughter."

"What do you do when she goes over his house?"

"First, I call ahead to make sure Malcolm is there. Then, I send one of her brothers with her. And they only get fifteen minutes to be there. It takes two to three minutes to walk there, so that's four to six minutes gone right there. And they know I want them back before the fifteen minutes is up so their visits typically last up to five minutes."

"I'm surprised all your kids just don't outright hate you."

"Why would they hate me?"

"Because what kind of relationship can last on five-minute visits, Torrance?"

"They've made it work this long."

"Yeah, but how much longer will they 'make it work'?"

"If they love each other–!"

"Boy, shut up! You of all people know that's a bunch of crap!" Mary snorted.

"Mary," said Mr. Brown. "Are you eavesdropping?"

"No sir," said Mary.

"You better not be," said Mr. Brown. "What do you think I should do Arty since you're such an expert on teen relationships?"

"I'm not an expert," said Mr. Lee. "But I trust my daughter and her boyfriend enough to at least let them hang out *inside* my house."

"I trust my daughter and I trust Derek. But I don't trust their teenage hormones together in my house."

"You know if they really wanted to, they'd find a way to be together without you knowing, right?"

"Speaking from personal experience?"

"I'm speaking from being realistic, from having a long career in working with children and knowing how they act, and from being the brother of a teen parent."

"Well, I'm the son of a teen parent so what's your point?"

"My point is you're being overbearing."

"And my point is you're being underbearing."

"You just don't want to admit that you know I'm right."

"I can say the same," said Mr. Brown. "But I am glad you found your birth family."

"Don't change the subject."

"It's my house, I can change it if I want. You know Mary's doing family research too."

"Yeah, I heard. How's it coming, Mary?"

"Good," answered Mary. She stopped playing and prepared to leave the room.

"Why'd you stop?" asked Mr. Brown.

"Because I'm done playing for the day," said Mary. "I'm going to my room."

Mary's room was actually her and Adrianna's room. When Karla lived with them, it had been her room too. Although they were sad when their older sister had moved out, both Mary and Adrianna had been excited to capitalize on the new space her leaving had given them. Sharing a space between three people had not been ideal. And once Drake moved out, the girls celebrated by trading their bunk bed for his bed. It felt like such a triumph to them to finally have separate beds.

Mary sat on her bed, which used to be Karla's, staring at all the research she had accumulated. She had family trees for each family – the Browns, the Joneses, the Allens, and the Brooks – that named who all was in the family. And she had some information on how her great-grandfather ended up in Creeke. But there was still much more for her to learn, and she knew the toughest family to learn about would be the Browns. Until she could get Mr. Leonard to finally share his story, Mary would have to focus on the other families.

Mr. Brown knocked on the door and entered after Mary told him it was okay. He used to enter without knocking because it was 'his house and he paid the bills', but Karla changed all that at eleven when he accidentally walked in on her while she was changing. Mary had never seen her father's face so red from embarrassment, nor had she seen Karla's face so red from anger. She believed it was the first time he realized his daughters were no longer little girls but were growing into women.

"What are you up to?" asked Mr. Brown.

"Family research," answered Mary. "I was trying to find more information about the Jones family. But I guess what I already have will have to be enough."

"What do you already have?"

"Well for starters, would you believe me if I told you that you were part-White?"

"Through who?"

"Great-Grandpa."

"How much?"

"He was one-eighth. That means you're like one-twenty-fourth."

"Girl," snorted Mr. Brown. "You had me thinking it was a lot."

"Did he ever tell you anything about his family?"

"I doubt he even knew anything to tell," said Mr. Brown. "And if he did, he wouldn't have told me. He didn't really like sharing about his life before he moved here."

"So, he didn't tell you anything about his childhood?"

"Nope. Everything I learned, I learned from other people. And even then, it still wasn't all that much."

"Oh," said Mary.

Mary found it ironic that all the men in her family were reluctant to share about their childhoods. What Mary knew of Mr. Brown's childhood had not come directly from him but from the people who had been around to witness it. The biggest shock to Mary had been learning that her father's facial scar was caused by Mr. Leonard smacking him into a table and not him tripping and falling into it as he had been told to say. He had not even shared that truth with his children. They had learned it from Drake, who had learned it from their cousins, who had learned it from confronting their own parents for answers. It was things like that that drew Mary to research the family history. She wanted to separate the truth from the lies and the secrets and get a clear picture of how the family got to be the way it was.

"Learn anything else interesting?" asked Mr. Brown.

"Not really," answered Mary.

"Dang," said Mr. Brown. He chuckled and said, "Well, keep digging. Maybe you'll uncover some huge deep dark secret."

Mary grimaced as she watched her father leave the room, wondering if he would still be laughing if he knew what she knew about the family.

Daddy's Baby

Out of all of my babies,
Mary was seriously Daddy's.
She was my little lamb,
Always where I am.
I didn't want her growing up like I did,
I made sure she knew she was my kid.
My baby girl is dark as night,
But her skin color was never my plight.
I just wanted her to know that I cared,
And that hurting her I'd never dare.
I gave my baby what love I had,
And did my best to be her dad.
I know she knows I love her,
And my love only grows stronger.
My sweet little lamb Mary,
Say you'll always be Daddy's baby.

-

Tuesday

After getting as far as she could with the Jones family, Mary decided to focus on her mother's families. Grandpap Jared came from the Allen family, one of the first families to settle in Creeke. Gran Ernestine's maiden name had been Brooks, and she had moved to Creeke after marrying Grandpap Jared. Mary had the facts about the Brooks from researching, and she hoped Gran Ernestine could fill in who the people were and what they were like.

Mary planned to visit her grandparents after work. She had told her father her plans, and Andre had expressed interest in joining her. Toward the end of her shift, Andre had biked to the library with a small backpack to wait for her. He browsed around while she finished the last of her work duties, and then they were off. When they arrived at their grandparent's house, Mary looked at their bikes, hers in her favorite color blue, and shook her head.

"I really need to get a car," said Mary.

"Me too," said Andre. "But we'll probably have to pay for them like Drake and Karla did theirs."

"True," agreed Mary. "What's the point of Dad letting us get our licenses if we can't at least drive his car?"

"That's a question for him."

"Well, let's go in," said Mary. They rang their grandparent's doorbell, and Grandpap Jared opened the door with a big grin.

"Come in, come in!" said Grandpap Jared in a comical accent. "We've been expecting you!"

"Do you ever take anything serious?" questioned Mary.

"Life is too short to not enjoy it while you have it dear granddaughter," said Grandpap Jared, continuing his accent. "Hello grandson!"

"Hello Grandpap!" answered Andre, mimicking the accent.

"Come with me to the back porch," said Grandpap Jared. "Let's give the women some time to talk."

"Okay," said Andre.

The pair went to the back porch, leaving Mary and her grandmother alone at the kitchen table.

"Grandpap is funny," said Mary.

"I wouldn't have him any other way," said Gran Ernestine. "Where do you want to start?"

"Anywhere you want."

"Well, you know the Allens are one of the oldest families in this town," explained Gran Ernestine. "Your great-grandfather was Deacon Marvin Allen Sr."

"A deacon?" repeated Mary.

"Mhmm," said Gran Ernestine. "In fact, he was one of the deacons who fired Pastor Harrison back in the day."

"What?" gasped Mary.

"Mhmm," said Gran Ernestine, nodding her head. "It was him, Deacon Timothy Haynes, and Deacon Tolbert. Deacon Tolbert was the one leading the charge and Deacon Haynes and your great-grandfather were his lackeys doing his bidding."

"Deacon Haynes was the current Deacon Haynes's father, right?" asked Mary.

"Mhmm," affirmed Gran Ernestine. "He was Titus's father. Titus is a lot nicer than his father was though."

"And Deacon Tolbert...," muttered Mary. "Wasn't that Lady Sophia's maiden name?"

"Sure was," said Gran Ernestine, her face darkening. Gran Ernestine had been Lady Sophia Perry's head maid for several decades and despised the woman. She scrunched her face up and said, "Deacon Tolbert was her grandfather. He was old as dirt sitting up, passing judgment meanwhile his low-down, conniving, gold-digging heifer of a daughter Miss Estelle had Sophia out of wedlock too. If anyone should've been sat down it should've been him!"

"Oop!" uttered Mary. "How'd you end up working for Lady Sophia?"

"Mrs. Allen used to work for that family, and she got me hired on," scoffed Gran Ernestine. "I worked for that woman for decades dealing with her foolishness and what do I get? I get replaced that's what I get!"

"Just terrible," said Mary.

"Mhmm," said Gran Ernestine, rolling her eyes. "Anyways. Where were we?"

"Uh," said Mary, looking down at her notes. "Deacon Marvin Allen Sr."

"Oh yeah," said Gran Ernestine. "That was your grandfather's father. Your grandfather's mother was named Julia. They were one of the first families to settle here in Creeke. Your grandfather's the only one of his family still here in town. His older brother Antoine went one way, and his other older brother Marvin Jr. moved to my hometown right next door to my family."

"And that's how you met Grandpap?"

"Mhmm. He and Antoine had come to visit. Marvin had come by to introduce them. They were only supposed to be there a few minutes, but your grandfather was a such a huge chatterbox that they ended up being there all evening. It was honestly my fault though because everything he talked about was so interesting and funny that I didn't want the conversation to end."

"And that's how you got together?"

"Mhmm. He later told me that his brothers told him not to let me get away because he might not find another girl who will let him talk her to death."

"Are his brothers still alive?"

"Marvin is but he's living in a retirement home. Antoine died right before our Antoine was born so your mother named him after them both."

"That's interesting. What about your side of the family Gran?"

"Honestly Mary, I don't know that much. I was an only child, and my family wasn't really keeping up with the family history like that. I was hoping you'd be able to tell me something."

"All I have is names and dates," said Mary. "I was hoping you'd be able to tell me about them."

"Sure, if I can remember anything," said Gran Ernestine.

Mary found that Gran Ernestine remembered more than she thought she would. She recalled her parents, aunts, uncles, and cousins easily and shared little anecdotes about them all. It was reminiscent of when Mary had received the letters from Grandma Marianne, which brought Great-Grandpa Gabriel back to her mind.

"Can I ask you something?" asked Mary.

"Anything baby."

"Did you know Great-Grandpa Gabriel?"

"Child, who didn't know Minister Jones?"

"What was he like?"

"Well, I was already grown when I came here to Creeke, so I wasn't as intimidated by him. But a lot of the people who grew up here like your grandfather were scared of him."

"So, he was mean?"

"I wouldn't say he was mean. He definitely didn't play, but he was far from mean. In fact, I'd even go so far as to say he was one of the nicest and most honest people in town as long as you didn't do anything to upset him."

"Hmm…"

"What's got you so interested in Minister Jones?"

"Nothing. I just learned some things about him in my research and I was curious what type of person he was."

Andre walked into the kitchen and began digging through his bag. Mary and Gran Ernestine watched him with keen interest. After a few seconds, Andre pulled out what looked like a brown-orange ball and grinned.

"Aha!" declared Andre. The brown-orange ball was an orange that had gone bad. Andre looked at it and frowned, saying, "Uh oh. It's rotted."

"How long has that been in there?" asked Mary.

"Uh... I don't know," answered Andre with a laugh. "I just remembered it was in there."

Mary was dumbfounded but unsurprised. Things like that were typical for Andre, and Mary had become quite used to them.

"Baby, throw that away," said Gran Ernestine. "I have some fresh ones in the fruit bowl over there."

"Okay," said Andre. He threw out his old orange, grabbed a new one, and dashed out the door, saying, "Thanks!"

"That boy is something else," laughed Gran Ernestine.

"Nothing about Andre surprises me anymore," said Mary.

Mary finished her talk with her grandmother and returned home with Andre. That evening, she went to dinner with her best friend Philomena James. Philomena had been one year ahead of Mary in school, and they had had speech class together. Although Philomena had hung around with Drake and his friends, she sometimes had felt like a fifth wheel, and it was during those times that she and Mary had grown close.

"Oh Patty's how I've missed you!" cried Philomena as they entered the restaurant.

"Don't they have good food in the city?" asked Mary.

"Yeah, but Patty's is one of a kind," said Philomena.

"Welcome to Patty's," said Charmaine Townsend, the daughter of Patty's owners Raymond and Patricia Townsend. "What can I get you?"

"Can I get a cheeseburger meal?" said Philomena.

"And I'll take the eight-piece wing meal," said Mary, which caused Charmaine to giggle. Mary looked at her peculiarly and asked, "What's so funny?"

"Nothing," said Charmaine, still giggling. "Your order just reminded me of something that happened today. Will that be all?"

"Yes," said Philomena.

The women paid for their food and settled into a booth to wait.

"I wonder what was so funny," said Mary.

"Girl, you know how Charmaine is," said Philomena. "She's always all smiles as opposed to that brother of hers."

"He's supposed to be shooting the music video for his new song tomorrow."

"Shoot, he better be working hard to get his music out there. The way his attitude is set up he won't be successful in any other career path."

"I think he's been improving."

"We'll see when he brings this food."

As if on cue, their food appeared in the window. Charmaine rang the bell and called for her brother to deliver it.

"Benji!" hollered Charmaine. "Food's ready!"

"Okay!" answered Benjamin.

"Okay, good start," said Philomena. "He's not going off on Charmaine anymore in front of customers. Now we just need a strong finish."

Benjamin retrieved the food and delivered it to the women.

"Enjoy your meal," said Benjamin.

"Okay growth!" said Philomena when Benjamin had gone. "That's what I'm talking about."

The women began eating their food.

"How's school?" asked Mary.

"These communications classes are no joke," said Philomena. "I thought those seven-page English papers in high school were rough, but I about fell out when my professor told us we were writing a twelve-to-fifteen-page paper. And it's worth forty percent of my grade!"

"Well Phil, I'm sure you can do it."

"Oh I know I can. I just don't want to."

"Well if you want that degree, you better start wanting to."

"I know," sighed Philomena. "Are you excited for your big audition next month?"

"I am," answered Mary. "I'm getting into this school."

"Okay confidence!" cheered Philomena. "And with that pretty sing-ing voice and all those different instruments you play, there's no way you won't get in."

"Thanks."

"How's your family research coming along?"

"It's going well. I've learned some very surprising things."

"Like what?"

"For starters, one of my ancestors is white apparently."

"How far back we talking here?"

"Before slavery ended."

"Child, that little bit of mess," chuckled Philomena. "You had me thinking you were about to say your mama was really a White woman with a tan or something."

"That's the crazy part though," said Mary. "The White ancestor is on my dad's side. Unless I'm missing something, everyone on my mom's side was Black as far as I can tell through my research."

"Well, Black does come in many shades."

"Okay, but all the shades on her side seem to be lightskinned."

"Well, that's a whole other conversation that I don't feel like getting into tonight. What all do you have left to research?"

"The Brown family."

"Oh Lord. The only person with information on that family's history is Leonard Brown."

"I know," said Mary. She debated whether she should tell Philomena she had been spending time with Mr. Leonard.

"What are you going to do?" asked Philomena.

"I'm going to talk to Mr. Leonard."

"You want me to go with you?"

"No? I'm not scared of him."

"Okay. What if your dad finds out?"

"I don't even want to think about that," sighed Mary.

Mary wanted to keep her dad in the dark as long as possible. She knew if he ever found out, he would not understand no matter how hard she tried to explain. Mr. Leonard was like a flame, and she was like a moth drawn to him out of curiosity. But there was more than just a desire to know about him brewing in her. A part of her was starting to care about him. And she knew that would be an even worse betrayal to her father than just talking to Mr. Leonard.

The Daughter's Rite of Passage

Mary Ann, Mary Ann, that's who I am,
And I'm here to remix my daddy's jam.
We've got the rite of passage for man and son,
But what about when it comes to someone
Like me? Because here's the trouble.
I go through all that and double.
And when I get into situations,
Everybody else takes elation,
In laying the blame on me,
Regardless of where the blame should be.
And I'm always having to fix everything,
And I risk my life a lot more than you'd think.
So, what exactly is my rite of passage?
Is it being the villain from a young age?
I don't want to always be strong,
Sometimes I also want to sing another song.

Wednesday

Mary was conflicted. She wished she did not have to go behind her father's back to get the information she needed. And she wished she had not begun to care about Mr. Leonard. But at the same time, she kind of enjoyed the thrill. Getting to know Mr. Leonard had been an interesting experience for her.

"Hey," said Aunt Marie Garza, approaching the circulation desk where Mary worked. "I'm returning this book for Alejandro."

"Okay," answered Mary.

"How is the family research?"

"It's going great. The only family I have left to do is the Browns."

"Wow. You work fast."

"Yeah," said Mary. She knew the best source for information on the Brown family history was Mr. Leonard. But his reluctance to share made Mary consider if there were other alternatives. Such as her Aunt Marie. "Do you know anything about the Browns family history?"

"Not really," said Aunt Marie. "The most I could tell you is about my grandparents. And even then, there's not much to tell about them."

"Something is better than nothing."

"All I really know is that my dad's father was really mean," said Aunt Marie. "And my dad's mother was very docile. That's really all I know because I didn't know them that well."

"Thanks."

"Sorry I couldn't tell you more."

"That's okay. What you said was helpful enough."

The information did not seem like much. But to Mary, it was the spark of curiosity that fueled her decision to push Mr. Leonard to share what he knew. She was determined to get answers from him as soon as possible.

When Mary arrived home from work, she found Mr. Brown practicing a song on the piano. His voice filled the house with its soulful melody.

"Hey Dad," said Mary.

"Hey!" said Mr. Brown. "Listen to this!"

Mr. Brown sang the whole song for Mary. He had been singing it all week whenever she heard him on the piano. As Mary listened to the lyrics, she realized it was a love song. But it was one she had never heard before.

"Sounds great," said Mary. "What song is it?"

"It's a song I wrote for Gretchen," explained Mr. Brown. "I'm going to sing it to her at the wedding."

"Oh," said Mary. "A serenade, huh?"

"Yeah," chuckled Mr. Brown. "You don't think it's too much do you?"

"It's your wedding," said Mary. "Nothing is too much."

"Okay," said Mr. Brown. "Let me keep practicing. I want it to be perfect on Saturday."

"And I'm sure it will be," said Mary.

Her father seemed so happy then. It was those moments of happiness that made Mary regret keeping so many secrets from him. He had been hurt repeatedly by Mr. Leonard, and Mary had dared to establish a connection with him and even worse, begin caring for him. As she listened to her father practice his love song, Mary felt like a guilty traitor for deciding to continue keeping him in the dark to preserve his happiness.

That evening at church, Mary could not focus. The pressure of the Mr. Leonard secret weighed on her, and she needed to share it with someone she could trust. So, she told Karla and almost immediately regretted it. Karla made Mary feel even more like a traitor. But the conversation had also steeled Mary's resolve to get the truth. She figured that if she did get caught, she would at least know the truth about everything.

"What were you and Karla talking about?" asked Mr. Brown when they were riding home from church.

"Family research," said Mary.

"Oh," said Mr. Brown. "You know, I've been thinking of having a family dinner instead of a wedding dinner. Just me and my kids. What do you think about that?"

"Will Karla be there?" questioned Mary.

"Is she not one of my kids?" retorted Mr. Brown. After a moment of considering her question, he added, "Do you think she'd come?"

"You'll have to ask her and see."

"I guess I will," said Mr. Brown.

In her room, she once again looked over her research. Great-Grandpa Gabriel had been a killer but was regarded by many as a nice and honest man. Her other great-grandfather Marvin Allen Sr. had been one of the deacons to fire Pastor Derrick Harrison but was known to be weak-willed. Mr. Leonard had abused her father. Mary noticed a common connection between all three men: Grandma Marianne. Grandma Marianne was Great-Grandpa Gabriel's daughter and Mr. Leonard's wife. And she had been one of the many reasons Pastor Derrick had been fired. So, Mary called her.

"Hello?" said Grandma Marianne.

"Hi Grandma," said Mary. "Do you have a minute to talk?"

"I always have a minute for my grandbabies. What's going on?"

"It's about Dad," said Mary, sneaking outside for privacy. "I haven't told him yet that I've been talking to Mr. Leonard and now I'm starting to feel guilty."

"Hmm," said Grandma Marianne. "Baby this is a tough one. I know the right thing to do is to tell him, but I also know how your father will react when you do."

"So, what should I do?"

"You can either tell him or take the secret to the grave."

"I don't want to have secrets from Dad though."

"I know how you feel," said Grandma Marianne. "Trust and believe I've been in your shoes several times before with my own father."

"And what did you do in those times?"

"Honestly, some secrets I told and some I tried to keep but he always found out. The times I told, he'd be more angry than hurt. But the times he found out, he'd be more hurt than angry. And it was those times he found out on his own that I ended up regretting."

"So, you think I should tell him."

"I think you'll have to make your own decision."

"I'll tell him after the wedding," decided Mary.

"You made that decision quick," noted Grandma Marianne.

"Can you be there with me when I tell him?"

"Of course. He won't act a fool if his mama is there."

"Thanks Grandma."

"Any time baby."

Mary felt relieved to have a plan for the secret regarding Mr. Leonard. But the secret regarding her great-grandfather would always have to remain one, even from Grandma Marianne. It was a burden Mary was willing to take to her grave to preserve the happiness of the ones she loved.

-

Secret Place

I've got a spot where I can hide away,
When I get worn down by a troublesome day.
A place known only to my heart,
And doesn't threaten to tear me apart.
I call it my secret place,
Because it's my sacred space.
Hidden in the shadow away from sight,
I expose my most inner plight.
I reveal what hurts me most,
And release the hard feelings that I host.
My secret place is where I dwell,
And it's where I get well.
It's where I go to hide,
And where I choose to confide.
Because what I keep inside myself,
I wouldn't trust to anybody else.

Thursday

It was Andre's birthday.

Mary was on her way to work but made sure to see Andre first. She, like everyone else, had forgotten his birthday the year before, and did not want to make the same mistake twice.

"I remembered this time," said Mary. "Happy birthday."

"Thanks," said Andre.

"I got to go. Have a good day."

"I will."

Mr. Brown was in the kitchen cooking breakfast. Mary could tell it was Andre's favorite by the smell.

"Dad, I'm going by Grandma's after work," said Mary. She had decided to get the truth out of Mr. Leonard that day, even if she had to drag it out of him.

"Why?" asked Mr. Brown.

"To visit," said Mary. "You said it was okay as long as I told you."

"I guess I did," said Mr. Brown. "Be careful."

"I will," said Mary.

The workday could not go fast enough. Mary wished she could fast-forward time and be at Grandma Marianne's already. She was determined to get Mr. Leonard's story and finish her family research. When she got there, Grandma Marianne was out. But Mr. Leonard was in.

"How's your family tree research coming?" asked Mr. Leonard.

"I think I'm just about done," answered Mary. She looked at Mr. Leonard and said, "All I need is the Browns."

"All you need is the Browns, huh?"

"Mhmm."

The two stared at each other. As Mary looked at him, she noticed her father favored Mr. Leonard heavily. There were minor differences that Mr. Brown had inherited from Grandma Marianne, but the only real major difference between Mr. Leonard and Mr. Brown was their skin tones. Mr. Leonard relented and sighed.

"Let's get this done and over with."

"Okay," said Mary. She started her recorder, pulled out her notepad and pen, and waited for Mr. Leonard to start.

"My father's name was Calvin, and my mother's Denise," began Leonard Brown. "I was an only child."

"What about your grandparents?"

"Didn't know them that well," said Mr. Leonard. "My parents moved here when most everyone else did and my dad worked in that factory in the city. I did too."

Mr. Leonard was beating around the bush, giving Mary basic facts she already knew. She wanted the stuff she did not know and realized she would have to initiate that conversation.

"What was your relationship with your parents like?" asked Mary.

"What you want to know that for?" questioned Mr. Leonard, his eyes squinting suspiciously the same way Mr. Brown's did.

"It's part of my research."

"What does my relationship with my parents have to do with building a family tree?"

"I'm not building a family tree. I'm compiling the family history to explain how we got here."

"Explain to who?"

"Our family."

"What they need to know all that for?"

"Because it's important."

Mr. Leonard frowned. Mary tilted her head and stared at him to let him know she would not bend. He shook his head and grumbled.

"I wish I had a picture of my mother to show you how much you look like her."

"Do you have one of her?"

"Around here somewhere but I don't feel like digging it out right now," said Mr. Leonard. He shook his head and continued. "My mother was like my Ladybug. Didn't say much, didn't really go anywhere, didn't really have friends."

"And your father?"

Mr. Leonard's eyes darkened the same way Mr. Brown's did when Mr. Brown talked about Mr. Leonard.

"He was a drunk," admitted Mr. Leonard. "I hated him, he hated me. I still really don't know why. He pushed us around a lot. My mother would make me leave the house when she knew he'd come home looking for trouble. I would just wander around until it was safe to go back. Sometimes that wouldn't be till the next day when he'd gone to work. That's how I became good friends with Derrick. He'd wander around with me until he had to go home. Then one night, I couldn't go back so he made me stay with him at his house. After that, I would just go to his house."

A small smile appeared on Mr. Leonard's face as he talked about his childhood with Pastor Derrick.

"I used to spend a lot of time down at Derrick's house," said Mr. Leonard. He chuckled and added, "He would always roughhouse with me and throw me around all over the place. Put me in all types of chokeholds and headlocks until I'd surrender."

Mr. Leonard continued laughing until it faded to a sad, regretful smile.

"He was like the brother I never had. The only person willing to be my friend and get to know me."

Mary could tell that Mr. Leonard missed having Pastor Derrick as a friend. The two had fallen out decades ago because of Mr. Leonard's actions.

"What happened to your parents?" asked Mary.

"Father drunk himself to death," said Mr. Leonard. "Mother died of a heart attack."

The two talked more about his background and his experiences working in the factory. Mr. Leonard said a lot of glowing things about

Uncle Jeremy-Micah and Aunt Marie, but Mary noticed he avoided talking about Mr. Brown, Uncle Terrence, and Aunt Ruth-Anne. She knew they would eventually have to address it, so Mary asked the dreaded question.

"Why didn't you believe my father was your son?"

Mr. Brown exhaled silently through his nose before answering.

"I didn't think he looked like me," said Mr. Leonard. "My father told me he looked like Parker's baby, and I was stupid enough to listen to him."

"Why?"

"Well, I... the way your grandmother and I got together... It didn't seem far-fetched to believe it..."

"Why did you abuse him?"

"I only smacked him one time!"

"But you also tried to get rid of him. You wouldn't claim him. You called him ugly. You made fun of his voice. You tried to pit him against his siblings. You did more than just smack him one time."

"And I told him I was sorry! But what about what my father did to me, huh? He smacked me and my mother around. I never put my hands on Marianne. He tried to kill me twice! First time he tried to let me drown in the creek, and the second time he tried to beat me to death. I never tried to kill Torrance. So, why am I getting all the blame when he was worse than I was?!"

"Because I'm asking you about what you did."

"Why?"

"Because if we just ignore it, it'll repeat itself. Your father hurt you and you hurt my father."

"Well, if that's the case then what'd Torrance do to you, huh?"

Mary heard the front door open. She figured it was Grandma Marianne returning home. But when she turned around, it was not Grandma Marianne standing in the kitchen entryway. It was a horrified Mr. Brown with an equally horrified Uncle Jeremy-Micah.

"What in the–?" gasped Mr. Brown.

"Dad!" yelped Mary, leaping up from the table.

"Dad, what are you doing here?" asked Uncle Jeremy-Micah, worriedly glancing at his brother.

"I live here," said Mr. Leonard.

"Dad, I can explain," said Mary.

"Where is your grandmother?!" asked Mr. Brown.

"She's not here," said Mary.

"Then why are *you* here?!"

"Torrey, calm down," said Uncle Jeremy-Micah. Mr. Brown shot him an angry look, but Uncle Jeremy-Micah was unfazed. "I'm sure there's a reasonable explanation.

"Why are you alone in this house with this man?" demanded Mr. Brown, glaring at Mary.

"We were talking," said Mary.

"What do you have to talk to him about?" demanded Mr. Brown. "I told you to stay away from him!"

"She's my granddaughter," said Mr. Leonard. "She can talk to me if she wants."

"Your granddaughter?" repeated Mr. Brown. "You don't even know her!"

"You're my son. That makes her my granddaughter."

"Jeremy-Micah is your son."

"You're my son too."

"Dad, stop," said Uncle Jeremy-Micah.

"It's the truth," declared Mr. Leonard. "Torrance is my son."

"No, I'm not."

"Can't you give me a chance?"

"No."

"The bible says you're supposed to forgive."

"It also says not to provoke your children to wrath and yet here we are."

"What can I do to make things right?"

"Leave me and my children alone. That's what you can do."

"Why won't you give me another chance?"

"Do you still have that scar on your foot?"

"Yeah."

"A scar from when your father tried to let you drown, right? I remember you telling me that because I had a scar too on my face that you gave me. I used to wear an eyepatch over it, and you told me how ugly I was with it. You tried to give me away to a whole other man who wasn't my father. And you mistreated my mother and my siblings. But I probably could've gotten past all those things except I witnessed how you treated who you said *was* your son."

Mr. Brown stood behind Uncle Jeremy-Micah and shook his shoulders.

"This is your son," continued Mr. Brown. "Your son that you love so much and would never do anything to hurt."

"Torrance," uttered Uncle Jeremy-Micah, uncomfortable with being the center of attention.

"You're his son, right?" said Mr. Brown. "His precious J-Man?"

"I think we should go."

"We can go after I'm through," said Mr. Brown. "Because you're his son. Not me. You're the one he loved. You're the one he cared about. You got all of it and I got nothing even though we're supposed to have the same father, right?"

Uncle Jeremy-Micah frowned.

"That's what I'm having such a hard time forgiving," said Mr. Brown. "The fact that my brother and I have the same father and I watched him get all the love while I got mistreated even though my supposed father knew how I felt. His father had treated him badly and knew how it felt to be in my shoes. But he treated me the same way, even though he knew how it felt. But it's okay because I still had a great father. He wasn't my grandfather; *he* was my father. He loved me, and raised me, and took care of me, and made sure I was good. And I loved him. He was my father. The man who scarred my face isn't my father. And that's why I don't wear that eyepatch anymore. Because I want everyone to see and know that the man who did this to me wasn't my father. You are Jeremy-Micah's father, Brown, not mine. You and I only have the same last name because it's my mother's last name."

"I just thought...," said Mr. Leonard.

"I know what you thought," said Mr. Brown. "You thought that if she accepted you then maybe I would too. But it doesn't work that way."

Mr. Leonard looked away.

"Now, we can go," said Mr. Brown.

He slammed the front door behind him, leaving everyone in shock at what had just happened. Mary knew she had messed up. She had messed up very badly.

-

Does Daddy Favor Me?

It's time to address the elephant in the room,
Because it's brought with it a bunch of gloom.
I've seen this side of him before,
But I've never felt it at my door.
I know I've committed a grievous sin,
Against the man I call my kin.
And I question whether the truth of life,
Was worth this great sacrifice.
My daddy's been like a mirror to me,
I'd hear what he'd hear and see what he'd see.
But this anger from him is something new,
It's my first time being the target of its view.
How can this be the first time,
That I experience my daddy's other side?
Is it true what my siblings believe?
Does my daddy favor me?

Friday

Mary awoke on Friday wondering if the day before had just been a bad dream. She hoped it had been because she did not want to believe her father had discovered her secret. When she entered the kitchen, she found her dad eating cereal.

"Morning Dad," said Mary.

Mr. Brown did not respond or even look at her. Mary sighed. Had she been more like Karla, she might have chucked her slipper near his head to get a reaction from him. But she was not like Karla. She was Mary, the quiet, obedient one. At least she had been.

After getting her hair done, Mary closed herself off in her room. As far as she could remember, her dad had never been this angry with her. She was not sure how to go about fixing the situation, so she called someone who might be able to help her.

"Hello?" said Philomena.

"I need help," said Mary.

"What happened?"

"My dad found out about me talking to Mr. Leonard and he's highly upset."

"Oh no. You told him you were just trying to get answers about the Brown family, right?"

"No."

"Why not?"

"Because that would have been a lie."

"How?"

"I've been talking to and regularly visiting Mr. Leonard since December."

"Girl what?!"

"This is really bad," sighed Mary. "I don't know what to do."

"You better call Jesus."

"Phil!"

"I'm serious! That's the only way you going to fix this!"

"I've really messed things up."

"In a way, yeah."

"What do you mean 'in a way'?"

"I mean, you should've told him what you were doing, so you messed up there. But at the same time, you're nineteen. You're not a child anymore and you should be able to talk to whoever you want whether he likes it or not."

"I wish."

"You should! Are you going to let your father dictate what you can and can't do for the rest of your life?"

"No. But if this had to happen this way, I wish it would've happened *after* the wedding."

"Well Mary, that part is your fault. Nobody told you to go over there and talk to that man two days before your father's wedding."

"I know...," groaned Mary. "But I just wanted to know the truth."

"Yeah, I know," said Philomena. "Just give your dad some time to cool off."

And that's what Mary planned to do. She planned to stay far away from her dad until his anger had subsided. But that did not make the wait any less painful. Mary knew the truth would come with a cost, and she was paying the price for it.

She considered Philomena's advice and decided she had nothing to lose by taking it. Mary got on her knees and began praying.

"Lord, I really messed up and I really need Your help," prayed Mary. "Please help me to make things right with Dad. I never meant to hurt him. I just wanted the truth. Please help. Amen."

That afternoon, Mary had the house to herself. Someone knocked on the front door. Mary did not know who she expected it to be, but the last person she thought it would be was her Uncle Jeremy-Micah.

"Hey," said Uncle Jeremy-Micah.

"Hey," said Mary.

"I came to talk about yesterday."

"You going to give me a piece of your mind too?"

"If you sass me again, then yeah."

"Sorry."

"Do you understand why your dad is so upset?"

"Yeah," said Mary. "He told me not to talk to Mr. Leonard, but I did anyway."

"Yeah, that's part of it," said Uncle Jeremy-Micah. "But the other part is that you hid it from him."

"I had to! Mr. Leonard is the only person who knows about the Browns's family history and Dad would've never let me talk to him if he knew."

"That wasn't the only way though. You could've asked me to help you get the information. That way you wouldn't have had to sneak behind your father's back."

"It doesn't matter what I would've done; I feel like Dad would've gotten mad either way," said Mary. She shook her head and sighed. "And you know what the worst part is? Now that I've gotten to know him, I actually care about Mr. Leonard. But I don't want to hurt Dad even more."

"Just know you're not alone," said Uncle Jeremy-Micah, hugging Mary. "I know exactly how you feel."

"Do you really?"

"Of course, I do!" exclaimed Uncle Jeremy-Micah. "This is my father we're talking about here! You think I like having to choose between my father and my brother?"

"No," said Mary. "I guess not."

"I one hundred percent love my father," said Uncle Jeremy-Micah. "But I also one hundred percent love my brothers and sisters. My father did a lot of terrible things to your father, and to your Uncle Thusi and Aunt Ruthie. He gave me and your Aunt RieRie special treatment but that only made us feel worse. That's the real reason your dad is upset.

He knows what my father is capable of and if something would've happened to you without him knowing, he would never forgive himself."

"What should I do?" asked Mary.

"Give your father some time," advised Uncle Jeremy-Micah. "He won't stay mad forever."

"Okay," said Mary. "There's something else I'm keeping from Dad."

"Something else?" repeated Uncle Jeremy-Micah, raising his eyebrows. "You've become quite the crypt keeper, haven't you?"

"It's... something about your grandfather."

"My grandfather? Grandpa Gabriel?"

"Yeah. I uh... I learned something really interesting about him."

"What'd you learn?"

"Um... well... his niece and nephew wrote me and told me what caused him to leave his hometown."

"You mean him killing his sister's fiancé?"

"You know about it?!" gasped Mary.

"Yeah," said Uncle Jeremy-Micah nonchalantly. "Grandpa told me when he was dying."

"Then you know what actually happened?"

"I know what he told me which is what Aunt Louise told Aunt Ophi," said Uncle Jeremy-Micah. "Aunt Louise had been secretly dating a White man. They had planned to run away together because back then it was illegal where they lived for White and Black people to marry. The night they planned to run away, her father wasn't home, and she hadn't told anyone she was leaving. She let her fiancé in the house to help her get her stuff, but Grandpa thought he was a robber, so he shot and killed him. Because it was a White man, they all had to flee the town forever or risk being lynched. He said his father Rosario handled the body, but he didn't know what his father did. His sisters and his mother all moved to the town where his oldest sister Susan was, while he and his uncle came here. After that, Louise got really sick. When he went to see her, she said she hated him and never wanted to see him again. She died after that, and he said Louise never forgave him. That tore him up for years and he always blamed himself for their deaths. He even believed Abel and Abigail being stillborn were God's punishment against him for their deaths."

"That's so sad," said Mary.

"Mhmm. I can't bring myself to tell your father about it because he and Grandpa were very close. It was kind of hard for me to process because I'd always known Grandpa as the saved and strict music minister."

"Why does everything we do have to revolve around Dad and what he wants?" asked Mary angrily. "What about what we want?"

"What I want will never happen," said Uncle Jeremy-Micah.

"What do you want?"

"For everyone to get along. But that'll never happen."

"Why can't it happen? Because Dad is stubborn and won't let it?"

"Don't talk like that," sighed Uncle Jeremy-Micah. "Your father has been through a lot. Probably even some things I don't even know about."

"It's not like he'll ever talk about it."

"Maybe not," said Uncle Jeremy-Micah. "And that's his decision. Besides, he's not the only reason I don't think the family will ever come together."

"What else is there?"

"Me."

"You?"

"I'm an affair baby," said Uncle Jeremy-Micah quietly. "I broke the family."

"You did not."

"Yes, I did," said Uncle Jeremy-Micah. "I guess that's why I want everyone to get along. To fix the fact that I broke the family. But I know it'll never happen."

"It could happen if everyone weren't so stubborn and trying to hide everything."

"That's true," agreed Uncle Jeremy-Micah. "Maybe it'll happen one day. But I don't see it happening in my lifetime."

"Does Grandma know... about what her father did?" asked Mary.

"If she does, I didn't tell her," answered Uncle Jeremy-Micah.

"I don't think we should tell her."

"I agree. At least not right now."

"It stays between us?"

"It stays between us."

Mary was grateful that she did not have to shoulder the burdens of the secrets alone anymore. But as she took her place at the dinner table that night, Mr. Brown still would not look at her. Grandma Marianne had been right. It would have been better for her to tell because he would have been more angry than hurt. She had hurt her father terribly, and Mary knew that if anything with the wedding went wrong, it would be all her fault.

-

Andre Brown

To Andre Joel Brown

You're a loud little baby,
And it's driving us crazy.
Every time you start to cry,
It makes me want to sigh.
Four kids in four years.
Guess I shouldn't have tears,
Since I'm the one that did it,
Cuz I'm addicted to kisses.
You might just break the bank.
I might need to cap my tank.
Four is enough for me and the wife,
And I should be thankful that you're alive.
My little baby boy named Andre.
Yet another name where I had no say.
You're a very loud baby boy,
But hearing you cry brings me joy.

Friday

Andre did not have to be at the 'say-no-to-drugs' assembly. He was a senior, and he could go home after sixth period. But since his father was his ride to and from school, Andre could not leave until Mr. Brown did. So, Andre attended the assembly.

Mariana and Adrianna both performed at the assembly. Andre's relationship with Mariana was not the typical, friendly one between cousins. Sometimes, he was fine with her, but sometimes she rubbed him the wrong way.

She sang the national anthem beautifully though. That was something Andre could not take away from her. Mariana had always been a great singer like her mother, Aunt Marie.

Aunt Marie could play the piano like Mr. Brown. But unlike Mr. Brown, Aunt Marie was very shy and preferred not to perform. She instead preferred math and science. So did Uncle Alejandro and Mariella.

Andre liked math too. He could play the piano too, but he did not consistently practice it. No matter how hard he tried, the piano did not interest him. Not like the guitar did.

His favorite genre of music was rock. Many people who had heard his singing voice said they could hear the rock influence in it. They described it as husky and gravelly.

Mariana's voice was warm and rich. She finished singing the national anthem, and then the school's Silver Divas varsity dance team performed.

It was Adrianna's first year as a Silver Diva. Andre watched as she performed on the back row of the formation. He smiled, believing that she was having the time of her life.

Adrianna could sing too. In fact, everyone in his family could at least sing. Everyone except Grandma Marianne. It was what his family was known for.

Watching the dance made Andre want to get up and dance too. He tapped his foot to the beat and bopped around in his seat. When the girls finished, Andre stood and applauded them. He was the only one.

Then came the main event.

Mr. Kasey Ferguson was the speaker. He had been drug-free for eight years and had made it his life's purpose to warn others of the dangers of drug use.

Drugs were something Andre knew he would never have to worry about. But Mr. Ferguson's story interested him.

Mr. Ferguson had grown up in Creeke. He had been a wide receiver for Creeke High's football team. But he had gotten hooked on drugs at eighteen.

Andre wondered why Mr. Ferguson had gotten hooked on drugs. During the whole presentation, Mr. Ferguson never said why he got hooked on drugs in the first place.

Even after the assembly ended, the question still burned in Andre's mind. He needed an answer. So, he did what any reasonable person would and approached Mr. Ferguson to ask.

Mr. Ferguson was talking to Vice Principal Christine Dow. Andre patiently waited until they finished talking. Vice Principal Dow was the first to notice him.

"I think you have someone who wants to talk to you," said Vice Principal Dow, motioning to Andre.

"I do?" said Mr. Ferguson, turning around.

"It's alright, go ahead," said Vice Principal Dow. "I'll give you the rest of the details later."

"Okay," said Mr. Ferguson. He smiled at Andre and said, "Hey. What's up?"

"Uh... hi," said Andre nervously. "I just... I had a question."

"I might have an answer."

"Why did you get hooked on drugs?"

"Why did I...?" said Mr. Ferguson, blinking with surprise. "Weren't you listening?"

"Yes," said Andre. "You said you got hooked on drugs at eighteen, but you never said why."

"Well, I don't want to tell all my business."

"Oh."

"What's your name?"

"Andre."

"Andre. Brown?"

"How'd you know?"

"You look like your father."

"You know my father?"

"Uh...," said Mr. Ferguson uneasily. "Yeah, I know Brown. If he's anything like I remember him being, you probably shouldn't tell him we talked."

"You two don't get along?"

"Nope."

"Why not?"

"He kept getting me in trouble," said Mr. Ferguson. "How is Brown these days?"

"Uh...," said Andre. "Good. He's getting married next weekend."

"Married? He and Lana aren't together anymore?"

"No, they divorced when I was six. My mom is married to Pastor Hall now, and my dad is marrying Ms. Nelson."

"Who's Ms. Nelson?"

"Her," said Andre, pointing to Gretchen. She was talking to her sister, Ms. Greta. "The one on the left."

"A twin?" said Mr. Ferguson. "I don't remember there being any twins around here growing up. At least not around our age."

"She's a teacher here. She and her sister moved here a couple years ago."

"I didn't know people moved *to* Creeke. Usually people move *away*." Andre laughed.

"How long are you staying in Creeke?" asked Andre.

"For good hopefully," answered Mr. Ferguson.

"Why'd you come back?"

"To meet my son."

"Who's your son?"

"I can't say yet."

"Why not?"

"He can't know about me until he turns eighteen."

"When is that?"

"Next week."

"I turn eighteen next week."

"Cool."

"Am I your son?"

"Nope."

"How do you know?"

"You look like Lana and Brown."

"Oh."

"Listen, it was nice talking to you," said Mr. Ferguson.

"You too," said Andre.

And then he was gone. Andre realized he still did not know why Mr. Ferguson had gotten hooked on drugs. But now he had a new mystery to ponder.

He wondered who Mr. Ferguson's son could be. It was someone born the same week and year as Andre. But he did not know if they were born before or after him.

It was also possible that the mysterious son did not live in Creeke. He could be living in the city, and Mr. Ferguson was just staying in Creeke because it was more convenient.

"Why do you look like that?" asked Antoine.

"Like what?" asked Andre.

"You're just laying there staring at the top bunk."

Andre sat up. He had been home from school for over an hour and done nothing but ponder the mystery.

"I was just relaxing," said Andre. "Did you have a good workout?"

"Yeah," said Antoine. "I'm going to see the new Drake Malone tonight."

"Okay," said Andre.

"You mind if I play the game for a bit?"

"Nope."

Andre watched as Antoine disappeared from the room, then returned and fired up his gaming system. His brother used to play *The Well* on his computer, but there had been some big controversy that caused the game to lose a lot of players. Antoine had tried to explain the whole situation to Andre, but Andre could not keep up with the twists and turns of the story.

He got up and went to the bathroom. Instead of having to fight with five other people over the bathroom, he only had to fight with three.

His most frequent opponent was Adrianna. She claimed he used the bathroom too long, but he knew for a fact she would be in there twice as long as he was. Drake used to mediate their conflicts, but he had moved out.

Drake moving out had turned out to be the best thing ever for Andre and Antoine. Andre was a night owl, so Antoine secretly gaming past curfew did not bother him as it had Drake.

Antoine was also not as demanding a brother as Drake was. He did not mind that Andre's area sometimes got a little cluttered or that Andre sometimes needed to pace around the room.

And Andre found that just being around Antoine helped him work better. He felt he got a lot more done as opposed to when he was by himself.

But Andre also missed having his older brother around. He missed hearing Drake sing and play the piano and missed the excitement Drake got when he was inspired to write a song.

He also missed the advice Drake used to give him. And he missed how Drake used to keep him on track and on top of things.

Andre wished he were not so easily distracted. But he could not help it. It was like his mind had its own mind and did what it wanted to do.

He wished he could be more like his older brother, who always had it together. Or even like his younger brother, who their dad never seemed to get onto.

He wished he could make his dad proud. And not be the son that was always messing up.

That was all Andre wanted. To make his dad proud of him for once.

-

My Daddy Was Perfect

My daddy was the perfect man.
Everything had to follow his plan.
If something went wrong,
His anger got strong,
So, I avoid failing if I can.

Monday

Mr. Ferguson's son was Samiel Dow Jr., who had turned eighteen that Sunday. Andre should have realized it sooner. Samiel had Mr. Ferguson's hazel eyes. He was glad his friend had finally learned who his biological father was.

But Samiel and Mr. Ferguson looked almost nothing alike. Samiel was dark-brown and slightly chubby, while Mr. Ferguson was light-brown and lean.

But Andre knew better than to judge family relations based on skin color alone. Half his siblings barely resembled their father, and he himself looked more like his father than his mother. And the same could be said for his other friends.

There was, for example, his new friend Tyler, whom he was on his way to visit. Tyler Graham-Hernandez was a year older than Andre and was the son of Mr. Zackariah Graham. And Tyler looked nothing like his father.

Unlike his sister Jada, who looked like an even mix between their parents, Tyler looked more like their mother, Mrs. Serafina. He had light tan skin, light brown eyes, and slick, wavy hair like her. The only things he had in common with his father were their noses and black hair color.

Tyler also differed in personality from his father. Mr. Zackariah reminded Andre of his Uncle Jeremy-Micah. They were both boisterous and funny.

But Tyler was more laid-back, though he could be snarky at times. He was a huge history buff and would major in history in the upcoming school year.

And he was also deaf.

When they first met, Andre had tried communicating with Tyler in sign language. After a few mistranslations and miscommunications, Tyler suggested they talk through text instead.

Their friendship quickly took off, which led to an awkward conversation between their fathers.

Mr. Zackariah had been one of the many people Mr. Brown had issues with when they were boys. With their sons becoming friends, Mr. Zackariah had decided, for their sons' sakes, to sort things out between him and Mr. Brown.

"Brown, we need to talk," said Mr. Zackariah when he had stopped by the house.

"Why?" responded Mr. Brown.

"It's about Dre."

"What about him?"

"Nothing bad," said Mr. Zackariah. "My Ty has really taken to him. I just wanted to let you know he's welcome to come by anytime he likes. But if our sons are going to be friends, I think we should have a level of understanding between us."

"I stay out of your way, and you stay out of mine. Got it."

"Brown, will you let me talk?"

"What is there to talk about? We don't have to be friends just because our sons are."

"Look, I just want you to trust me when I have Dre at my house. Because if Ty ever comes over here, I'm going to have to trust you with him."

"I don't have an issue with your son."

"But you do with me."

"So?"

"I don't want you taking your issues with me out on my son."

"Can you get to the point please?"

"Look Brown, I know things back then were a mess and I know I wasn't the nicest to you."

"You weren't."

"And I'm sorry about how roughly I treated you. But you've got to admit you had your part in it too."

"I don't have to admit anything."

"Come on Brown. You were the one always starting the fights."

"So? If I feel threatened I'm going to defend myself."

"You were the one making the threats half the time!"

"Did you come over here just to start with me?"

"No," said Mr. Zackariah, refocusing. "No. I came over here to make sure our issues don't ruin our sons' friendship. I'm apologizing for my role in things."

"Okay."

"And I want to make sure I can trust you with my son."

"I should be asking you that."

"We're moving past the past."

"You want me to move past you letting me get beat up so many times?"

"My father always taught us don't start anything you can't finish. Like I said, every fight you had, you started, and you needed to learn your lesson."

"So, if your son got in a fight, you'd just let him get beat up to learn his lesson?"

"Tyler wouldn't be in a fight, and neither would Jada. I raised my children better than that."

Andre was unsure how, but Mr. Zackariah's sincerity seemed to soften Mr. Brown.

"Then you won't let anything happen to my son?" asked Mr. Brown.

"Not while he's under my roof," said Mr. Zackariah. "Can I trust you with my son as well?"

"He can come by."

"Alright."

"I just want to make it clear again that this doesn't mean there will be some kind of friendship between us because of this."

"I have my own friends. As long as nothing happens to my son, you don't have to worry about me coming around here."

Since then, Andre had a great friendship with Tyler. Andre found him in his room, intently reading something on his laptop. His back was to the door, so Andre texted him to get his attention.

"Hey," texted Andre.

"Hey," responded Tyler.

"Turn around."

Tyler turned around wide-eyed and then chuckled.

"What you doing?" asked Andre.

"Learning about Creeke. Found some interesting stuff."

"Like what?"

"Did you know part of this town was built on a former plantation?"

"I think Allison told me that once. The Perrys' mansion was the main house."

"I wonder how this place went from a plantation to a town."

"I don't really know. You'd have to ask the Harrisons. They're the most knowledgeable about the town's history."

"I would hope so since their family founded it."

Andre snorted.

The boys hung out for a few hours. Tyler shared everything he had learned so far about Creeke. There were many things Andre had not known about the town he lived in.

"ZACK!"

Andre jerked his head around to the door.

"What is it?" texted Tyler.

"Someone is yelling downstairs," responded Andre.

"Is it my grandfather?"

"I don't think so."

"Let's go see."

As the boys reached the living room, Andre found Mr. Ferguson wheeling a wheelchair to Mr. Riley Graham Jr.

"ZACK!" yelled Mr. Ferguson.

"Boy, stop all that hollering!" chastised Mr. Graham.

"Well, how else do you expect to get to the bathroom Mr. Graham?" said Mr. Ferguson.

"Don't get mouthy with me, Kasey," said Mr. Graham. "I don't take it from Trip, Han, or Zack and I'm not taking it from you."

"Why are you yelling my name like that?" sighed Mr. Zackariah.

"Your father needs to use the bathroom," said Mr. Ferguson.

"Help me get him in his wheelchair," said Mr. Zackariah. "Can't even get a day off in peace..."

"What did you say?!" snapped Mr. Graham.

"Nothing."

The men helped Mr. Graham into his wheelchair, and Mr. Zackariah wheeled his father away. Tyler had told Andre previously that the Grahams had moved back to Creeke so Mr. Zackariah could help care for his father, who had become unable to care for himself. Mr. Zackariah had been the only one willing to return while his two older siblings, Riley III and Hannah, had still not visited their father.

"Hey!" said Mr. Ferguson, noticing Andre. "What are you doing here?"

"Visiting Tyler," answered Andre. "But I need to be getting home."

"I can take you," said Mr. Ferguson. "I just dropped by to see Zack real quick anyways."

Andre said his goodbyes to Tyler and left with Mr. Ferguson. Mr. Ferguson drove a used white car and liked listening to the old-school radio station.

"Coming up next we've got a classic straight from the eighties!" announced the radio announcer. "It's The Boombox Boyz's first ever hit 'Boomin Down Yo Block'! That's right, we're taking you back to those days when King Roy was still in the group and Tony-P was rapping the hooks instead of singing them. The Boombox Boyz, Boomin Down Yo Block."

"I love this song," said Andre.

"What you know about this?" asked Mr. Ferguson.

"That's The Boombox Boyz. They're my dad's favorite group."

"Really?" said Mr. Ferguson. "I figured Brown only listened to hymns all day like his grandfather."

"No," chuckled Andre.

"Man, I grew up listening to The Boyz," said Mr. Kasey. "They got me through some hard times."

"Mr. Ferguson," said Andre.

"Kasey," said Mr. Ferguson. "Mr. Ferguson is my father, and I don't like to be reminded of it."

"Mr. Kasey," said Andre. "What happened to your parents?"

"They moved away from here. I don't know where. Don't even know if they're still alive really. They were embarrassed to have a drug addict as a son."

"You still never answered my question about why you got hooked on drugs."

"Like I told you, I don't go around telling all my business."

Mr. Kasey pulled in front of Andre's house.

"Here we are," said Mr. Kasey.

"Here we are," echoed Andre.

Mr. Brown came outside and approached the car. He peeked inside, and his eyes shifted between Andre and Mr. Kasey.

"Hey Brown," said Mr. Kasey.

Mr. Brown didn't respond. Andre noticed the disapproving frown on his father's face and exited the car.

"I hope you don't mind me giving Dre a ride home," added Mr. Kasey.

"Get inside," said Mr. Brown to Andre.

"Yes sir," said Andre.

Andre obeyed his father, who followed behind him without speaking to Mr. Kasey. Mr. Brown shot one final look at Mr. Kasey as he closed the door.

"Why would you accept a ride from a stranger?" demanded Mr. Brown.

"He's not a stranger," said Andre. "I met Mr. Kasey on Friday."

"I know who he is. I don't want you talking to him anymore."

"Why not?"

"*Because I said so.*"

"Yes sir," said Andre. "But what do I do if he talks to me first?"

"Andre, don't get smart with me."

"I'm not."

"You're my son," said Mr. Brown. "If I don't want you talking to him, then that's final."

"Why don't you like him?"

"Don't worry about it," said Mr. Brown in a tone that indicated the conversation was over.

Andre knew his father might never tell him what he wanted to know. But he knew who would. And she was only a short bike ride away.

"ANDRE!" hollered Layla gleefully when Andre entered his mother's house.

"LAYLA!" hollered Andre as he caught the running six-year-old.

"Lord have mercy," griped First Lady Hall. "This all the proof I need that seven is *it*. And I mean it this time."

"Hi Mom," said Andre.

"Mommy, mommy!" said Layla, hopping up and down. "Andre's here! Andre's here!"

"I see him, Layla," said First Lady Hall. She hugged Andre and asked, "What'd your father do now?"

"Ma'am?"

"I'm just saying," said First Lady Hall. "It seems like my children only come visit me when their father has done something wrong."

"He didn't do anything," said Andre. "But I do need to talk to you about him."

"Here we go."

"Do you know Mr. Kasey?"

"Mr. Kasey who? Only Mr. Kasey I know is Kasey Ferguson."

"That's him."

"Why are you asking me about him?"

"I was talking to him and he said you knew him."

"You talked to Kasey Ferguson?"

"Yeah. He did a presentation at our school last week."

"He did? When did he get back in town? Nobody told me nothing."

"Well Mom, that's kind of embarrassing. Aren't you the First Lady of the church?"

"You shut up!" said First Lady Hall, whacking Andre on the arm. "What does this have to do with your father?"

"I want to know why Dad doesn't like him. He doesn't want me talking to Mr. Kasey but he won't tell me why."

"Typical," grumbled First Lady Hall. "Your father doesn't like Mr. Kasey because Mr. Kasey used to bully him."

"He did?"

"Yeah."

"Why?"

"You're going to have to ask him that."

And Andre would.

I Don't Know Who This Man Is

Son, I know you don't understand,
Why it is I don't like that man.
But you've never felt his foot in your side,
To help another try and make you cry.
You didn't have him chase you up the street,
And try to put your head through concrete,
All because he was mad,
That he got in trouble for being bad.
Son, the man before you isn't familiar,
This man to me is very peculiar.
I wish I could believe he's truly changed.
That this new man is real and isn't a fake.
But I can't seem to do it because I know the truth.
I knew who this man was to me in our youth,
And I can't trust him to be around you.
Because I fear he'll hurt you in the same way too.

Tuesday

Andre was visiting his grandparents with Mary that Tuesday to get of out the house.

Mary got off from work at five in the evening. So, Andre went to wait for her around four-thirty.

He browsed the aisles, looking at all the books. Although Andre did not read as much as Mary, he still did like the occasional book. But he found them easier to focus on if he listened to them over physically reading them.

Beverly Boyd stood in the classics aisle, cradling an armful of books and searching for more. She waved to Andre with her free hand, and he waved back.

He liked Beverly. She was cute and always volunteered to help at the church.

And she was also dating Marcellus Campbell. According to Derik, a lot more boys and men had started visiting the Campbell household after Marcellus and Beverly had gotten together. Andre wondered what it was like to date.

A lot of people thought he should date Allison. He knew his mother would especially love it if he did because she was best friends with Allison's mother.

Allison was pretty. And also pretty smart. She was way smarter than Andre was. He was convinced he was only second in the ranking because of how much she helped him with his assignments.

A lot of people thought they would make a great couple.

But he did not like Allison in that way. He saw her as a good friend, and that was it.

Andre ended up near the video section of the library. Mr. Kasey was there.

"Hey Andre," said Mr. Kasey.

Andre waved.

"How's it going?"

Andre shook his head and motioned that he could not talk.

"You can't talk?" said Mr. Kasey. "Is something wrong with your voice?"

Andre shook his head. He repeated the motion and pointed at Mr. Kasey.

"Me? You can't talk to me?"

Andre nodded.

"Why?"

Andre frowned. He was unsure how he could explain what his father told him not to do without saying it.

"Did I do something wrong?"

Andre shook his head frantically.

"Then... what's wrong?"

Andre pointed at himself and then motioned like he was playing a piano.

"Piano? You play piano?"

Andre shook his head. But then he nodded because he could play the piano. Then he shook his head again because that was not what he meant.

"You can or you can't?"

Andre nodded.

"You can?"

Andre nodded.

"What's that got to do with why you can't talk?"

Andre rubbed his temples.

"You look like your dad when you do that," laughed Mr. Kasey.

Andre pointed excitedly at Mr. Kasey.

"What?"

Andre repeated the 'no talking' motion and then re-rubbed his temples.

"You can't talk because your head hurts? But you just said nothing was wrong."

Andre slapped his forehead and exhaled frustratedly.

"I'm confused," said Mr. Kasey. "What are you trying to say?"

"My dad said I can't talk to you," whispered Andre.

"Oh," said Mr. Kasey. "*Oh*. That's what the piano motion was."

Andre nodded.

"Alright, so you can't talk to me," said Mr. Kasey. "But he didn't say I can't talk to you, and he didn't say you couldn't listen."

Andre smiled. He had not thought of that.

"So, I hear you're slated to be salutatorian," said Mr. Kasey.

Andre nodded.

"You going to college?"

Andre nodded.

"Which one?"

Andre held up his hand.

"A hand college?"

Andre shook his head and pointed to his hand.

"A brown college...?"

Andre nodded.

"What's a brown college?"

Andre pointed between the two of them.

"Why are you pointing at me? I didn't go to college. Well... not for school anyways."

Andre rubbed his temples. Feeling his hair, an idea sprang to mind. He pointed at Mr. Kasey's hair.

"My hair?"

Andre nodded.

"What about it? Is something in it?"

Andre shook his head and motioned above his head to simulate patting his hair.

"Afro?"

Andre nodded.

"An afro college?" said Mr. Kasey. "You're going to hair school?"

Andre tilted his head and stared at Mr. Kasey.

After thinking about it, Mr. Kasey gasped and said, "Oh! A black college!"

Andre nodded triumphantly.

"Dre, I'm not going to lie," said Mr. Kasey. "This is silly. I feel like I'm playing a bad game of charades."

"It is kind of silly," agreed Andre. "But I don't want to get in trouble with my dad."

"How about this?" said Mr. Kasey. "If you get in trouble, then you can tell him that I told you to talk to me."

"He'll still get mad at me."

"Ah. He's strict like that, huh?"

"Yeah."

"I get it. I had strict parents too."

"You did?"

"Yeah. I couldn't bring home anything under an A. I couldn't be out past eight at night unless it was school or church related. My dad wanted me to go pro in football."

"That's like my dad. He has all these rules and it seems like I can't do anything without him getting mad at me for something. And he's always getting on to me about not paying attention and not trying hard enough, but I do try. But it feels like no matter how hard I try, everything still ends up a big mess."

"Well, you must be doing something right because you're going to be salutatorian."

"I don't know how I pulled that off to be honest."

"Because you're smart."

"I don't feel very smart most of the time."

"Do you feel overwhelmed?"

"Sometimes I feel like I am."

"Then you need to tell your dad you feel overwhelmed."

"I can't do that!"

"Yes, you can and you should," said Mr. Kasey, placing his hands on Andre's shoulders. "You wanted to know why I got hooked on drugs right? It's because I felt overwhelmed too. And I didn't tell anyone because I thought I could handle it. But I couldn't. I don't want to see you go down the same road."

Andre stared at Mr. Kasey. He found it hard to believe this nice, encouraging man had once bullied his father.

"Did you bully my dad?" asked Andre.

"Er...," said Mr. Kasey, removing his hands from Andre's shoulder. He rubbed the back of his neck and said, "I guess there's no point in avoiding it. Yeah, I did."

"Why?" questioned Andre surprisedly.

"There's never really a good reason to bully someone," said Mr. Kasey. "But I guess you could say I used him as a punching bag for all my problems."

"Hmm..."

"It caught up with me though. That brother of his came home from college and beat me so badly I thought he was going to put me in the grave."

"Uncle Mikey?"

"Mhmm. Don't let all that joking fool you. You piss him off enough and you going to wish you hadn't."

Andre believed it. With how hot-tempered his father and Uncle Terrence were, it did not surprise Andre that his Uncle Jeremy-Micah could be just as hot-tempered when pushed.

"But yeah, that's why your dad doesn't like me," said Mr. Kasey. "And frankly, I don't blame him."

"I see," said Andre. "Do you regret bullying my dad?"

"Do I regret it?" repeated Mr. Kasey, scratching the back of his neck again. Andre figured he did that when he was uncomfortable. "I try not to live with regrets but I'm definitely not proud of it."

Andre did not know what to say. His father had a valid reason to dislike Mr. Kasey. And yet, Andre still found him interesting.

Once Mary finished her shift, Andre accompanied her to visit their grandparents. While she stayed inside to conduct her research with Gran Ernestine, Andre went outside with Grandpap Jared.

"So, how's my favorite grandson today?" asked Grandpap Jared with a wink.

"I'm fine," answered Andre, returning the wink. Grandpap Jared did not actually have a favorite grandchild. It was just a running joke between Andre and his grandfather because everyone said they were a lot alike.

"You ready to leave me in the fall?" asked Grandpap Jared.

"It's only March."

"Fall will be here before you know it. Of course, I'm going to lose my fishing buddy but that's okay."

"I'm excited for college. The school I'm going to has a great engineering program."

"You're going to make some money doing that boy I'll tell you that much."

"You think so?"

"Yeah! Better money than I made working in that factory all those years."

"I thought you liked working in the factory."

"I liked to eat and have a place to sleep."

The mention of eating made Andre aware that he had not eaten anything since breakfast. And he was beginning to feel it. He remembered he had an orange in his orange bag. His bag was orange because orange was his favorite color.

"My orange!" exclaimed Andre, darting into the house to retrieve it.

The orange had rotted. Things like that always happened to Andre. He would put something somewhere and then forget about it until it randomly reappeared in his mind one day.

Andre got a new one from his grandmother's fruit bowl and returned to his grandfather.

"Got your orange?" asked Grandpap Jared.

"Yes sir," answered Andre.

"Good. Very good. Oranges are good for you. A lot better than junk food."

"Yes sir."

Things like that always happened to Andre. He would put something somewhere and then forget about it until it randomly reappeared in his mind one day.

"Life is like an orange," said Grandpap Jared, looking out over his backyard. "First you have to remember that it's been gifted to you by The Creator. You might get a really good, ripe orange or you might get an orange that's already been through some things and you'll have to make it work. But what you do with the orange is what's important. You can choose to unpeel it and see its potential, or you can throw it away and waste it. You have to put some effort in to get to the good part of it. Pieces of it might get under your nails, make your hands sticky, stain your clothes. The smell of it might irritate those around you. It's not a pretty process. Then once you make it to the good part, you can either dive right in and take a huge bite out of it like I do, or you can take your time savoring it. But don't take too much time or it'll lose its flavor. And then parts of the peel get stuck to it, so you have to put more effort in to get those off, or you can just accept that they're there and eat them. And then there are the seeds. You can either choose to risk planting them and watch them grow or die, or you can let them go to waste and miss out on what they'll become. And then once it's gone, that's it."

"Do you really just take a bite out of the orange?" asked Andre.

"Yeah. Try it."

Andre tried it. Orange juice ran down his chin and had already begun to dry and become sticky.

"Good ain't it?" asked Grandpap Jared.

"Mhmm."

"Mhmm," said Grandpap Jared. "You've got a good orange there. And you're going to do just fine with it. I can feel it."

That evening, Andre attended youth bible study, which was held every Tuesday. The boys went with Pastor Derrick Harrison, while the girls went with Mrs. Kiana Harrison.

"Tonight's topic is titled 'My Brother's Keeper'," explained Pastor Derrick. "We're going to talk about brotherly love and why it's important. Some of you in here have been blessed with a biological brother."

Andre nudged Antoine, who subsequently smiled.

"And some of you, like me, don't have biological brothers," continued Pastor Derrick. "But the good news is you don't need a biological brother to share brotherly love. The Bible tells us in the seventeenth verse of Proverbs seventeen that friends love at all times, and brothers are born for adversity. A friend is someone who loves you at all times, and The Word tells us that the greatest friend is one who is willing to lay their life down for you as Jesus did for us.

"A friend can be a brother because we just learned that a brother is someone who is born for adversity. They are willing to go through thick and thin with you. They do as we are commanded in Romans chapter twelve verse fifteen and rejoice when you rejoice and weep when you weep. They don't have to be related to you to do this. For example, I have many men in my life that I would call my brothers because they've been there for me through my hardest times. Like the men I served in the military with, my friends from college, and we can't forget good old Mr. Damian."

The boys laughed.

"To share brotherly love with someone is a powerful thing," said Pastor Derrick with a smile. Andre thought the smile looked kind of sad. "And it's not restricted to only loving men like brothers. Brotherly love is meant to be shared with everyone.

"The reason why this is important can be found in the first verse of Psalms Chapter One-hundred thirty-three. It tells us that brethren dwelling together in unity is good and pleasant. To dwell somewhere is to live there. Therefore, it is good and pleasant when you live in unity with one another. It is good and pleasant when you care about and show someone you love them.

"Tonight, we're going to practice brotherly love. I'm going to pair each of you up with someone, and I want you to talk about what's going on with you. I want you to listen to the concerns of your brother and show them that you care."

Andre was paired up with Samiel. Since Samiel was already his friend and liked to talk, Andre figured Samiel would have no problem with the assignment. But Andre was concerned whether he would be able to focus long enough to pay attention.

"Hey Sami!" said Andre.

"Hi," said Samiel. Andre noticed he said it kind of dryly but brushed it off.

"How are things with you and Mr. Kasey going?"

"Good," said Samiel quickly, almost as if he were daring Andre to believe otherwise.

"That's good," said Andre. "Is everything okay?"

"I'm fine."

Andre waited for Samiel to continue. When it became obvious Samiel would say nothing more, Andre decided to take the lead.

"I'm doing good too," said Andre.

"I'll bet," snorted Samiel.

"You're sure everything's alright?" asked Andre, his mouth slowly forming into a frown.

"Yeah," answered Samiel, not even bothering to look at Andre.

Andre stopped bothering after that. It was clear to him that Samiel was not in a talking mood, so he went and sat off to the side by himself, and listen to one of his favorite rock groups, Rotten Teddy Bears. And that's how he remained until it was time to go.

Mind Games

I don't really know what's going on here.
I feel trapped inside my mind.
I feel like I'm in someone else's skin,
And playing a game that isn't mine.
Mind Games – Rotten Teddy Bears

I don't know what is happening to me.
And I don't understand the reason why.
It feels like everything in life's a lie,
And I'm the only one with eyes to see.
But I know that's not true, it just can't be.
There must be someone who hears what I hear,
There must be someone who's vision is clear.
Someone who sees this stuff for what it is,
Who sees that life isn't filled with pure bliss.
I don't really know what's going on here.

My friends no longer appear to be friends,
But instead appear to be enemies.
And though I'm begging them to tell me please,
What exactly led to our friendship's end,
They laugh at me like it's all in my head.
But I know if I do a rewind
for the truth I seek, it I shall find.
But what if I find that my eyes aren't true?
If that be the case, then what will I do?
I feel trapped inside my mind.

Can it be that I am going crazy?
That my mind is not within my control?
It takes flight and goes where it wants to go.
And it's easier to just let it be.

Could it be that something is wrong with me?
Am I not like those that I call my kin?
Is this a battle that I'll never win?
My focus has a mind of its own,
And when I need it most is when it roams.
I feel like I'm in someone else's skin.

Why do I forget what's important?
But remember every single detail,
and get so excited I want to tell
of things that excite me for a time that
lasts until my mind moves to its next plan?
How is it that I know that I am fine,
when my own mind turns against me at times?
Why does my life have to be such a mess?
And why do I feel that I am hopeless,
And playing a game that isn't mine?

-

Wednesday

Benjamin was shooting the music video for his new song 'Home Team' at the park's basketball court. He wanted everyone on location at nine in the morning.

Andre had not planned to go to the shoot, but Adrianna had gotten them invited the day before. It ended up being just him and Adrianna because Antoine was busy.

When they arrived at the park, Adrianna ran straight to Derek, who was dressed like a referee. Andre took a seat in the bleachers with everyone else.

"Alright guys," said Benjamin, getting everyone's attention. "We'll get started soon. I'm pretty sure you guys have already signed my hoodie, but make sure you do it if you haven't. And thanks for coming out. I really appreciate it."

The Brown siblings were the only ones who had not signed the hoodie. Andre made sure to sign Antoine's name too.

He wondered how his brother was doing. Antoine had gotten himself into a predicament with their father and had to earn money to fix it.

Andre wondered if he should also be trying to make money. He had not taken a job because he had wanted to focus on his grades. But with him getting ready to be on his own soon, he wondered if he should consider working over the summer and in college.

College. Andre had heard many things about college. Some people called it the best years of their lives while others said it was on another level from high school.

People had also said his particular university was a notorious party school. Uncle Jeremy-Micah had attended the university and said those rumors were untrue. He stated that it was only a party school if all you did while you were there was party.

Andre was excited for college. He was excited for his first real taste of adulthood. But he was also nervous.

His high school life was already complicated. He worried that college would be even worse and that he would be a complete and utter failure.

Andre's thoughts were interrupted by someone repeatedly rapping on his head.

"Anybody home?" asked Derek.

"Yes, I'm home," answered Andre.

"If we're taking turns knocking Andre upside the head, I call next," laughed Samiel.

"Nah," said Derek. "I would never hit Rockstar for real. Just like he'd never hit me for real."

"You don't know what he would do," said Samiel.

"Sure, I do," said Derek. "Andre's a nice guy."

"Maybe a little too nice."

"You can never be too nice," said Derek.

"Sure, you can," disagreed Samiel. "In fact, it's the super nice ones you have to watch the most because they tend to be the biggest backstabbers. Don't you agree, Andre?"

There it was again. Samiel's remarks came across stingingly. But Andre did not understand why.

"I think some people are really just nice people," said Andre. "And some people are just really good at pretending."

"You made that sound so smart," said Derek. "If I was smart like you Andre, I could've been salutatorian."

"You might still can since they're just giving diplomas away," said Samiel. "It shouldn't be that hard for you to overtake him."

"Aw," cackled Derek. "Why'd you do me like that?"

"I'm just saying."

Andre gave a small smile.

"Well Sami, if that's the case why aren't you salutatorian?" asked Adrianna. "Since you're so smart and got so much to say."

Samiel frowned.

"Baby chill," said Derek. "It was just a joke."

"I'm just saying," said Adrianna, mocking Samiel's tone. "You'd think with that smart mouth and the vice principal as his mama he'd at least be in the top ten of his class."

"Adri!" cried Derek. "It's not that serious. I know I'm not dumb."

"Andre, I'm ready to go," said Adrianna, ignoring Derek.

"Alright," said Andre.

Andre followed Adrianna out of the park. As they neared the entrance, Andre heard someone calling his name.

"Andre!" called Samiel, running after them. When he reached them, he said, "Can I holler at you for a minute?"

"Sure," said Andre. "What's up?"

"Uh...," said Samiel, glancing at Adrianna. "Can we talk alone?"

"No," said Adrianna, crossing her arms.

"It's alright," said Andre. "It won't take too long."

Adrianna glanced at him before wandering away. Andre figured that Samiel was going to apologize.

"I don't want this to come across wrong but... could you not spend so much time with Kasey?"

"Huh?"

"It's just that... he's supposed to be here to get to know me, but it seems like he's spending more time getting to know you."

Andre was surprised. He had not thought he had spent so much time with Mr. Kasey that it interfered with Samiel's relationship with him.

"I'm not trying to be mean or anything," laughed Samiel. It was not a genuine laugh like the ones he shared with his friends, but a polite one. "But you know... let the man spend a little more time with his *own* son? Okay?"

"I understand," said Andre.

"Thanks."

Samiel returned to the court while Andre walked home with Adrianna.

"What'd he say?" asked Adrianna.

"Nothing," said Andre. "He just had something to tell me."

"It better have been an apology," ranted Adrianna. "The nerve of that Samiel! Trying to imply you aren't smart! He's just mad because you're smarter than him!"

Andre half-listened as Adrianna ranted about Samiel and Derek. He figured the whole thing was just one big misunderstanding.

To Andre Joel Brown: Eighteen Years Later

Here we go again.
You're a loud young man.
And this eighteen-year ride,
Has been a wild time.
How do I describe Andre?
What is it that I can say,
About my son,
That I adore a ton?
A is for adventurous.
N is for notorious,
Due to you being,
Rambunctiously leaping,
Everywhere you can find.
But I guess I don't mind.
Because you leap for the stars,
And that's just who you are.

-

Thursday

It was Andre's birthday. He was finally an adult.

His birthdays over the past few years had sucked. The fourteenth one was the last one he had enjoyed. It had also been the last time he saw Simon.

Simon. In a week, it would be four years since his friend had died. Andre wondered what Simon would have been like if he were still alive.

Like his older brother, Simon liked and was liked by everyone. And he had been Andre's best friend.

Simon never got upset with him. Never tried to make him feel like he was stupid. He would not have treated Andre the way Samiel had been treating him.

Andre could not wrap his head around it. He had always considered Samiel a friend. But things between them had changed in only a few days.

Samiel wanted Andre to stay away from Mr. Kasey. Mr. Brown wanted Andre to stay away from Mr. Kasey. Everyone wanted him to stay away from Mr. Kasey.

Andre wondered what was so bad about Mr. Kasey.

It was not his fault Mr. Kasey talked to him. And whatever issue Mr. Brown had with Mr. Kasey had nothing to do with Andre.

He just wanted to have a good birthday.

His fifteenth one had been a painful reminder that Simon was gone. He missed Simon a lot.

Simon would have been eighteen and preparing for college like him. Andre remembered that Simon had been unsure about his future.

He had felt a bit in Andrew's shadow because Andrew was smart, and everyone thought he would be a professional basketball player.

Feeling overshadowed by their older brothers was something Simon and Andre had bonded greatly over. For all his accomplishments, Andre felt he could never live up to Drake's legacy. Drake was talented and organized, while Andre could barely focus on one thing for an extended period.

Drake had also been the first to wake him up and wish him a happy birthday that morning.

Andre could hardly believe he was eighteen. He remembered when his parents unsurprisingly could not get him a car for his sixteenth. And he especially remembered when everyone forgot his seventeenth, including himself.

Andre hoped the eighteenth would be different. He lay in bed, hoping his eighteenth birthday would be the best one yet when he noticed Antoine stirring from sleep.

Antoine sat up and looked at him. At least, Andre thought Antoine looked at him. He did not have his glasses on, so he could not tell.

"Happy birthday!" cheered Antoine. He shot up from his bed and dove at Andre. "Time for birthday licks!"

The brothers wrestled with each other until Antoine successfully landed eighteen hits on Andre. The taps were playfully light, but Andre could feel the growing strength in them.

His younger brother was becoming a man. Just like Andre had become that day. Andre was a man. A grown man.

"I wish I could hang out with you today," sighed Antoine. "But I've only got a few days left of spring break to make this money back for Dad, and I need all the time I can get."

"It's alright bro," said Andre. "Go get paid."

"Thanks bro," said Antoine. "I'll make it up to you."

Andre felt strange watching Antoine leave the room. He could not describe the feeling, but it disappeared when Allison called him.

"Hello?" said Andre.

"Happy birthday!" said Allison.

"Thanks. I'm glad you remembered."

"What do you mean? I remembered last year."

"No, you didn't."

"Yes, I did. Because when I called you were like 'it is my birthday!', remember?"

"Oh yeah."

"What are you going to do today?"

"I don't know. Want to do something with me?"

"Sorry, I can't. I've got to work today."

"Oh. That's okay."

The feeling came back when the conversation ended. Tyler texted him, 'Happy birthday!', but could not hang out either.

Andre went to the kitchen, wondering why he felt so strange on his birthday. He hoped he was not sick. The last thing he wanted to be was sick on his birthday.

Simon had gotten sick after Andre's fourteenth birthday. A week later he had died. The strange feeling grew stronger when Andre thought of Simon.

It went away when he saw his father making breakfast.

"Happy birthday son," said Mr. Brown.

"Thanks Dad," said Andre. "Do you want to do something with me today?"

"Can't," said Mr. Brown. "Mr. and Mrs. Nelson are flying in today and I'm going with Gretchen to meet them at the airport."

"Oh. That's okay."

"Maybe we can do something when I get back."

"Okay."

"I made breakfast for you."

"Thanks."

The strange feeling returned as Andre ate his French toast and scrambled eggs.

Andre found that everyone said the same thing. They all remembered his birthday, but they had something to do and could not hang out with him. And with each person he talked to, the strange feeling grew stronger.

He had no one to spend his birthday with. But he would at least be able to do something later with his father. There was at least something to look forward to.

Andre thought to pass the time by tidying up the house a bit. It was mostly clean but needed some minor cleaning. He knew it would be helpful and make everyone happy. But for some reason, he could not do it.

Things had always gone like that for Andre. He would want or need to do something but for some reason, could not until the last possible minute when it became urgent. Instead, he would find himself doing something unrelated but more interesting.

For instance, instead of cleaning, Andre ended up watching television.

By the time Adrianna came home, Andre had watched four episodes of 'The Lukas McKinney Show' and had cleaned none of the house. The show was an old sitcom starring Baby Luke, but his character's name was Lukas Shaw.

Adrianna said hi, 'Happy birthday!', grabbed her dance bag, and left.

Andre watched a few more episodes of 'The Lukas McKinney Show' before changing the channel. Another channel was showing a 'Brethren' marathon. On that sitcom, Baby Luke played OG, the main character's father. The new season had just finished airing and would begin filming the next one that fall.

A third channel was running the first Drake Malone movie. Andre figured all the stations were trying to cash in on the release of the sequel by running everything they had relating to Baby Luke.

Mary had arrived home next. She seemed in a bad mood, so Andre left her to herself and watched a rerun of the latest 'Legacies of Hip Hop' episode.

Mr. Brown came home right when the drinks started flying. Andre would finally be able to do something for his birthday.

"Hi Dad," said Andre.

Mr. Brown looked at him. There was anger in his eyes. It seemed it took him a moment before he responded.

"Hi," said Mr. Brown.

Andre knew then his father was not in the mood to celebrate with him, so he did not bother asking him to. He rode his bike over to Patty's to finally get out of the house.

He had spent his birthday alone.

That was the strange feeling he felt. Loneliness. Everyone had been unable to spend time with him on his birthday, and it made him feel lonely.

"Welcome to Patty's," said Benjamin. "What can I get you?"

"Can I just have a water?" answered Andre, avoiding Benjamin's eyes.

"Sure," said Benjamin. "You know, you left my video shoot kind of early yesterday."

"We couldn't stay long."

"Yeah, but you guys weren't in any of the shots."

"That's alright."

"If that's how you want it," said Benjamin. "Here's your water. Happy birthday."

"Thanks."

Andre took the water and sat down in a corner of the restaurant. He looked out the window at Creeke. There had been many changes there in the past few months.

New people. A new gravel road to the high school. New streetlights so people did not have to wander around in the dark anymore.

Creeke was changing. The town that Andre had grown up in was changing. And so was he.

He was eighteen. Eighteen and lonely, and soon would be out on his own. Andre was not sure if he was ready for such a big change.

"One order of burger and fries just for you," said Charmaine.

"I didn't order this," said Andre.

"I ordered it for you," said Charmaine. She sat down and stuffed a fry in her mouth. "And paid for it too. Consider it a birthday gift."

"Thanks," said Andre, unsure what to do with the random act of kindness.

"I have a gift of knowing what people like," said Charmaine. She ate another fry and said more quietly, "And also what they don't like."

"What do you mean?"

"I just notice things," explained Charmaine. "Like what happened yesterday. I know the real reason Adrianna got upset."

Andre looked at Charmaine. He noticed for the first time how much she looked like Benjamin. They favored each other heavily, and he wondered if his sisters favored him as much.

Karla definitely did not. If anything, she favored Antoine more than she did Andre. Or maybe it was the other way around.

Mary did not really favor him either. But Adrianna did. Maybe that's why she was the sister he felt closest to.

Out of all his siblings, he and Adrianna got into it the most. But Andre could not deny that she, along with Antoine, were typically the first to rush to his defense.

"I hope you don't blame Benji for what happened," said Charmaine. "He couldn't have known Sami would treat you like that."

"It's fine," said Andre. "It's not his fault."

"It's not fine," said Charmaine. "You're mopey and sad on your birthday. That's not the Andre I know."

"And what's the Andre you know?"

"The Andre I know is funny, and smart, and always smiling.

"I've had a lot on my mind."

"Do you want to talk about it?"

"Not really."

"Okay," said Charmaine. She stood up and added, "But if you ever want to, I'm always willing to listen. I'm sure Benji would say the same too."

Charmaine walked away to tend to the other customers. Andre looked at the plate of food she had left him before resuming looking out the window.

It was his eighteenth birthday. And he was celebrating it all alone.

Andre sighed and bit into a fry. It had been another crummy birthday.

Does Daddy Like Me?

Does Daddy like me?
Or does he like me not?
Everything must be perfect for him.
Sometimes, I feel like I don't measure up.
Daddy claims I don't try hard enough.
And I wonder if that's true.
Does everything I do end in
disaster because I don't try hard enough?
Yet, I know I always try my hardest.
Life has just been unkind to me.
If I could figure how to control my focus, then I
know that I could make Daddy proud of me.
Even if it only happened once,
Making him proud once would be enough for me.
Everything would be alright after that.

Friday

Andre had expected the day before the wedding to be a stressful one. But the day had started surprisingly calm.

Mr. Brown was in one of his moods. They went to the wedding rehearsal at the church that morning.

The rehearsal was going well, but Andre noticed Antoine, Mariana, and Mariella all had attitudes for some reason. He knew why Antoine was annoyed, but he could not explain why his cousins were too. And he was not the only one to notice their attitudes.

"What's the matter?" asked Aunt Marie when the rehearsal ended.

"Why do we have to be here?" asked Mariana.

"Because it's your uncle's wedding."

"The wedding is tomorrow," griped Mariana. "Why did we have to be at the rehearsal?"

"What else did you have to do?" asked Aunt Marie.

"I could be sleep!" exclaimed Mariana.

"So could I!" echoed Mariella.

"Here they go again...," mumbled Uncle Jeremy-Micah.

Aunt Marie closed her eyes and took a deep breath. She released it through her nose and looked at her daughters.

"Miran," Aunt Marie began in her whispery voice. "Entiendo que están fastidiada porque no visitamos la familia de sus padre para la vacación. Mariana, lamento que no ganaste el concurso de canto. Mariella, lamento que te roban los Paynes. Pero este es la boda de sus tío. Necesitan estar feliz porque si quieren respeto de la gente, necesitan tener actitudes mejores."

Andre did not know what Aunt Marie had said. But it quickly caused his cousins to get their act together.

"What'd she say?" asked Mr. Brown.

"I don't know," answered Aunt Ruth-Anne. "I don't know Spanish."

"And as for you four," said Aunt Marie, turning toward her siblings. "I don't appreciate you talking badly about my daughters and talking badly about how I'm raising them. You don't see me saying anything negative about any of your children. So, the next time you want to mutter something under your breath about them Jeremy-Micah, or say how disrespectful they are Torrance, or talk about how my daughters are future inmates Terrence, and whatever you be saying Ruth-Anne–!"

"I don't be saying nothing!" objected Aunt Ruth-Anne.

"Whatever!" said Aunt Marie. "The point is if you don't have anything nice to say do like your mama taught you and shut up!"

Aunt Marie turned and exited the church with her very shocked husband and daughters.

"Who was that?!" exclaimed Uncle Jeremy-Micah. "That couldn't have been RieRie!"

"It only took her forty-two years!" added Mr. Brown. "But she should've directed that at her girls and not us!"

"Forget all that!" griped Aunt Ruth-Anne. "Why am I being fussed at for what you three did?!"

"Girl, you're always being fussed at over us," said Mr. Brown. "Don't act like it's anything new."

The three siblings argued and discussed Aunt Marie's outburst until they left. Andre noticed Uncle Terrence never said anything. He just stared into space with a frown until it was time to go.

Mr. Brown returned home in a slightly better mood than the one he left home with. Around noon, he took Andre and Antoine with him to get their hair cut. Before heading to the barbershop, they stopped by Uncle Arnold's.

Uncle Arnold Green had taken the day off from running the Creeke Courier to help with wedding prep. He was forty-seven like his wife, Aunt Ruth-Anne, and always had a big cheesy grin.

His forty-four-year-old brother, Mr. Alfred, was the same way. Mr. Alfred was the football coach and a history teacher at Creeke High School, so he had spring break off.

"Did Marie really go off on everyone like Ruthie said?" asked Uncle Arnold.

"I don't know if she did her girls, but she for sure did on us," said Mr. Brown. "I was shocked!"

"You can probably count how many times Marie has raised her voice on one hand," laughed Uncle Arnold.

"I sure can!" agreed Mr. Brown.

"You ready for the big day tomorrow?"

"Yeah. I have to pick Mr. Nelson up when we leave from here."

"Ah, the father of the bride," said Uncle Arnold. "You know, it's a good idea to have a good relationship with him."

"Trust me, I know," said Mr. Brown. "Mr. Jared was not a happy camper when me and Leilana divorced. He fought as hard as I did for us to stay together. I do not want a repeat of that with Mr. Nelson."

"Freddie, what are you looking at?" asked Uncle Arnold. Mr. Alfred had been staring at Mr. Brown during the whole conversation.

"His scar," answered Mr. Alfred. "Every time I see it, I think back to that day when we were kids tossing my football around. Arnie had me out there playing wingman with you while he pushed up on Ruth-Anne."

"Well, it worked since they'll be hitting twenty-eight years this year," laughed Mr. Brown. Andre noticed him turn his head so the scar was less visible. It had always been a sore spot for him.

"Freddie, I don't know what to do with you sometimes," sighed Uncle Arnold, the smile fading from his face. He wet a rag and began wiping the counter.

"I already cleaned that Arnie," said Mr. Alfred.

"I'm just making sure you didn't miss anything," said Uncle Arnold. "I don't want Ruthie having a conniption."

"It's always Ruthie and Mimi with him," said Mr. Alfred, leaning back in his chair. His eyes filled with memory as he recounted the days of his youth. "Man, that day was so hot. I still remember when you got thirsty, and I suggested we drink out of the water hose. The face you made before you went in the house still cracks me up to this day."

"Freddie, I doubt Torrance wants to hear this," said Uncle Arnold, moving from wiping the counter to inspecting the glasses for spots. "Change the subject."

"I don't mind," assured Mr. Brown. "I had fun that day with Freddie. It was the best part of that day."

Mr. Alfred pursed his lips into a regretful smile.

"I should listen to Arnie," said Mr. Alfred. "Because when I think of that day, I think of how I should've tried harder to keep you outside. Because if I had..."

Mr. Brown's smile melted into a frown as Mr. Alfred looked down at his hands.

"This is why I told you to drop it," said Uncle Arnold, throwing the dishrag in the sink. "Well, since we're on it. Torrey, that scar pisses me off."

"I can't do anything about that," said Mr. Brown. "It's either show the scar or hide it and I don't want to go back to the eyepatch."

"And I don't want you to either," declared Uncle Arnold. "But that scar pisses me off because it shows loud and clear what you went through in that house. Makes me think the whole thing could've been avoided if I hadn't shown up. Makes me mad when I remember seeing those poorly-covered bruises on my Ruthie. He did all of that for ultimately nothing."

Uncle Arnold sank into a kitchen chair and exhaled.

"How could you want to hurt your own child?" asked Uncle Arnold. "I can't understand how he could look in your face, see his face, and do that."

"Beats me," said Mr. Brown, looking at the clock. "I better get going. Come on boys."

Andre looked at his father as they left. Mr. Brown seemed a bit down himself, no doubt caused by the conversation he had just had about his childhood. Although Andre could say many things about his father, one thing Mr. Brown had never done was deliberately try to harm Andre or his siblings.

The Browns picked up Mr. Gerald Nelson and went to the barbershop. Mr. Nelson talked the entire ride there.

"This is a really nice town," said Mr. Nelson. "It's a lot bigger than I expected it to be."

"What'd you expect?" asked Mr. Brown.

"Well, usually when I think of small towns, I think of places where if you blink you miss it. And I don't typically stop in them."

"Yeah, well this town has an interesting history, that's for sure," said Mr. Brown.

"Hmm," said Mr. Nelson. "I'd like to hear it one day. I wonder if Gretchen's done any photography out here."

"Not as much as she could be doing," answered Mr. Brown.

"Why not?"

"I don't know."

"I'll have to ask her about that."

Mr. Nelson went on about how excited he was for the wedding. Andre wondered how someone as levelheaded as Gretchen could have such excitable parents.

The barbershop was packed when they arrived.

"Brown, don't jump on me," said Mr. Zackariah as he shot Mr. Brown an apologetic look.

"What?" asked Mr. Brown.

"Marlin is going to cut you."

Mr. Brown's face went blank.

"He's a licensed barber if that's what you're worried about."

"But why is he cutting me?!"

"Because I had to call in reinforcements. Everybody's trying to get cut for this wedding tomorrow.

"But why is he cutting *me*?!" repeated Mr. Brown. "I'm the groom! I should be getting cut by the best person here!"

"Well... you didn't set an appointment," said Mr. Zackariah. "But I knew you'd be coming in today at some point, so I asked him to take care of you. He's pretty good with a pair of clippers. He cuts all the men in his family. It'll be alright. I'll let him know you're here."

"This don't make no sense," huffed Mr. Brown, dropping into a chair.

When Mr. Harrison entered the shop, he and Mr. Brown stared at each other. Then Mr. Harrison moved toward his chair.

"Come on, Brown," said Mr. Harrison.

"Don't make no sense," muttered Mr. Brown, walking over to the chair.

"I heard it was your birthday yesterday," said Mr. Kasey, standing near Andre.

"It was," answered Andre.

"Well, happy birthday! What'd you do?"

"I watched TV."

"That's it?"

Andre noticed Mr. Brown glance at him.

"I think you should get back to work," said Andre.

"Well, when some hair hits the floor, I'll get back to work."

"Here's some hair for you," said Mr. Zackariah, shaking out his previous customer's smock. He prepared the seat for Andre, saying, "Come on, Andre."

Andre settled into Mr. Zackariah's chair while Mr. Kasey began sweeping the hair around it.

"What am I doing?" asked Mr. Zackariah.

"What I usually get," answered Andre.

"Is that what you want?" whispered Mr. Zackariah. He grinned and added, "I can do the mohawk if you want since you're eighteen now."

Andre had wanted to try out a mohawk like the lead singer of THE CA113D. He had told Tyler about it, and they had consulted Mr. Zackariah on whether it would work for his head. Although Andre was tempted to say yes, he glanced at his father and decided against it."

"Dad's paying for me to get what I normally get."

"Okay. Same old boring haircut it is."

By that point, Mr. Brown was engaged in conversation with Mr. Harrison. Andre was not sure what they were talking about, but the conversation looked friendly. Antoine was sitting next to them, getting cut by Deidrick, so Andre figured he would get the details from him later.

"Aw, look at them getting along," whispered Mr. Kasey to Andre.

Again, Andre noticed his father glance at him.

"Work," whispered Andre.

"Ain't no hair to sweep," answered Mr. Kasey.

"Go see if Leya has some for you to sweep," said Mr. Harrison. "I don't pay you to just stand around."

"Oh alright," grumbled Mr. Kasey.

The appointment did not last very long. After dropping Mr. Nelson off at Gretchen's, Andre looked at his father through the rearview mirror.

"You know Dad, for someone who doesn't like Mr. Harrison, you sure were talking to him a lot," said Andre.

"What else am I supposed to do while getting my hair cut?" said Mr. Brown. "You don't have to like somebody to have a conversation with them."

Andre could hear the truth in his father's words. That week, he had talked with a multitude of people. Some conversations had been friendly, others not so much.

And yet, he still felt lonely.

But it was not the time to feel lonely. His father was getting married in less than twenty-four hours, and that was supposed to be a happy occasion.

So, Andre decided he would be happy the next day. And he hoped by then the lonely feeling would be gone.

Adrianna Brown

To Adrianna Ernestine Brown

Hello there baby number five.
You sure picked a time to arrive.
A second job is what I'll need,
Before we're all put out on the street.
But when will I get to see you grow,
If I'm always out on the go?
How did life become like this?
Is it because I love to kiss?
There's no use in complaining now.
Because you're here, and I don't know how,
but I'll make sure you don't go hungry.
And if I'm not there I hope you'll forgive me.
I've got to do what's best for you,
Because doing my best is what I do.
You'll be taken good care of that I sure,
So, welcome to the family baby girl.

-

Friday

Adrianna had always loved dancing. She loved the energy when she moved herself to the rhythm of the music. And she loved giving that energy to others through performance.

She was one of the many varsity Silver Divas performing at the assembly. The previous year, she had danced with the junior varsity Maroon Marionettes.

Since it was her first year, Adrianna danced in the back row. But she one day hoped to be front and center.

After the assembly, the girls returned to the dance classroom, where their teacher, Mr. Jonathan Haynes, praised them on their performance.

"You all did a great job today," said Mr. Haynes. "I'm glad those times you guys made me go hoarse paid off."

The girls giggled. Adrianna loved Mr. Haynes, and he was her favorite teacher. He was so caring and thoughtful towards his students.

Some of the students even found him a little cute. But not Adrianna. She had Derek for that.

"Enjoy your spring break but not too much," said Mr. Haynes. "I need you all back here for the spring showcase. Class dismissed."

Adrianna said goodbye to her friends and went across the hall to her father's classroom.

"Thank you, thank you, thank you, thank you!" said Mariana, hugging Mr. Brown. "Thank you for letting me perform today!"

"You're welcome," said Mr. Brown. "You did good."

"Did I really?"

"Yeah."

"Thank you!" said Mariana, hugging her uncle again. She left to find her mother, cheerfully greeting Adrianna as she passed her.

The Garza sisters were always like that. Sometimes, they remembered the Browns were family and treated them like it. Other times, they acted like their family members were random people on the street staring at them.

"You did good too," said Mr. Brown.

"But you think I could've did better," said Adrianna.

"I'm not a dance teacher."

"But you are my dad."

"Your dad says you did good."

"But he thinks I could've done better."

"If I say you did good, then you did good," griped Mr. Brown. "Stop trying to put extra words in my mouth."

Adrianna knew her father. He was prone to critique because he was a perfectionist, especially regarding anything music-related. She got in the car with him and Andre and began driving home.

"Why didn't you sing at the assembly?" asked Adrianna.

"I didn't feel like it."

Adrianna received a text from Derek.

You, me, dinner, six o'clock.

Adrianna smiled.

Where?

Nik's. I want to try this special while they have it.

"Dad?" said Adrianna. "Can I go on a date tonight?"

"Tonight? Why are you just now telling me?"

"I just found out."

"Good grief Dria," grumbled Mr. Brown. "What time?"

"Around six. He wants to take me to dinner."

"Where?"

"Nik's."

"That's in the city," said Andre.

"Thank you Captain Obvious," said Adrianna, rolling her eyes.

"You want me to drive you into the heart of downtown on a Friday night?" asked Mr. Brown.

"It was just a suggestion," said Adrianna. She texted Derek, *Patty's.*

> *Patty's isn't romantic though.*
>
> *Dad doesn't want to drive that far.*

Derek replied with a photo of his face looking highly annoyed. Adrianna chuckled.

"What's so funny?" asked Andre.

"Nothing," said Adrianna. "Dad, we're going to go to Patty's."

"For a date?" snorted Mr. Brown.

> *He agrees with you. It's not very romantic.*
>
> *I'm about to square up with your old man.*

Adrianna stifled her laughter. Derek sent his next suggestion.

> *What about a picnic in the park?*
>
> *Who's making the food?*
>
> *Me.*

"Never mind, we're having a picnic in the park," said Adrianna.

"The boy needs to make up his mind," said Mr. Brown.

"That's his final decision. He's going to make the food."

"Alright," said Mr. Brown.

> *He liked that one.*
>
> *Tell him I want my round with him as soon as this cast comes off.*

Six o'clock came faster than Adrianna expected. She needed something cute to wear. Something that was park-appropriate but would still make Derek go mad over her. And then she looked in her closet.

Even though she liked her clothes, everything she owned made her look church-ready at any moment. It was a side effect of being financially dependent on her father. He did not like attention-grabbing clothes. Adrianna found it ironic, considering he had worn an eyepatch for most of his life up until recently.

But Derek differed from Mr. Brown. He was known to wear outlandish clothes. And the more outlandish it was, the more Derek wanted to 'make it work'.

She settled on a denim dress with a white t-shirt. It was the best she could do with what she had to work with. And she was glad she had when she saw what Derek wore.

He wore a gray shirt that had maroon and gold trim on the collar and sleeves. His black shorts were flame-themed, matching the flame-styled lettering on his shirt and his black multicolored shoe.

In typical Derek fashion, he had on a black cap with a dog bone symbol that he had stuffed his reddish hair into.

"Nice flames," teased Adrianna.

"Thanks," said Derek with a sheepish grin. "They go well with how I'm feeling right now looking at you."

"Boy stop," giggled Adrianna.

"Let's go get ourselves a table," said Derek.

Derek had prepared a dinner of ham and cheese sandwiches for them. They sat next to each other, watching one of the games on the basketball court.

"Dinner and a show," joked Derek. "Maybe one day we can do this type of thing for real."

"Maybe," agreed Adrianna. "Sorry you couldn't get Nik's."

"Who said I couldn't get Nik's?" said Derek.

"We couldn't go like you wanted."

"Yeah, we couldn't go tonight. But I'm still getting it."

"Well then."

"Eat your sandwich," encouraged Derek. "I worked hard on it."

"I'm sure you did," giggled Adrianna.

"So, what's the plan for your birthday next month?"

"I don't know. I haven't decided yet on whether I want a sweet sixteen or not."

"Is your dad going to let you have one?"

"I don't see why not."

"Then you should have one."

"What did you do on your sixteenth birthday?"

"Dad let me skip school."

"I wish," snorted Adrianna. "Mom might let me do that, but Dad would never."

"Why is your mom so much more chill than your dad?"

"I don't know," said Adrianna. "She just is."

"Are you excited about next weekend?"

"I sure am. I don't know about everybody else but I'm excited to have Gretchen as a stepmom."

"I think it's hilarious that your dad fell in love with her when he has more in common with her sister."

"Well, you know what they say. Opposites attract."

"How'd we end up together then?"

"You asked."

"You're right, I did ask."

"Are you excited for college?"

"I don't know yet. I have to see how my leg will be first."

Adrianna looked at the cast on Derek's leg. She had witnessed the deliberate hit-and-run in which Derek had been mistaken for his eponymous lookalike cousin, and she had been so scared he would die.

"When does the cast come off?" asked Adrianna.

"July or August," said Derek. "Then I've got to do physical therapy."

"Do you think you'll be able to dance again?"

"I better or I'm knocking heads off. It's already bad enough I had to change to attend the local community college because I'll probably still be in physical therapy when the schoolyear starts."

"What's wrong with the local community college? Karla goes there."

"Nothing's wrong with it. It just wasn't what I originally planned to do."

"What if you're not able to dance anymore?"

"I'm staying positive."

Adrianna let the subject drop. She knew how important dance was to Derek. It was dance that had brought them together.

Derek had never been a stranger to her. He had been friends with Andre since kindergarten, but that's all he had been to her. Andre's loud, hyperactive friend who sometimes spoke to her.

Things had changed when he started dancing at Adrianna's dance studio in the city. They were the only ones at the studio from Creeke, so naturally they had ended up becoming close with each other.

But things had changed again during her freshman year. That year she had left the studio to join the Maroon Marionettes. Derek had continued to dance at the studio. But the two would encounter each other in the school hallways and at the gym.

At first, Adrianna had not thought anything of the encounters. She had figured the school run-ins normal since they were both students. And the gym run-ins had not been odd to her either. It was a public place, and Derek had run on a similar schedule to her.

But then school had ended. Her summer schedule had run differently from her school schedule. Yet, she had still encountered Derek almost every day.

Sometimes, she would spot him jogging past the house, and he still showed up at the gym almost every time she was there. And almost every time, no matter the place or time, she always noticed him look at her at least once.

Then, one day, it happened. It had been in July when she was sitting on her porch. He had jogged past the house, and she waved to him like normal. But instead of waving back, he had jogged up onto the porch.

"Hi," said Adrianna confusedly. He had looked down at her, breathing heavily. She smiled and asked, "What you doing?"

"I need to see your dad," said Derek. "Is he home?"

"Yeah," said Adrianna. "What you need to see him for?"

"To see if he'll let me take you on a date," said Derek.

Adrianna had waited for him to laugh as if he were joking. But he had not. He had smiled at her, but he had not laughed.

Once she had realized he was serious, everything had clicked into place. He had purposely been putting himself in her path the whole time because he liked her.

Adrianna had not thought her father would go for it. She had just turned fifteen, and Derek had been four months away from turning eighteen. There would have been no way her father would let her date at all, let alone date a boy two years older than her.

But he had. Her father had not only let her go on a date but had allowed her to be Derek's girlfriend.

Eight months later, Adrianna and Derek were going strong. But things were starting to change.

Derek would graduate high school soon, and Adrianna's already short time with him would grow shorter. Her busy schedule and overly strict father already caused her to rarely see Derek, and it was brief when she did see him.

And Derek himself was also changing. Since his accident, Adrianna noticed that he got more easily annoyed and had increasingly more moments of sadness and anger. Adrianna figured it stemmed from his leg, and he would be back to normal once he was fully healed.

Not getting to see her man regularly was one of the most frustrating things in Adrianna's life. But she chose to cherish the moments she did get with him.

"If my leg wasn't all busted up, I could've drove us to Nik's," griped Derek.

"That's alright," said Adrianna. "I like this. It's nice and peaceful."

"Well, I'm glad you like it," said Derek, licking Adrianna's cheek.

"Dee!" squealed Adrianna, swatting him away.

"What?" laughed Derek. "I told you that's how dogs kiss."

"Are you a dog Derek?"

"You bring out the big dawg in me," said Derek, grinning. "Aroooo!"

"Oh my gosh," snorted Adrianna, placing her hand over Derek's mouth. "Stop. People are staring."

Derek licked her hand.

"Derek!" exclaimed Adrianna. She wiped her hand on his shirt and said, "Why?!"

"Because I'm a nice big dawg. A mean big dawg would've bit it."

"Boy, you better not be biting people!" scolded Adrianna, cleansing her hands with sanitizer.

"No one's given me reason to," said Derek. "Yet."

Adrianna glared at him.

"You're so cute when you look at me like that," teased Derek. He leaned toward Adrianna, and she put her hand up to stop him.

"Why do you keep wanting to lick me?" questioned Adrianna. "Can't you just kiss me regularly like other guys do?"

"What other guys?" said Derek, furrowing his brow.

"That came out wrong," said Adrianna, wincing.

"It better have," said Derek. "For your information, I actually was going to give you a regular kiss. But since you asked, I like licking your face because you taste like fruit."

"Fruit...?" said Adrianna. Then it struck her. Derek had been tasting her moisturizer. She looked at him and cried, "Boy, you licking my lotion off! Oh my gosh! Am I ashy?!

"You don't look ashy to me."

"I cannot believe you!"

"Sorry. How was I supposed to know your lotion is the reason you taste so good?"

"That's it. You are banned from licking my face."

"Alright," sighed Derek. "You know, I'm naming our first child after my grandfather."

"Excuse me?" choked Adrianna.

"I'm naming our first child after my grandfather," repeated Derek. "You can name all the other ones."

"How'd we go from lotion to kids?"

"Because we're talking about our future. When we're older and married. Like in our twenties."

"Oh."

He was already planning for their future and thinking about their adult lives. Another sign for Adrianna that things were changing. But she hoped that through all the changes, their relationship would remain intact.

Because there was no one she would rather be with than with him.

-

My Daddy Was Loving

My daddy was the first man I adored,
Because he taught me how to be loving.
He demonstrated for me its meaning,
By showing that he wanted me to soar.
My daddy was like a lion that roared.
He was alert and always protecting,
Keeping me safe and sound from life's trappings.
That's what I'm thankful to my daddy for.

To this day, loving is how I describe,
My daddy who's never stopped being so.
And though I'm the fifth child of his tribe,
And sometimes tend to get lost in the flow,
And feel like a forgotten number five,
I love my daddy that much I do know.

Monday

Two days had passed since Adrianna had last heard from Derek.

They had talked through text for a bit on Saturday. But the conversation had been so brief that it barely classified as one to Adrianna.

Derek was not at church on Sunday. Adrianna had noticed his church attendance slacking recently.

By Monday afternoon, Adrianna still had not heard from him. She decided to march around the corner to his house and confront him. All she had to do was get her father's approval first.

"You can't go," said Mr. Brown.

"Why not?" asked Adrianna.

"Because there's no one here to go with you."

"You're here."

"I'm going to visit your Uncle Al," said Mr. Brown. "And you're coming with me."

"Why do I have to go?" said Adrianna. "I'm fifteen. I'm old enough to stay home alone."

"And old enough to sneak off unsupervised too," countered Mr. Brown. "You're going and that's final."

It annoyed Adrianna that her father constantly felt the need to observe her every movement. She sometimes wished he would trust her more to follow his rules when he was not around. But she reluctantly and annoyedly accompanied him to visit her Uncle Alejandro.

Uncle Alejandro Garza was the easygoing fifty-one-year-old husband of Aunt Marie. He spoke Spanish and English, and his accent placed him as being from the northeastern region of the country. Like Adrianna, he was a middle child, which they bonded over. His older brother was named Armando, and his younger Alonzo.

His skin was medium-brown, and he had thick black eyebrows the same color as his afro. But the feature that garnered him the most compliments were his blue eyes he had passed down to Mariana.

They were a recessive gene in his family, and he and Mariana were the only ones in his immediate family to have them.

Aunt Marie had met Uncle Alejandro when she was in college. He was working towards his master's degree while she, her bachelor's degree. Uncle Alejandro had been the teacher's assistant in one of her math classes and had noticed her quietly sitting in the back.

Things had progressed from there, and they had married after she graduated at twenty-two. They had settled in Creeke so she could remain close to her family. She taught math at Creeke High while he taught math at Creeke Middle School.

"Hola," said Uncle Alejandro.

"Hola," answered Adrianna.

"¿Como estás?"

"Estoy bien. Y tú?"

"Estoy bien. ¿Estás disfrutando Spring Break?"

"Sí," answered Adrianna, hoping she had answered correctly. The only thing she had really understood was 'I'm good' and 'Spring Break'.

"Bien. ¿Qué planes tienes para hoy?"

"Uhn uhn," said Adrianna, stopping her uncle. "We're not there yet."

"Okay," laughed Uncle Alejandro. "Hola Torrance."

"Hey," answered Mr. Brown.

Before Uncle Alejandro could speak again, Mariana entered the room carrying her purse.

"Papá, me voy," said Mariana.

"¿Te llevas a tu hermana?" asked Uncle Alejandro.

"No," answered Mariana.

"Okay," said Uncle Alejandro. "Llévate a tu prima contigo."

"Pero Papá," whined Mariana. "Estoy andando con mi amiga hoy."

"Puedes andar con tu amiga y tu prima," said Uncle Alejandro. "Torrance y yo necesitamos hablar y ella estará aburrida por su misma."

"¿Por qué necesitas hablar con a él aquí?" griped Mariana. "Ya estamos faltar a nosotros vacación porque de él."

"Mariana, no digas cosas malas sobre tu tío," said Uncle Alejandro. "Él es el hermano de tu mamá y no faltamos a su boda. Ahora llévate a tu prima contigo."

"Pero Papá."

"Mariana, por favor. ¿Hacer esto para mí, okay?"

Mariana huffed and rolled her eyes.

"What are they saying?" whispered Mr. Brown. "I think I heard my name."

"Dad, I don't know," answered Adrianna. "I'm in Spanish I. I only know 'me llamo' and 'uno, dos, tres'."

"Come on," grumbled Mariana. "You have to go with me."

"I do?" answered Adrianna.

"Yes," huffed Mariana. "Hurry up."

Adrianna looked at her father, who shrugged and nodded his approval.

"Why do I have to go with you?" asked Adrianna when they were in the car.

"Because my dad said so," said Mariana. "He didn't want you sitting there looking all pitiful."

"I don't have to go with you."

"It's too late now."

They ended up going to the mall in the city. Adrianna would have asked her father for money had she known they would be shopping. Mariana walked ahead of Adrianna into the food court, where Jada waited for them.

"Hey!" said Jada when she spotted Mariana. Noticing Adrianna, she smiled bigger and said, "Oh hey! I didn't know you were coming too!"

"Neither did I," grumbled Mariana.

Adrianna looked Jada over. She had slicked her curly brown hair back into a ponytail, and her tannish-brown skin had started darkening similarly to Karla's.

"So," said Jada. "Where to first?"

"Wherever you want," answered Mariana.

"I kind of want to look at the prom dresses real quick to get some ideas for next month," said Jada. She looked at Adrianna and added, "You know Mariana's running for prom queen."

"You are?" said Adrianna surprisedly.

"Why'd you say it like that?" griped Mariana. "I can't run for prom queen?"

"I didn't say you couldn't," said Adrianna. "I was just surprised."

"Hmph!" said Mariana, stomping ahead.

"Maybe I shouldn't have brought that up," said Jada, wincing.

"Don't mind her," said Adrianna, waving a dismissive hand toward her cousin. "She's always been overly dramatic for no reason. I thought you two had stopped hanging out."

"Yeah, for like a week," said Jada. "But then I thought about it and decided Dani wasn't the boss of me. I'm going to be friends with who I want to be friends with. And I want to be friends with Mariana."

"I think you're the only one that does," joked Adrianna.

"Oh well," said Jada. "Wouldn't be the first time I had to stand on my own."

The girls caught up with Mariana and followed her into a dress store. Mariana went one way towards the blue dresses, while Jada went the other towards the black ones. Adrianna decided to go with Jada.

"Are you going to prom with Derek?" asked Jada.

"Probably," answered Adrianna.

And then it struck her. Prom was approaching, and Adrianna would likely be Derek's date because she was his girlfriend. She needed to look at dresses too.

The problem was Adrianna did not know what Derek would wear. His outlandish fashion choices aside, Derek would be spending prom in a wheelchair because his leg would still be in its cast. Adrianna could already see him wearing something that was half-pants and half-shorts to accommodate him and cringed.

Derek's favorite color was red, which he would likely wear. Knowing this, Adrianna went to look at the red dresses. She could always wear her favorite color, pink, for her prom.

As she sifted through the dresses, Adrianna wondered how much fun Derek could really have at prom on a broken leg. He would not be able to dance, which meant she might not get to do any dancing either.

"I'll probably have to bring him to my senior prom to make up for it," chuckled Adrianna.

But then Adrianna stopped chuckling. She wondered if Derek would even want to attend her senior prom. He would be twenty by that point. Already two years into adulthood when she would just be graduating high school.

Then a darker thought entered Adrianna's mind. She wondered if she and Derek would even still be a couple by that point. With the difficulties they were currently facing in their relationship, she wondered if they would even last up to his prom, let alone her senior prom.

"No," said Adrianna, snapping herself out of it. "Of course we're going to last. He loves me and I love him."

"Thank you for that PSA," said Mariana sarcastically. "We're so glad to know he loves you and you love him."

"Girl, don't sneak up on me like that!" snapped Adrianna.

"Girl, I've been standing here this whole time!"

"Then you need to speak up then!"

"Did you find a dress?" asked Jada, approaching them.

"No," said Mariana.

"Oh," said Jada. "Well, I found one. I'm going to go try it on."

"Okay," said Mariana. Once Jada was gone, Mariana eyed Adrianna and said, "You can't tell anyone that I was hanging out with Jada. If Dani finds out–!"

"I know full well you ain't scared of no Danielle Lee," said Adrianna.

"I'm not scared of her," said Mariana. "But I need her as a friend. Just a little while longer. If she knows I'm still hanging with Jada, she'll drop me."

"You need to start from the beginning because I'm lost," said Adrianna.

"Lord Dria," grumbled Mariana. "Being Dani's friend makes me popular... popular enough to win prom queen."

"So... you're using Dani?"

"What else am I supposed to do? Nobody likes me enough to vote for me, not even my own cousins."

"Because you be being mean to people," said Adrianna. "And being friends with Dani makes people like you even less. People aren't going to vote for someone they don't like."

"They will if Dani convinces them to. Especially now that she's dating Derik. They're popularity has skyrocketed since they got together, and if he endorses me, I'll for sure win prom queen."

"So, this whole friendship is a lie? You did all this to be prom queen?"

"No! I like Dani but she's been spending all her time lately with 'her man'. If I'm going to be pushed aside, I might as well get something out of it for myself."

"Does Jada know you're hiding your friendship with her?"

Mariana looked away guiltily.

"How sad," said Adrianna. "So sad. Very sad. Very very sad."

"You just don't understand," muttered Mariana. "Everyone likes you."

"Everyone would like you too if you were nicer to people," said Adrianna. "You make yourself unlikable."

"I'm likable!"

"You are not. You always say rude things."

"Like what? Give me an example."

"Girl, you said my dad's marriage wasn't going to last! Who says that about their own uncle?!"

"I said I wouldn't be *surprised* if it didn't last. If you're going to throw something back in my face at least have it right."

"The point is what you said was mean and rude. You always say mean and rude things then get mad when people don't like you."

"It's not my fault that I'm brutally honest."

"Well, you being 'brutally honest' is why no one likes you."

"If you think what I said was mean and rude you should hear some of the things Papá's family says," scoffed Mariana. "You wouldn't last thirty seconds with them being all sensitive like you are."

"I might get that dress," said Jada, returning to them.

"Jada, am I likable?" asked Mariana.

"Yeah."

"See? Dria says I'm not and claims I say rude things."

"Erm...," murmured Jada. "Sometimes you do say things very... bluntly."

"Told you," said Adrianna.

"Oh shut up," snapped Mariana.

The girls walked around the mall. Jada bought herself a new video game from the gaming store. Mariana bought Adrianna lunch, and Adrianna assumed it was because she wanted to prove she was likable. While they were eating, a man holding a bunch of flyers approached them.

"Hello ladies," said the man. "How are we today?"

"We're doing good," said Jada.

"What you trying to sell us?" asked Mariana.

"Mariana!" grunted Adrianna.

"I'm just trying to get to the point," said Mariana.

"I'm not selling nothing, I'm just handing out flyers," laughed the man. He handed a flyer to Mariana and said, "The Lounge is holding a singing contest this Thursday. Come out if you can."

"You should enter!" encouraged Jada when the man walked away.

"No way," said Mariana. "There's no way I'd win."

"You could totally win!" said Jada. "And you could even get discovered!"

"Yeah right."

"I'm serious!" said Jada. "Tell her Adrianna!"

"You could win," agreed Adrianna.

"You think so?" asked Mariana with a slight smile.

"Yeah, there's a chance," said Adrianna.

"I'll consider giving it a shot then," said Mariana.

Hours later, Mariana dropped Adrianna off at home, where Mr. Brown had returned after leaving Uncle Alejandro's.

"Dad, I'm home," said Adrianna. Her father scowled, and Adrianna winced, "I can not be home."

Mr. Brown rolled his eyes and walked away.

"What's wrong with Dad now?" asked Adrianna.

"Your brothers," said Mary.

"What did they do?"

"I don't know what Andre did, but Antoine did something that caused Dad to take his video games away."

"Oh, that's bad."

"Mhmm."

Adrianna went to her room and decided to call Derek. She wanted an answer to his lack of communication.

"Hey," said Derek.

"Don't hey me," said Adrianna. "I haven't heard nothing from you for the past few days. Are we broken up and you just forgot to tell me?"

"Aw I'm sorry," said Derek. "It's been a busy past few days."

"Why weren't you at church yesterday?"

"Dad didn't go, and I can't exactly take myself right now."

"Why didn't he go?"

"Well, you know he's still kind of... wary of the church folks."

"What about Saturday?"

"I texted you."

"Barely."

"I was busy. My dad's cousin Joe and his wife had returned home so we were visiting."

"And today?"

"We're talking right now."

"Because I called you."

"Well, phones do work two ways."

"Don't give me that!"

"Well, they do. You don't always have to wait on me to call you first."

"You're the man in the relationship. You're supposed to call me. Don't start slacking off now."

"I'm not!" griped Derek. "I was just busy."

"Well, I would appreciate it if you'd at least tell me you're busy," complained Adrianna.

"Fine, I will," said Derek.

Adrianna shook her head as she and Derek continued talking. Sometimes, Derek could be a lot like her dad with his lack of communication. And it was moments like that when Adrianna questioned if their relationship would last.

Daddy's Little Girl

When my baby girl wanted to be a dancer,
I readily made that happen for her.
But when she decided to try romance,
I didn't really want to take that chance.
My baby can't be ready to date,
She's only fifteen for goodness' sake!
I didn't date till I was eighteen,
But then again, I don't think anyone wanted me...
My baby girl is growing up to fast.
Where's the baby girl of my past?
The one with cute hairbows,
And not this teen with her eye rolls.
The one that was sweet,
And used to call me daddy.
I used to be her number one guy,
And losing my spot to him makes me sigh.

Tuesday

Adrianna found that she was the only Brown child without plans that Tuesday. But she did not have to wait long for plans to find her.

Gretchen had started moving her stuff in ahead of the wedding. Adrianna accompanied her and her bridesmaid, Ms. Shirley, to help them.

"Are you excited?" asked Ms. Shirley.

"I am," said Gretchen. "After this Saturday, I will officially be Mrs. Nelson-Brown. I think the only people more excited for this than me are my parents."

"I'm not surprised."

"They're coming in on Thursday."

"I'm surprised they didn't come earlier."

"Oh, they wanted to," said Gretchen. "But I was the one purchasing their tickets."

"Smart," laughed Ms. Shirley. "Get in and get right back on out."

"Exactly," said Gretchen, joining in on the laughter.

"You're a very quiet girl," observed Ms. Shirley, looking at Adrianna.

"All the kids are like that," said Gretchen. "Well... maybe except Andre..."

Adrianna snorted.

"Oh, that got something out of her," giggled Ms. Shirley. "But this means Mr. Right is a good parent with how well-behaved all his kids are."

"Mhmm."

"And speaking of kids, how many do you think your mother wants?"

"I'll tell you how many she's going to get."

"How many?"

"One."

"Only one?"

"That's what me and Torrance agreed on. He's forty-one and he already has six kids. And my thirty-sixth birthday is coming up soon."

"Your mom had you around that age, right?"

"Mhmm. She was thirty-six and Dad was thirty-two. I'm hoping I won't have the same experience she had. I don't think I could have twins in my late thirties like she did."

"That's fair."

"There's Patty's," said Gretchen as they drove past the aforementioned restaurant. "You hungry?"

"Not really."

"Adrianna?"

"Uh," said Adrianna. She was not all that hungry. But she knew of someone who might be. "Sure, I'll get something."

Gretchen and Ms. Shirley waited in the car while Adrianna went inside to place her order.

"Hey," greeted Charmaine. "What can I get you?"

"I need a ten-piece wings and a blue sports drink," said Adrianna. "And it's to go."

"Alright, I see you," teased Charmaine. "Taking your man a little something special?"

"Girl," laughed Adrianna. "Yes, it's for Dee."

"I still can't believe someone ran him over like that," said Charmaine. "That was scary. I still see it sometimes when I close my eyes."

"I know," said Adrianna. "But at least he's still alive. And he'll be back on his feet in a few months."

"You think he'll still be able to dance? He was supposed to dance in Benji's video but now he's going to be the whistle guy."

"The whistle guy?"

"The guy who blows the whistle on beat. It's a part of the beat to Benji's song."

"Oh. I'm hoping he'll be able to dance but his doctor said it's a slim chance."

"What'll he do if he can't dance anymore?"

"I'm not sure. He's hoping he'll be able to."

"I hope so too. Are you going to be in the video?"

"Benji didn't ask me to be in it."

"What?" gasped Charmaine. "Benji!"

"What?" said Benjamin, approaching the counter.

"You didn't ask the Browns to be in your video?"

"No."

"Why not?"

"I didn't think Mr. Brown would let them do it so I didn't make jerseys for them. I'm not going to waste money on getting them jerseys just for them to not be there."

"You could've at least asked."

"You think your father would let you do it?" asked Benjamin.

"I don't know," said Adrianna. "I could ask."

"See?" retorted Benjamin to Charmaine.

"Whatever Benji," griped Charmaine. "Ask your dad. And if he says yes, the video is going to be shot at the park tomorrow at nine AM. Wear black."

"Okay," said Adrianna, collecting her food. "Thanks for the food."

Gretchen dropped Adrianna off at home. Her father was home and allowed her a short visit to Derek's house. When she arrived, she found Derek lying in bed with his shirt off.

"Where are your clothes?" asked Adrianna.

"What I need clothes for?"" answered Derek. "I'm in my room and the only people that live here are me and my dad."

"What if you have visitors?"

"Then they'll just have to see my chest," said Derek. "But I'll put a shirt on if it'll make you happy."

"It will."

"Alright, but first," said Derek. He pointed to his left pec and said, "This is where your name is going."

"What?"

"I'm getting your name tattooed over my heart so I can always carry you with me."

"What made you want to do that?"

"Because I love you," said Derek. "My dad has my name tattooed in the same place."

Adrianna was flattered.

"What's that?" asked Derek. "It smells good."

"Something I got for you," said Adrianna, handing Derek his food.

"You got me food?" squealed Derek. "Thanks Adri! You're the best girlfriend in the world!"

"I try."

"Want to be the best girlfriend in the universe?"

"That depends on what you want me to do."

"Well, if you want me to cover up, I need a shirt," said Derek, biting into a wing. "Mm! This is good!"

"Okay, I'll get you a shirt while you enjoy that," chuckled Adrianna. She opened the top drawer of Derek's dresser.

"Not that drawer!" cried Derek.

"Why not?" asked Adrianna. She looked inside and saw it was his underwear drawer. She would have closed it, but she noticed one of Derek's underwear had a hot dog on it.

"Hot dog?" asked Adrianna, holding up the underwear.

"Well, I am a hot dawg," joked Derek.

"Okay...," said Adrianna. She was about to close the drawer when another pair of underwear caught her eye.

"Money?"

"D-Money?"

"I...," said Adrianna. She held up a pair of white boxers covered in red lips and exclaimed, "These ones are covered in kisses!"

"I didn't put them there."

The next pair of underwear Adrianna saw was horrendous. They were tattered plaid boxers.

"You need to throw these away," said Adrianna.

"Why?" said Derek. "They're still good to wear."

"There's a hole in the bottom and the elastic is poking out!"

"Are you going to go through all my draws or are you going to get me a shirt?" asked Derek.

"Yeah, let me get you that shirt," said Adrianna.

"Second drawer."

"Okay." Adrianna grabbed a shirt off the top but noticed something seemed off about it. She unfurled it and said, "This looks a little small."

"That's because it's fitted."

"Oh," said Adrianna. The next thing she grabbed was a mesh tank top. "What is this?!"

"What?" said Derek innocently.

"Where would you even wear this?"

"Where do you like me to wear it?"

"No where."

Adrianna handed Derek a white t-shirt, but she was curious about the rest of his wardrobe. She went through his clothes, marveling at the things her boyfriend believed he could 'make work'. Some of his most outrageous pieces included: a sports cap with literal dog ears attached, a pair of jeans with white bandanna patterns running down the sides, and a black bulletproof vest that was not functional.

"Baby, what do you be wearing?" said Adrianna. "You need to let me dress you."

"That's alright."

"What you mean 'that's alright'?"

"Your family just dresses so... boring," said Derek.

"Our clothes aren't boring," whined Adrianna. "We just don't wear all those loud colors like you do."

"Maybe I like being loud," said Derek. "If you're complaining now, wait until you see what I'm wearing to prom."

"Should I be scared?" questioned Adrianna.

Derek showed Adrianna his outfit inspiration. It was a red plaid buttoned vest with matching pants and a white flat-brimmed hat.

"You've got to be kidding me," said Adrianna.

"What?" said Derek. "I like it."

"There's no way they're letting you in dressed like that."

"Sure they will," said Derek. "I wear the suit jacket when they check our tickets, then I take it off once we're inside. While you're in my closet, can you get my referee shirt and my gold shorts?"

"Why gold?"

"To go with these," said Derek, motioning to the golden grill he had gotten for his birthday.

"So, you're going to wear a black and white striped shirt, gold shorts, with red hair," said Adrianna.

"My shoes will tie it all together," said Derek triumphantly. Then he frowned a little and added, "Well, my left shoe anyways."

"Okay then."

"You're going to be at the shoot, right?"

"Benji didn't invite us. He wasn't sure Dad would let us go."

"You've got to go!" whined Derek. "Call your dad. I'll convince him to let you go."

"How?"

"What do you mean 'how'?" asked Derek. "You're my girl. As your man, I take care of you when he can't."

Adrianna glanced at Derek's leg.

"Oh, you think I can't do anything just because my leg is broke?" snapped Derek.

"I didn't say that," said Adrianna.

"Your face did."

Adrianna had never been more thankful for her phone to ring than when it did at that moment.

"Hello?" said Adrianna.

"Dria, you need to come home so you can get ready for bible study," said Mr. Brown.

"Yes sir," said Adrianna. She hung up and said, "I got to go."

"Oh, I see," said Derek. "Running off when things get to hot to handle, huh?"

"Don't be a jerk," said Adrianna, kissing his cheek. "And you better be at bible study tonight."

"Maybe, if my broken leg doesn't get in the way," remarked Derek.

Adrianna sighed and left Derek to himself and his mood. She had not meant to insinuate that his leg was an issue.

But it was the truth. There were certain things he was not able to currently do because his leg was broken. And she figured the sooner he accepted that, the better off he would be.

The topic for girl's bible study that evening was 'My Sister's Keeper'. Mrs. Kiana was teaching the girls the importance of being a good sister to one another.

"A lot of you in here know what it means to be a sister, and all of you know what it means to be a Sista," said Mrs. Kiana. She chuckled and added, "In fact, some of you know so well that you created a club about it."

Adrianna smiled at the mention of The Little Sister Society. It had been her and Tamara's idea because they had wanted to do something positive in the community. They had named it The Little Sister Society because all the founding members were ironically little sisters.

But the club had recently been facing some issues. Although everyone had apologized to Jada for misjudging her when she had first moved to Creeke, Latasia and Nicole had continued being standoffish toward her. It had caused a divide among the girls.

Jada herself did not want the girls fighting over her. Although Madame President Adrianna was supposed to remain neutral as Althea had chosen to, she did not like how Jada was being treated. So, she sided with Allison and Charmaine against Latasia, Nicole, and Kameryn, who sided with her sister out of loyalty.

No one knew how Tamara felt about the situation because she was never around anymore. The only time anyone ever saw her was at school. Any other time she was at home tending to her mother. Adrianna felt bad that the club they had started to help others was involved in drama when Tamara needed them most.

"As the oldest sister of three, I not only know what it means to be your sister's keeper, but also how hard sisterhood can be sometimes," continued Mrs. Kiana. "But those hard and testy moments are when you find out who your true sisters are. Biological and spiritual. My sisters and women I call my sisters were right by my side through some of the hardest moments in my life. Like the Bible tells us, friends love at all times and brothers are born for adversity. True sisters rejoice when you rejoice and weep when you weep. They don't kick you while you're down, they don't talk about you behind your back, and they don't do things to try and harm you. True sisters love you and outdo themselves showing you honor like the tenth verse of Romans twelve instructs. They check on you, they help care for you, they make sure you're okay. And that's what all of us in this room should be trying to do. So, today we're going to do an exercise..."

The exercise was one where the girls would be randomly paired and talk about their issues. Althea got paired with Danielle. Adrianna figured that was the best possible pairing for her. Only Althea had the patience and kindness to talk with Danielle and was the only one in the room outside of the Garza sisters who did not have an issue with her.

Adrianna was paired with Danielle's former best friend, Priscella Payne. Although Allison claimed Priscella had improved since parting with Danielle, Adrianna was not exactly rushing to be friends with her.

"So...?" said Adrianna awkwardly. "Got anything that's bothering you?"

"Yeah," said Priscella. "My parents think I shouldn't be friends with Allison."

"Why not?"

"They think she's not a good influence on me."

"Why do they think that?"

"They say she's too rough and unladylike."

"Who do they think is a good influence?"

"Dani."

Adrianna stared at Priscella dumbfoundedly. She could not believe Priscella's parents thought Danielle was a better influence over Allison. Danielle had treated Priscella like a dumb shadow and had constantly gotten her into trouble, while Allison did the complete opposite.

"What do you think?" asked Adrianna.

"I don't know," said Priscella. "I like having Allison as a friend. She doesn't treat me like I'm stupid and she's one of the only people willing to talk to me. But my mom is best friends with Mrs. Tasha, and she wants me and Dani to be friends again."

"Do you want to be friends with Dani again?"

"Not really," said Priscella. "Is there anything bothering you?"

"No," answered Adrianna. She was not about to tell all her business to a girl she barely liked.

After finishing up, Adrianna waited with the other girls for her father to pick her up. Mariana and Mariella waited off to one side, while Priscella waited off to another alone. Althea was still talking to Danielle. Adrianna found it weird to not see the 'mean girls' together like they normally were.

"Do you know Prissy's parents think I'm a bad influence on her?" cried Allison. Adrianna realized she was not the only person Priscella had complained to.

"Who do they think is a good influence then?" asked Jada.

"Dani."

"I know you lying!" hollered Latasia. "I know you are lying to me!"

"I wish," griped Allison. "Her mom claims I'm too rough of a person to be hanging with. Apparently, Dani is more in line with how they want Prissy to be."

"How do they want her to be?" asked Nicole.

"Strong and assertive," said Allison.

"Are you not strong and assertive?" asked Latasia.

"She's definitely strong the way she be throwing her brothers around like it's nothing," said Nicole.

"You make me sound like I'm a superwoman or something," said Allison.

"Girl, every Preston High coach needs to be glad you chose looks and books over sports," said Latasia.

"Mhmm," agreed Nicole. "Your granddaddy was a linebacker, your granny was a cheerleader, your father was a quarterback, your older brothers played basketball, your cousin is basically an acrobat. You come from a family of athletes. No wonder you're so strong."

"I–!" gaped Allison.

"What are you guys talking about?" asked Althea, joining the group.

"Allison rejecting her destiny as an athlete," teased Nicole.

"You sure were talking to Dani a long time," said Latasia.

"It was an interesting conversation," said Althea.

"What'd she talk about?" said Nicole. "How everyone hates her and how nothing is ever her fault?"

Latasia and Nicole giggled.

"What we talked about is between me and her," remarked Althea crossly.

"Althea chill," said Latasia. "It was just a joke."

"A very bad one," said Althea, walking away from the group.

"What's gotten into her?" asked Nicole.

"You know how she is," said Latasia. "Always got to be Miss Friend of The World."

"Mean girls," coughed Allison.

"What now?" huffed Latasia. "What'd we do now?"

"Why are you talking about your friend behind her back?" questioned Allison. "We literally just got done talking about being your sister's keeper."

"People are strict around here," joked Nicole. "Can't say nothing!"

"Not when it's disrespectful, you can't," said Allison.

"I'm not doing this tonight," sighed Latasia. "Come on Nicki. We'll wait over there."

Latasia and Nicole walked away with Latasia's sister Kameryn in tow.

"Every now and then I see why they were friends with Danielle," griped Allison.

"Mhmm," agreed Allison's best friend, Stacy Gilbert.

"Jada," whispered Adrianna. "Come with me."

Adrianna led Jada away from the group.

"What's going on?" asked Jada.

"I was talking to Mariana, and she told me to keep you and her being friends a secret," said Adrianna.

"A secret from who?" asked Jada.

"Danielle."

"I kind of figured," said Jada, shaking her head. "Honestly, I don't care whether Dani knows or not, but I'll respect her wishes."

"Doesn't that bother you though?" asked Adrianna.

"I mean I would prefer to not have to hide who I'm friends with," said Jada. "But Mariana was friends with Dani first. If that's an important friendship to her then I can't do nothing about that."

"You're so nice to her and look how she repays you," griped Adrianna.

"It's fine," said Jada "If it comes down to it, I'm perfectly fine with not having any friends."

"Well, that's never going to happen because I'll always be your friend," said Adrianna.

"Okay," chuckled Jada.

"Adrianna," said Mariana, coming up to them. She cast a friendly glance at Jada before adding, "Uncle T is here."

"Alright," said Adrianna. "Bye Jada."

"Bye," said Jada.

Danielle was standing near the exit. Mariana rushed past her without looking at her. But Adrianna looked her directly in the eye as she passed her, and the look on Danielle's face said it all. She knew something was up and was not happy about it.

All My Love

To all that I love this one is for you.
To my parents who brought me to this place,
And my stepparents who have joined the race,
My siblings for whom anything I'd do,
And to my friends who always keep me cool,
To the people in town who show me grace,
And to my man who likes to lick my face,
I love you all with all my heart, it's true.

I know love is patient and that it's kind.
I know it spreads joy and it never fails.
The love that I feel isn't hard to find,
And it's something that isn't hard to share.
This love that I feel isn't only mine,
I share it with you and know it prevails.

Wednesday

Wednesday had started well and ended in disaster.

Adrianna had only been at Benjamin's video shoot a short while before things had gotten ugly. Samiel had tried to embarrass Andre, and worse, Derek had unknowingly egged it on. The latter upset Adrianna more because Samiel would not have had ammunition to use against Andre if Derek had just shut up.

She had planned to be at that video shoot most of the day, but instead, she was at home. Benjamin had been right not to have jerseys made for them. It would have been a waste of money.

Gretchen had brought more of her stuff to the house, so Adrianna and Andre helped her organize it.

"Adrianna," said Gretchen. "Is something wrong?"

"I'm fine," said Adrianna, trying to hide her irritation. She held up a picture and asked, "Where do you want this?"

"Just set it there," said Gretchen, pointing to the dresser.

"Were you goth?" asked Andre, holding up a spiked choker. "And can you get me one of these too?"

"I don't think your dad would let you have one," said Gretchen. "And what do you mean about me being goth?"

"I mean your favorite color is black, you like skateboarding, you like rock music, you're super artsy, but you were also a cheerleader, and you like dresses."

"To be quite honest, me doing cheerleading was a dare," said Gretchen. "And dresses aren't limited to girly girls."

"A dare?" said Adrianna.

"Yeah. I never expected to make the team, let alone become captain of it."

"If it was a dare, how were you able to do all the flips and stuff?" asked Andre.

"My mother had us in gymnastic classes when we were little," explained Gretchen. "I liked them more than Greta did, so I stayed in them while she did other things."

"You just get more and more interesting," said Andre with a laugh. He pulled out a rock album and gasped. "You have a limited edition?!"

"I stood in line for hours to get it," said Gretchen with a grin.

"You are the coolest person ever!" exclaimed Andre.

Adrianna could not understand it. Andre had been insulted, yet he was being his regular self like nothing happened. Meanwhile, she was angry in every possible way for him.

"Do you think you'll get another skateboard?" asked Andre. "I think it'd be cool to learn."

"My skateboarding days on these knees are over," chuckled Gretchen. "But if your dad says yes, I'd be more than willing to teach you."

"Yes!" cheered Andre.

Adrianna did not understand it one bit.

That evening, she went to church in a terrible mood. She also noticed most of the people who had been at the video shoot were not at church. Including Derek.

Adrianna could not understand why Samiel had been so rude to her brother. And she could not understand how her brother just brushed it off like it was nothing.

She really could not understand why Derek had not listened to her demands for him to stop. He should have respected that the conversation was taking a turn she did not like and ended it. But he had not.

Adrianna sat through the service, stewing over it all. And she was sure it was written all over her face because her mother kept glancing at her throughout. As soon as the service ended, it seemed like First Lady Hall made a beeline straight for Adrianna.

"Okay, what's wrong with my little Dria?" asked First Lady Hall.

"Nothing," said Adrianna. "Just some mess today."

"Some mess, huh? Want to talk about it?"

"No."

"Okay. If you ever do, you know I'm always available."

"I know."

Adrianna did not want to talk about it. She wanted to understand it.

Adrianna called Derek when she got home. He picked up on the last ring.

"I know I wasn't there tonight," said Derek before Adrianna could say anything. "The shoot went longer than expected."

"I'm not surprised," said Adrianna.

"Why'd you leave so early?" asked Derek.

"Because I wanted to."

"But why?"

"Because I didn't like the conversation."

"Adri, they were just jokes."

"They were not."

"Yes, they were. Sami and I joke like that about each other all the time."

"You just don't get it."

"What am I not getting?"

"The jokes weren't about you!" snapped Adrianna. "Sami was talking about Andre and you're just hee-hee ha-ha-ing like the mess is funny!"

"How was I supposed to know?!"

"Because I told you to stop! Everything Sami was saying was aimed at Andre and you're just encouraging it!"

"Well, I thought they were about me! Rockstar knows I wouldn't make fun of him like that."

"All I know is you better check your friend or I will!"

"Adri, I don't think it's as serious as you're making it to be."

"It's that serious to me. And if you want me to be happy, then it needs to be that serious to you too!"

"Why?"

"What do you mean 'why'? My brother was insulted by your friend!"

"Well, if Rockstar has an issue with it then he needs to speak up."

"You cannot be serious right now."

"Adri, I'm telling you. I don't think it's as serious as you're making it. It's probably all just a big misunderstanding."

"Calling my brother dumb is not a misunderstanding. And now I'm wondering if you think the same way since this is your best friend and you're defending him."

"Why would I ever think Rockstar is dumb?"

"Because you're sitting up here acting like what Sami did is not that big of a deal! That must mean that you agree with what he said."

"That doesn't even make sense! All I'm saying is if Andre has an issue with what happened, then he should handle it! You don't have to fight his battles for him!"

"Andre is my brother and I'm not going to let nobody disrespect him! Not you or your raggedy friends!"

"My raggedy friends are your raggedy friends too!"

"Well, they don't have to be! I got three brothers, three sisters, and a whole bunch of cousins! That's more than enough friends for me!"

"Well, good for you."

"You know what I'm done with this," said Adrianna. "If you can't see why this is such a big deal to me, then maybe we just don't need to be together."

Derek did not answer.

"Hello?" snapped Adrianna.

"Goodnight Adrianna. Goodnight."

Derek hung up the phone before Adrianna could respond. She threw her phone down and stared at the ceiling.

Adrianna just could not understand why she was the only one who seemed upset about this. She lay in bed trying to figure it out until she fell asleep.

The Boyfriend

It's not that I don't like her boyfriend.
In fact, I wouldn't mind if he was her future husband.
But the poor boy unfortunately comes with a curse,
That makes him seem the worst of the worst.
I know that he's sweet boy,
And that with my daughter he wouldn't toy.
But I also know that when emotions get involved,
All other senses tend to devolve.
The boy's father is a teen parent,
And to be fair that's the same way my mother went.
But I want these two to avoid that fate.
Especially because it's my daughter at stake.
I don't care if others say I'm wrong,
Because the run I'm looking at is long.
And I have in mind the big picture,
That this boy won't be a teen parent with her.

Thursday

It was Andre's birthday. Instead of being happy that her brother had finally reached adulthood, Adrianna was still highly annoyed.

But she had to at least pretend she was in a good mood. Gretchen's parents were flying into town, and Adrianna was going with her father and Gretchen to meet them. They sat outside the city airport, waiting for the plane to land.

Adrianna was still annoyed with Derek. But she wanted him to know she had not meant what she said about them breaking up, so she texted him 'good morning'. He had not responded yet.

"I think that's them coming out now," said Gretchen.

Mr. Gerald Nelson and Mrs. Myrtle Nelson engulfed their daughter in a hug. They greeted Mr. Brown and Adrianna too, and the group drove back to Creeke.

"Where's your sister?" asked Mrs. Nelson.

"At home sleep," said Gretchen.

"Well, this is a first," laughed Mr. Nelson. "Usually, she's the early bird and you're the one missing the worm."

"We traded places today."

"I hope you've been getting plenty of rest."

"I have Dad."

"You're a very quiet girl," observed Mrs. Nelson of Adrianna.

"All my kids are like that," said Mr. Brown. "Well... maybe except Andre..."

Adrianna snorted harder than she had when Gretchen said the same thing earlier that week.

"Kids," said Mr. Nelson dreamily. "You know, that's the next step after marriage."

Adrianna noticed her father's reflection glance at Gretchen.

"I think I only want one more brother or sister," said Adrianna.

"Only one?" said Mrs. Nelson. "You sure you don't want like two or three more?"

"No," said Adrianna. "I already have six of them. I can only take one more."

"I guess one would be okay," said Mr. Nelson.

"You both do know you have more than one daughter, right?" said Gretchen.

"Well, we have to get your sister down the aisle first!" complained Mrs. Nelson. "And by the time that happens she might not be able to have any kids!"

"I don't think things with her and Bud will take that long."

"Well, I'm ready to meet this Bud," said Mr. Nelson.

"Me too!" agreed Mrs. Nelson. "And if he's anything like that evil Brad then your sister would just be better off being an old maid!"

"Trust me, Bud is nothing like Brad," said Gretchen. "The only thing they have in common is that they're names start with B and end with D."

"So does the word, 'bad'," observed Mr. Nelson.

"And that's too much in common for me!" griped Mrs. Nelson. "She need to get her a good man like Torrance!"

Mr. Brown blushed, and Adrianna started giggling. She could already hear Karla's *a man with six kids?!* response to that declaration.

"I... uh... Bud's a good man," said Mr. Brown. "He just turned forty and uh... he's uh... starting his own business."

"Doing what?" asked Mr. Nelson.

"Catering."

"That's smart," said Mrs. Nelson. "It's always somebody that likes to eat so he shouldn't have a problem in that area."

Mr. Brown dropped Gretchen and her parents off at Gretchen's house.

"Why'd you start laughing when Mrs. Myrtle said I was a good man?" asked Mr. Brown.

"It was funny."

"Mhmm. You want to talk about that argument I heard last night?"

"No sir."

Derek still had not texted her back.

"Listen, if you're going to argue with your little boyfriend, you need to do it before the sun goes down. I'm not trying to hear arguments while I'm trying to sleep."

"Yes sir."

Having a lot of siblings was both a blessing and a curse.

It was a blessing to Adrianna when her father was preoccupied with her other siblings because then he was not so concerned with her. But the downside was sometimes she got no attention from him at all.

The curse came when her father had no other child to focus on. Then he zeroed in on Adrianna and focused all his attention on her. But the upside was that she had his attention.

That evening, First Lady Hall drove Adrianna to praise dance practice at the church. She had something to handle there but would leave before Adrianna's practice finished.

"Make sure you let your father know that he's picking you up from practice," said First Lady Hall.

"Yes ma'am," said Adrianna.

Creeke Church's praise dance ministry was directed by Mrs. Lydia Haynes. Mrs. Haynes was Mr. Haynes's mother, and she was married to Deacon Titus Haynes.

Adrianna entered the practice room and placed her sneakers in a designated crate by the door. She was the only one who had to do so because of her father's infamous reputation of throwing shoes in anger. But Adrianna knew her father had not thrown a shoe in seven months. Still, she abided by the rule and quietly slipped into her dance shoes.

At fifteen, Adrianna was one of the youngest members of the praise dance ministry. But being one of the youngest did not allow her any excuses. She was expected to be just as good and seamlessly synchronized with the adults of the team.

Although Adrianna loved dancing in general, she especially loved liturgical dance. It was the style she was most comfortable with, and she always felt she could let out all her stress as she danced. And that's what she did at practice.

By the end, she felt refreshed and renewed. Her annoyance with the previous day had subsided. But Derek still had not texted her back.

Adrianna stood outside, waiting for her dad to pick her up. She had done as her mother had instructed, but it was unusual for her father to be so late.

"Still here?" asked Mrs. Haynes when she exited the building.

"Yes ma'am," said Adrianna. "I think my dad is running late."

"That Torrance," snorted Mrs. Haynes. "Here, I'll take you home."

"Thank you."

"I'm just waiting on Miki. She had to use the bathroom."

As if on cue, Mikayla rushed through the door.

"Girl, you sure took your time," said Mrs. Haynes.

Adrianna called her father to update him, but he did not answer. She texted him just in case and got in Mrs. Haynes's car. As they were driving, Mrs. Haynes's phone began ringing.

"Hello?" said Mrs. Haynes.

"MOOOOM!" said Mr. Haynes. "Are you on your way home?"

"Yes. Why?"

"Do you want to do me a favor?"

"Oh Lord. What you want Jonny?"

"Can you stop at the store and get me some juice. I ran out."

"Why can't you do it? You have a car."

"But you're already out. Besides, I know you're going that way anyways because you always take Mikayla home."

"Boy, why are you bringing me into it?" cried Mikayla.

"To prove a point!"

"You are so childish."

"Nuh uh."

"You know we have one of your students in the car while you sitting up playing."

"Who?"

"Jonny how many students you got on the praise dance team?" asked Mikayla sarcastically.

"Why is she in the car though?"

"Because her father didn't show up and we had to go!" explained Mikayla. "I'm on first shift at the store in the morning! I can't be out here all night waiting on Mr. Brown to get his life together!"

"Did he call and say he was coming to get her?"

Mrs. Haynes and Mikayla looked at Adrianna. Her father had not called her back or answered her text. She shook her head.

"Nope."

"Something must be wrong. He wouldn't just leave his child out there like this."

"Aw look at you sounding all concerned for your student."

"Wait, I'm not on speakerphone, right?!"

"You are."

"Uhn uhn, why you guys play me like this?!"

"Because your mother is driving."

"Oh my gosh this is so embarrassing! Have I been on speaker the whole time?!"

"Yeah."

"NOOO! OH MY GOSH WHY?!"

"Jonny you're so dramatic," teased Mikayla.

"TAKE ME OFF SPEAKER! NOW!"

"Alright, alright," laughed Mikayla as she took Mr. Haynes off speakerphone. "No need to get your briefs all in a twist."

Mikayla finished the conversation with Mr. Haynes and then relayed the information to Mrs. Haynes.

"Jonny is funny," laughed Mikayla.

"You want him?" joked Mrs. Haynes.

"Nope," said Mikayla. "He can go be with his play cousin Brianne."

"She don't want him either."

"Well," said Mikayla.

The trio arrived at Brewer's grocery store. Brewer's had been a staple in Creeke for decades, and Adrianna did not see it going anywhere soon. The Brewer family passed it down to each generation like an heirloom.

"Welcome in!" called Nicole. Upon seeing who it was, she said, "Oh. It's just you."

"Rude!" said Mikayla.

"What?" said Nicole. "You're not a customer."

"You don't see Mrs. Lydia and Adrianna standing behind me?"

"Hi, welcome in!" said Nicole with a smile.

"Where's Ralphie?" said Mikayla annoyedly.

"Still at work," said Nicole.

"This late?"

"Mhmm."

"Did something happen?"

"I don't know," said Nicole. "I don't work there."

"Where's Mom and Dad?" huffed Mikayla.

"Where do you think?" said Nicole, pointing to the 'employees only' room.

"Sometimes you are so impossible," griped Mikayla as she walked away to the room.

"Look in the mirror sometime," called Nicole.

Adrianna browsed the aisles. She did not need anything out of Brewer's. And neither Derek nor her father had responded to her.

As she was about to go find Mrs. Haynes, Adrianna noticed the underwear. Thinking back on Derek's tattered underwear, she grabbed a three-pack of plaid boxers and bought them along with a card for Andre.

When Adrianna arrived home, she found Mary on her bed reading a book.

"Where's Dad?" asked Adrianna as she signed Andre's card. "And sign this card for Andre."

"I don't know where Dad is," sighed Mary as she did what Adrianna said. "But he's in a very bad mood. Very bad."

"What happened this time?"

Mary did not answer, but Adrianna noticed she shrunk behind her book.

"Mary?"

"I don't want to talk about it."

Adrianna left it at that, figuring she would find out soon enough. She decided to enjoy the calm before the hurricane that was her father's temper came blowing in.

Peeking into her brothers' room, Adrianna saw Andre lying on the bed. Antoine motioned for her to keep quiet and followed her into the hallway.

"Is he sleep?" whispered Adrianna. "Sign this."

"Yeah," whispered Antoine as he signed the card. "I'll put this on his nightstand."

"Did he have a good day?"

"I don't think so. He seemed kind of down when he came home and just went straight to sleep."

"Stupid Sami," grumbled Adrianna.

"What'd Sami do?" questioned Antoine.

"Be a birthday-ruining idiot."

Adrianna heard the front door slam.

"Adrianna!" hollered Mr. Brown.

"Oh Lord," sighed Adrianna. "Here we go."

"What'd you do?" asked Antoine.

"I didn't do anything. Dad's the one that messed up."

"Adrianna!"

Adrianna met her furious father in the living room. He looked angrier than usual, and Adrianna wondered if it was because of her or something else."

"Where were you?!" snapped Mr. Brown. "I pull up to the church and you're not there!"

"I waited for you, and you never showed up, so Mrs. Lydia brought me home," explained Adrianna.

"You could've told me!"

"I did! I called and texted, and you didn't answer!"

"Don't yell at me Adrianna, I'm not in the mood!"

"You had me standing out there forever. Where even were you?"

"Where I was is none of your business!"

"It is when you're my ride home!"

"If I was your ride home then you should've waited until I showed up no matter how long I took!" said Mr. Brown. "You didn't tell me nothing! For all I know you could've been down at that boy's house doing God knows what!"

"Well, I wasn't," countered Adrianna. "And even if I was at his house, it wouldn't be a big deal. You let me go over there any other time."

"With someone else with you!" argued Mr. Brown. "Or when his Dad is home! Never at nighttime and never alone!"

"What does this have to do with you not showing up to get me from practice?"

"It has to do with it because I should know where you are at all times!" said Mr. Brown. "Do you want people to think you're out here being fast?!"

"What?!" choked Adrianna.

"You heard me! Because that's what people are going to think if you're out here at all hours of the night doing what you want to do! That's what people will think if I let him in this house!"

"Why would say that?!"

"Why would *I* say that? Dria, those people out there expect Derek to be just like his father and get you pregnant!"

"But you know me, Dad. You know I wouldn't do that."

"Yeah, because he's not coming in this house!"

"So, you don't trust me."

Mr. Brown stopped to take a breath and eyed Adrianna. She could tell he was seeing red, but she still was unsure why.

"I do trust you," said Mr. Brown, calming down a bit.

"Then you don't trust Derek."

"Look, I think Derek is great. He's very respectful, a bit rambunctious but overall, a good guy. But I also know he's a teenage boy, and sometimes teenage boys let their emotions get the best of them. And because you're my daughter, it's my job to make sure you're not the girl he loses control of his emotions with. I'm not letting that happen if I can help it."

"So that's what you think of him? That he's only interested in sleeping with me?"

"Of course not! But I'm not going to give him the chance to put my trust to the test either and that's final. Now get out my face!"

Adrianna went to her room, confused about what had just happened. Mary had shrunk even farther behind her book. Derek still had not texted her back.

Adrianna was over it. And when she thought about it, she still had no idea what her relationship had to do with her dad not picking her up from praise dance practice. But what she did know was she was in an even worse mood than before.

Does Daddy Know Me?

How hurtful is it to hear that you're fast,
When that is far from the reality.
What have I done to have charged against me,
This terrible lie that's left me aghast?
My daddy treats me like a girl who's rash,
And not like the woman I'm becoming.
Does my daddy really see and know me?
Or does he see who I was in his past?

I am no longer that young little child.
I am blossoming into something more.
And I don't want Daddy getting riled,
Because he's made this his personal chore.
I would like his trust once in a while,
And that's what I feel down in my core.

Friday

The argument with her father had seriously affected Adrianna. The insinuation of being considered 'fast' made her sad. And mad.

Adrianna had been nothing but respectful of her father's rules and wishes. No matter how ridiculous she thought they were, she obeyed them because she respected her father. For him to say what he said made Adrianna question whether even having a boyfriend was worth the stress.

Adrianna went to get her hair done for the wedding with her mother and sisters. She was having a weave installed, which meant she would be at the salon for a while.

As she waited for her turn to sit in Mrs. Harrison's chair, Allison motioned for her to come to the receptionist's desk.

"What's the matter with you?" asked Allison.

"I'm going through it with your cousin," sighed Adrianna.

"What'd he do?"

"Nothing too bad. It's my dad."

"What is it?"

Adrianna considered telling Allison. She knew Allison would not spread her business around. But Allison was also Derek's cousin, and Adrianna knew Allison did not like getting in the middle of her family's relationship drama.

"It's nothing. You know how my dad can be sometimes."

"Yeah. But he shouldn't have nothing to worry about as long as D-Money's treating you right."

Adrianna knew Allison was right. And in a perfect world, her father would be like that. But it was not a perfect world and instead, her father had called her 'fast'.

"Adrianna, I'm ready for you," called Mrs. Harrison.

After having her hair washed, Adrianna settled into Mrs. Harrison's chair for the long session ahead of her.

"How are things in school?" asked Mrs. Harrison.

"Good," answered Adrianna.

"That's good. How are things between you and my nephew? Your mother here was telling me how happy she was that you were dating such a nice boy."

"Mom," whined Adrianna.

"What?" teased First Lady Hall. "I am."

"Things between us are okay."

Adrianna noticed Mrs. Harrison and her mother glance at each other. The rest of the appointment was relatively uneventful. Mr. Kasey entered the salon at some point looking for something to sweep, but there was nothing there, so he talked to First Lady Hall.

"I'm glad to see your hair isn't lopsided anymore," said First Lady Hall.

"I'm going to let that slide because you're Dre's mother," said Mr. Kasey.

"Oh yeah, he told me he talked to you. What were you two talking about?"

"Drugs."

"Drugs?"

"He wanted to know why I got hooked."

"That boy is so nosy," sighed First Lady Hall. "Honestly though, I am glad to see you doing well for yourself."

"Thanks. I just take it a day at a time. And don't worry about Dre. He's a good kid."

"I know. I raised him."

"You said that with such confidence," snorted Mr. Kasey.

"Because it's the truth," said First Lady Hall.

"Kasey, I don't have anything to sweep over here," said Mrs. Harrison. "You can go back to the barber side."

"Alright," said Mr. Kasey, disappearing back into the barber's side of the salon.

"Now that I get a good look at him, I can see the resemblance between him and Sami," said First Lady Hall.

"Would you believe that Marlin knew the whole time?" remarked Mrs. Harrison.

"Yeah. That's his best friend."

"He knew about everything though," said Mrs. Harrison. "The drugs, the rehab, Sami. He knew where Kasey was the whole time. He's the one that got Kasey into rehab."

"Again. That's his best friend."

"It just doesn't make sense to me."

"Maybe Marlin has different standards for his best friends from his wife."

Mrs. Harrison exhaled through her nose and shook her head.

Several hours later, Adrianna's hair was completed, and she was on her way home with her mother. As they pulled in front of Mr. Brown's house, First Lady Hall motioned for Adrianna to wait a bit.

"I want to know what's going on with you," said First Lady Hall. "You seem like you've been in a bad mood all week."

"My whole life is falling apart," said Adrianna.

"Sweetheart, you're fifteen. You've barely lived life for it to be falling apart already."

"Well, it is."

"What exactly is falling apart?"

"Everything."

"What's everything?"

"My relationship, The Little Sister Society. Everything."

First Lady Hall waited for Adrianna to elaborate. Adrianna considered telling her mother about the argument between her and Mr. Brown. But she decided against it.

"Mom, what do you think?" asked Adrianna. "Should I just break up with Derek?"

"Do you want to break up?"

"No."

"Then don't break up."

"But being in this relationship is hard because of Dad's rules."

"Well, Dria, you know your father is a little... strong-minded," said First Lady Hall. "But at the end of the day, this is your relationship not his. What you think is best is entirely up to you."

"Why doesn't it feel like it then? I feel like if Dad had his way, I wouldn't have a boyfriend at all."

"Your father and I both agreed that you could date. He wouldn't have agreed if he didn't want you to date."

"He's not acting like he wanted me to though."

"He *is* your father, after all. He's going to do what he thinks is best for you even if it is a little annoying. But again, this is your relationship, not his. You determine whether it continues or not."

"But–!"

"Listen. I'm not going to tell you what to do. But I will say this. A relationship depends on the level of commitment from both you and Derek. If you feel like you're not committed to it anymore, then there's no point in staying. You've got your whole life ahead of you and I don't want you wasting it trying to make something work with a boy."

"Okay," said Adrianna. "Thanks Mom."

"You're welcome," said First Lady Hall. "And don't let your father's ways get to you either."

Adrianna exited the car feeling a little better. But only a little.

As she sat beside her father and across from Mary at dinner, Adrianna's feelings were still hurt by what her father had said about her. But his words and her mother's advice had given Adrianna something to think about. She knew she had to decide about her relationship. And soon.

-

Antoine Brown

For Antoine Marvin Brown

O my Father who art thou in Heaven,
I thank thee Lord for this child before seven.
I still have no son who bears my name,
But it no longer matters this late in the game.
Antoine Marvin is great I suppose,
For it is the name his mother chose,
To honor an uncle who's gone off to glory,
And another who's still walking his story.
I pray to thee Lord over my son,
That one day he will be someone.
I pray he'll be smart and pray he'll be wise,
I pray that he'll bring delight to my eyes.
I pray he'll be kind and pray he'll be strong,
And ask that all of his days be long.
O Lord please guide and preserve my son's tale,
So that one day it will be worthy to tell.

Friday

Antoine was ready for spring break. He would spend the next seven days relaxing and gaming away on his video game console.

That was not all he would do during spring break though.

Antoine had learned that as a man, the most important things to him should be finances and fitness. He was still too young to have a job but not too young to exercise.

Every Monday, Wednesday, and Friday after school, Antoine went to the recreation center's gym with his best friend, Derik Harrison. That's where he had gone when school let out after the assembly ended.

Derik's father, Mr. Harrison, managed the recreation center. It was ironic to Antoine that he and Derik were best friends when their fathers practically hated each other. The two had never gotten along and had fought as recently as the beginning of the school year.

Mr. Brown had a tiny scar on his arm from that battle. One had to squint to see it. It was not as noticeable as the one that split his left eyebrow in two, but it was there.

Just like the ones on Derik's back. Tiny scars marking up his best friend's back. Antoine glimpsed them in the locker room before Derik quickly covered them with a shirt.

"Ready?" asked Derik.

"Yeah," answered Antoine.

Derik drove him home in his new silver car. Ever since he had gotten it, all Derik wanted to do was drive around blasting his music like his older brothers.

"Man, this beat is too good," asked Derik, bopping his head along to the beat of KV's Rite of Passage. "Have you seen the video to this song?"

"No," answered Antoine.

"Man, you've got to see it."

"Was it good?"

"The women were good."

"The women?"

"You'll understand when you see the video."

Antoine glanced at Derik, who had changed a lot since February. His previously black shoulder-length hair was short and blonde, and his ears pierced. He had regained some of his weight and started developing muscles from his consistent exercise.

He had also developed anxiety. It was a permanent reminder of his time being abducted, just like the scars on his back.

"What are you doing over the break?" asked Derik.

"Playing the game," said Antoine. "My dad and I made a deal that if I got all A's, he'd buy me a new game."

"Wow."

"What are you doing?"

"I don't know. Probably hang out with Dani."

Derik had been dating Danielle for two weeks and had gone girl crazy. Antoine wanted Derik to be happy, but he barely saw his best friend anymore. While Danielle loved all the attention that Derik gave her, Antoine hated it.

Many wondered why Antoine continued being friends with Derik after Derik had disrespected Mr. Brown back in September. The truth was Derik had done something Antoine only wished he could do: he had stood up to Mr. Brown.

Antoine did not fear his dad by any means. But sometimes, his dad could be hard to talk with about certain things.

"I'm going to see the new Drake Malone tonight," said Derik. "Want to come?"

"Is Dani going too?" grumbled Antoine.

"Nah, not this time. It's just me and my brothers. A guy's night out."

"Why am I going then?"

"Are you not a guy?"

"Yeah, but it's you and your brothers hanging out though."

"You're my bro. And I want you to go."

A smile spread across Antoine's face. It made him happy to know his best friend still remembered he had a best friend.

"If my dad lets me, I'll go."

"Cool. Let me know."

Antoine went straight to his father when he arrived home.

"Dad, can I go see the new Drake Malone with Derik tonight?"

"That depends on your report card," said Mr. Brown, holding out his hand expectantly. Antoine handed his father the report card and waited for his reaction. Mr. Brown nodded approvingly and said, "Okay, you can go."

"Yes!" cheered Antoine. "Now, about my game…"

"You could at least go put your stuff down first," snorted Mr. Brown.

"I'm just so excited!" said Antoine. He sat his stuff down in his room and returned to his father.

"I'm giving you my card to buy your game," said Mr. Brown, as he pulled a plastic card from his wallet. "You said it was fifteen dollars, so you get twenty dollars. Alright?"

"Yes sir."

"And bring my card right back when you finish."

"Yes sir."

Antoine raced to his room to claim his prize. After questioning why Andre was zoned out, Antoine powered up his console. He realized he did not have his glasses on but decided he did not need them because he had done the purchasing process enough times to do it without them.

"Two," said Antoine, inputting the number two. He scrolled over to the zero and began inputting it. "Ze–!"

His phone rang.

"Hello?" said Antoine.

"Hey," said Derik. "Did he say you could go?"

"Yeah, I can go."

"Okay. We're coming to get you at seven so be ready."

"Alright," said Antoine.

He inputted the zero and confirmed his purchase.

"Antoine!" called Mr. Brown.

Antoine went to the kitchen where his father was.

"Antoine!" hollered Mr. Brown again as Antoine rounded the corner.

"Sir?"

"Boy, get these glasses!" scolded Mr. Brown. "These things are too expensive for you to be losing track of them!"

"Yes sir," said Antoine. He exchanged the glasses with his father's card, saying, "Here you go."

"You got your game?"

"Yes sir."

"Okay. What time are you going to the movies?"

"Derik said they're coming to get me at seven."

"They're?"

"Him and his brothers."

"Hmm...," uttered Mr. Brown, scratching his chin. Antoine feared he would reconsider letting him go, but Mr. Brown said, "Alright."

Antoine was glad. He showered, picked out his hair, and changed into jeans and a polo that was his favorite color, gray. Then he sat in the living room and waited with his father.

While he waited, he watched KV's video with the sound off. An ad for the army ran before it. The video was one giant pool party that looked wild and fun.

He heard the car before he saw it.

"Dad," said Antoine.

"I hear them," answered Mr. Brown. "You got everything you need?"

"Yes sir."

"Go on then."

"Okay. Bye."

"Bye."

Antoine stepped out onto the porch. The candy-red car rounded the corner and stopped in front of the house. As he neared it, Antoine saw the car vibrate from the force of the speaker in the trunk blasting a gospel rap track.

"Hi," said the Harrison brothers when Antoine got in.

"Hi," answered Antoine.

"What time does your dad want you home?" asked Matthias.

"He didn't say," said Antoine.

"Then we can stay out," joked Deidrick.

"I don't think so," said Matthias. "I'm not about to have the whole Brown clan come down on my head. We'll bring you straight home after the movie."

The song ended.

"Your turn Cornbread," said Matthias.

Deidrick picked a song about stealing girls and playing stepdaddy, and the two older Harrisons began talking sports.

Antoine looked over at Derik, who quietly stared out the window. He wore a white undershirt with gray shorts and a black durag.

"Were you sleep?" asked Antoine.

"No?" answered Derik.

"Then why are you dressed like that?"

"Dressed like what?"

"Like you just woke up."

"Because we're going to a movie," said Derik. "I want to be comfortable."

"You still have your durag on."

"And?" said Derik. "It's not a fashion show."

"But you should want to look your best at all times," said Antoine. "You never know who you could meet."

"Well, whoever I meet tonight is going to meet me with my durag on. And if they don't like it that's too bad."

The song ended.

"Your turn Dee-Three," said Deidrick. "What you want to hear?"

"Obnoxious," muttered Derik.

"Should've known you'd pick that," snorted Matthias. "That girlfriend of yours must be driving you crazy."

"I just like the beat," said Derik, though Antoine noticed a smile creeping onto his face.

Baby girl thought it was love
That I was sent from above
But she ain't know what she got into
And she ain't know what I like to do
Don't she know I'm obnoxious
That I'm just a bit toxic
That the sign says beware
Of the dog that's in there
But don't get frightful
Cuz I won't bite you
Like a vamp in the night
Cuz I'm out in the light
You can see me as I am
I'm a wolf and not a lamb
Baby girl can handle me
Cuz with you for life is where I plan to be

"How you like your new job?" asked Deidrick.

"It's cool," said Matthias. "This new shop pays way more than the one in Creeke. John really hooked me up. I might need to get Uncle Falcon to work there."

"Uncle Falcon's not leaving his job," said Deidrick. "He's too loyal."

"He might leave for the right price."

"Maybe. But it'd have to be a big one."

"Here Brown," said Matthias, handing Antoine the phone after the song ended. "Pick a song."

Antoine picked a gospel rap song that ended when they arrived at the movie theater. Derik grabbed a navy-blue sports cap from the back window and put it on his head. Exiting the car, Antoine realized Derik was dressed similarly to his brothers.

Antoine was the one who stood out from them. He suddenly felt bad for getting on Derik's case. Here he was, insulting the friend who had chosen to take him out over Danielle when he was the oddly dressed one.

"Why are you looking like that?" asked Derik.

"Like what?" answered Antoine.

"All sad and pitiful."

"I don't look sad and pitiful."

"Boy, you look like you about to bust out crying."

"Why you picking with me?"

"Because I can," laughed Derik.

Antoine laughed too. He knew then that everything between them was alright.

"I saw the video by the way," said Antoine.

"What'd you think?" said Derik with a grin.

"I had to watch it with the sound off because my dad was right next to me."

"You're a brave man Antoine Brown."

"She is bad," said Deidrick, licking her lips. He eyed the cashier, who was light tan with back-length black curly hair tied in a ponytail.

"She also looks really young," said Matthias warningly.

"Only one way to find out."

"Look man," said Matthias. "I came to see a movie."

"Man, you know it ain't going to take me too long to get her number."

"Don't you think you should hold off on dating for a while though?"

"No. Why?"

Matthias gave Deidrick a knowing look. Antoine looked at Derik for an explanation, but Derik shrugged.

"I already told you that's got nothing to do with me," said Deidrick.

"You don't know that for sure," said Matthias.

"What are you two talking about?" asked Derik.

"Nothing!" said Matthias and Deidrick together quickly.

"Hmm," uttered Derik suspiciously.

"Next in line!" called the girl.

"Hey, how you doing?" said Deidrick smoothly, approaching the counter.

"I'm good," said the cashier with a smile. "What can I get you?"

"Your name," answered Deidrick.

"Excuse me?" said the cashier, her smile faltering.

"What's your name?" asked Deidrick.

"Uh... Esperanza...?" said the cashier, pointing to her nametag.

"Esperanza," repeated Deidrick. "What's that mean?"

"It means hope."

"That's very fitting because I hope you'll give me your number."

"Oh my gosh," snorted Esperanza.

"Cornbread," said Matthias. "Let her do her job in peace."

Esperanza smiled gratefully at Matthias.

"Can we have four popcorns and four drinks please?" said Matthias.

"I get my own?" whispered Antoine excitedly.

"Why wouldn't you?" whispered Derik.

Antoine was used to having to share with at least one of his siblings, usually Adrianna, Andre, or sometimes both. He did not tell Derik that though.

"How old are you, Esperanza?" asked Deidrick.

"I don't think that's any of your business," said Esperanza as she began making the popcorn buckets.

"I know it's not, but my brother here thinks you're a teenager. I don't think you are so I was hoping you could put this debate between us to an end."

"I just want to make it clear I have nothing to do with this," said Matthias. "I'm just trying to get my snacks and see a movie."

Esperanza giggled.

"Is it me or does she seem to like Matthias better?" whispered Antoine.

"Maybe," agreed Derik. "But he's not interested though."

"What drink would you like?" said Esperanza.

"Whatever drink will get me your number," said Deidrick, causing Esperanza to purse her lips.

"Four lemonades," said Matthias.

"Four lemonades," repeated Esperanza, making the drinks.

"What's our damage?" asked Matthias.

Esperanza told Matthias the price, and he paid. Deidrick shoved his fists in his pockets and slightly frowned. He put a grin back on for his final attempt with Esperanza.

"So, how about that number?" said Deidrick.

"I'll give you my number," said Esperanza to Matthias. "And you don't have to worry about me being a teenager. I'm twenty-one."

"I uh... okay," said Matthias. He glanced at Deidrick, who eyed him and said, "But don't be surprised if he ends up with it."

"I'll take that risk," said Esperanza, putting her number in Matthias's phone. "Have a nice day."

The boys rounded the corner into the hallway leading to their theater, and Deidrick exploded.

"Bro!" said Deidrick. "How could you do me like that?!"

"It's not my fault you fumbled her," said Matthias.

"All because you had to be Mr. Comedian."

"I was just trying to get my stuff."

"Bro, I can't believe this!"

"You do know I'm not interested in her, right?"

"Why'd you get her number then?"

"She gave it to me."

"I thought you were my bro!"

"I am. I got her number for you."

"Oh."

"I'll give it to you later. What you do after that is your business."

"Thanks bro."

"Now, shut up and let me enjoy my movie."

"What just happened?" said Antoine.

"Matthias saved the day," said Derik.

The Drake Malone sequel was even better than the first movie. It took place twenty years after the first movie ended.

"That movie was awesome!" said Derik. "And that Irina Frazier? Man, I wish I could've been that security guard she was distracting in that one scene. I would've gone crazy if she had been all over me like that."

"You know that was the director of the movie in that scene, right?" said Antoine. "He's her husband in real life. And don't you have a girlfriend?"

"I know who Morgan Abernathy is," scoffed Derik. "And her being married and me having a girlfriend doesn't make Irina Frazier any less hot. Ask any Black man what he thinks of her, and they'll all say the same thing whether they're single or not."

Antoine returned home a little before eleven that night. Mr. Brown was up waiting for him.

"Did you have fun?" asked Mr. Brown.

"Yeah."

"That's good," said Mr. Brown. As Antoine prepared to go to his room, Mr. Brown called him back.

"Sir?"

"You only took twenty dollars off my card, right?"

"Yes sir."

"You sure?"

"Yes sir."

"You're absolutely sure? You didn't accidentally mistype it?"

"Positive."

"Alright."

Antoine wondered why his father had questioned him like that. He was positive he had only taken twenty dollars off his father's card.

Thinking back to Derik's statements about Black men's views on Irina Frazier, Antoine decided to test it for himself.

"Dad, what do you think of Irina Frazier?"

"What do I think of her?"

"Yeah."

"She's a great actress if that's what you mean?"

"Do you think she's hot?"

"I'd say she's an attractive lady," said Mr. Brown as his face turned slightly pink.

"Is that your way of saying yes?" teased Antoine.

"Boy go to bed," said Mr. Brown, clearing his throat. "And don't try to sneak and play that game with the volume off either. I don't care if it is spring break."

"Yes sir."

Antoine went to his room. Andre was turned in for the night, but he was still awake.

"Andre, I have a question," said Antoine.

"What?" answered Andre.

"Do you think Irina Frazier is hot?"

"Yeah," said Andre. "Do you?"

"Yeah," said Antoine. He grabbed a towel and stuffed it in the crack of their bedroom door.

"What are you doing?" asked Andre.

"I need to see something real quick," said Antoine, turning on his gaming console.

He wanted to know why his father had kept questioning him about the twenty dollars. As he went to where his funds were, he noticed something was off.

He saw a one, an eight, and a four before the decimal. His heart dropped.

"Oh no," gasped Antoine. "Oh no!"

"What?" said Andre.

"I made a big mistake," said Antoine.

Antoine had not taken twenty dollars off his father's card like he thought. He had taken two hundred.

My Daddy Was The Man

My dad possessed a fiery spirit.
I never knew him any other way.
My dad was a man who knew no limit,
He always went headfirst into the fray.

I don't know what else there is I can say,
Except to admit that I am his fan,
Because my dad has always been the man.

Monday

Antoine had been a basket of nerves all weekend. He was sure his father would pounce on him about the two hundred dollars missing from his bank account.

But Mr. Brown had not said anything.

"You scammed your dad out of two hundred dollars?" said Derik as they ran on treadmills.

"I didn't scam him!" exclaimed Antoine. "I accidentally took too much out."

"How do you accidentally take out too much?"

"I wasn't paying attention, and I didn't have my glasses on. What am I going to do?"

"Have you told him?"

"No."

"Why not?"

"Because he'll get mad at me."

"But if you tell him it was an accident–!"

"You know how my dad is."

"Dang," said Derik. "If I could, I would give you the money but my parents have cut off all our allowances until they get the house rebuilt. And my job at The Courier is minimum wage."

Antoine did not know what to do. He knew he could not hide it forever. But he hoped he could hide it for a little longer until he figured something out.

Danielle sauntered past the boys. Derik's eyes followed her as a grin spread across his face. The two had spent the whole weekend together, and it made Antoine want to gag.

"Did you have fun on your little date?" said Antoine.

"Yeah. I had lots of fun. Her room is really pink."

"Her room? How do you know what her room looks like?"
"I was in it."
"Why were you in her room?"
"Why do you think?"
"I don't know.
"Her bed is really comfortable. She's got this gigantic teddy bear that takes up like half the bed."
"You were on her bed?"
"Yeah."
"Why?"
"That's where we hang out. And talk. And kiss."
Antoine resisted the urge to hurl.
"I can't believe you kissed her," said Antoine.
"You know Dani isn't the first girl I've kissed, right?"
"Yeah but... it's Dani."
"So?"
"Why do you like her?"
"What do you mean 'why do I like her'? She's my girlfriend."
"But why her?"
"I like her."
"But she's–!"
"*My girlfriend,*" said Derik, a hint of warning in his voice. "There's another side to her that people don't know. That's the side I like."
"I'll believe it when I see it."
"Then come see it."
"What?"
Derik turned off his treadmill and led Antoine over to Danielle, who was preparing to leave.
"Hey," said Derik.
"Hey," said Danielle.
"Want a ride?"
"Sure."

Before he knew it, Antoine was sitting in the backseat of Derik's car. He had not even gotten to finish his workout all because of Danielle's supposed nice side.

"So, how do you like your new grandma?" asked Derik.

"That lady is not my grandma," griped Danielle.

"You don't like her?"

"That lady knew exactly where my daddy was this whole time and said nothing," complained Danielle. "She gave him up because she was tired of being broke and never came back for him. Got married and everything and was just living her life like she didn't have a whole child down the street."

"Sounds like he was adopted out of pity then," said Derik, causing Danielle to grimace. He teased her, saying, "Don't make that face. You said it."

"So, what if I did?" said Danielle.

"It wasn't a nice thing to say."

"I wasn't in the mood to be nice."

"Why do you always have to be mean?"

"Sometimes you've got to be a little mean," said Danielle. "That's what my mom always says."

"Why'd she say that?"

"Because you can't let people walk all over you or else they'll think they can play with you."

"So that's why you're so mean?"

"I'm not mean," argued Danielle. "I just don't accept less than what I deserve."

"What do you think Ant?" asked Derik. "Is Dani mean?"

"Don't bring me in this," said Antoine.

"Aw come on! You know you want to say 'yes'."

Antoine did want to agree with Derik. He despised Danielle because of how mean she was. But one look at her staring him down in the rearview mirror stopped him from saying so.

"I plead the fifth," said Antoine.

"I'm going to take that as a yes," said Derik.

"Well, if I'm so mean then why are you dating me?" snapped Danielle.

"Maybe I like mean girls," said Derik.

"That explains a lot," scoffed Danielle.

"Like what?"

"Like how Ms. Nelson is your favorite teacher."

"Ms. Nelson isn't mean."

"Yes, she is. She's just good at hiding it."

"Antoine, do you think your future stepmother is mean?"

"Nope," said Antoine. "Gretchen is one of the nicest people I know."

"Well Dani, it seems like you're the only one who thinks she's mean."

"You know what, let me out here," demanded Danielle. "I'll walk home."

"Alright," said Derik, pulling over.

Danielle got out and slammed the door. Antoine watched as she started walking up the road.

"Is she really going to walk?" asked Antoine.

"I guess," said Derik. "We'll let her have her little hissy fit until her feet get tired and she decides to get back in the car."

"What if she doesn't?"

"Well, either way she'll get home."

Danielle never got back in the car. What should have been a short drive from the recreation center to her house became a half-hour journey of the boys riding alongside her all the way home. When they reached her lawn, Derik rolled down his window to get her attention.

"Enjoy your walk?" called Derik.

"Shut up!" hollered Danielle. "You and your stupid little sidekick are a pair of jerks!"

"I love you too," laughed Derik. "Can I get a goodbye kiss?"

"Can you get a goodbye kiss," huffed Danielle. She stomped over to the car and kicked the passenger door, hollering, "There's your goodbye kiss!"

"Hey girl!" screeched Derik. "Don't you dent my car up now!"

"Or what?!" argued Danielle. "What you going to do about it, huh?!"

Derik's nostrils flared and his lips upturned into a snarl. But Antoine was focused on Derik's eyes. His eyes had gone dark and filled with anger.

"Hey," said Antoine, placing his hand on Derik's shoulder. Derik flicked those angry eyes to him. "I need to get home."

Derik shot one final glare at Danielle and pulled off. Once they were down the road, he pulled over and told Antoine to get in the front passenger seat.

"Can you believe that girl?!" ranted Derik when they were driving again. "Kicking my car like that!"

"That's your girlfriend," snickered Antoine.

"Shut up!" snapped Derik.

"That was a little intense though," admitted Antoine.

"What are you talking about?" asked Derik annoyedly.

"The face you made after she kicked your car," whispered Antoine. "I thought you were going to do something to her."

"What?" said Derik, like he was startled. "Ant, I don't hit girls."

"You didn't see your face," said Antoine. "Your eyes looked... they looked like your dad's."

"He doesn't hit girls either, so I don't know why you thought I'd do something like that to Dani."

"I just didn't want something bad to happen."

"Nothing bad would've happened. We probably would've just argued, and I would've left."

The conversation died after that. But Antoine knew he would never forget the look Derik had had in his eyes.

Derik dropped Antoine off at home. Mr. Brown was watching an episode of 'Brethren'.

"Hey Dad," said Antoine.

"Antoine," said Mr. Brown, muting the television.

"Sir?"

"How long are you going to wait before you tell me you stole two-hundred dollars out my account?"

Antoine froze.

"You must've thought I was a special brand of stupid not to notice something like that," said Mr. Brown. Antoine looked down guiltily, causing Mr. Brown to snap out, "Look at me when I'm talking to you!"

Antoine reluctantly raised his head and looked at his father, who stood before him with his hands on his hips. The infamous scar above his father's eye seemed more imposing than ever.

"You lied to me," accused Mr. Brown, glaring into Antoine's eyes. "I specifically asked you if you took twenty dollars from my account and what did you say?"

Antoine did not answer.

"What did you say?" repeated Mr. Brown, holding a hand to his ear.

"I said yes," muttered Antoine.

"You said yes," confirmed Mr. Brown. "So, why is there two-hundred dollars missing from my bank account?"

"It was an accident!" blurted Antoine.

"Now it was an accident."

"It was. I really did think I only took twenty dollars when you asked but when I went back and checked it was two-hundred."

"Then why didn't you tell me?" questioned Mr. Brown. His angry figure towered over Antoine, demanding an answer. "Why did you continue lying to me?"

Antoine did not answer. He did not want to say he was afraid his father would get angry like he was then.

"You need to get my money back," declared Mr. Brown.

"It's non-refundable," admitted Antoine.

"Well, then I'll just have to hold on to your gaming system until you give me my money back," said Mr. Brown. "I want it in my room within the next five minutes. You'll get it back when I get my two-hundred dollars."

"How am I supposed to get two-hundred dollars?"

"You better figure it out."

-

Father Of The Year

There was once a time before I was a man,
When I was a boy who believed 'I can'.
I believed I could be anything,
And all I long to do was to sing.
But as I began to grow,
And feel myself becoming old,
Everything I dreamed and all that I saw,
For myself began to grow small.
Now, I'm in charge of six young men and women,
And it's my job to recognize when,
They start to see less for themselves,
And stop them from putting their dreams on shelves.
Sometimes that's easier said than done,
And sometimes I have to be the tough one.
But through it all I hope and pray,
That they'll appreciate what I've done one day.

Tuesday

Antoine had spent the night coming up with a plan. Andre had helped some, but he had gotten distracted, so Antoine did most of the planning.

He figured he could easily raise the money by charging people twenty dollars to cut their lawns. All he needed was ten people to say yes, and he would have the money and, more importantly, his gaming system back in no time.

He started with his aunts and uncles. First was Aunt Francine Brown.

Aunt Francine was cleaning the kitchen when Antoine arrived. He sat at her table, watching her wash dishes.

"Aunt Franny, can I cut your grass for twenty dollars?"

"You can cut it for ten," answered Aunt Francine, her back still turned to him.

"No, it's got to be twenty. I won't do it for anything less."

"Quite the businessman, aren't we?" laughed Aunt Francine. Antoine beamed with pride until she said, "But there's just one small issue that hurts your negotiating."

"What?"

"Alex."

"What does Alex have to do with me cutting your grass?"

"I'll show you," said Aunt Francine. "Alexander!"

"Ma'am?" answered Alexander when he entered the kitchen.

"I need you to cut the grass."

"Yes ma'am," said Alexander. It had seemed like he wanted to protest. Antoine figured he was working on a new beat or maybe felt it was too hot outside. But he had simply agreed and disappeared.

"See?" said Aunt Francine with a smirk. "I could get it done for free but I'm trying to help you out Nephew. So, ten dollars or nothing. Final offer."

"Alright," sighed Antoine.

"Alright," said Aunt Francine. She hollered to Alexander, "Never mind, Alex! Antoine's going to do it!"

"Okay!" answered Alexander, sounding pleased.

It had not taken long to cut Aunt Francine's yard. Two hours and ten dollars later, he stood in Aunt Marie's living room, asking her the same question.

"I'm sorry sweetie," apologized Aunt Marie. "Your uncle just cut the grass this past weekend."

"Is there anything else I can do?"

"Not that I know of," said Aunt Marie with a frown. "I'm sorry. I wish there was something I could do."

"It's alright," sighed Antoine.

He left. Halfway down the road, he heard someone running behind him, calling his name.

"Hey!" called Mariella. "Wait!"

"What?" said Antoine when Mariella caught up with him.

"I'm going with you."

"No, you're not."

"Yes, I am. I'm bored out my mind."

"What's that got to do with me? Don't you have friends to hang out with?"

"Mariana keeps going out without me and Dani has been spending all her time with Derik."

Antoine pursed his lips and exhaled through his nostrils. He knew firsthand just how much time Danielle had spent with Derik. It was more than enough to ensure his best friend had no time to hang out anymore.

"What are you doing?" asked Mariella.

"I'm making money," answered Antoine.

"I want to make money too."

"Fine," grumbled Antoine. "Come on."

"Let me get my bike," said Mariella.

The two biked to their Uncle Terrence's house, where Aunt Sarah sat on the porch in a rocking chair. She had just won a big case for her law firm and was taking some much-needed time off.

"Hi Aunt Sarah," said Antoine.

"Can we cut your grass for fifty dollars?" blurted Mariella, causing Antoine to glare at her.

"That's a lot of money to cut a lawn," said Aunt Sarah.

"Twenty-five for the front, twenty-five for the back," said Mariella.

"I could always get Junior or Mike to do it for free," reasoned Aunt Sarah.

"You would've done it by now," countered Mariella. "You can keep waiting for them to do it, or you can have a nice-looking lawn by the end of today for fifty dollars. Your choice."

"How about twenty and I feed you?"

"She don't want her grass cut for real," said Mariella.

"She don't," agreed Antoine "Let's go."

"Last chance Aunt Sarah before we leave," said Mariella. "Imagine how grateful Uncle Thusi will be when he comes home and sees he doesn't have to worry about the grass. And I know you've got fifty dollars because you just won that big case and lawyers aren't broke. And you don't look broke Aunt Sarah. Are you broke?"

"No."

"So, you can afford to pay fifty dollars to get your grass cut, right?"

"Yeah."

"So, you're going to pay us to cut your grass for fifty dollars, right?"

"Baby, we need to work on your negotiating skills," chuckled Aunt Sarah. "You can't insult your client into paying for your services. But since you're so persistent, I'll let you cut my lawn for fifty dollars. But if you mess it up, you're going to have to deal with Mr. Parker."

"We won't mess it up," said Mariella. "Antoine, you get to work while I secure the money."

"Okay," said Antoine. "Uh... can I use your lawnmower Aunt Sarah?"

"You can rent it for ten dollars," said Aunt Sarah. "It's in the shed."

Four hours and forty dollars later, Antoine had cut Aunt Sarah's lawn. She had been kind enough to prepare him a sandwich at lunchtime. When the job was finished, Mariella handed him his money.

"Here you go," said Mariella.

"This is only twenty," said Antoine.

"That's your cut."

"My cut? You took half my money!"

"I did half the work."

"Where? Last time I checked I was the one slaving out in the sun while you were in the house with Aunt Sarah."

"I negotiated the deal. And you showed up unprepared and lost us ten dollars."

"If I'd known you were going to take half my money, I would've left you where you was!" griped Antoine. "I'm never working with you again! Taking half my money...!"

Antoine and Mariella knew it was pointless to stop by Aunt Ruth-Anne's. Her house was always neat, inside and out. And since Antoine had no lawnmower with him and was out of aunts and uncles, it was less likely anyone else would let him cut their grass with their equipment.

He had no choice but to call it a day.

Antoine had made thirty dollars off his aunts. It was not what he had hoped to make, but he still had five days left of spring break. He was sure he could make the money back before school resumed.

That evening, Antoine went to boy's bible study and got paired up with Derek for their assignment.

"It's funny," said Derek. "I'm dating your sister, but I feel like we barely talk."

"Probably because we barely see each other," answered Antoine. "How's your leg?"

"It's getting there," said Derek. "So, how can I be your keeper today?"

"I'm not sure," said Antoine. "Know anyone that's hiring?"

"Not for your age," said Derek. "You trying to make money or something?"

"Something like that."

"There's got to be something you can do," reasoned Derek. "Maybe the church bulletin board will have something. People are always posting things they need on there."

"That's an idea," said Antoine. "Thanks."

"You're welcome," said Derek. "As for me, I don't need any keeping tonight."

"Okay."

Derik was talking to Justin Holmes. Justin was a senior and had been the quarterback of the football team. He had signed to play college football at a big university and hoped to one day make it into the league.

After bible study ended, Antoine sat beside Derik.

"Me and Dani made up," said Derik.

"That's nice," said Antoine.

"I told her what you thought was going to happen. She thought I was going to get out and try and kiss her."

Derik chuckled, causing Antoine to shrink in his chair.

"What were you and Justin talking about?" asked Antoine, changing the subject.

"School newspaper. We're partnering on an article."

"You are?"

"Yeah. Justin writes for the sports section."

"He's part of the school paper?"

Derik grew quiet.

"What?"

"Do you not read the paper?"

Antoine blushed.

"Wow," said Derik.

"I–!"

"No," interjected Derik. "Don't dig yourself deeper."

Antoine knew how important the school newspaper was to Derik. Derik was the editor-in-chief of The Creeke High Gazette and worked part-time at The Creeke Courier. He hoped to go into a full-time journalism career after graduating college.

Antoine did not yet know what he wanted to do with his life. He was still only a freshman. His current goal was to just make it through high school.

He did have interests though. Antoine liked making music mixes. And he also liked video games. His recent favorite was a first-person shooter where he played as a soldier.

"Justin has been part of the paper since his freshman year," said Derik.

"Oh."

"How goes your quest to pay your father back?"

"I made thirty dollars today," reported Antoine. "It would've been fifty, but Mariella stole half my money."

"Thirty is not half of fifty," said Derik quietly.

"I know," said Antoine. "I got ten from cutting Aunt Franny's lawn, and I was going to do Aunt Sarah's for twenty. But then Mariella negotiated her to fifty, then Aunt Sarah took off ten to rent her lawnmower, and then Mariella took twenty talking about some it was her cut."

"Ant, you've got to do better than this," said Derik, shaking his head. "That's thirty dollars that you lost."

"I know," sighed Antoine.

Mr. Brown arrived to take his children and nieces home before Antoine had a chance to check the bulletin board. Mariella sat next to Antoine, and he tried not to glare at her.

"Want to make fifty dollars tomorrow?" asked Mariella.

"You mean twenty-five since you're going to take half?" scoffed Antoine.

"I mean fifty," repeated Mariella. "The job is paying one hundred but I'm subtracting my cut from it."

"Why do you get half my money?"

"I'm doing half the work!"

"What's the job?" grumbled Antoine.

"Mr. Payne needs his garage cleaned out and I told him we could help," explained Mariella. "Mrs. Rachel will be there to help us."

"How'd you find out about this?"

"The church bulletin board," said Mariella. "He had just put it up there when he came to pick Priscella up and I snatched it down before anyone else could see it."

"That was smart," said Antoine.

"I know," said Mariella haughtily. "So, what do you say?"

"Okay," said Antoine after giving it some thought.

If things went according to plan, he would have eighty dollars and be almost halfway to his goal. He felt confident he would have his father's money in no time.

Trials Of The Son

There comes a time in the lives of young men,
When who they are must be put to the test,
And they must wake up the warrior in them,
And prove that his manhood isn't hopeless.
At fourteen, Antoine awoke from his rest,
To contend with a man who was so tough,
And full of fire, and passion, and zest,
A man who's childhood had been so rough,
That his manhood could not be called a bluff.

This tough man which Antoine had to contend,
Had been raised by a man tougher than he.
Who, when his time had arrived at its end,
Had ensured his charge was tough as could be.
This tough man on Antoine had been easy,
Until Antoine told a lie to his face,
And the tough man realized, and he could see,
That upon his hands he now had a case,
To toughen his boy and do it with haste.

But the tough man still had in him a heart,
And knew well from his own test of manhood,
That the trials ahead could get real hard.
So, he did what only a tough man could,
And started smaller than his mentor would,
And gave Antoine something simple to win,
And decided that all that Antoine should
do is repay what it is that he spent.
So now Antoine's test of manhood begins.

Wednesday

Antoine and Mariella were at the Payne residence bright and early on Wednesday.

"Well, good morning," said Mrs. Rachel Payne in her sugary, sweet voice. "Don't you two look ready to work hard today?"

"We are ma'am," answered Antoine.

"Good," said Mrs. Payne. "I'll show you to the garage."

The Paynes' garage was big enough to hold two cars. And it was filled with junk and boxes.

Mrs. Payne wanted Antoine and Mariella to separate everything into three piles. One for things the Paynes still wanted, another for things they could give away, and the third for trash.

It took a while for Mrs. Payne to go through everything she wanted to keep. By the time she finished, it was nearing lunchtime. But unlike Aunt Sarah, Mrs. Payne did not offer any refreshments.

"I believe that's everything we're keeping," said Mrs. Payne. "You two can carry the trash to the curb and load up what we're giving away on Mr. Payne's truck."

Taking the trash out was the easy part. Loading the giveaway items was the hard part. Some of the items were just too heavy for two fourteen-year-olds to handle.

"I need a break," said Mariella.

"You can't take a break," cried Antoine. "I need this money."

"I need a break and I'm taking it!" snapped Mariella. She sat down on the ground, looking annoyed. "The least she could've done was give us some water!"

Priscella entered the garage with her dog Leafy in tow. Leafy ran toward Mariella and began trying to lick her sweaty face.

"Hi Leafy!" squealed Mariella, playing with the dog. "Hi boy!"

Neither Antoine nor Mariella were particularly fond of Priscella. Antoine disliked her because she had been Danielle's sidekick for years and had only recently seen the light a few months ago. Mariella disliked her because Priscella had gotten her in trouble when she saw the light.

"What are you doing?" asked Priscella.

"Working," said Antoine.

"On what?"

"Nun'ya."

"What's nun'ya?"

"Nun'ya business," said Antoine.

Priscella blinked. Then she tilted her head and confusedly asked, "What's that?"

"Lord," muttered Mariella, petting Leafy.

"Did you just come in here to bother us?" questioned Antoine.

"Bother you?" replied Priscella.

"We're trying to work here."

"I don't see any work being done," said Priscella. Antoine knew she more than likely meant it literally than mockingly, but he was still annoyed.

"That's because you've probably been sleep all day," said Antoine.

"No, I've been cleaning the house," explained Priscella.

"Don't you think you should get back to it?" questioned Antoine, wanting her to go away.

"Rude!" said Priscella. "How sad!"

"So sad," said Mariella.

The girls stared awkwardly at each other.

"Uh... very sad?" said Antoine.

"Ugh," uttered Priscella, rolling her eyes. She snapped her fingers and commanded, "Leafy! Potty!"

Leafy ran off into the yard, pottied, and returned inside with Priscella minutes later.

"I don't see any work being done," mocked Antoine. "I can't stand her, Dani, or her minions!"

"Now wait a minute!" whined Mariella. "I am not a minion!"

"Why'd you even become friends with them?" asked Antoine. "Were you that desperate?"

"First of all, Dani wanted to be *our* friend," corrected Mariella. "She came to *us* and started hanging out with *us*."

"Does it matter? Either way everyone thinks you're her follower."

"Let's just get this done so we can go," said Mariella, standing up. "I'm not about to listen to you talk smack about me all day."

Cleaning out the garage took most of the day. By the time they finished, Antoine and Mariella were exhausted. Mrs. Payne stood in the garage with Priscella and nodded her head.

"Well done," said Mrs. Payne. She handed dollar bills to Antoine and Mariella, saying, "Here's your pay."

"This is only twenty-five dollars," said Mariella, counting her cut. Antoine counted his cut and discovered he too only had twenty-five dollars.

"That's all Mr. Payne left," said Mrs. Payne.

"I was told we were getting a hundred," said Mariella.

"Well, that's all he left," said Mrs. Payne. "Take it or leave it."

"Let's just take it," said Antoine.

"No," said Mariella. "We worked for a hundred dollars. I want my money."

"Do you have it in writing?" asked Mrs. Payne with a smirk.

"No but–!"

"Then you can't prove that you were supposed to be paid one hundred dollars. You could've made that up for all I know."

"I did not make anything up!" said Mariella. "Mr. Payne told me we were getting a hundred dollars and that's what I want! I done sat up here and slaved all day in this hot garage! Somebody going to pay me my money!"

"You better get out of here before I call the police," said Mrs. Payne.

"Call them!" declared Mariella. "I'll call them for you because you're ripping us off!"

"That's all Mr. Payne left," reiterated Mrs. Payne. "I'm not going to say it again."

Mariella stared long and hard at Mrs. Payne. Then she grabbed Antoine's hand and led him out of the garage.

"I can't believe this!" ranted Mariella as she mounted her bike. "All that hard work just to get ripped off!"

Antoine was just as angry. He had half a mind to go back and demand the rest of his money. As he contemplated, he saw Priscella standing in the yard, watching them go. And he decided to let it go, believing God would get them for their ugly.

As Antoine and Mariella biked home, they heard someone beep a car horn at them. Uncle Terrence pulled up beside them in his police car.

"What you two out here doing?" asked Uncle Terrence.

"We just got done cleaning out the Paynes's garage," explained Antoine.

"Alright," said Uncle Terrence. He looked at Mariella and said, "You better not be getting in no trouble out here or I'll have to put you in the back of the car."

"We're not," grumbled Mariella.

"Alright," said Uncle Terrence, pulling off.

"You see how they do me?" complained Mariella. "I'm just out here riding my bike and they assume the worst from me."

"He was talking to both of us," said Antoine.

"But he was looking at me," countered Mariella. "They always do that to me like I'm just the worst niece in the world.

Mariella pedaled off in a huff, and Antoine followed her to her house. Uncle Alejandro sat in the living room watching a baseball game.

"¡CORRE!" hollered Uncle Alejandro at the batter running the bases. "¡CORRE!"

"Hola Papá," said Mariella.

"Hola, hola," said Uncle Alejandro, waving the pair away without even glancing at them. "¡CORRE!"

Antoine followed Mariella to the kitchen, where Aunt Marie typed away on her computer.

"Hola Mamá," said Mariella. "What are you doing?"

"Taxes," said Aunt Marie. "Hi Nephew."

"Hi," said Antoine.

"We ran into Uncle Thusi today," said Mariella. "He threatened to put me in the back of his police car."

"What were you doing?" asked Aunt Marie.

"Riding my bike."

Aunt Marie scrunched her face and looked at Mariella.

"Riding your bike?"

"Mhmm."

"Let me call him," said Aunt Marie, grabbing her phone. Moments later, she was in conversation with Uncle Terrence.

"Hello?... Thusi, why did Mariella tell me you threatened to put her in the back of your police car?... Mhmm... Mhmm... What was she doing?... Mhmm... If that's all she was doing, why did you say it like that?... You could've just said, 'Oh make sure you're staying out of trouble'... I'm not arguing, I just want to know what's going on... You don't have to yell at me, I was just calling to see what the issue was... Okay bye."

"What'd he say?" asked Mariella.

"He said he was just making sure you guys weren't getting into any trouble," answered Aunt Marie.

"Mhmm. Okay."

"How did cleaning the Paynes's garage go?"

"Terrible," complained Mariella. "It was terrible, and they ripped us off!"

"By how much?" asked Aunt Marie.

"Fifty dollars!" said Mariella. "We were supposed to get a hundred!"

"Mhmm," said Aunt Marie. "They did the same thing to your father when he helped Mr. Payne move all their new furniture in. Claimed they would pay him and sent him home empty-handed. They almost found out where your father was from that day, but I told him not to worry about it."

"Mamá, why didn't you warn me?!" cried Mariella.

"I thought it was a good opportunity for you and Priscella to talk and try to make up," said Aunt Marie.

"I don't want to make up with her!" ranted Mariella. "I want my hundred dollars!"

"Okay," said Aunt Marie. "No need to yell at me about it."

"You knew this would happen and you didn't say anything!"

"Sorry," apologized Aunt Marie. "I'll give you your money if you want."

"Ugh!" scoffed Mariella, stomping off to her room. She slammed the door, and Aunt Marie continued working on her taxes.

Antoine was awed by what he had witnessed. He knew that if he had talked and acted toward his parents like Mariella had with Aunt Marie, the outcome would have been vastly different. Sometimes though, he wished he could do what Mariella had done and face no consequences.

Friendship?

Who ever thought a Brown and a Harrison,
Would turn out to be best friends?
Or that another Harrison and a Brown,
would fall in love in this town?
In my day, those two things didn't mix,
Unless there was a face to fix.
A Harrison was a Brown's worst enemy.
Friendship was never something that could be.
Of course, not all the Harrisons were terrible,
Just like how certain Browns are unbearable.
But the Harrison closest to I,
Was one with who I couldn't see eye to eye.
But with his son my son has grown close.
And he's the best friend my son has chose.
And seeing them together makes me question,
Is this what friendship with him would have been?

-

Thursday

It was Andre's birthday.

Antoine had wanted to go all out for his brother's eighteenth birthday. But he had to make his money. The best he could do was give Andre birthday licks.

Dealing with The Paynes's shadiness had taught Antoine another business lesson. In addition to showing up prepared, he had started requiring people to pay him fully upfront.

Unfortunately, he found that people were less willing to employ him when they had to pay upfront. They claimed if they paid him before the work was done, he would not do as good a job. Antoine tried to get them to understand why he had adopted the new policy, but it was no use.

By noon, Antoine was unsure of what to do. He was ready to give up and go home when Derik called him.

"Hello?" said Antoine.

"How goes your quest?" asked Derik.

"Not good," sighed Antoine. "I've only made fifty-five dollars so far."

"You're one-fourth of the way there."

"Yeah, but I've only got today left because tomorrow's wedding prep, the wedding is Saturday, church on Sunday, and we're back in school on Monday."

"Well, what you doing today?"

"I don't know. Nobody wants to pay me upfront so I can't get no work."

"So, you just going to give up?"

"I just don't know what to do anymore."

"Where are you?"

"Walking home."

"Alright."

That was the end of the conversation. Antoine figured Derik did not want to hear about his problems. But ten minutes later, Derik pulled up beside him.

"What are you doing here?" asked Antoine.

"I'm taking you to make some money," said Derik. "Get in."

"Make some money where?" asked Antoine. "And how did you know where I was?"

"I just drove around till I saw you," said Derik. "My granddad needs help clearing out the church storage room. We're going to get you to at least a hundred by the end of the day."

And that's what Derik did. He and Antoine cleared out the storage room and got fifty dollars each for it. But Antoine noticed Derik looked troubled during the whole ordeal.

"What's the matter?" asked Antoine while they took a break.

"This is where I was," whispered Derik. "Where I hid at in the church when I escaped from Hakeem. I slept right over there in the corner behind those boxes."

Antoine looked where Derik pointed, then looked back at his friend. Derik stared at that spot with a pained expression, then stood up.

"Let's get this done so we can get out of here," said Derik.

They finished right before dinnertime, and Derik drove him back home. Sitting in his driveway, Antoine marveled at the fifty dollars in his hand. He had reached the halfway point.

"Why did you do this for me?" asked Antoine.

"What you mean?" said Derik. "You're my boy. I can't just let you go out sad."

"I don't know how I can make this up to you."

"Don't worry about it."

Antoine stared at his best friend. His best friend, who had come through for him and brought him closer to his goal.

"What you looking at me like that for?" asked Derik.

"Because I just don't get you," said Antoine.

"You don't get me?"

"You're just so... free," said Antoine, unable to describe what he meant. "You just do whatever you want. And you're never scared of anything or anyone. I just don't get it."

"I just have a different view of life, that's all," said Derik. "I realized I don't have time to waste on stupid stuff anymore because anything can happen to me at any moment. But things aren't any less scarier. In fact, things are more scary because I'm more aware of the danger around me."

Derik made the same pained expression again.

"You don't know how good you have it," said Derik. "To still be so innocent about the world."

"Innocent?" questioned Antoine.

"Everything about the world has changed for me," said Derik. "I feel like someone hit the fast forward button on my life. And the sad part is, all of this happened because my dad couldn't answer a simple stupid question. I wish my dad was more like yours."

"You do?" asked Antoine, furrowing his brow.

"Don't look at me like that," said Derik. "I know I got into it with him at the beginning of the school year but it's true. Your dad cares about you. He's always telling you he loves you. My dad doesn't do that. He never has."

"You don't think he loves you?"

"He told me he doesn't hate me," answered Derik. "He told me I was a part of his life. But that doesn't mean he loves me either."

"What does it mean then?"

"I don't know," sighed Derik. "I never know what he's thinking. Everyone always know what your dad thinks and how he feels."

"It's not always a good thing," said Antoine. "Especially when he's disappointed in you."

"I'd even take your dad being disappointed over my dad's nothing," said Derik. He shook his head, then let out a small chuckle. "Derek has a better relationship with him than I do. Isn't that funny? He has a better relationship with the Derek that isn't his son."

Antoine did not know what to say.

"You better go inside," said Derik.

"Why?" asked Antoine.

"Your dad will be looking for you."

But Antoine discovered that Mr. Brown was not looking for him, nor was he home. He lay on his bed thinking about what Derik had told him and found that he agreed. Even though his father could be over-bearing at times, he knew there was no one else he would rather have as a father. And for the first time, he felt like he had failed as a son.

Does Daddy Raise A Man?

This wasn't how things were supposed to go.
Things weren't supposed to be this difficult.
This life has become a powerful foe,
And I am not yet even an adult.
I long for the days of childish glow,
Before I received this most vicious jolt.
I don't know how much more I can withstand.
Is this how my daddy raises a man?

Friday

By Friday, Antoine had managed to make it halfway to his goal. But he was out of time.

The whole weekend would be dedicated to the wedding. Therefore, Antoine would not have any time to make money. Knowing this had annoyed him the whole morning.

Antoine ended up getting his hair cut by Deidrick at the barbershop. Since he was sitting next to his father, he could hear every word of their conversation.

"You better not slice my throat," warned Mr. Brown when he first sat down.

"I'm not a murderer, Brown," said Mr. Harrison, as he tied the protective smock around Mr. Brown's neck.

"You're not a friend either."

"Don't need to be a friend to give you a cut."

"Just don't mess up my hair."

"Don't mess up my payment."

"You'll get your money."

"And you'll get a good cut."

Antoine noticed that Mr. Kasey kept trying to talk to Andre. Mr. Brown noticed too. He felt bad that his brother could not even have a conversation like he obviously wanted to.

After Mr. Kasey went into the salon and came back, the barbershop conversation shifted to the new Drake Malone.

"Man Fina, Kasey, and I went to see that new Drake Malone yesterday and that movie was good!" exclaimed Mr. Zackariah. "And that Irina Frazier? Man if I wasn't already married–!"

"You still wouldn't have a chance," joked Mr. Kasey. "I don't know how you managed to pull Fina but you better hang on to her."

"What you mean 'how I managed'?"

"Boy I remember that time you tried to pull Leya and she called you broke," laughed Mr. Kasey.

"Well, I ain't broke now," said Mr. Zackariah. "And I know you ain't talking because you couldn't pull Leya either. She looked you up and down and busted out laughing!"

"Sirs," said Mrs. Harrison, coming into the barbershop. "Why do I keep hearing my name?"

"We're just talking," said Mr. Kasey.

"Mhmm," muttered Mrs. Harrison. "Do you get paid to talk or to work?"

"Now Leya."

"Just do your job and leave my name out of it," said Mrs. Harrison, disappearing back into the salon.

"Dummies," said Mr. Harrison.

"You can't tell me you don't think Irina looks good, Marlin," said Mr. Zackariah. "Even you've got to admit she's bad."

"I don't got to admit nothing."

"Well, I'll say it," said Mr. Zackariah. "It's a lot of pretty women on this earth and I'd be doing them a disservice not to take notice."

"You talk like you're not married," said Mr. Harrison.

"I'm happily married with kids," said Zackariah. "And Fina is everything I've ever wanted in a woman. You think I'd mess something like that up?"

Antoine realized that Derik had been right. Every Black man he had heard talk about Irina Frazier loved her.

'Rite of Passage' came on.

"Now, this right here is the joint!" laughed Mr. Zackariah. "Not that new mess they playing these days."

"That Rite of Passage remix was hot garbage," said Mr. Kasey. "I ain't never turned off the radio so fast in my life."

"See? That's what you get for trying to keep up with these young bucks. You need to stick to the good music that you're used to."

"Aw, hold on now," said Deidrick. "It's some good artists out here."

"Name me one good artist that's out right now," challenged Mr. Zackariah.

While Deidrick, Mr. Zackariah, and Mr. Kasey debated about the sorry state of the music industry, Mr. Brown and Mr. Harrison engaged in a different conversation.

"I didn't know you liked this song," said Mr. Brown.

"I didn't know you liked it either," said Mr. Harrison.

"How could I not like 'Rite of Passage'?

"How should I know what you like? We're not friends."

"I used to sneak and listen to it when my grandpa wasn't home."

"I used to sneak and listen to it too," said Mr. Harrison. "The whole album. Especially 'Draws'."

"You're not going to put it on, are you? I don't want my sons hearing that."

"I wouldn't put it on even if you wanted me to. Leya would kill me if I played something like that during business hours."

"Okay."

"Rite of Passage is a good song though," said Mr. Harrison. "King Roy's son sampled it for his new song. My daughter put it on while we were playing chess, and it was so crappy I had to cut it off."

"I'm not surprised. A lot of music these days just seems terrible."

"Yeah."

Another one of The Boombox Boyz's songs started playing.

"This is the song that–!" began Mr. Harrison before suddenly stopping.

"What?" questioned Mr. Brown.

"That night you had that panic attack. This was what was playing."

"You remember that?" asked Mr. Brown, his face growing pink from embarrassment.

"I remember a lot of things," said Mr. Harrison.

"Even the night when...?"

"Yeah."

Mr. Harrison spun Mr. Brown to face him. As he began shaping Mr. Brown's hairline, Mr. Brown looked at him with uneasy eyes.

"What?" asked Mr. Harrison.

"Why do you remember those things about me?" questioned Mr. Brown.

"Because I learned some things those nights."

"To use against me?"

"No," answered Mr. Harrison. "Remember the first time we fought in junior high? Because you got me in trouble?"

"Why?"

"My dad told me after that fight that I could really hurt you because I was a lot stronger than you. Don't move or you'll mess your hairline up!"

"I don't want to hear this! And you're not stronger than me! I've beaten you before!"

"You mean the one time I didn't fight back because I didn't feel like it?"

Mr. Brown became silent.

"If you want to know why I remember all that stuff then you need to listen," continued Mr. Harrison. "Like I said, my dad said I was a lot stronger than you. So, every time you wanted to fight, I went easy on you. But that one time you threw your shoe at my head, I decided not to go easy on you because you pissed me off with that."

"Well, I wouldn't have thrown my shoe at you if you wouldn't have called my sister a pig!"

"I didn't call her a pig," griped Mr. Harrison. "I got dared to use a pickup line on her using the word 'pig' because she had on a pink bathing suit."

"Then why didn't you just say that?"

"I was young and dumb, and I was getting tired of fighting with you," said Mr. Harrison. "I knew you'd come after me, but I wasn't expecting a shoe to the head. So, when you did that I decided to show you how badly I could really hurt you. But that night you had that panic attack showed me what my dad really meant."

"Why are you telling me all this?" asked Mr. Brown.

"You asked," said Mr. Harrison.

"But what does it have to do with why you remember that stuff about me?"

"Because I learned stuff about myself those nights."

"About yourself?"

"You're done," said Mr. Harrison, giving Mr. Brown a mirror to look at himself.

"What'd you learn about yourself?"

"None of your business," said Mr. Harrison. "Where's my money?"

"Here," said Mr. Brown, handing Mr. Harrison the payment for his haircut. He looked at Mr. Harrison again with uneasy eyes before leaving.

That evening, Antoine and his siblings sat around the table for dinner, tension filling the room. He was not sure what was wrong with everyone else, but he knew for himself that he felt down because he had failed to repay his father before the break ended.

He had disappointed his dad and himself. And that made him feel like a failure as a son and a man.

-

Interlude

The Last Supper

I just wanna know where I went wrong,
Cuz I always figured we all got along.
On the eve of my wedding at my dinner table,
The tension in the air was so unstable.
So, I said, "Why is everyone so quiet?"
But I didn't know that that would start a riot.
Cuz none of you paid me no mind,
Until I asked Andre if he'd be so kind,
As to pass the salt from his hand to mine,
But of course, the boy don't never give me his time,
So, I had to let him know who the boss was here,
Cuz how he ain't hear me when he sitting so near?
But he wasn't the only one who couldn't hear tonight,
Cuz everyone was looking like something just wasn't right.
I figured the issue was my incoming wife,
But I knew she wasn't trying to ruin a life,
Or six, so I tried to spread a little hope.
But Miss Karla over there had to be a dope,
And say "Gretchen's not the problem. The problem is you."
And I'm like "How am I the problem? What did I do?"
You see, this isn't surprising coming from Karla,
But it's really surprising when it comes from all of ya.
Drake, I thought we already talked about this,
Last fall when you threw your little hissy fit.
Karla always got a darn problem with me.
And I don't understand why she won't let me be.
Out of some strange allegiance she got for her mother,
And whole time her mother's in love with another.
Mary Ann, Marianne, both of you are traitors,
Both studding that man who wouldn't bother to save you.
And speaking of men that I just can't stand,
Kasey's found in Andre a number one fan.

What's Adrianna even mad for?
Cuz I won't let her little boyfriend in the door?
And Antoine chose to be a liar and a thief,
So, I don't understand why he's mad at me.
I just think it's really funny,
How everyone's suddenly got a problem with me.
And if you meant to hurt me with your foolishness,
Well, congratulations, you got your wish.

Sister, Sister

Today's the big day
and I'm nervous as can be.
Will I make him happy?

Today's the big day
and I'm nervous as can be.

Will I be set free?

I wasn't supposed to be here,
Beyond that of a single year.

I wasn't supposed to find him,
My heart was meant to be sealed.

And yet, here I have,
A man who loves me
As I am.
Even when I doubted his love

And yet, here I have,
A man who loves me
As I am.
Even when I doubted his love
And called him a liar

And called him a cheater

Called him silly.

Moody.

Sweet.

Sour.

For loving me
Because I thought
I had no more love to give

I thought I'd be single
As long as I live
He came along

He held on strong
And loved me for me
And changed my song.
But now I'm scared

And loved me for me
And changed my song.
But now I'm scared
That I'll disappoint him

That I'll chase him off

He's been married before
And that ended in divorce

Once left at the altar

Will I run that same course?

His kids are all lovely
But will I suffice?
Or will they all hate me
As time goes by?　As time goes by
He's chasing his loves
And that includes mine
But will he grow tired?
Is this path of mine right?　Is this path of mine right?
It's my big day　It's her big day
And I'm worried about me

Am I getting cold feet?

Let me go see her
And make sure she's complete

Can I really do this?
Is there anyone who could?
Love a man with anger like fire?
Accept his kids without any ire?
He wants another with me at his side
Can I love them all
Knowing only one is truly mine?
My parents seem to think so
But a grandkid is their end goal
Am I truly up to this task?
I'm scared that I'll fail
Scared that I won't last

"Gretchen."

Let me throw on a mask
"Hey!"

The fear is written all over her
"You look like you're about to high tail it
right out of this church!"
"So I'm a little nervous."
"I'd be too if I were marrying Torrance."

It was meant to be a joke
As I checked her corset

Does she know something I don't?
Is everything not all set?
Is Torrance really the right one?
I saw her panicked face in the mirror
Lord, what have I done?
"I was joking."

"But what if you're right?
What if he decides
I won't be his wife?"

"That won't happen to you.
Your story won't be mine.
Besides, he loves you too much
To leave you high and dry."

"How do you know?"

"Because you'll see it
The moment you look in his eyes."

His eyes.   His eyes.
Those brown eyes   Those green eyes
Will they truly be full
Of the love he has?

At the sight of me they light up
Lord, please don't let this be
A repeat of my past.
My heart's been unsealed

And I'm giving my love   And I've given my love
To a man I believe   To a man I believe
Is sent from above   Is sent from above
How could I have ever   How could I have ever
Doubted his love?   Doubted his love?
                            When his smile is kind
                            And his demeanor is sweet

When he sings his love for me

And his shoes stay on his feet
Yes I've decided
This choice is right
I will marry Torrance

And I will be alright

"Ready as I can be."

"I'm really getting married."

Yes I've decided
This choice is right

I will give Bud my heart
And I will be alright
"You ready sister?"

"Then let's do this."

I Do

Tell me
Do you?
Tell me
Will you?

Many say that I'm unlovable,
And for a time, I believed so.
Once married before,
But that's no more.
Left bitter and broken,
With hard feelings unspoken.
I've been said to have a fiery spirit,
And to be a bit overdramatic.
But it's only because I was alone.
Where I was no light could've shone.
It was dark and cold,
My life felt weary and old.
I saw no way out,
Saw no need to scream and shout.
This was how things would remain,
But then along you came.

Tell me
Do you?
Tell me
Will you?

Many say that something's wrong with me.
How could I have made it this far without some loving?
Who would have me at my age?
My time had passed as they'd say.
I tried my best not to listen,

But one got through every now and then.
But out of the one's that got through,
The only important one was you.
How could she love a man like that?
He's got six kids, he's not exactly a catch.
But they can't see what I see,
Are you only something of my dreams?

Tell me
Do you?
Tell me
Will you?

What I love most about you is that you make me smile,
I'm doing so as you walk down the aisle.
And I love that you hold on,
Because there's been chances when you could've gone.

What I love about you is you don't give in,
What you want you always get.
And I love that you take me as I am,
Because there's been time for you to scram.

I love that you keep me together.
I love that you want me forever.
I love that my mistakes,
Don't cause our relationship to break.

That's because I've made them too.
And I forgive them like I hope you do.

Nothing you do will ever make me leave.
I am your prize for you to keep.

And if you love me as long as I live,
Then love is what I'll always have to give.

Do you?
I do.
Will you?
I do.

Pillow Talk

Let me hear you say, "Tonight's the night!"
Tonight's the night!
Let me hear you say, "Life's alright!"
Life's alright!
Let me hear you say, "Tonight's the night!"
Tonight's the night!
Let me hear you say, "Life's alright!"
Life's alright!

Got the house to myself,
Love life been up on a shelf,
Twelve years with no wife,
But that all changes tonight.
She laying on the bed,
Just one thing needs to be said,
"Hey honey, how you doin'?
Are you ready to get to it?
"Yeah sweetie, I'm just fine,
But I need to talk right now."
"We can you do what you like,
Cuz we got all night."
"I'm glad you feel that way,
Cuz I have something to say.
Before you get a kiss,
We gotta talk about the kids.

Let me hear you say, "Tonight's the night!"
Tonight's the night!
Let me hear you say, "Life's alright!"
Life's alright!
Let me hear you say, "Tonight's the night!"
Tonight's the night!

Let me hear you say, "Life's alright!"
Life's alright!

"Do we have to talk about this tonight?"
"Yes, cuz I want to start things off right."
"I did my best for them kids."
"Everybody knows you did."
"Then why are they all mad at me?"
"Look at things differently.
Did your mama do her best?"
"Yeah, but she was a mess.
But that's not her fault though.
She just had a tough go."
"But her choices affected you?"
"Yeah I guess that part is true."
"Ever tell her your feelings?"
"Tried but they made her angry,
Said I called her a terrible mother,
But I wasn't trying to hurt her."

Let me hear you say, "Tonight's the night!"
Tonight's the night!
Let me hear you say, "Life's alright!"
Life's alright!
Let me hear you say, "Tonight's the night!"
Tonight's the night!
Let me hear you say, "Life's alright!"
Life's alright!

"Want to know something real?
No matter how it makes you feel?"
"Always be straight with me,
Even if I get angry."
"Baby the truth is,

You're your mother in this.
And they can't tell you,
Cuz you get upset too."
I just don't understand,
I did better than my mother had,
I kept them safe and fed,
Childhood better than what I led,
I've always had their back,
And they've never felt lack.
Wasn't that enough?
Or was my love a little too rough?

Let me hear you say, "Tonight's the night!"
Tonight's the night!
Let me hear you say, "Life's alright!"
Life's alright!
Let me hear you say, "Tonight's the night!"
Tonight's the night!
Let me hear you say, "Life's alright!"
Life's alright!

"Baby you've got to fix this,
We can't start this off with brokenness.
You can't be sweet to me,
And sour to them, it just can't be.
Until you fix it,
You'll have to go without your night kisses."
"But I've waited twelve years!"
"I've waited thirty-five and I ain't shedding no tears.
You'll be alright,
But for your kids you've got to fight."
"Why's it gotta be me?"
"Cuz you're the one that's the daddy.
Now goodnight.

Don't forget to turn out the light."
Then she turned over,
That's when I knew I'd lost my night lover.

Let me hear you say, "Tonight's the night!"
Tonight's the night!
Let me hear you say, "Life's alright!"
Life's alright!
Let me hear you say, "Tonight's the night!"
Tonight's the night!
Let me hear you say, "Life's alright!"
Life's alright!

Sunday Service

Gathered we are on Sunday morn,
To come and hear His voice.
O that my soul will bless The Lord,
As I start to rejoice.

First, we must offer up our praise,
In spirit and in truth.
Amongst the others I will raise,
My heartfelt song to You.

I cry out Lord with this burden,
That has left me quite uncertain.
Raise it from my shoulders please,
As I pray for the pain to cease.
Lend your ear to my lament,
As I pour out my regret.
Through this song I share with my father,
I sing from the heart of a remorseful daughter.

"Glory Hallelujah! Praise The Lord Saints!"
I watch as mommy addresses the church,
And see how she in a showcase of strength,
Talks to a crowd who've shown they dislike her.

It is time to hear the church announcements,
And learn what will soon benefit the town.
I watch as mommy does her assignment,
For a group who'd enjoy bringing her down.

I've always tended to my mommy's needs,
From the time when I was a little girl.
To me she's always been my first lady,

And nothing can replace her in the world.

I'll protect my mommy at every chance.
But now it's time to watch my sister dance.

Lord, I pray that you order all my steps,
Not only the ones I do in this dance,
But also, the ones I take in romance.
What will it take for my dad to accept,
That he can trust me with all his precepts.
Why did he allow me to take this chance,
With my heart if it he was so against?
How I wish things were easy except,

I've allowed love to grow in my heart.
I've watered and tended to all its needs,
I've done my best to do what is my part,
And tried to make everyone be appeased.
Lord, please accept this dance as more than art,
As it is my secret place for release.

They're passing around the collection plate.
I must add to it my share of spoil.
I give my ten percent of what I made,
From a week's worth of laborious toil.
I add an extra seed to the soil,
And water it with bitter tears of hope,
That my fate will change and won't recoil.
I gave fifteen and I'll try not to mope,
But I feel I'm at the end of my rope.

I listen to the sermon that is preached,
About how The Lord has the final say.
'It ain't over' is what is being teached,

But it's hard to believe those words today.

Is that what it means to hold onto faith?
That even when things seem out of control,
You believe The Lord will still make a way?
If so, I must continue to hold.

Even in the moments I feel alone,
And feel downtrodden and feel forgotten,
I'll hold on because of what I've been told.
That he heals those who are brokenhearted.

I pray Lord that you do not pass me by,
Because only on You can I rely.

B-Side

I Might As Well Have

I might as well have been who it,
Is you say that I be.
You say that I am the villain,
So, I guess that is me.

You ask how you are the problem.
But the truth is I can't,
Seem to trust you to do what's right,
For you've said that you shan't.

I might as well have been who it,
Is you say that I be.
You say that I am the villain,
So, I guess that is me.

You were who I called my hero.
You were my shining star.
But now I see that I was wrong,
And see you as you aren't.

I might as well have been who it,
Is you say that I be.
You say that I am the villain,
So, I guess that is me.

I might as well have,
Been who you say I am.
I gave you a place in my heart,
And loved you from the start.
And the way you repay me,
Is by turning on me.
What'd I do that was so wrong,

To make you feel this strong?
Why have you cast me as the villain,
If the hero's who I've always been?
How is it I lost your trust,
When I've given away my love,
And made sure you were always straight?
Has your love for me turned to hate?
What's happened to us my son?
What is it that I've done?

I might as well have been who it,
Is you say that I be.
You say that I am the villain,
So, I guess that is me.

If you are truly the bad guy,
It's hard for me to say.
I'm burnt from loving your fire,
That's why I couldn't stay.

I might as well have been who it,
Is you say that I be.
You say that I am the villain,
So, I guess that is me.

Drake

Drake was the first of his siblings to speak to his father after the disastrous dinner. And he only did so because he was heading back to the city and did not want to leave on bad terms again. He and his siblings had spent the night at their grandparents', hoping to give their father and his new bride some privacy. But upon returning, it seemed Mr. Brown was in an even worse mood than he was before the wedding.

His father was eating lunch with Gretchen at the kitchen table. It was weird having a grown woman in the house after so many years. Gretchen had already begun adding her touch to the place, livening it up again after it had been left vacant by his mother's departure over a decade earlier.

"Hey," said Drake. "I'm about to head out."

"Already?" asked Gretchen.

"Yeah. I just wanted to talk to Dad before I left.

Mr. Brown did not respond or acknowledge Drake. Gretchen glanced at her new husband, and Drake watched as the table slightly jiggled.

"Ouch!" yelped Mr. Brown, grabbing his shin. He stared at his wife and cried, "What'd you kick me for?!"

Gretchen glared at Mr. Brown, and he blew frustrated air through his nostrils.

"Sit," said Mr. Brown to Drake. Drake obeyed, and Mr. Brown said, "Speak."

"He's not a dog," said Gretchen.

Mr. Brown pursed his lips.

"Do you mind if I talk to Dad one on one?" asked Drake.

"Go ahead," said Gretchen. She shot a sharp look at Mr. Brown and said, "I'll be here in the living room if you need me."

"What?" said Mr. Brown when they were alone.

"I just wanted to say I'm sorry before I left."

"You should be," grumbled Mr. Brown. "Can't even sleep with my own wife because of you."

"What'd you say?"

"I don't understand how you have an issue with me when you don't even live with me anymore."

"I'm sorry," said Drake. It was all he could say. He did not know how to express to his father what was wrong.

"Is that all you have to say? 'I'm sorry'?"

"What do you want me to say?"

"How about what your so-called issue with me is? Can you tell me that?"

"I'm sorry."

"Of course you are," uttered Mr. Brown, throwing his hands up in defeat. "If you can't tell me what's supposedly wrong, then we have nothing to talk about."

Mr. Brown was right. Drake did not feel comfortable telling his father about his financial issues, and his father obviously was not going to talk about anything but that. So, Drake left.

Before leaving town, he had one more Harrison issue to confront. He wanted to know once and for all what the trouble was between Derek and Andre and whether he should still call Derek a friend.

"I know you did something to Andre," said Drake, sitting beside Derek's bed.

"Then they told you," said Derek.

"I had to piece it together. But I still don't know exactly what you did. But what I do know is if you're picking on my brother–!"

"Then what?" challenged Derek. "I'm not scared of you, Drake."

"Dude, what is your problem?"

"It's starting to seem like the Brown family is my problem."

"I could say the same about the Harrison family."

"What has my family ever done to you?" argued Derek.

"What has mine done to you?" retorted Drake.

"Why are you even here?"

"Because I want to know what happened. And if we're friends like we say we are, then you'll tell me."

Derek glared at Drake. Then he turned his head and sighed.

"I hurt Andre's feelings," muttered Derek. "We were just joking around, and I guess some of the jokes hurt his feelings."

"You guess?"

"Adri told me he was hurt, but he himself hasn't said anything."

"Did you apologize?"

"I haven't had a chance to yet."

"You should if it was just a case of jokes going too far."

"Yeah. But I thought they were about me."

"You weren't making the jokes?"

"I was but Sami was too."

"Sami was part of it too?"

"Yeah. It was his jokes that hurt Andre's feelings."

"Then why is everyone mad at you?"

"Because I kept egging him on after Adrianna told us to stop. And me and her argued over it and I haven't texted her back yet."

"When's the last time you spoke to her?"

"When we had the argument. That was Wednesday."

"You shouldn't go this long without talking to your girlfriend," advised Drake. "And honestly, this isn't as bad as you guys all made it seem. All of you were acting like you beat Andre up or something."

"You know I'd never do that," said Derek.

"Yeah, I know," said Drake.

"I'm sorry for snapping at you like that."

"Me too."

"We good?"

"Yeah. We're good. Talk to Dria."

After leaving Derek, Drake decided to take his own advice. He had not spoken to Tamela himself in a few days and wanted to have an understanding with her before he returned to the city.

He called her and asked her to meet him at the park. Fifteen minutes later, a tired-looking Tamela approached the park bench where he sat.

"Hey," said Tamela.

"Hey," said Drake.

Drake held Tamela close. He felt her sink into him and latch onto him like he was the only thing anchoring her to the ground.

"Tam," said Drake. "I want you to know that I love you."

"I love you too," whispered Tamela.

"I know you do. And I know that's the reason you won't tell me how bad things really are with Mrs. Reesy."

"So, that's what this is about," sighed Tamela, letting go of Drake.

"Yeah," said Drake. "Do thought I knew more than I did. I'm not forcing you to tell me about your mother's condition. I'm just telling you that whether you choose to or not, I'm here for you."

Tamela looked at Drake and deflated.

"She's dying," said Tamela. "My mother is dying."

Drake's heart dropped.

"I just didn't want you worrying because I know how you get with situations you can't fix," explained Tamela.

"You not telling me made me even more worried."

"Everything has just been very hard and very frustrating," said Tamela. "And I'm scared. I'm not prepared to lose my mother. I still need her here. It's not fair!"

Drake offered Tamela his shoe. She eyed it warily before taking it and angrily chucking it. Then she took his other shoe and threw that one too. After that, she threw her shoes.

"This doesn't work," said Tamela. "I'm still angry."

"I know."

"Then why do you do it?"

"Habit?"

"Why did this have to happen?"

"I don't know."

Tamela shook her head and sighed.

"It just feels like everything is on my shoulders," said Tamela. "I'm trying to take care of her, I'm trying to take care of Em and let her still enjoy being a kid, I'm trying to finish school. It's just a lot that I wasn't ready for."

"I know," said Drake, taking Tamela's hand.

Tamela laid her head on Drake's shoulder and silently cried. He did not have to say anything else. His presence was enough to let her know he was there. And he always would be.

Drake kept his promise and visited his mother before leaving. It was not a long visit, but she did send him off with a generous amount of food and a kiss on the forehead. He did not know what he would do without his mother and wished his relationship with his father could be as easy to navigate. While driving back to the city, Drake received a phone call from Matthias.

"Hello?" said Drake.

"See, that's what I like to hear," said Matthias. "Now you see how you were respectful and started off with hello? Do that more often."

"Okay...?"

"Anyways, I'm calling to tell you that you don't have to worry about the money anymore."

"I'm going to pay you back."

"It's already been paid."

"What?"

"I've got a check in my hand for five-thousand dollars. Your debt is paid."

"How?"

"I guess the Big Guy answered your prayers."

"But I didn't write a check."

"Oh, I know. It was written on your behalf."

"By who?"

"I was asked not to tell. Just know that it's taken care of."

Drake was shocked. Then elated.

He was free.

With the responsibility of paying Matthias back suddenly resolved, Drake felt a huge burden lifted off his back. He could focus his energy elsewhere. And he knew just where to start.

"This is Vincent."

"Uh, hi," said Drake nervously. "This is Drake Brown. We spoke about me possibly singing background for you. You told me to call you if I was interested in setting up an audition."

"You said all that like I haven't been expecting your call," laughed Vincent. "You sure did take your time considering it, that's for sure."

"I wasn't sure you'd remember me."

"Fair enough. I am a busy man."

"If the offer still stands, I'd like to accept it."

"Great," said Vincent. "I'll send you the info for the auditions."

Drake was excited and nervous. Everything seemed to be falling into place for him. Except his relationship with his dad. The debt had been paid off, yet Drake still felt like he and his father were in an awkward place. He hoped one day, they would get to a place of trust and understanding between them.

Fight Song

I think I can say I've hit rock bottom.
                    Rock bottom is a place I've visited,
                    I'll never return as long as I live.
I regret what I've gotten myself in.
                    There are things in this life that I regret,
                    But I can't change them and this I accept.
My life has become very troublesome.
                    Troublesome things are nothing new to me,
                    And every time I have the victory.
I feel like I've been made its harlequin.
                    Life has tried to turn me into its clown,
                    But I always come out wearing the crown.
I have failed and its left me feeling glum.
                    There have been times when I've not been my best,
                    Those were the times when I needed to rest.
And there's no possible way I can win.
                    My son, going through your test of manhood,
                    I know you can do it because I could.
Life looks on me with a smile so coy.
                    Don't give up yet there's still some fight in you,
                    You've got to show life that you are not through.
For it knows I'll always remain a boy.
                    Pick your head up like I know that you can,
                    And start fighting back like you are the man.

-

Antoine

After church, Antoine remained behind to help Uncle Terrence with his music selections for the next service. Although Antoine was not as musically inclined as his father, he was more than willing to use whatever he needed to avoid returning home. Being around his father reminded him how much of a failure he had become.

"Sometimes I wonder why I was chosen to do this," said Uncle Terrence. "Everybody knows I'm the last person who should be doing this."

"Who do you think should be the music minister?" asked Antoine.

"Your dad," said Uncle Terrence. "But he was in his early twenties when the position became open, and the elders didn't think he was mature enough for it at the time. So, they chose me. But I think they forgot you had to have musical talent to be a music minister."

"You have musical talent," said Antoine, arranging the selections by how well he thought they would flow into each other. He always did that with his music because he liked smooth transitions between songs, and because he liked experimenting with different mixes.

"Not like your dad though," sighed Uncle Terrence. "Compared to him I feel like an untalented loser."

Antoine understood how his uncle felt. His father tended to cast a long shadow when he was good at something. And sometimes, being in that shadow was not the best feeling.

He had only raised half the money he needed to repay his father. And he had just given ten percent of it in tithe. Antoine wanted to be done with the whole thing and figured he would have to do something drastic.

"Uncle Thusi?" said Antoine. "Can I ask you a favor?"

"You know you can ask me anything Nephew."

"Will you buy my gaming system for a hundred dollars?"

"Buy you a gaming system?"

"No," said Antoine. "Buy my gaming system that I have at my house."

"What?" said Uncle Terrence confusedly. "I thought you liked that thing."

"I do but... I need a hundred dollars."

"Why?"

"I made a mistake and now I need a hundred dollars to fix it. I've tried to earn the money but..."

"But...?"

"But...," repeated Antoine. He carefully considered whether he should tell his uncle everything that transpired. He knew his uncle had zero tolerance for wrongdoing and had no problem addressing it directly. "Will you buy it or not?"

"I might if you tell me what's going on."

"Well...," said Antoine. "Like I said, I made a mistake."

"What was the mistake?"

"Dad let me use his card to get a game on my system. I was only supposed to take twenty dollars, but I accidentally took two hundred. When I realized what I'd done, I was scared to tell Dad so I... I pretended I didn't know. But Dad found out, and he took my system and all my games and said I'll get them back when I repay him his two-hundred dollars."

"That's not unreasonable considering you lied," said Uncle Terrence.

"I know," said Antoine. "I wish I could take it back."

"That's good," said Uncle Terrence. "That means you're remorseful. Everyone's done things they weren't proud of and wish they could take back, so know you're not alone in that."

"Even you?" asked Antoine.

"Even me," said Uncle Terrence, scratching the back of his neck. "The biggest thing I regret ever doing is telling your father something that was very mean when we were kids. It affected our relationship badly, and even though we've talked about it and made up from it, he still has somewhat of a wall up with me. And I think he always will."

"That's how I feel," sighed Antoine. "I feel like he doesn't trust me anymore."

"Yeah, that's possible," said Uncle Terrence. "And knowing your father, it might take him some time to get over this and trust you again. But I'll have to back him on this. It's better for you to earn that two-hundred dollars through your own hard work and pay it back yourself."

"I've tried," muttered Antoine. "But I've only made a hundred so far."

"That's halfway there."

"Yeah, but I made that money off family and friends," said Antoine. "And I barely made that. With school starting back up, it could take forever to pay Dad back."

"Sometimes things get harder than expected Nephew," explained Uncle Terrence. "But that doesn't mean you give up."

"I'm not giving up," said Antoine. "I'm just taking an easier way."

"The easier way isn't always the best way," cautioned Uncle Terrence.

"Uncle Thusi, I just want this whole thing to be over," said Antoine. "Will you buy my system?"

"You do know if I buy your system, it'll be mine, right?"

"Yes. I just want this to be over."

"Are you sure about this?"

"Uncle Thusi," pleaded Antoine. "If you don't buy it, I'll sell it to someone else who will."

"Hmm," said Uncle Terrence, scratching his chin. "Alright."

Uncle Terrence drove Antoine home. His father had gone with Gretchen to take her parents back to the airport. Antoine retrieved his gaming system from his father's closet and traded it for the hundred dollars. When his father and Gretchen returned home, he was waiting for them with the money.

"Hey Antoine," said Gretchen. "Having a good day?"

"Yeah," said Antoine.

"That's good," said Gretchen. She kissed Mr. Brown on the cheek and said, "I'm going to go change. See you in a bit."

When Gretchen was gone, Antoine stood and faced his father.

"Here's your money, Dad," said Antoine, placing the money in his father's hand.

"Oh?" said Mr. Brown. He counted the bills and said, "Yep. It's all here. Wait right there."

Mr. Brown left to discover what Antoine already knew.

"Antoine, where's your gaming system?" asked Mr. Brown when he returned. "I can't find it."

"It's right there," muttered Antoine, pointing to the money in his hand.

"Where? I don't see it."

"The two-hundred dollars. That's the gaming system."

"I don't understand."

"I sold it."

"You what?"

"I sold it."

"You... you sold the gaming system that your mother and I bought you?"

"Yes sir."

"To who?"

"Uncle Thusi."

"Why?"

"So, I could repay you your money."

"Let's go."

"Where?"

"To get the system back."

"It's Uncle Thusi's now."

"No," said Mr. Brown. "That was not your system to sell. That was my system that I bought with your mother for you to play on. You cannot sell that system without my permission. We are going over to your uncle's house. You are going to give him his money back, and he is going to give back that system."

"What if I don't want it anymore?"

"What do you mean you don't want it anymore? The whole purpose was for you to earn the system back because you lied to me!"

"I lied to you because I knew how you'd react."

"First of all, you don't lie to me period, little boy," said Mr. Brown. "I don't care how you *think* I'd react, you don't lie to me ever."

"This is why. Because you get mad."

"I'm getting mad because you stepped outside of your place!" griped Mr. Brown. "I'm the father and you are the child! You do not lie to me! You do not sell stuff without my permission! You do not make a single move until I know about it first! Do you understand?"

"Yes sir," sighed Antoine.

"Now, like I said earlier, you are going to return this money to your uncle, and he is going to give back that system. Now, let's go."

The ride to Uncle Terrence's was a quiet one.

"I figured I'd be seeing you before the end of the day," said Uncle Terrence with a smile when he saw his brother.

"Give me my system back," demanded Mr. Brown. "You had no business 'buying' it in the first place."

"You're right, I didn't."

"Then why'd you do it?"

"Because I knew you'd want it back," said Uncle Terrence." Plus, it'd bring you around to see me. You know, out of all our siblings, you visit me the least. I want to see my baby brother too."

"Terrence, this isn't funny!"

"I know," said Uncle Terrence. "I figured I'd take the Mikey approach than my usual approach. His approach requires way less screaming. Besides, you really do visit me the least."

"Who cares how much I visit you?!"

"I care."

"It's always you stirring up drama where there doesn't need to be any!"

"Oh no! You need to point that finger at yourself. Because every time you have drama, I'm the one that ends up fixing it."

"I don't care about none of that! Give me my system back and stay out my business! This is between me and my son and has nothing to do with you!"

"Torrance, you're holding my money in your hand and standing in my house. That makes me a part of it."

"Well, you don't have to be!" declared Mr. Brown, shoving the money into his brother's hand.

"Half of this is yours," said Uncle Terrence, giving Mr. Brown half the money back. "I only gave him a hundred."

"I can't believe you did all of this just because you 'wanted to see me'!" ranted Mr. Brown. "What kind of stupidness is that?!"

"It's not stupid!" argued Uncle Terrence. "I shouldn't have to resort to schemes to get you to come see me!"

"You just saw me yesterday!"

"Oh yeah," mocked Uncle Terrence. "At the wedding you didn't want to pick a best man for."

"Are you still on that?!"

"Yes! Because you know you wanted to pick Mikey! Talking about some 'I didn't want to pick between my brothers'. You know you wanted him as your best man because that's your favorite brother!"

"I don't have a favorite brother!"

"I'm the brother you like the least then."

"What are you talking about? I like you!"

"Yeah now. But what about back then?"

"What about it?"

"You didn't like me back then."

"We already talked about that."

"Just because we talked about it doesn't mean I'm not still affected by it!" argued Uncle Terrence. "I have to go through life knowing you thought I didn't love you and that I failed to protect you."

"You were a kid."

"No, you were a kid! I was big enough to do something and I didn't!"

"What could you have done?"

"I should've done something! And I should've never said what I said to you. No wonder you didn't like me. I was a terrible half-brother."

"Don't say that!" cried Mr. Brown. "We're brothers! Period!"

"Mikey is your brother," said Uncle Terrence. "I'm your half-brother because that's all I've been to you. Half a brother that hurt you like everyone else."

"I've never blamed you for anything that happened to me in that house," said Mr. Brown. "All I ever wanted from you was for you to like me. And I got that a long time ago."

"You should've gotten that from the beginning," said Uncle Terrence. "Our relationship is a mess and it's my fault."

"Where is all this coming from?"

"I don't know it just...," began Uncle Terrence. "It just seems like everything that goes wrong is somehow my fault."

"Like what?"

"Like us," said Uncle Terrence. "Like Marie getting upset at me over her girls. Like Bud quitting on me to 'pursue other opportunities'. Do you want to know what the last thing he said to me before he left was? He told me he was sorry that he had disappointed me. After almost two decades of working with me all he could say was that he was sorry for disappointing me."

Mr. Brown did not respond. But Antoine noticed his demeanor had softened.

"I guess he figured I'd let him do more after that whole situation with the Kelly brothers, but I couldn't," continued Uncle Terrence. "Bernard has been trying to catch me messing up so he could replace me with Bud and control the department through him. But I couldn't let that happen so I restricted what Bud could do. Now he's quit and he probably thinks I hate him, but I don't."

"Well, you were in a tough spot," said Mr. Brown. "You did your best."

"It always seems like me 'doing my best' messes everything up."

"Then stop doing your best."

"What?"

"Stop doing your best," repeated Mr. Brown.

"I can't do that," said Uncle Terrence. "I have too many responsibilities to start slacking off now."

"You have a responsibility to yourself first."

"You just don't understand," sighed Uncle Terrence. "I feel like I'm having to take care of everyone and in return everyone hates me for it."

"If you think I don't understand how that feels you're sadly mistaken," said Mr. Brown.

"Here," said Uncle Terrence, handing Mr. Brown the gaming system. "This is what you came for."

"Methuselah, if you really want to see me all you have to do is say so," said Mr. Brown. "You don't have to resort to doing stuff like this."

Mr. Brown hugged his brother and returned home. As they were in the car, he looked at Antoine curiously.

"So, you've raised half the money," said Mr. Brown.

"Yes sir," said Antoine.

"You're halfway there."

Antoine pursed his lips and nodded.

"Look," said Mr. Brown. "One day, you'll understand why I didn't let you sell this system."

"I didn't mind," said Antoine.

"Okay but I minded," remarked Mr. Brown. "Your mother definitely would've minded. You know gaming is one of her things and you're her only child that seriously shares that interest."

"I know."

"Still," continued Mr. Brown. "I appreciate that you were willing to sacrifice what you liked to pay me back. Maybe I'll give you your gaming system back a little early. How's that sound?"

Antoine did not feel as excited as he probably should have been. Instead, he felt annoyed.

"Then what was the point of all this?" questioned Antoine.

"All what?" asked Mr. Brown.

"Making me go out here and do all this work, and deal with all these people!" ranted Antoine. "People not paying me, people talking to me crazy, missing out on my whole spring break, Mariella stealing half my money talking about some it's her cut!"

"Who didn't pay you?!" said Mr. Brown. "And who's been talking to you crazy?! And what do you mean Mariella stole your money?!"

"It doesn't even matter anymore," griped Antoine. "Just keep the system. I don't even want it no more. Sell it for all I care."

"Antoine."

"I'm serious! I'll pay you back the rest of your money and that'll be it."

"Now you're just being overdramatic."

Antoine did not care anymore though. He was over everything.

But another part of him was also glad that his father had acknowledged what he had done. It made him feel like less of a failure. And that feeling made him want to press on and get the rest of his father's money.

Ebb and Flow

How is it that love came to be for me,
Like a tide that came and went in my life?
I thought together we would always be,
But now I find myself holding the knife.
My heart wails for you releasing her cry,
For I hold the knife that will bring our end.
And she's worried that she will be left dry,
When her love flows out from my tearing rend.
I want to remain always by your side,
And bask in the light that you've brought my way.
And on the wings of love I want to glide.
I can't, because Dad's made it hard to stay.
How funny that my love began to leak,
Right when his reached its most glorious peak.

How is it that love has turned out to be,
Like a tide that went and returned to me?
I never thought I'd feel the light again,
Or feel the warmth of this most cherished friend.
I never thought I'd escape the rough times,
When my broken heart sang it's wretched rhymes.
I never thought that I would leave behind,
The confused hurt that plagued me in my mind.
But now I've been given a second chance,
To try again at the wheel of romance.
And I hope that I navigate this sea,
And steer myself into life's bliss and glee.
There's no greater feeling than to find love,
Especially one ordained from above.
And I hope my daughter will also speak,

Of this joyous love that I've let her seek.
I did not think that it would end so soon,
Because I thought that we would always last.

He's taken the harmony from my tune,
And locked it away where no man can pass.
I want you to know that it's not your fault,
For to me you are still very much dear.
But now comes the time that will make us halt,
For the inevitable end draws near.
I feel the love flowing out of my heart,
But it's residue I feel left behind.
And though for now our love's been torn apart,
I pray that one day happiness we'll find.
There's only one task left for me to do,
To tell you what's broken my heart in two.

Adrianna

Monday was somber for Adrianna. After talking with her mother, she had decided what to do about her relationship with Derek. She had not seen him all day at school, but he had finally texted her, apologizing for not talking to her for the past few days.

As the school day neared its final class period, she and Tamara walked up the hallway, catching up.

"I think Tam and Drake made up," said Tamara.

"I didn't even know they were fighting," said Adrianna.

"They weren't fighting," clarified Tamara. "She just wasn't telling him everything."

"Oh," said Adrianna. "How's your mom doing?"

"Um...," said Tamara. "Honestly? Not too good."

"Oh no."

"Yeah."

"Aw Em. I'm sorry."

"It's fine. She keeps trying to be positive and looking on the bright side. She's already making plans for my graduation next year but honestly..."

"What?"

"I... I'm not all that confident she'll be at my graduation."

"Where do you think she'll be?"

"In the ground."

"Em, don't say that!"

"I'm just being honest. I can tell it's taking a toll on her. She's holding on but I'm not sure how much longer she'll be able to."

"You!" said Mariana, storming toward the girls.

"Me?" said Adrianna, pointing to herself.

"I cannot believe you!" ranted Mariana. "I can't believe I trusted you! I should've known you wouldn't have my back! You're fake just like everyone else in this family!"

"Girl, what are you talking about?" asked Adrianna confusedly.

"You told Dani about me and Jada being friends! Now she's making me choose between being friends with her or Jada! How could you do this to me?!"

"Why would I tell Danielle anything?" asked Adrianna. "I don't talk to her!"

"Because you don't like me, and you want me to be miserable just like you!"

"First of all, my life does not revolve around you. And second of all, I didn't tell that girl anything."

"Then how'd she find out then? Because you're the only one who knew!"

"Mariella knew. Jada knew."

"Mariella is my sister! She wouldn't do that because she actually acts like my family unlike you! And Jada's my friend! She wouldn't do it either! That leaves you!"

"Well, all I know is I didn't say anything. So, you need to take all that anger somewhere else."

"I can't believe you!" cried Mariana. "You're the worst cousin ever!"

Mariana stormed away, and Adrianna rolled her eyes. She knew she had not said anything to Danielle.

"I swear that whole group of girls is nothing but drama," said Tamara annoyedly. "The only person I feel bad for in the situation is Jada."

"Not even Lala and Nicki?" asked Adrianna.

Tamara eyed her.

"Em!" cried Adrianna with laughter.

"I'm sorry but no," said Tamara. "Lala and Nicki were her friends for years and making excuses for her behavior. The only reason they fell out is because they wouldn't do what she wanted them to do. I guarantee if she came around talking about some, 'I'm sorry! I was wrong!', they'd forgive her and go right back to being her friends like nothing happened."

"Mhmm," agreed Adrianna. "I agree."

As they kept walking, the girls came across Jada, who was preparing to leave for the day.

"Hey Jada," said Adrianna. "I think I should warn you Mariana is in one of her moods again."

"What happened?" asked Jada.

"She claimed I told Dani about you guys being friends. I don't know how Dani found out, but it wasn't from me."

"I told her," said Jada.

"Oh!" choked Tamara.

"You did?" gasped Adrianna.

"Yeah," said Jada. "She asked me was I friends with Mariana and I said yeah."

"Does Mariana know you told?"

"Not yet. I'll tell her though. See you later."

"And that's why I like her," said Tamara as they watched Jada walk away.

"Yeah," agreed Adrianna. "Well, we better get moving before we're late to class."

"I'll see you later," said Tamara.

"See you later."

Adrianna seemed to have a harder time in dance class than usual. She missed steps, sometimes got offbeat, and even forgot part of her dance at one point. Her mind was unfocused because of everything going wrong in her life, and it showed in her dancing.

"Adrianna, I need to speak to you," said Mr. Haynes when class ended.

Adrianna blushed as the other girls teased her with 'ooohs'. She stepped into Mr. Haynes's office and waited to be reprimanded for her poor performance.

"I'm just going to be honest," said Mr. Haynes. "You were terrible today. You were a beat behind in some parts, cutting off some of your moves. At one point you just stopped dancing altogether. I've never seen you dance this badly before."

"I know," sighed Adrianna. "I'm sorry. I'll do better."

"I hope so. Is everything okay?"

"Yes sir."

"You sure?"

"Yes."

Mr. Haynes stared at her and shook his head.

"Want to know a secret?" said Mr. Haynes. "You have the same weakness as your father and brother."

"I do?"

"You sure do. Anytime they get stressed, they start slacking. Tell me I'm lying."

Adrianna had to agree. But she had not realized she did the same thing.

"Your silence means you know I'm right," said Mr. Haynes. He smiled impishly and said, "And I know I am because I've used that weakness to my advantage before."

"Well then," said Adrianna.

"So, what's making you dance so badly?" asked Mr. Haynes. "Dad troubles? Boy troubles?"

"Uh...," uttered Adrianna. "Both?"

"Both?" choked Mr. Haynes. "How is it both?"

"My dad is causing the boy troubles."

"What's he doing?"

"He just has all these rules for my relationship. And I'm following them, but it just seems like he doesn't trust me."

"Hmm," muttered Mr. Haynes. "Well, there's only one thing you can do."

"What?"

"You've got to decide which relationship is more important to you."

"I already have," sighed Adrianna.

"Why do I get the feeling I'm going to have a few more days of bad dancing from you?" said Mr. Haynes.

"I'll do my best," said Adrianna.

"Okay," said Mr. Haynes. "Just remember, this isn't the end of the world."

"Then why does it feel like it?"

"Because you're young."

Adrianna went home and got her dad's permission to visit Derek. He was happy to see her and was as apologetic in person as he was in text.

"This time I mean it," promised Derek. "I'll talk to you every day from now on. I promise."

"Don't promise that," whispered Adrianna.

"Why not?"

"Because we need to talk."

"I don't like the sound of that," said Derek. "Look, if you're still upset about what happened with Andre–!"

"I am. But that's not what I need to talk to you about."

"Then what is it?"

"Derek," said Adrianna. She looked him in his worried brown eyes, and said, "I'm breaking up with you."

Silence.

"Why?!" cried Derek.

"Because our relationship isn't working."

"What do you mean it isn't working?"

"Let's be real with ourselves," said Adrianna. "We barely see each other as it is, and after you graduate, we probably won't see each other at all."

"Adri, if this is about your dad's rules then–!"

"It's more than that," said Adrianna. "We barely see each other and..."

"And?"

"And you've become... different... since your leg broke."

"No, I haven't."

"You have too. You're not the same guy I started dating back in August."

"So, I'm the reason we're breaking up?"

"No, it's just…"

"Then what is it? Why are you giving up on us?"

"Because 'us' is impossible right now."

"But I love you."

"I know," said Adrianna. "And I love you too. But we've got to admit when something isn't working."

"I guess it's a good thing I haven't had time to get that tattoo yet," said Derek.

"This is so unfair," said Adrianna, choking up with tears.

"What is?"

"This! I don't want to break up but we have to!"

"Not if you don't want to."

"Yes, we do! People think… they think I'm… that I'm fast. And because of that my dad is trying to make it so nothing has a chance of happening."

"Nothing is going to happen," assured Derek. "I'm sure you already know this but that stuff grosses me out because my dad scarred me for life with his puberty talk."

"I know," said Adrianna. "But I still think it's best that we just break up. It'll make everything easier for me."

Derek frowned and bowed his head in defeat.

"Alright," said Derek. "We're broken up."

"I'm sorry."

"I know. I'm sorry too. I didn't mean to make your life hard."

"You didn't," corrected Adrianna. "You were the best part of my life."

"I uh… I think you should go now," said Derek, clearing his throat. Adrianna could see his eyes starting to water. "Your fifteen minutes is probably almost up."

"You're right," sighed Adrianna. "Goodbye."

"Goodbye."

Adrianna had done a good job holding back her tears. But when she got home, both her father and Gretchen noticed her and became worried.

"Hey, what's wrong?" asked Gretchen.

"Did something happen?" questioned Mr. Brown. "Do I need to go over there?"

She could not hold it any longer.

"Dee and I broke up!" sobbed Adrianna.

"Oh no!" cried Gretchen.

"Aw," said Mr. Brown, hugging her. "I'm sorry."

Adrianna stopped crying. Her dad was sorry they had broken up. But *he* was the reason why they had broken up. And he had the nerve to hug her and say he was sorry.

"It's fine," said Adrianna, pushing her dad away. "I'm fine. I just need time to myself."

"Uh okay," said Mr. Brown, caught off guard by the mood change. "We're... we're here if you need us."

"Okay," said Adrianna.

She hurried off to her room and curled up in her bed where she could cry in peace.

-

Loneliness

Loneliness is a bitter thing,
To one who's always known a friend,
Or has family to no end.
And yet, lonely am I feeling.

To be alone is bittersweet,
Because sometimes I need to breathe.
But then I find that there's no sound,
And it's because no one's around.

I just want to be understood.
But instead, I feel pushed aside,
And feel like I'm losing my mind,
And deemed no longer any good.

I just want to be understood.
I've always done the best I could.
But then, why am I full of shame.
Am I really the one to blame?

Where in the world did I go wrong,
To make everyone that I know,
Decide to turn around and go,
Against me and not get along?

Did I create the loneliness?
Am I the one who made this mess?
Have I pushed everyone away?
Am I why no one wants to stay?

I feel like I'm about to break.
Am I so stupid to believe,

I don't deserve what I've received?
I don't know what more I can take.

How bitter is being alone.
It's enough to make a heart stone.
What will I be,
If that happens to me?

Andre

That Monday, during the final class period, Andre did not wait in his father's classroom. Instead, he sat alone in front of the school, watching as the other seniors went home for the day.

"Hey Andre!"

It was Mr. Kasey calling from his car. Andre figured he was there to pick up Samiel and waved back.

Samiel walked up to the car and looked back at Andre. Andre could not tell if Samiel was glaring at him because of the distance, but it felt like it. Another silent warning to stay away from Mr. Kasey.

Soon, everyone was gone except Andre. Sitting in front of the school, Andre realized how lonely he really felt.

He had no one to talk to. And the one person interested in talking to him was off limits.

"What you doing out here by yourself?"

Allison sat beside him.

"I thought everyone had left," answered Andre.

"I'm about to as soon as Derek wheels himself out here," said Allison. "I can't wait till his leg heals up."

"Yeah."

"Only a few more months and we'll be free," said Allison.

"Mhmm," agreed Andre.

"Are you ready for college?"

"I think so."

"Well, I definitely am. I'm ready to get out there and see the world."

Andre was ready to see the world too. But it seemed like the closer the time got, the more unprepared he felt.

"I'm ready," said Derek, wheeling up beside Allison. He looked at Andre and said more quietly, "Hey."

"Hey," answered Andre.

Things between them were still awkward. Contrary to what Adrianna felt, Andre himself was not angry at Derek. He was not sure what he felt about the situation, but he knew he was not angry.

"Listen," said Derek. "I wanted to tell you I was sorry about what happened at the video shoot. I didn't know some of the jokes hurt your feelings. I'm sorry."

"Okay."

"No hard feelings, right?"

"Sure."

"We've got to get going before I'm late for work," said Allison. She began wheeling Derek toward her car, saying to Andre, "I'll see you later."

"Bye," said Andre.

Soon, school ended, and Andre was at home in his room. Adrianna had disappeared for a little while and returned home very unhappy. Andre thought it best to leave her alone.

Antoine returned from his workout in a good mood. Andre was glad at least someone in the house was happy.

"Hey Antoine?" asked Andre.

"Yeah?" answered Antoine.

"Can you explain The Well to me again?"

"The Well? Like what it is or what happened?"

"What happened."

"Alright," said Antoine. He lay beside Andre on the bed, saying, "Let me get comfy. This is going to take a while."

Andre liked having his brother beside him. He liked that his brother never questioned his whims and just went along with them. It made him feel less lonely.

"So, it all began back in December when the latest DLC released," began Antoine. "Andrew and his friend were busy, so me, Jada, and Stacy formed our own little guild to explore the new area."

"This was after you found out that you and Jada had already been playing together, right?"

"Yeah. I'm still amazed by that. And then Allison connected her with Stacy. But yeah, so the new area featured a limited time boss that would drop a rare item for only about a week. But there was this guild that had been a problem for a little while in the game who used to block other players from accessing the limited time bosses so their members could be the only ones with the rare items. They did the same with this boss and attacked anyone who came near them."

"You can attack other players?"

"In player versus player zones yeah. So, what ended up happening is someone decided to create this huge alliance that would attack the guild and it started a war in the game. But then, two of the players met up outside the game and got into an actual fight."

"They fought... over a video game?"

"Yeah. But that's not the crazy part. The person who lost the fight ended up suing the video game company.

"Why?"

"They claimed the game created a toxic environment that started the fight and wanted his medical bills paid. He didn't win but it caused such a huge negative reaction against the game that no one plays it anymore."

"And that's why you've moved on to playing that shooter game now?"

"Yeah," said Antoine. "What's got you so interested in The Well all of a sudden?"

"It just crossed my mind."

They heard someone knock on the front door.

"Who is that?" asked Andre.

"I don't know," said Antoine. "Let's go see."

The boys crept up the hallway and peeked into the living room. Mr. Kasey was talking with a very displeased Mr. Brown.

"What are you doing here?" asked Mr. Brown annoyedly.

"I need to talk to you," said Mr. Kasey.

"Last time you said that to me, it ended with you trying to bash my head into the concrete."

"It... it did?" said Mr. Kasey surprisedly. "I... I don't remember that."

"Well, I do," said Mr. Brown bitterly. "One minute I'm minding my business walking home and next thing I know I'm on the ground begging for my life because you're trying to crack my skull open on the sidewalk!"

"Wow, I...," said Mr. Kasey. "Why did I do that?"

"You tell me!"

"Did we argue or something?"

"No! You called my name, I ignored you because I don't like you, and you jumped on me and tried to kill me!"

"When was this?"

"It was around the time I had that fight with Marlin where you kicked me in the side while he held me down."

"Oh," muttered Mr. Kasey. "No wonder I don't remember... I must've been high..."

"I still want to know what you're doing here."

"Well, first I want to say I'm sorry for how I treated you when we were kids," said Mr. Kasey. "You don't have to forgive me, but I want you to know that I'm sorry."

"Okay."

"And I came over because I want to talk about Andre."

"We have nothing to talk about regarding my son," said Mr. Brown. "Actually, I want you to stay away from him."

"If that's what you want," said Mr. Kasey. "But that'll really hurt him, you know."

"What do you care? I thought you were here to be part of your son's life not mine."

"I am here to be part of my son's life," said Mr. Kasey. "It just so happened that your son needed someone to talk to and I was willing to listen."

"He doesn't need you to listen. That's what I'm here for."

"Good. I would hope that you're listening to him."

"What are you talking about? I always listened to him!"

"So, you know that he feels overwhelmed?"

"Overwhelmed by what? What does he have to be overwhelmed with? If anyone should feel overwhelmed, it's me!"

"Brown, that's not funny. Your son is struggling."

"What do you know? You've never raised a child before!"

"You're right, I haven't. But I have spent time listening to Andre and how he feels."

"My son is fine. He's smart, he's kind, and he's talented. There's nothing wrong with him."

"You have to admit he's a little different from your other kids."

"No, he's not!"

"I'm not saying something's wrong with him. I'm just saying he's different from them. He thinks and learns differently than they do."

"He does not!"

"Brown, you're not listening."

"Why should I listen to you? You drift into town and all of a sudden you think you know my own son better than I do? You don't know the first thing about being a parent!"

"You're right. My son was born when I was locked up and I couldn't have contact with him until he was eighteen. But you've had the chance, and you take it for granted."

"I take it for granted?!"

Andre decided he had heard enough.

"Mr. Kasey," said Andre, entering the living room.

"Andre," said Mr. Kasey.

"Andre, why is this man in my house talking to me crazy?!" demanded Mr. Brown. "I told you I didn't want you talking to him no more!"

"I'm sorry," said Andre. "Mr. Kasey, can we talk outside?"

"Uh, sure," said Mr. Kasey.

"You don't have anything to–!"

"Dad," said Andre. "Please."

Mr. Brown pursed his lips as Andre walked outside with Mr. Kasey.

"You shouldn't have come here," said Andre.

"I came here because I was concerned about you," said Mr. Kasey. "You looked upset earlier. And I'm glad I did because your father's not listening to you. He's in denial about you struggling and–!"

"Mr. Kasey," said Andre. "I appreciate that you talked with me when I felt down. But you can't come around here anymore. And you probably shouldn't talk to me anymore either."

"You can't expect me to just stop caring about what's going on with you. Your father clearly doesn't listen to you and expects things of you that aren't realistic. I don't want to see you go down the same path I did."

"I'm not going to," said Andre. "It's just like my dad said, I'm smart and talented. I'll be okay."

"Andre."

"I'll be okay," repeated Andre, his voice cracking. On the inside, he wanted to scream and tell Mr. Kasey he was right. He wanted to yell at the only person willing to listen to him that he was not okay. But Samiel had made it clear Mr. Kasey was his and his only. So, with a heavy heart, Andre said, "Please don't come by here anymore."

Andre watched as the realization sank in for Mr. Kasey that Andre had set fire to their bridge.

"If that's what you want," said Mr. Kasey. "But if you ever need someone to talk to again, don't be afraid to come find me."

"I understand," said Andre.

He watched as Mr. Kasey got in his car and drove away, then returned inside to his angry father.

"Why was that man here?" demanded Mr. Brown.

"I didn't ask him to come here," said Andre.

"I thought I was very clear that you were not to talk to him anymore," said Mr. Brown.

"You were," said Andre. "And I'm sorry. It won't happen again."

"Why would you bring a man to my house that I don't like?" ranted Mr. Brown.

"I didn't bring him here!" cried Andre.

"Well, he came here for a reason Andre!" snapped Mr. Brown. "And that reason was you!"

"I already said I was sorry! What more do you want me to say?"

"I want you to say why you didn't listen to me! Like what is wrong with you? It seems like sometimes you just don't think at all!"

"Look Dad, I get it!" hollered Andre, losing his temper. "I'm a screwup and an idiot, okay?! You don't have to keep reminding me!"

Andre did not wait to hear his father's reply. He stormed out the front door and mounted his bike.

"Andre!" called Mr. Brown from behind him. "Andre! Come back!"

Andre ended up biking to his mother's house, where his grandfather happened to be visiting.

"What'd your father do this time?" asked First Lady Hall when she saw Andre. She was in the middle of cooking dinner and turned around to tend to the food on the stove.

Andre did not answer. He was trying to get his frustration under control before it spilled out.

"Lana, I think this time might be serious," said Grandpap Jared, noticing Andre's silence.

First Lady Hall turned to look at Andre. She looked at him closely with worried eyes, and it was enough to crumble Andre.

"Uhn uhn!" hollered First Lady Hall, rushing to Andre. "What the heck did your father do?! I'm going over there!"

"Girl, you ain't going nowhere," said Grandpap Jared. "I'll handle this."

"Yeah, you handle it while I go over there and give this man a piece of my mind!" ranted First Lady Hall. "I'm going to break my foot off in his behind! There's no reason my kids should be coming from his house to my house in tears!"

"Leilana," said Grandpap Jared more firmly. "Go calm yourself down and let me handle this. The last thing we need is for the First Lady of the church to be giving the whole town a show with her ex-husband. I'll call you back in here when I get everything sorted out."

First Lady Hall huffed and stormed out of the kitchen.

"Come sit down," said Grandpap Jared, leading Andre to a kitchen chair. He wiped Andre's tears and asked, "What happened?"

"I'm the screwup of the family," said Andre.

"No, you're not."

"Yes, I am," said Andre. "I'm always messing everything up, and everything's always my fault."

"What'd you mess up?"

"Everything."

"What's everything?"

"Everything. I just can't seem to do anything right. And it seems like every time I try, all it does is make things worse and everyone just gets mad at me and treat me like I'm stupid."

Grandpap Jared frowned. Then he nodded and took hold of Andre's hand.

"I know how you feel," said Grandpap Jared. "I used to think I was the family screwup."

"You did?" asked Andre, his tears slowing down.

"Oh yeah!" said Grandpap Jared. He took on a mocking tone and wagged his finger, saying, "You can't tell Jared anything. If you do, all your business will be all over town before the sun sets."

Andre giggled.

"But you know what I learned?" said Grandpap Jared. "There is no screwup of the family. Not when you're being yourself. Not when you're being who God made you to be. God doesn't screw up and He knew the type of person he meant for you to be when He made you."

Andre stopped crying. It made him feel better that someone did not think of him as a screwup.

"Now, I want you to answer me honestly," said Grandpap Jared. "Did your father ever say out of his mouth that you were the family screwup?"

"No," sighed Andre.

"Then why do you think he thinks that about you?"

"I just feel like a disappointment to him."

"Has he ever said you're a disappointment?"

"No."

"Then that settles it. You're not a disappointment."

"But–!"

"No buts," said Grandpap Jared. "You're not a disappointment. End of story."

"Okay, I've waited long enough," griped First Lady Hall, marching back into the kitchen. She placed a hand on the kitchen table and leaned over Andre, wedging herself between him and his grandfather. "What'd your daddy do? Do I need to go over there?"

"It's taken care of," said Grandpap Jared. "He just had a misunderstanding with Torrance, and he's going to go over there and get it straightened out."

"Do I need to go with you?" questioned First Lady Hall.

"No ma'am," said Andre.

"Alright," said First Lady Hall, stepping back. "Alright."

"Satisfied?" quipped Grandpap Jared.

"Uhn uhn, don't do that," remarked First Lady Hall. "Do not do that. Because it's been a few times when I came home in tears, and you got riled up."

"Why you think I told you to go calm down?"

"I just don't like seeing my children in tears."

"No caring parent does," said Grandpap Jared. "You think you're okay to go back home now?"

"Yes sir," answered Andre.

"Good," said Grandpap Jared. "And remember what we talked about."

Andre returned home and went to his room. A few minutes later, Mr. Brown knocked and entered.

"Andre?" said Mr. Brown.

"If you're going to say I told you so, then I'll save you the trouble," said Andre. "I... I should've never spoken to Mr. Kasey. All it did was cause a bunch of trouble."

"I wasn't going to say I told you so," said Mr. Brown. "I was going to ask if you were alright."

"I'm okay."

A strange look crossed his father's face.

"I'm glad you're okay," said Mr. Brown before leaving the room.

"Where'd you go?" asked Antoine.

"I don't want to talk about it," said Andre.

It had been a tiresome day for him. All Andre wanted then was to be left alone.

-

Daughter vs Father

Let me tell you about a man I call my dad.
For a few days now he's been real mad,
Because of a choice that I made,
He's been real silent the past few days.
Let me tell you about my second daughter,
Who betrayed me with a phony father.
She knew what that man put me through,
And yet she did what she wanted to do.
He hasn't made a sound.
How could she be so proud?
Can't he see I'm grown?
How couldn't I have known?
Can't he see I don't want to fight?
I should have told her going wasn't right.
Getting through to my dad is sometimes hard,
But I hope that this doesn't tear us apart.

-

Mary

By that Tuesday, Mr. Brown still had not spoken to Mary. She sat with Gretchen at breakfast before leaving for work.

"Where's Dad?" asked Mary.

"He's still getting ready," answered Gretchen. "Has he spoken to you yet?"

"No."

"I don't like this," said Gretchen, shaking her head. "You shouldn't go five days without speaking to your child."

"It's fine," said Mary. "One time, he and Karla went a whole month without speaking to each other."

"That's terrible," said Gretchen. "Do you want me to get him to talk to you?"

"That's alright," said Mary. "He'll talk to me when he's ready."

Mr. Brown entered the kitchen, and Mary got up and left. She knew there was no point in even attempting to speak to him.

After work, Mary went to visit Grandma Marianne. She needed someone to talk to who knew what it was like to be in her shoes.

"What happened to us telling him together?" asked Grandma Marianne.

"He found out sooner than I expected," answered Mary. "Now he won't talk to me."

"Mhmm," said Grandma Marianne. "I know how that feels."

"He's given you the silent treatment too?"

"He wouldn't dare," answered Grandma Marianne. "But my daddy on the other hand. We went eight years without talking to each other."

"Eight years?"

"Yeah. And then when we finally did start talking again, he died the next year."

"Oh."

"I hope you and Torrance don't plan to go that long without speaking."

"I hope so too. But it's up to him."

"It could be up to me if you want."

"No, that's alright."

They heard the front door open, followed by the familiar thump of a cane coming to the kitchen. Mr. Leonard appeared in the entryway and looked at Mary.

"Didn't think I'd be seeing you again," said Mr. Leonard.

"Hi," said Mary.

"Want to go somewhere with me?"

"Go where?" questioned Grandma Marianne, placing a hand on Mary's arm.

"To Derrick's."

"What you going over there for?"

"I want to talk to him."

"You're wasting your time. He won't talk to you."

"He talked to you."

"I'm not you."

"I'm going."

"Go on then. Don't say I didn't warn you."

"You coming Mary?"

"What's she need to go for?"

"I want her to. She might learn something for her research."

"It's alright Grandma," said Mary. "I'll go."

Grandma Marianne shook her head and let go of Mary's arm. Mary rode with Mr. Leonard to Pastor Derrick's house. She knew the real reason he wanted her to go was because he did not want to go alone. When they arrived, Pastor Derrick was sitting out on the porch.

"Derrick," said Mr. Leonard.

"What are you doing here?" questioned Pastor Derrick, narrowing his eyes at Mr. Leonard.

"I came to talk," said Mr. Leonard. He ascended the porch, and looked around, "This reminds me of when I used to visit you after church, and you'd tell me what you preached on that day."

"What do you want to talk about?" asked Pastor Derrick, still looking warily at Mr. Leonard.

"I want us to be friends again," said Mr. Leonard. When Pastor Derrick began to protest, Mr. Leonard stopped him, saying, "You told me you still cared about me. If you still care about me, then there's still a chance. If you can be friends with Marianne again, then why can't you be friends with me again?"

"How can I be friends with someone who did what you did?"

"I've tried to make things right. I've tried to do better. Isn't that enough?"

"Things can't be fixed that easily, Leonard."

"Derrick," pleaded Mr. Leonard. "I need you."

Mary watched as Pastor Derrick's face went through several emotions. He stood up and leaned against his porch railing, looking out over his land.

"No," said Pastor Derrick.

"Derrick!"

"Stop," commanded Pastor Derrick. "I can't... I won't let myself get close to you."

"Why not?"

"You... you broke my heart," said Pastor Derrick, turning to face Mr. Leonard. "And you bring out a side of me that I don't like. Someone like you, who's mean and hurtful. I don't like him... and you bring him out."

"Derrick please!" begged Mr. Leonard. "You're all I got left!"

Mr. Leonard stepped forward and lost his balance. He fell into Pastor Derrick, who caught him and held him for a moment.

"No!" said Pastor Derrick, shoving Mr. Leonard away. He turned away from Mr. Leonard and gripped the railing. "Go away!"

"Derrick..." whimpered Mr. Leonard.

"Now!"

Mr. Leonard looked sadly at Pastor Derrick's back before leaving. As they left, Mary turned to look at Pastor Derrick, noticing he looked very troubled.

"Nobody loves me," said Mr. Leonard as they drove home.

"Pastor Derrick loves you," said Mary. "He loves you a lot."

"If he loves me so much, why'd he push me away?"

"Because the love he feels for you is the kind that hurts."

"Then I can't be loved?"

Mary did not answer because she could not tell him she felt that same love. To love Mr. Leonard meant to betray her father. It meant to ignore everything her father had been put through for a man that she barely knew. And she could not do that to her father.

"I guess not," sighed Mr. Leonard. They pulled in front of her house, and he said, "Well, this is where you get off."

"Yeah," said Mary. She wanted to say more, but she did not know what to say.

"This is for you," said Mr. Leonard, holding out two small glossy papers.

Mary took it and stared at them in awe. The first was an old black and white photo of a woman who heavily resembled her. In the second, the woman stood with a heavyset man who resembled Mr. Leonard."

"Those are my parents," muttered Mr. Leonard. "I figured you'd want them for your research."

Mary looked at Mr. Leonard with gratitude. But he would not look at her. He stared straight ahead.

"Goodbye Mary," said Mr. Leonard. He would not look at her.

"Goodbye Mr. Leonard."

And he was gone. Just like that, their time together ended. And Mary knew it would remain ended. She figured that's why Mr. Leonard would not look at her. Because he also knew it was over, and looking at her would make it harder to accept.

Mr. Brown was in her room reading her family history notes. Normally, she would not have minded because it was his family history too. But he had not spoken to her since that disastrous dinner, and she felt it rather rude for him to go through her stuff without even speaking to her first.

"Hey Dad," sighed Mary, unwilling to argue with her father over her privacy.

"Is this everything he told you about himself?" asked Mr. Brown. Those were the first words he had spoken to Mary in five days. Mary accepted them, figuring it to be better than silence.

"Who?"

"Brown."

"Yes, that's everything he's told me."

"What is it about him you like so much?"

"I just found him interesting."

"How long has this been going on?"

"Since December."

"December?! It's March!"

"I know."

"I just don't understand how you can befriend this man knowing everything he did to me," said Mr. Brown.

"That's why I got to know him," said Mary. "We've only got your side of the story and you've barely given us that. I wanted the full truth about everything."

"All you had to do was ask and I'd tell you."

"No, you wouldn't," said Mary. "When Drake asked you got mad at him and told him it wasn't his business."

"It wasn't!"

"You would've said the same thing to me."

"No, I wouldn't!" argued Mr. Brown.

"Why not?" challenged Mary. "What makes me so different from Drake that you'd tell me about your past but not him?"

"I don't...," said Mr. Brown, trying to find a reason. "Look, the point is you had no business talking to that man. But if you want to talk to him so badly, then go ahead."

"I won't be talking to him anymore."

"Why not?"

"There's nothing left to talk about," said Mary. "And I asked him, you know. Why he stopped believing you were his. He said his father told him you didn't look like him."

"He still had a choice to do the right thing," said Mr. Brown. "Just because your child doesn't look exactly like you doesn't mean they aren't yours."

"Is that why you treat me the way you do? Because I look nothing like you?"

"Who said you look nothing like me?" answered Mr. Brown. "Because I know my nose when I see it."

"But our skin isn't the same."

"So?"

"Dad, tell me the truth," said Mary. "Am I your favorite child?"

"Yes," said Mr. Brown sarcastically. "Out of all my children you are my favorite. Satisfied?"

"You could've just said no."

"I've *been* saying I don't have a favorite, but nobody listens to me," griped Mr. Brown. "You are my child. Period. How much darker you are than me doesn't determine how much I love you. I love you because you're my child."

Mary was relieved. But her relief did not last long. Her father had resumed looking through her research documents and had picked up the dreaded letter.

"Not that one!" shouted Mary.

"Why not?" asked Mr. Brown. Mary could not come up with an excuse and helplessly watched as her father learned the truth. Once he finished reading, he set the letter down and uttered, "Hm."

"I didn't want you to know," said Mary.

"That my grandfather killed someone?" said Mr. Brown, a hint of amusement in his voice. "That doesn't surprise me."

"It doesn't?"

"Your grandmother told me he had a past. She probably wouldn't be all that shocked by this either. Plus, I can finally solve a mystery I've been trying to figure out for years."

"What mystery?"

"He had this passage highlighted in the family bible. The one about David and Bathsheba. It's starting to make sense. Grandpa killed someone, and believed God punished him with stillborn children. That's why he blamed himself for them not living. But if I'm right, which I'm pretty sure I am, then that would mean Grandpa killed two people. I wonder who the second person was..."

"Louise," admitted Mary.

"Louise?" said Mr. Brown. "You think he killed his sister?"

"Not purposely," said Mary. "He thought she died of a broken heart, and he blamed himself."

"That makes sense," said Mr. Brown. "How do you know?"

"Uh... an anonymous source told me."

"An anonymous source?" said Mr. Brown. "So, someone else knows about this already?"

"I don't reveal my sources."

"It's a lot of things you don't reveal apparently," said Mr. Brown. "What's that in your hand?"

"Some pictures," said Mary, handing the pictures to Mr. Brown. "These were his parents."

Mr. Brown frowned at the pictures. He kept looking between them and Mary.

"You do look like her," noted Mr. Brown.

"Did you know them?"

"Not personally. But I knew of them. You really do look like her."

Mr. Brown set the pictures aside, his mouth gritted angrily.

"Look Dad," said Mary. "I didn't mean to hurt you. But I'm nineteen now. I should be able to make decisions for myself."

"And you can," said Mr. Brown. "But every decision has consequences, good and bad."

"So, what are we doing here? You just going to be mad at me forever?"

"I might if you get smart like that again," said Mr. Brown. "Go ahead and do what you want since you're so grown. Don't let me stand in your way."

Mr. Brown left the room, and Mary rolled her eyes. The first time she talked to her father in five days, and all that came from it was more revealed secrets and her father still having an attitude. Mary was over it and more determined than ever to get into music school and get out of her father's house.

What Happened?

If I could ask my father one question,
About something I'd really want to know,
Something that would have him in reflection,
Then I know exactly where I would go.

I'd ask him to tell me what is for real.
To tell me his deal and to tell me why,
Whenever we're together that it feels,
Like a battle even when we don't try.

This isn't how I want things between us.
I wish we could go back to that time when,
Things between us were not so serious.
When we got along and we were friends.

Tell me what's happened to us, my father.
Am I your enemy or your daughter?

If there was one thing I never wanted,
It was to have issue with my kid.
But somehow or another,
And it really makes me wonder,
Just how did it happen,
Can someone tell me when,
I became father of the year?
Not the one making smiles ear to ear,
But the one making children cry.
The one making them ask why.
When did I become the villain,
To all of my children?
Someone make it plain for me,
Because I really just don't see,

What I did that was so bad,
That makes me the worst dad.

Karla

The difference between Karla and Mary was that Mary cared if their father stopped talking to her. She had listened to Mary's complaints about her first experience with the silent treatment, trying not to roll her eyes. Karla had experienced it from him so many times that it no longer fazed her.

Karla had no intention of reconciling with her father first. He would have to take the first step if he wanted things fixed between them. She was tired of always having to be the bigger person in their relationship when he was supposed to be the parent.

"I need you to do something, and you might not like it," said Forrest on Tuesday afternoon.

"What is it?" asked Karla.

"I need you to go make up with your father."

"Why do I always have to make up with him? Why can't he ever come make up with me?"

"I can call him over here if you want."

"Why are you always so nice to him?" griped Karla. "Even back then you were nice to him when he deserved to get beat down for how badly he treated you."

"I'm a pastor, I can't beat people down," laughed Forrest. "I admit I was nicer to your father than most men in my position would've been. But I also knew where he was coming from. I've known your father a long time. I even gave him dating advice when he was dating your mother, and I was at their wedding. So, I imagine he felt very betrayed and hurt when I ended up with your mother. That's why I was and still am nice to him."

"Well, if it were me, he would've gotten slapped," said Karla.

"Then it's a good thing I'm not you," said Forrest. "So, did you want me to call him over here?"

"No, that's alright. I'll go over there."

Karla did not know what she was going to say. Over the past week, she had learned how much of herself she had sacrificed throughout the years. She had also learned how alike she was to her father. The last thing she wanted to do was talk to the man who had turned her into who she had become.

When Karla arrived at the house, she noticed Mary's bike was gone. She knew Mary was off work and had hoped Mary would be there to act as a buffer between her and Mr. Brown. Karla released a heavy sigh, realizing she would have to go at it alone, and knocked on the door. It was Gretchen who answered.

"Hi," said Gretchen cheerfully. "Come to see your father?"

"Yeah," answered Karla. "How have things been going?"

"There's been a few things we needed to get straight, but overall, I'd say things are great," said Gretchen.

"That's good," said Karla. She was glad Gretchen was happy. But a small part of her wondered how long the happiness would last. "Do you know where Mary is?"

"She just left a few minutes before you arrived," said Gretchen. "She and Torrance finally talked, but I don't know how well things went. They both seem pretty annoyed."

"Isn't that just great," muttered Karla. The last thing she needed was to have her father in an annoyed mood when she was trying to make up with him.

"I'll let him know you're here," said Gretchen. She disappeared into Mr. Brown's room and, minutes later, reappeared with Mr. Brown.

"I'm going out right quick," said Gretchen. "I'll be back."

After Gretchen left, Karla and her father stared at each other in awkward silence. Karla steeled herself for the battle she was sure was coming.

"Why are you here?" asked Mr. Brown.

"Forrest asked me to come talk to you," said Karla.

"About what?"

"He wants us to make up."

"What I need to make up for?" said Mr. Brown. "I'm not the one with the problem."

"Well, I can't leave until we make up," said Karla annoyedly.

"That's sounds like a 'you' problem."

"Why do you hate me?" asked Karla.

"I could ask you the same question," said Mr. Brown.

"I don't hate you."

"I'd say the same."

"Then why are you always the angriest with me?"

"Every question you ask me is a question I could ask you too."

"Here's one you can't ask: why am I your least favorite child?"

"Why am I your least favorite parent?"

"I don't have a least favorite parent."

"I don't have a least favorite child."

"Why are you always so difficult?"

"Why are you?"

Karla closed her eyes and exhaled through her nose. Then, she stared out the screen door. She could not leave because Forrest expected her to make up with her father. But her father was being petty, and her patience with him was growing thin. So, she stared out the screen door like she had when her mother had left.

"Karla," said Mr. Brown.

"Sir?" answered Karla, not turning to face him.

"Let's talk."

"I'm listening."

"I'm not going to talk to your back."

Karla rolled her eyes and turned around.

"I don't hate you and you know I don't," began Mr. Brown.

"I don't hate you either," replied Karla.

"So then, what's the problem?"

"You tell me."

"All I know is you started disliking me after the divorce," said Mr. Brown. "At the dinner you said I chased your mother away."

"You did."

"I didn't. She left. But I didn't want her to."

"She left because you couldn't get it together. And after she left you put me in her place and took everything out on me."

"That's not true."

"It is too. I can't count how many times I've heard you yell 'you're just like your mother' at me."

"You are just like your mother."

"So?"

"Karla, I don't understand," said Mr. Brown. "What did I do to you that was so bad that you have all this animosity toward me?"

"You made me take on Mom's role after she left!"

"I was thirty and suddenly found myself with six kids to raise alone," said Mr. Brown. "So, yeah I asked you and your brother to help me a little."

"It wasn't just a little," argued Karla. "You basically made me the new mom of the house. Everything she did except the romantic parts, you made me do. And you took all your anger out on me. I didn't know which Dad I was getting when you came around. And I couldn't tell you anything because you'd get upset. It was too much living with you."

"I did the best I could."

"Oh my–!" ranted Karla. "You're not getting it!"

"I am too getting it!" said Mr. Brown. "Everything you're saying is the same thing your brother said when he left. But I wish you'd both understand that I was literally doing this alone. I didn't have anyone to turn to."

"You had Grandma and your siblings."

"Your aunts and uncles had their own families to worry about. And I love your grandmother but..."

Mr. Brown shook his head. He shoved his fists in his pockets and sighed.

"I thought I had done a great job raising all of you," admitted Mr. Brown. "In fact, I still think I did a great job."

"So that's it," said Karla. "You don't care."

"I do care!" snapped Mr. Brown. "But I couldn't have been as terrible as you say I was. You wouldn't be here if I was. I had to have done something right at some point."

Karla felt herself getting more and more frustrated with her father. And though she tried to stop them, the tears started falling.

"Why are you crying?" asked Mr. Brown.

"Because you're not listening to me!" snapped Karla. "I'm trying to tell you how you treated me and you're not listening! You never listen!"

"You said I told you that you were like your mother."

"It's how you said it!" said Karla. "You'd say it with this disgusted look on your face like it was the worst thing in the world to be like her! It made me feel like you hated me like you did her and you didn't want me around!"

"That's not true!"

"Yes, it is! Just say it so I can leave, and we'll never have to speak to each other again! Just tell me you hate me already!"

Mr. Brown walked away, and Karla returned to staring out the screen door. Things were not resolved yet, so she still could not leave. After staring out the screen door for a good ten minutes, Karla exhaled and went in search of her father. She found him sitting on the back porch and silently sat beside him.

"Why is everything always my fault?" said Mr. Brown. He sounded like a child when he said it, and when he turned to look at Karla, she realized he was crying.

"Are you serious?" scoffed Karla. "What are you crying for?"

"Because for the past few days all I've heard from all my kids is how terrible a father I am. Do you know how that makes me feel? It makes me feel like crap!"

"Oh really?"

"Oh yeah, just rub it in! The worst father in the world feels like crap, and I get to celebrate after ruining his wedding! Why don't you go ahead and tell me you hate me while you're at it!"

"Don't turn this around on me! You're the one who hates me!"

"No I don't! If I hated you, I wouldn't have bothered raising you!"

"Ooh!" grumbled Karla. "Sometimes I can't stand you!"

"Sometimes I can't stand you either!" screamed Mr. Brown.

Karla wanted to leave and go home but could not because they still had not made up.

"You know what your problem is?" ranted Karla. "You don't like to take responsibility for what you've done!"

"What I've done?!" cried Mr. Brown.

"Everything is your fault!" said Karla. "You chased Mom away. You put me in her place. You're the reason I am the way I am. You did this!"

Mr. Brown did not respond. He stared straight ahead, tears rolling down his face.

"Well?" demanded Karla. "What do you have to say for yourself?"

"What do you want me to say?" said Mr. Brown. "All of you say the same thing. That everything that's gone wrong is all my fault. I'm tired of explaining myself. So, if I'm the bad guy for trying my best, then I'm the bad guy."

"This is what I mean by you're not listening," complained Karla. "Nobody is saying you're the bad guy. You keep saying you did your best, and we know you did your best. But you also did some things wrong, and we want you to take accountability for them."

"Ahem."

Karla and her father turned around to see Gretchen looking at them.

"I'm back," said Gretchen. "Did you two make up?"

"If by 'make up', you mean Karla blaming me for everything, then yeah," scoffed Mr. Brown.

"He just doesn't listen to anything I say!" griped Karla.

"Okay, let's all pause," said Gretchen. "What's wrong?"

"He won't take accountability for his actions when he was raising me," said Karla.

"She claims I was the worst father in the world but I know I wasn't," said Mr. Brown.

"Okay," said Gretchen. "Torrance, you remember what we talked about on our wedding night? About your relationship with your mother?"

"Why you got to bring that up?" grumbled Mr. Brown.

"Because that's what's wrong here," said Gretchen. "Remember, you're your mother in this situation."

"But I didn't do things the way she did!" argued Mr. Brown. "I didn't let the same things happen to my kids!"

"True," said Gretchen. "But just because you didn't repeat her mistakes doesn't mean you didn't make any of your own."

"Hmph!"

"Don't be hardheaded. You know I'm right."

Mr. Brown looked down at his hands and frowned.

"I'm going to give you two some privacy," said Gretchen. "Hopefully, you two can resolve this."

Gretchen left the pair alone.

"What did I do wrong?" sighed Mr. Brown. "Why is it so hard for us two to get along?"

"I'm not repeating myself," said Karla.

"If I was that bad then why are you here?"

"Because Mr. Forrest wanted us to make up," answered Karla. After a short pause, she added quietly, "And because I love you."

"I love you too, Karla," said Mr. Brown. "I'd never do anything to purposely hurt you."

"But you did hurt me," said Karla. "That's why I left."

"I didn't mean to," said Mr. Brown.

Karla nodded, accepting it was probably the closest she would get to an apology from her father. By that point, she could hold onto her issues or let them go. She chose to let them go.

"So, where do we go from here?" asked Karla.

"I want us to get along," said Mr. Brown.

"Then, let's get along," said Karla.

"Okay," answered Mr. Brown. He took off his glasses and began cleaning them, and Karla did the same. Mr. Brown looked at her and said, "I can't see you."

"I can't see you either," giggled Karla.

The two laughed.

"Ah," said Mr. Brown, half-sighing. "Even that's my fault. All my kids got their mother's eyes but got my terrible eyesight."

"We'll just blame it on the tears this time," said Karla.

Mr. Brown put his glasses back on his face. He looked at Karla and smiled.

"Ah, there you are," laughed Mr. Brown. "My beautiful baby girl."

"And there you are too, Dad," said Karla, placing her newly cleaned glasses on her face.

"I've never hated you Karla," said Mr. Brown. "And I'm sorry that I ever made you feel like I did. I never meant to hurt you like that."

"I forgive you," said Karla, surprised he had apologized.

She hoped that she and her father could get along like they said they would. There were still a lot of things to mend between them, but Karla was at least glad for the start. Her daddy was gone for good. But Karla found that her dad did not seem like such a bad guy either.

Man of Honor

I'll admit I was knocked down for a bit,
And figured that I was down for the count.
But now I've got myself a second wind,
And I'm ready to continue the bout.
Where life thought it had taken me on out,
I have picked myself up off of the floor,
And I'm raising up a valorous shout.
And though it may be a battle of gore,
I'll fight with heart like a man of honor.

Antoine

By Wednesday, Antoine had already begun planning for how he would earn the rest of his father's money. He had decided to return to mowing lawns and would put all of the lessons he had learned the previous week to use.

During one of the passing periods, Antoine was making his way to his next class when Priscella approached him.

"Antoine," said Priscella.

"Huh?" answered Antoine.

"This is for you."

Priscella handed Antoine an envelope.

"What is this?" asked Antoine.

"It's the money my parents owe you," said Priscella. "A hundred dollars each for you and Mariella."

"So, they had a change of heart, huh?" scoffed Antoine, choosing not to correct Priscella about how it was supposed to be a hundred dollars split between him and Mariella. He figured they deserved it after what the Paynes had put them through.

"No, it came from my piggy bank," said Priscella.

"Your piggy bank?" repeated Antoine. "Your parents didn't give you this?"

"It's my allowance that I've been saving," answered Priscella.

"Why are you giving it to me?"

"Because I felt bad," said Priscella. She pursed her lips and continued, "Sometimes, they do that to me too and I hate it. They'll promise to do one thing if I do something for them, then act like they don't remember. Sometimes, I feel like they think I'm stupid."

"Oh," said Antoine, unsure of what to do with the outpour of information. "Uh... thanks, I guess."

"You're welcome," said Priscella.

Antoine found Mariella at her locker, exchanging her books for her next class.

"Want to make a hundred bucks?" asked Antoine.

"Oh, now you want to work with me?" said Mariella. "I thought you didn't like me taking half *your* money."

"You just have to do one simple thing and the money is yours," said Antoine with a smirk.

"What?"

"Tell me I'm the best cousin in the world."

"You're the best cousin in the world," said Mariella dryly. She held her hand out and said, "Now hand over the money."

"You didn't even mean it!"

"You didn't say I had to mean it. You just said to tell you."

"Touché," said Antoine, handing Mariella the money.

"Where'd you get this from?" asked Mariella.

"Priscella."

"She gave you a hundred dollars?"

"She gave me two hundred," corrected Antoine. "That's your cut for helping clean out the garage."

"What's the catch?"

"No catch. She felt bad. Apparently, her parents do her dirty too, so she knows how it feels."

"Well, I'm not complaining."

Derik and Danielle passed by them, holding hands, and Derik looked back at him and grinned. Antoine gave him a thumbs up.

"Ugh," said Mariella.

"What'd you make that noise for?" asked Antoine.

"Because Dani dropped me and Mariana as friends."

"What'd you do?"

"I didn't do anything!"

"So, now you don't have any friends?"

"I don't know," said Mariella. "Do you consider yourself my friend?"

"I'm your cousin."

"And?" said Mariella. "Andre and Mariana are cousins, and they aren't friends like that."

"That's because Mariana, and *you*, act like brats sometimes," said Antoine. "But I'd say we're friends, even if you do get on my nerves sometimes."

"Then, there's your answer," said Mariella.

Antoine ended up working out alone after school. Derik had gone to hang out with Danielle. Although Antoine still disliked Danielle, he had accepted the relationship. Danielle was Derik's girlfriend, but Antoine knew that if he really needed him, Derik would have his back.

Since Derik had skipped the workout, Antoine had to walk home. He had begun getting used to and even liked being more independent. As he made the trek home, a car horn honked at him.

"Hey Nephew," said Uncle Terrence. He was driving his regular car and had his sons with him. "Where are you off to?"

"Home," answered Antoine. "I just got done working out."

"Getting big and strong huh?" laughed Uncle Terrence. "You need a ride?"

"Sure," said Antoine, getting in his uncle's car.

"We're going to stop by Bud's new food truck first," explained Uncle Terrence.

Mr. Bud's food truck, Flowerbud's, was outside the park. He had had his grand opening that Monday and people who had tried his food gave positive reports. When they arrived, Mr. Bud was tending to a few customers.

"Hey Boss!" said Mr. Bud when they finally got to the window. "What can I get you?"

"Surprise us," said Uncle Terrence.

Mr. Bud ended up making them grilled chicken sandwiches.

"This is really good!" exclaimed Terrence Jr.

"It is!" agreed Michael.

"It is really good," said Uncle Terrence.

"Thanks Boss," said Mr. Bud, blushing.

"How are things going?" asked Uncle Terrence.

"Things are going good," said Mr. Bud.

"That's good," said Uncle Terrence.

There was an awkward silence until Uncle Terrence went to throw his trash away.

"He's sorry for how he treated you all these years," said Terrence Jr.

"Junior!" scolded Michael.

"What?" said Terrence Jr. "He's not going to come out and say it so I will."

"It's not your place."

"Well, what am I supposed to do Mike? Just leave Mr. Bud in the dark?"

"You're supposed to shut up and let Dad handle it when he's ready."

"Well, he's taking too long."

"You don't get to decide that!"

"What are you two going on about now?" asked Uncle Terrence.

Terrence Jr. and Michael both became quiet.

"Boss," said Mr. Bud. "Can I tell you a story?"

"A story?" repeated Uncle Terrence.

"Mhmm," said Mr. Bud. "You know when I was growing up, I lived in a gated community, and went to private school, and pretty much all my friends were White."

"Is this the story?" questioned Uncle Terrence.

"Yeah," said Mr. Bud. "Me and my friends always used to play cops and robbers. But I began noticing that they always made me a robber. So, one day when we were playing, I said I wanted to be a cop and they told me I couldn't be one because I looked like a robber. And I asked, 'what's a robber look like?', and they said brown like you."

Everyone waited for Mr. Bud to continue in stunned silence.

"And I was confused at first because I thought we were all the same," said Mr. Bud. "They all had White dads just like I did. But apparently, me having a Black mom, unlike them, meant I couldn't be a cop. So, I went home and told my parents, and they got very upset. My dad told me I could be a cop if I wanted to be. When I finished college, he asked me did I still want to be a cop. I thought he was joking so I said sure. Next thing I know, he's telling me I've got a guaranteed spot waiting for me in the town down the road. He tells me the new chief just restructured the whole department, so I shouldn't have any issue fitting in down there. There was an issue though. I didn't actually want to be there. But my dad was so proud and eager to show that I could be just as good as everyone else's sons that I stayed for about seventeen years.

Uncle Terrence frowned.

"I just want you to know that it's not your fault that I left," said Mr. Bud. "I was glad to work under you all these years. I thought you were a great boss actually. Even with how hard you were on me, I always knew it was only because you a lot cared about the community."

"Oop," said Terrence Jr. "Plot twist."

"Always instigating," grumbled Michael.

"I left to pursue my own dreams and what made me happy," said Mr. Bud. "This is honestly what I've always wanted to do. I appreciate you and thank you for putting up with me all these years. And I hope I can count on you to be a regular customer of mine."

"Yeah," said Uncle Terrence. "You can."

"Great," said Mr. Bud. His phone rang, and he answered it. "Hello?... What?!... What are they doing here?!... Now?!... Jana wai–! Ugh!"

"What's wrong?" asked Uncle Terrence.

"My parents are coming," said Mr. Bud.

"Here?"

"Mhmm," said Mr. Bud. "They want to see the food truck I left my nice-paying job for."

"We'll leave you to it," said Uncle Terrence.

As they walked away, they passed an older couple moving toward the food truck. The man was pale and green-eyed, while the woman was light-brown. Both were gray-haired and wore looks that were a mix of curious and concerned.

"We're those his parents?" whispered Terrence Jr.

"Mhmm," answered Uncle Terrence. "Judge Darwin Vaughn and his wife Mrs. Deborah Vaughn."

"I've heard of Judge Vaughn," said Michael. "Isn't he a really strict judge?"

"Yes," said Uncle Terrence.

Antoine cast a final glance at Mr. Bud. He was talking to his parents, but it seemed he was no longer nervous to see them. There was even a smile on his face.

"Alright Junior, what'd you say?" asked Uncle Terrence when they were back in the car.

"Why does it have to be me that said something?" cried Terrence Jr.

"When I left, we were talking about food. I come back to you fussing with Mike, and Bud telling me he appreciates me. What'd you say?"

"I just told him you felt bad," muttered Terrence Jr.

"You could've at least let me do it myself."

"You weren't going to."

"How do you know?"

"Because I know you."

"Sometimes you can be a real knucklehead."

Mr. Brown was lying on the couch when Antoine entered the house. Uncle Terrence came in behind him and stood over his brother.

"Torrance," whispered Uncle Terrence.

Mr. Brown's eyes flew open, and he stared at his brother with bleary eyes.

"Hi," said Uncle Terrence. When Mr. Brown did not respond, he furrowed his brow and asked, "Why are you looking at me like that?"

"Just for a second when I opened my eyes, you looked like Grandpa," said Mr. Brown.

"Nope. Just your horrible half-brother."

"I really wish you'd stop saying that," griped Mr. Brown.

"Why?"

"Because if you're my half-brother, what does that make me to you?"

"Uh...," uttered Uncle Terrence, his face growing pink with embarrassed realization.

"Uh...," mocked Mr. Brown. "Exactly. I don't even disrespect you like that so I don't even know why you'd do that to me."

"Sorry."

"What are you doing here?"

"Dropping Antoine off," said Uncle Terrence. "Where's Gretchen?"

"At cheer practice," answered Mr. Brown.

"How are things going?"

"Great."

"That's good," said Uncle Terrence. "I took Antoine to try out Bud's food."

"How'd it taste?"

"It tasted great. I think he'll do well for himself. His parents had dropped by right when we were leaving."

"Oh," said Mr. Brown. "Jana said they weren't too happy about him leaving his job."

"Yeah, but I think he'll be able to convince them."

"You still feeling bad about yourself?"

"You didn't have to ask it like that."

"Look man, we've had a rough time recently. I just want to know if you're okay."

"I'm good. You?"

"I'm always good."

"No, you're not."

Antoine watched as his father and Uncle Terrence bantered with each other. He remembered hearing them talk about how hard they had fought to get to their level of brotherhood. It reminded him of Pastor Derrick's brotherhood lesson and how true brotherhood was often tested.

Antoine was glad for his brothers. And he was glad for the friends he could call brothers. He realized they were essential to helping shape him into the man he was becoming.

After Uncle Terrence left, Antoine presented his father with the hundred dollars.

"This is for you," said Antoine.

"I knew you could do it," said Mr. Brown. "You didn't try to sell your gaming system again, did you?

"No sir."

"Good," said Mr. Brown. "Let me get it for you."

Antoine was glad to have his gaming system back. He felt proud to have earned it back after enduring a hard lesson.

But Antoine was also glad for the lesson. He had learned so much within the past week that Antoine decided he would go into business for himself. Antoine planned to start a lawnmowing business and continue making money for himself.

Antoine loved the feeling of independence and realized his father had been right about him one day appreciating the hard lesson. He hoped as he continued to grow, he would become a man that his father could be proud of.

-

If And When

My senses left when I bid you adieu.
Should you ever come back I'll still be here.
I long to see your smile reappear,
In my life in that special way you do.
I wonder that I'm still in love you,
And wish I'd never let it disappear.
For in my heart there is one thing that's clear,
I still want you and hope you want me too.

Will you return to the sight of my love,
And mend the pieces of our broken heart?
For I believe you are sent from above,
Please say that we will not remain apart.
That life together is what you dream of,
I pray that one day we'll have a fresh start.

Adrianna

Adrianna had not planned to visit Derek again so soon after their breakup. But she had noticed his underwear sitting on her nightstand and realized she had never given them to him.

He did not frown when he saw her, but he did not smile either.

"Uh... hi," said Adrianna awkwardly.

"Hi," said Derek just as awkwardly.

"These are for you," said Adrianna, handing Derek the underwear.

"You bought me underwear?"

"It was before we broke up. I forgot to give them to you."

"Oh. Thanks."

Silence filled the room.

"Look," said Adrianna. "I don't want things between us to be awkward. I still like you. It's just... things between us weren't working right now."

"I know," said Derek. "I'm not mad about it. I still like you too."

Adrianna blushed. He still liked her.

"We can just be friends for now," said Derek.

"Yeah," agreed Adrianna. "We'll just be friends."

"And who knows?" added Derek. "Maybe when things are better, we can give ourselves another shot."

"Maybe," said Adrianna. "But for now, we'll just be friends."

"Yeah," said Derek. "We'll just be friends."

He grinned at her, and her heart fluttered. His toothy smile lit up his face in the way that she liked. She carried the memory of it home with her.

As she walked home, Adrianna received a call from Mariana.

"Hello?" said Adrianna.

"Hi," said Mariana. "Uh... Jada told me what happened."

"Mhmm."

"I'm uh... I'm sorry."

"Okay. I forgive you."

"You do?"

"Sure. But you really should stop treating us like we're all your enemies. We're your family."

"Okay," sighed Mariana. "Thanks."

"Mhmm."

Adrianna found her father sitting on the porch with Gretchen. She had not told her father where she had gone and started to turn around to avoid another confrontation.

"You do know we already saw you, right?" called Mr. Brown.

Adrianna sighed and ascended the porch.

"Where are you coming from?" asked Mr. Brown.

"Derek's," answered Adrianna. "I had to give him some stuff back. We're just going to be friends."

"You're handling this pretty well," said Mr. Brown. "It's a shame too. I liked Derek."

"Oh well," said Adrianna. "At least you won't think I'm fast anymore."

"Excuse me?" said Gretchen. "What is she talking about?"

"That's not what I said!" whined Mr. Brown. "I said people in the town expected her to be fast because of who she was dating!"

"Why?!"

"Uh..."

"Do I need to unmarry you?"

"No!"

"Then you need to get this right. I don't like that."

"Okay, I will!"

"You better."

Gretchen got up and went into the house.

"Why?" griped Mr. Brown. "We finally get things good around here and here you come with this."

"I was just saying," said Adrianna.

"That's not even what I meant, and you know that!"

"Well, what was I supposed to think?" asked Adrianna. "You don't pick me up from dance practice, and then you come home yelling and screaming about how I probably snuck off to my boyfriend's house against your will when I didn't."

Mr. Brown did not respond. Instead, he pursed his lips and stared at the ground.

"Dad, that really hurt my feelings," continued Adrianna. She no longer cared if he got upset with her. He would know how he had made her feel. "I'm trying to follow your rules and respect you, and then you still get mad at me and accuse me of something I didn't do. And I still don't know why."

"I wasn't mad at you," muttered Mr. Brown. "I was mad about something else."

"So, I'm your new punching bag," said Adrianna. "Good to know."

"You are not a punching bag, you're my daughter."

"Okay, so I'm your new Karla. Even better."

"Adrianna don't get smart. I shouldn't have taken my anger out on you. But what I said is true and I'm not going to apologize for telling you the truth."

"But Dad, you know me, and you know I wouldn't do that. Why can't you trust me to make good decisions?"

Mr. Brown chuckled.

"What's so funny?" asked Adrianna.

"I remember saying that to my grandfather once," explained Mr. Brown. "How the tables have turned."

Adrianna watched as her father's amused smile slowly melted into a frown.

"The tables have turned," repeated Mr. Brown more seriously. "You're right. I haven't trusted you to make good decisions, have I?"

Adrianna was so taken aback by her father's admission that she forgot to answer.

"Well, I guess it's too late to start now that you and Derek have broken up," sighed Mr. Brown. He perked up and added, "I hope I wasn't the reason you did."

"There were several reasons," said Adrianna, not wanting to admit her father was one of them.

"Oh," said Mr. Brown. "Okay. Well, if you decide to date again, I'll try harder to trust you. But that doesn't mean you test how much I'll be willing to try."

"I won't because I don't plan on dating again anytime soon," said Adrianna.

"Okay."

Adrianna was glad she had gotten through to her dad about trusting her. And she was sure she had made the right decision about breaking up with Derek, even if it hurt for the time being.

But Adrianna knew it would not always hurt. And she figured they could always give love a second chance in the future, as Derek had said. Only time would tell, and Adrianna found herself hoping it would tell her that love was possible for them again.

My Friends Ain't Real

I hate to say it but my friends ain't real.
Our friendships are over as it would seem,
But having no friends ain't that big a deal.

When I was their friend, I was full of zeal,
Cuz I thought I was a part of their team.
I hate to say it but my friends ain't real.

Upon our friendship they have placed a seal,
That's marked me an outsider as they deem.
But having no friends ain't that big a deal.

I wondered just how loneliness would feel.
It's bitter to wear its badge of esteem.
I hate to say it but my friends ain't real.

Now that I'm alone I should let out a peal,
To drown out the pain that makes my heart scream.
But having no friends ain't that big a deal.

As time goes on, I am sure that I'll heal,
And this to me will fade like a bad dream.
I hate to say it but my friends ain't real,
But having no friends ain't that big a deal.

Andre

Thursday was the fourth anniversary of Simon's death.

Andre stood staring at Simon's grave. It read 'Beloved Brother and Son. Simon Peter Stone'. He had only lived fourteen years.

He placed the flowers he had brought next to the ones already there. The Stones had been there earlier.

Andre left the graveyard without saying anything. His father had told him previously that talking to graves was pointless because the person was not there anymore. Their spirit had left the world.

It made Andre sad that Simon was no longer around. Four years had passed since his death, but it did not make things any less painful.

As he biked home, Andre rode past the Grahams's house. Tyler and Jada were sitting on their porch. Andre decided to stop and visit.

"Hey Andre," said Jada when he neared them.

"Hey," answered Andre.

Tyler waved and signed something to Jada, who then nodded her head.

"Tyler wants to know what's wrong," said Jada. "He said you look down."

"Oh," said Andre, slightly flustered. He wanted to say he did not have friends and felt alone. But he thought that would hurt Tyler's feelings. "I uh... I just miss my friend. Today is four years since he died."

Jada translated Andre's answer, and they watched as Tyler signed his response.

"He wants to know if you want to talk about it," said Jada.

"No," answered Andre, shaking his head.

As Tyler signed his response, Andre wondered if Tyler actually cared. Tyler probably had his own friends and did not have time to bother with Andre's issues.

Andre wondered who his friends truly were. He could not for sure list any, aside from his siblings and cousins. And maybe Allison. He was unsure of all the relationships in his life.

"He says he's if you need a friend he's here," said Jada.

"Okay," said Andre.

"I'm here too, by the way," said Jada. "That's from me, not him."

It was confirmed. Tyler was his friend. Possibly his only one. Aside from his siblings. And Allison and apparently Jada.

As he got closer to home, he rode past Derek's house. Derek was sitting outside in his wheelchair, and when he saw Andre, he started hollering.

"Andre!" called Derek. Samiel and Benjamin were with him. Andre had intended to keep riding like he had not heard, but again Derek called out, "ANDRE!"

Andre groaned and warily approached them. He did not know if he was walking into a circle of friends or a den of snakes.

"Yes?" said Andre.

"I feel like we didn't get to finish our talk Tuesday because Allison had to go," said Derek. "Like I said, I'm sorry for hurting your feelings."

"I said it was fine," said Andre.

"I just wanted to make sure there were no hard feelings. Benji wishes you guys could've been in the video."

"I can speak for myself you know," griped Benjamin. "And I already told him."

"Benji, you're always such a grouch," said Derek.

"Well, you and Sami haven't exactly been balls of sunshine lately either," countered Benjamin.

"Whatever Benji," sighed Derek. "We just wanted to say sorry Andre."

"Okay," said Andre.

"Friends?" said Derek, extending his hand for Andre to shake.

Andre stared at the hand. Shaking it would mean that Andre accepted the offer of friendship. But Andre did not believe the boys in front of him were his friends.

Benjamin and Derek treated him nicely, but he did not feel like a close friend to them. And Samiel treated him like they were competing for Mr. Kasey's attention. Andre could feel himself starting to dislike Samiel for that.

None of them were truly his friends. Not like Simon had been.

"My hand's getting kind of tired hanging here all alone," joked Derek.

"Thank you for your apology," said Andre, offering a small smile.

The smile faded from Derek's face. Realizing Andre would not shake his hand, he slowly dropped it.

"You're sure we're good?" asked Derek.

"I'm okay," said Andre.

"If something's wrong, tell me."

"I'm... okay," said Andre again, the words starting to sink in for him. They were not his close friends, but that was okay. He was okay with that. "Yeah. I'm okay."

"Hmm...," murmured Benjamin, his mouth setting into a line.

"You're okay?" said Derek. "What does that mean?"

"It means that I'm okay," said Andre more confidently. "Is that it?"

"Yeah, that's it."

"Okay," said Andre.

He walked off the porch and went home. He had not accepted that handshake because he knew he was better off alone. And it was not until he was in his room that he realized Samiel had not even apologized.

"Hi Gretchen," said Andre when he arrived home.

"Hi," said Gretchen. "We're having pizza for dinner tonight.

"Okay," said Andre.

"I talked to your father about skateboarding," said Gretchen. "He said it'd be okay if you learned."

"Yes!" cheered Andre.

"He's in the kitchen if you want to talk to him."

Andre went to the kitchen, where Mr. Brown sat at the table, grading papers. He and Mr. Brown had not spoken much since their argument.

"Hey Dad," said Andre quietly.

"Hey," answered Mr. Brown.

Andre decided to address the elephant in the room. He needed to know for sure what his father thought of him.

"Dad? Is something wrong with me?"

"No!" said Mr. Brown quickly.

"Then why do I feel like there is?"

"What do you think is wrong with you?"

"I... I just feel like I can't ever focus or get anything done. And I always say things at the wrong time. And I always make people mad at me."

"Lots of people do those things," said Mr. Brown. "It doesn't mean there's anything wrong with you. It doesn't mean you're an idiot. Or a screwup."

"Yeah but..."

"Andre," said Mr. Brown, moving to stand near Andre. "I don't ever want you to believe that there's something wrong with you. And I especially don't want you to believe I think there's something wrong with you."

Andre did not answer.

"I've never thought you were an idiot or a screwup. I do think that sometimes you don't apply yourself fully, and give up too easily on things sometimes, but never an idiot or a screwup. I think you're one of the nicest, smartest, most-talented people I've ever met. And I'm proud to be your father."

Andre started to cry.

"I've always been proud of you," said Mr. Brown, taking hold of Andre's shoulders. He wiped the tears from Andre's face. "You're going off to college soon and after that you'll be your own man. But no matter what happens, just know that I'll always be here for you, and I'll always love you. Okay?"

"Okay."

His father held him close, and Andre could hear his father's heartbeat. At that moment, Andre felt his father's love as he never had before. It did not matter then if he had no friends or that he tended to

be all over the place. He had made his father proud of him, and Andre
was glad.

-

Like You Never Met Me

The world continues to spin.
It doesn't stop whether you're in,
My life or not around.
It keeps on going as it's bound,
To spin until it can't no more.
And I can't help that I feel sore,
If you want me out, then just say so,
All I need is a word and I'll go.
I planned on leaving anyway,
But it's no problem to be out today.
But I don't want things to be like this.
When I leave, I want it to be with a hug and a kiss,
And with the knowledge that you'll be there,
And that your heart will be in it to care.
But if it's not possible for that to be,
Then when I leave it'll be like you never met me.

Mary

Thursday afternoon, Mary returned home from work and prepared to practice her composition for her audition. Getting into that school was Mary's one-way ticket out of her father's house. She did not want to give the school any reason to deny her admission and was determined to deliver her best performance yet.

Mary felt like she was on thin ice with her father. Although the two were back on speaking terms, she could tell her father still felt sore about what she had done. She knew it would be a while before the two would have the relationship they had previously had.

Halfway through her rehearsal, Grandma Marianne visited.

"Hey there," said Grandma Marianne to Gretchen. Mary continued practicing her piece. "How's my new daughter-in-law doing?"

"I'm doing good, ma'am," said Gretchen.

"That's good," said Grandma Marianne. "Can you tell Torrance to come here. I want to talk to him."

"Of course," said Gretchen, leaving to fetch Mr. Brown.

"Baby, you sounding real good over there," complimented Grandma Marianne.

"Thanks Grandma," said Mary.

"You think you can stop to take a break?"

"Okay."

Mary ceased playing and sat beside her grandmother on the couch.

"Girl, do you know you are a trip?" laughed Grandma Marianne. "Why were you trying to hide the truth about my daddy from me?"

"I didn't want you to be sad," said Mary, blushing with embarrassment.

"Be sad about what? I know who my daddy was."

"You do?"

"He always had a gun on him," said Grandma Marianne. "I was there when he fired that warning shot at Mr. Calvin. And I was there when he shot Leonard."

Grandma Marianne nodded her head, and her eyes misted over with memory.

"Mhmm," said Grandma Marianne. "I was there alright. I'll never forget the blank look he got when Leonard told him to shut up and mind his business. He calmly pulled that gun out and fired it straight at Leonard's knee like it was nothing."

Mary watched as Grandma Marianne nodded her head again.

"Yeah, I know who my father was," sighed Grandma Marianne. "That day I knew for sure who he was. He did his best to live right but when he fell off the path, he fell all the way off. It doesn't surprise me to learn that wasn't his first time shooting someone."

"How'd you find out?" asked Mary.

"Torrance told me," said Grandma Marianne. "He's been trying to figure out who your 'source' is. I had to let him know it wasn't me."

"You wanted to see me, Mama?" said Mr. Brown, entering the living room.

"Mhmm," said Grandma Marianne. "Sit down. We going to get this resolved."

"Mama!" protested Mr. Brown.

"Sit down," said Grandma Marianne more forcefully.

Mr. Brown sat down in a huff.

"Did Gretchen put you up to this?" demanded Mr. Brown.

"No," said Grandma Marianne. "You and your hard head did. If you're going to walk around mad at Mary, then you might as well walk around mad at me too because I'm the one let her talk to him."

"Why?" demanded Mr. Brown. "You knew I wouldn't like that."

"You're right, I did," said Grandma Marianne. "But Torrance, you can't keep these kids under your thumb for the rest of their lives. Eventually, you're going to have to let them make their own decisions."

"That doesn't mean I have to like them."

"You're right, you don't. You've made some decisions I didn't like, and I'm sure I've made some decisions you didn't like. But we're still here. We're still talking to each other. We still love each other."

"I still love her," said Mr. Brown. "But she shouldn't have went behind my back."

"Maybe she shouldn't have," said Grandma Marianne. "But it's done, and you can't change it."

Mr. Brown released a frustrated sigh.

"Now, in light of what we've recently learned about my daddy, I've brought something for both of you to share," said Grandma Marianne. She placed a big, worn Bible and a notebook on the table, and Mr. Brown lit up with recognition.

"His family Bible?" gasped Mr. Brown.

"Mhmm," said Grandma Marianne. "The only reason I'm giving this to you is because what's in the back."

Grandma Marianne flipped to the blank pages at the back. At least, the pages should have been blank. But Mary saw they were filled with writing, and that there were other papers stuffed inside.

"What is this?" asked Mary.

"Songs that he wrote," answered Grandma Marianne. "I want to give this to you both, so we can remember who my daddy was. He wasn't perfect, but he wasn't a terrible person either."

Mary read over the songs. Some were choruses, others were verses, and others were complete, but all were written from the heart. She noticed her father also looking.

"I had a similar situation with him," said Grandma Marianne. "Torrance, you should remember. You're the one that helped solve it."

"Yeah," said Mr. Brown quietly.

"I went eight years without speaking to my daddy," said Grandma Marianne. "Eight years that we could've spent enjoying each other and getting along. After those eight years, I only got to spend one year with him before he died."

Mary noticed that Grandma Marianne and Mr. Brown looked somber at the mention of Great-Grandpa Gabriel's death.

"When you both look at this Bible, and you look at these songs, I want you to remember what it means to be family," said Grandma Marianne. "Being family means loving one another, through good times and bad. Okay?"

Mary and Mr. Brown nodded.

"Now, both of you hug," said Grandma Marianne.

Mary stood up and hugged her father. At first, it was awkward, but it slowly morphed into a real, loving hug.

"Dad, I'm sorry," said Mary.

"I'm sorry too," said Mr. Brown. "You know I love you, right?"

"I do," said Mary. "And I love you too."

Mary was glad to be back on good terms with her father. The time for her to leave his house was approaching. And she was glad that when it came, it would be a happy departure and not a bitter one.

First Lady

She never thought she'd be a First Lady.
She never thought she'd be a pastor's wife.
She thought her only love would be Daddy,
But a different path is now Mommy's life.

Will that happen to me with this church boy?
Is my future tied to this pastor's son?
Or are we each only to be a toy,
For each other that'll last a short run.

I find it strange that I'm interested,
To see how my life is going to change,
Due to this intriguing man that I've met.
Yes, it is indeed to me very strange.

Is this what my life is moving toward?
Will this be for me a new way forward?

Karla

Friday afternoon, Karla was nervous. She was hanging out with Hosea. They had both agreed it was only a friendly outing and not a date as her mother kept annoyingly referring to it.

"Oh, I'm so excited!" squealed First Lady Hall. "My baby's going on her first date."

"It's not a date," griped Karla, smoothing out her favorite-colored green shirt. "We're just hanging out. That's it."

"You can call it what you want, but the way I see it, you and a boy are hanging out alone," said First Lady Hall. "In my book, that's a date."

"Okay Mom," sighed Karla.

"Mommy?" asked Layla. "What's a date?"

"It's when two people who like each other go out and have fun," explained First Lady Hall.

"Oh," said Layla. She looked at Karla and said, "Can we go on a date too?"

"Some other time," laughed Karla.

It would be the second time that Karla had a day to herself. But unlike the first time, she would not spend it worrying about Layla. She had vowed to enjoy her day with Hosea.

The two planned to go skating. Then they would go see the new Drake Malone movie. When Karla arrived at the skating rink, she found Hosea inside, waiting for her.

"Hey there!" said Hosea, giving Karla a side hug. "I was going to get your skates, but then I realized I didn't know your shoe size."

"That's okay," said Karla.

Hosea was a smooth skater. In fact, everything he did was smooth to Karla. He was completely different from their first interaction, where he had seemed awkwardly cute. And Karla found that she was becoming more comfortable with him.

At one point, he took her hand and rolled with her around the rink. And Karla let him. Although it was for something as small as skating, it felt good to let someone else take the burden of leading for once.

Once they finished skating, they headed for the movie theater. Hosea paid for everything. As they watched the previews for the other upcoming movies, Karla decided to make small talk and let Hosea in on her little secret.

"Want to know something funny?" said Karla.

"What's up?" said Hosea. He smiled when he said it, and Karla found she liked his smile.

"My mom actually named me after Karla Klein."

"No way!"

"I'm serious!"

"Why?"

"She's a huge nerd."

"Didn't you say she was a First Lady though?"

"Yeah."

"She must be an interesting First Lady then."

"I'd say she is."

"You know it's funny. There's a guy at my church whose mom named him after Drake Malone."

"Really?"

"Yeah. He's one of our newer members and he's in the choir. I was curious about his name, so I asked one day and that's what he told me."

"That's interesting," said Karla, struck by how eerily similar Hosea's Drake was to her brother. She did not want to reveal all the details about herself so quickly, so she chose to keep her Drake to herself.

There were so many things Karla wanted to know about Hosea. She knew he was a preacher's son and was beginning to preach himself. But she wanted to know about his dreams, his goals, and his values. Karla wanted to know if Hosea would only be a friend or if he would become more than that.

She figured he was aiming to become the latter. But whether he would, depended on the type of man he was. They watched the movie and then went out to eat.

"That movie was incredible," said Hosea. "But I wonder why they're drawing out Drake and Karla getting together. We all know it's going to happen."

"Apparently, it was drawn out like that in the comics too," said Karla, repeating what her mother had told her. "They had a bunch of other relationships before they became a couple. But I think they were in their mid-thirties when it happened in the comics. I'm not sure how things will go in the movies."

"Well, I think we're for sure going to get a third one," said Hosea. "And hopefully they don't start straying into territory I'll have to preach against. That one scene with Karla Klein and the security guard was towing the line very heavily."

"I'm pretty sure that was her real-life husband playing that role," said Karla.

"But in the movie universe he was just a random security guard," said Hosea.

"True."

"I will say though that this has been aa fun day," said Hosea.

"I agree," said Karla. "I've enjoyed spending time with you."

"Enough to maybe do it again?"

"I'd say I'd be okay with that."

"Cool."

Karla was still unsure about how things with Hosea would play out. But she was certain of one thing: she was glad their paths had crossed. When she returned home, everyone was waiting for her.

"Well?" said First Lady Hall.

"Well, what?" said Karla.

"How did it go?" said First Lady Hall. "Was he nice? Was he cute? Do you think you'll date him?"

"Mom please," laughed Karla. "We just went out as friends. But he did say he'd like to hang out again."

"You hear that, Forrest?" squealed First Lady Hall. "That means it was a success!"

"Yay!" said Forrest, jokingly clapping his hands.

"Yay!" said Layla, copying her father's motions mixed with her mother's excitement.

First Lady Hall hugged Karla excitedly. But Karla found herself sharing in her mother's excitement. Not because Hosea could potentially become a romance for her. No, Karla was excited because her life was moving forward. She had done something for herself and had enjoyed herself. And for the first time, she felt like she did not have to shoulder the weight of the world.

It Ain't Over

Sometimes I want to give up when,
I see no way forward.
I won't quit till I see it change,
Till then it ain't over.

Sometimes life will get you down and
may seem impossible.
In those times of trouble I say,
I need a miracle.

Sometimes I want to give up when,
I see no way forward.
I won't quit till I see it change,
Till then it ain't over.

Sometimes the vision may seem like,
It will never come true.
But I say put your faith in Him,
And see what He will do.

Sometimes I want to give up when,
I see no way forward.
I won't quit till I see it change,
Till then it ain't over.

There are times that will test your faith,
You've got to keep pressing.
Don't lose hope and don't get dismayed,
You've got to keep fighting.

Sometimes I want to give up when,
I see no way forward.

I won't quit till I see it change,
Till then it ain't over.

Drake

It was Friday, and Drake was full of nerves. That evening, he would be auditioning for Vincent. He had an off day from his first job, so Drake spent the morning resting. If he landed this gig, it could lead to new possibilities for him.

One of the local channels showed the first Drake Malone movie, and Drake watched it in preparation for the sequel. He, Andrew, and Quentin were going to go see it after Drake finished his audition.

During one of Karla Klein's scenes, Drake noticed she tilted her head a particular way. It was familiar to him, and as Drake paid more attention, he noticed that Irina Frazier had a lot of similar mannerisms to Camille, and kind of eerily resembled her. But he did not have time to dwell on it because he had to prepare for work soon.

Around lunchtime, Drake started heading to the radio station. While driving, he received a call from his father. He had not talked to Mr. Brown since Sunday.

"Hello?" said Drake.

"I'm in town," said Mr. Brown. "Got time for lunch with me? I need to talk to you."

"Okay."

Mr. Brown brought Drake a meal from Nik's Barbecue. They sat in his car eating and the food was as good as it had been reported to be. Since neither one of them were at work, Drake and his father had no need to rush through lunch.

"I thought you had work today," said Drake.

"I had a doctor's appointment," answered Mr. Brown.

"Oh."

There was a small moment of silence while both men ate.

"I paid the rest of that money you owed Matthias," said Mr. Brown.

Drake almost choked on his food. His father had given no indication of knowing about his financial situation. And he had given no warning about bringing it up either.

"How'd you find out?" coughed Drake.

"Alex," said Mr. Brown. "He thought Matthias was running you for money, so he came to me the day after you left, and we confronted Matthias. He didn't want to tell us at first but then Alex told him he was supposed to be a changed man. That set Matthias off and before we knew it, he told us that you had borrowed money from him and had come to pay some of it back. Alex felt bad for accusing him and I paid the money for you so you wouldn't go bankrupt trying to pay him back."

Mr. Brown wiped his lips clean of barbecue sauce.

"Why didn't you tell me about it?"

Drake looked down at his lap.

"Were you embarrassed?"

"No."

"Then why?"

"You told me not to come to you if I got into trouble," mumbled Drake guiltily.

"I did?"

"You said it during the argument before I moved out."

"I...," uttered Mr. Brown. "Is that what's been wrong the whole time?"

Drake did not answer.

"Look at me."

Drake did not want to. But he also did not want to know what would happen if he did not. He looked at his father's confused face.

"Why is it that every time something is wrong, you don't tell me?" said Mr. Brown. "You just walk around mad at me like I'm supposed to be a mind reader."

Drake could say the same about his father, but he dared not to.

"Why didn't you say something?"

"Because you said–!"

"I was upset when I said that!" snapped Mr. Brown. He wearily ran a hand over his hair and looked out the window.

"I'm sorry," said Drake. "I should've told you."

"Yeah, you should've!" griped Mr. Brown. "I mean, what kind of father do you think I am? Do you really think I would leave you to fend for yourself like that? Is it that hard to tell me when something's wrong?"

"I was trying to handle it on my own."

"Yeah, well look how that turned out! What'd you even need that much money for anyways?"

"I needed it to move out."

"To move out? To move out where?"

"Out of your house."

"Living with me was that bad for you?"

"It wasn't bad, I just... needed to get out..."

Mr. Brown closed his eyes and shook his head.

"Look," said Mr. Brown. "Whenever you have a problem, you can come to me. Okay? I'm not the big bad wolf, you don't have to hide from me."

"Okay," said Drake. He was not sure how he felt. Part of him felt embarrassed that he had not been able to do it by himself. But another part of him was relieved, not only because it was over, but also because he realized he could trust his dad after all.

It was about time for Drake to go inside the radio station. Mr. Brown followed him inside because he needed to use the restroom. Minutes later, when Drake was showing his father back out of the building, they ran into Mr. King.

"Hey Mr. King," said Drake.

"Hey," said Mr. King. He eyed Mr. Brown and said, "Who's this?"

"My dad."

Mr. King gasped and stared at Mr. Brown. Drake noticed his dad was doing the same.

"Can I have your autograph?" said both men.

"Why do you want my autograph?" questioned Mr. Brown.

"You're Torrance Brown of The Brown Family Band!"

"Oh my gosh," laughed Mr. Brown. "I didn't think anyone outside of Creeke would remember that."

"I remember!" cried Mr. King. "I've got to get you on the air!"

"I don't know about that," said Mr. Brown.

"It'll be fine," said Mr. King. "I make the rules here so who's going to complain?"

Fifteen minutes later, Mr. King was going on air with a very nervous Mr. Brown.

"Good afternoon, everyone," said Mr. King. "This is Mr. King here, the owner of this wonderful gospel radio station. I'm interrupting the programming today because I have a surprise special guest. Now, if you were in the area back in the mid-nineties and especially in the church, then you know this man. I have with me *the* Torrance Brown of the Brown Family Band. You guys remember the family band who performed at all the different churches in the area, and they had the little boy who's shoes didn't fit? And he's here!"

"Uh… hi," said Mr. Brown.

"So, Mr. Brown turned out to be the father of one of my employees and was visiting today, and I just could not let this opportunity pass by without him telling us what he's been up to lately. It's been a long time."

"Yeah," said Mr. Brown, getting more comfortable. "It's been a long time since those days."

"There were six of you, right?"

"Yeah, me, my brothers, my sisters, and our grandfather."

"So obviously we all know everyone can't stay in the spotlight forever, but I just want to know what happened. It's like you guys just disappeared."

"Well, life happened," said Mr. Brown. "I don't want put too much of my business out there, but our home life just wasn't ideal to maintain the band anymore."

"Ah," said Mr. King. "So, do you still sing?"

"Yeah," said Mr. Brown. "I got a little rusty along the way but I'm still singing. I have my son over there to thank for that. But let the family tell it, I tend to lean more towards rap."

"Your son told me that."

"Yeah," said Mr. Brown. "You were one of my biggest inspirations. I'm a huge fan of The Boombox Boyz and you couldn't tell me nothing when you transitioned to gospel rap. Your music has really gotten me through some tough times."

"Wow. I don't know what to say. Your music has definitely gotten me through some rough times too."

"We only made one album though," laughed Mr. Brown.

"Listen, I played that album until it wouldn't play no more," cackled Mr. King. "But I'm curious. What about rap was so impactful on you."

"Well, my grandfather loved music but he hated rap. He said it was devil music. But he always told me that music was a tool that could bring people together and I just never understood why he believed that only certain genres of music could be used to do that."

"I have to agree with your grandfather," said Mr. King. "I believe rap leads people into lifestyles that don't glorify God."

"I believe it's a matter of the heart," countered Mr. Brown. "There is music that glorifies the devil and tries to paint him in a positive light. In that way, I agree that devil music does exist. But I also believe God created all forms of music and they draw us to him when used properly. When used improperly, they draw us away from Him."

"Hmm...," muttered Mr. King. "You know you've given me a lot to think about. And I want to thank you for agreeing to come on air with me."

"You're welcome."

"And thank you to the listeners for allowing me to interrupt. Now back to your regularly scheduled programming."

After the interview ended, Drake accompanied his father and Mr. King back to the parking lot.

"Do you mind telling me exactly what my music got you through?" asked Mr. King.

"Lord, where do I start?" laughed Mr. Brown. "Well, I had a troubled home life and ended up being raised by my grandfather. My biological father didn't like us traveling and singing, and he used to make fun of my singing to the point that I stopped. Last year at our church revival was the first time I sang publicly since I was fourteen and it was only because Drake convinced me to."

"Praise The Lord for that," said Mr. King. "A voice like yours shouldn't go to waste."

"And then I ended up getting married right out of high school, but that didn't end well."

"Oh."

"Yeah, I've had my days of trouble. But your music helped me get through them."

"Thank you for sharing that with me. I'm glad my music was able to do some good for someone."

"You're welcome," said Mr. Brown. "I guess I'll let you both get back to work."

"Of course," said Mr. King. "It was nice meeting you."

"You too."

Drake watched as his father drove away, awed by the whole experience.

"I can tell your daddy is strict," chuckled Mr. King as they returned to the station. "You ain't say not one word the whole time he was here. I ain't never seen you so quiet and sat up in all my time of knowing you."

"I...," said Drake, unsure of how to respond.

"But I must admit, I feel a little inspired by him," said Mr. King. "I didn't think my music had that much impact."

"Mr. King, I think you underestimate how big of a deal you are," said Drake.

"I think you might be right," said Mr. King. "These past few weeks, I've experienced such an outpour of love over appearing on that soundtrack. It's all just so inspiring."

"Can I ask you something?" asked Drake. "We're you serious about mentoring me if I asked?"

"Of course," said Mr. King. "Is that something you'd be interested in?"

"Yes sir," said Drake.

"Okay then."

The time for the big audition had arrived. It was being held in a theatre space, and Drake stood in the wings nervously awaiting his turn. Before he knew it, it was his turn to sing.

Drake stepped onto the stage and peered out into the audience. Vincent and his cousin, Zion, were serving as the judges, and the other people there had been brought by the auditioners for moral support.

"Whenever you're ready," said Vincent.

Drake nodded and took a deep breath. Then he let the gospel song he had prepared flow out of him. It was a song about new beginnings and Drake had chosen it not only because it suited his voice, but because he felt it suited the situation. When he finished, Drake stood soaking in the moment.

"Thank you," said Vincent.

Drake rushed off the stage. Once the auditions were over, Vincent thanked everyone for coming out, and let them know he would contact the chosen ones within a week. Then, Drake was off to the movie theater with Andrew and Quentin.

"How'd I do?" asked Drake.

"Uh," said Quentin. "You definitely ushered in The Spirit that's for sure."

"Is that good or bad?"

"Good," said Quentin. "Definitely good."

"Bro, I swear at one point you were literally glowing," added Andrew. "Que isn't lying. You turned the audition into a praise and worship session."

"Well, from a saved standpoint that's good," said Drake. "But do you think I'll get picked?"

"Vince is crazy if doesn't pick you," declared Quentin. "You were literally the best singer and I'm not just saying that because you're my friend."

"Wow guys," said Drake, feeling himself blush. "Thanks."

Drake looked ahead to the future, and for the first time, it looked brighter to him than ever before.

We Are Family: A Postlude

Each of us are as leaves when on our own,
And we share the branches of the same tree,
Because together we are family.

Love is the thread that's used to keep us sewn,
Together and it comes without a fee.
Each of us are as leaves when on our own,
And we share the branches of the same tree.

Family is more than a shared skin tone,
It's more than sharing blood lines and a gene.
Family is love that is given free.
Each of us are as leaves when on our own,
And we share the branches of the same tree,
Because together we are family.